SHOTGUN

THE BLEEDING GROUND

SHOTGUN

THE BLEEDING GROUND

C. COURTNEY JOYNER

PINNACLE BOOKS
Kensington Publishing Corp.
www.kensingtonbooks.com

PINNACLE BOOKS are published by

Kensington Publishing Corp.
119 West 40th Street
New York, NY 10018

All Kensington titles, imprints, and distributed lines are available at special quantity discounts for bulk purchases for sales promotions, premiums, fund-raising, educational, or institutional use. Special book excerpts or customized printings can also be created to fit specific needs. For details, write or phone the office of the Kensington sales manager: Kensington Publishing Corp., 119 West 40th Street, New York, NY 10018, attn: Sales Department; phone 1-800-221-2647.

PINNACLE BOOKS and the Pinnacle logo are Reg. U.S. Pat. & TM Off.

ISBN-13: 978-0-7860-3234-1
ISBN-10: 0-7860-3234-0

First printing: July 2016

10 9 8 7 6 5 4 3 2 1

Printed in the United States of America

First electronic edition: July 2016

ISBN-13: 978-0-7860-3235-8
ISBN-10: 0-7860-3235-9

INTRODUCTION

From a journal left by Dr. John Bishop:

I write this as a dead man. My own life ended with the death of my wife and son. I existed only to find their killers and see them draw last breaths. It was a long and bloody trek, and with the help of White Fox, I have done it. But revenge has led me to my own family, and to my own brother, and a group of terror-riders worse than anything I saw in the War Between the States.

My mission is to stop my brother—and his followers.

I used to be a doctor, and now I'm a killer, with a gun where my right arm used to be. I am a monster of my own making, stitched together when I should have died. I have become what I am because to win this fight I must become something feared by the outlaws and killers who plague the decent families like my own used to be, and I must wipe that plague out any way that I can.

I set this down so that others will understand that I spilled blood, so that no one else will have to exist as I exist.

That is my mission, as a dead man, until I find my final peace.

CHAPTER ONE

Dead Memories

The special bandolier was designed perfectly. Cut from beaver skin and holding six .12-gauge shells, it fastened tight around the upper part of John Bishop's half-arm with two leather ties. The oil from the pelt let the shells slide easily from their pockets into the double-barreled, swivel-breech shotgun that replaced the rest of the right limb he'd sacrificed defending his family.

Bishop's one-handed prep of the weapon was all skill and adrenaline; quick motion to open the breech, pop the shells into place with his thumb, then a jerk of the wrist to snap it shut. It was load, fire, shuck brass, and load again. He could do it in fifteen seconds; less, if he fell into a rhythm, facing enemies from any direction.

At the moment, only one enemy was facing him, but with two guns. A shadowed figure stood on a frozen ledge jutting from the side of an unforgiving mountain, its peaks twisted like diseased muscles.

The sun was behind him, making him a dark specter.

Blowing snow masked his face, but he held a Navy Six in each hand, his stance daring Bishop's approach from below. A horse couldn't make it that far off-trail, and a man, just barely. He kept the Navies hammered back, waiting. He knew Bishop was there, someplace, waiting for his chance.

Bishop stayed out of sight in a deep wound in the mountain's side—an opening in the rocks, hidden by tufts of dead grass. Without showing himself, he could see the man on the ledge twenty feet above him. The wound was good cover, but lousy aim, especially for a shotgun. He scrubbed the snow from his eyes with his left palm, looking for a better position, judging his odds of making it.

Shreds of winter light threw a hint of the man's shadow at Bishop's feet. He watched him inch to the other side of the ledge, ready to open fire as soon as Bishop stepped away from the mountain's protection.

Filling his lungs with the cold, Bishop followed the shadow. The enemy on the ledge had the advantage, but at least he was finally a clean target. Bishop raised his half right arm, the elbow joint bringing the shotgun rig instantly into place, the metal supports on either side of the prosthetic locking its firing position.

Flexing his shoulders, he drew tight the silver chain that ran from the gun's two triggers to the leather harness that fit snugly across his back. The chain looped through the leather and was anchored to a band on his left wrist so the triggers could be pulled with a simple tug or a half-move of the body. His body and the special weapon acted and reacted as one.

To goad Bishop out of the wound in the mountain, the figure yelled, "Your ma never . . ." but his words were murdered by the high wind. The second attempt was a shot into the sky, followed by whoops of laughter.

Bishop blocked his howls and screams, letting the sound of his own calm fill his ears, while keeping his eyes fixed on the man's shadow, his moves.

The man leaned forward, trying for a glimpse, and then fired twice more, angry wild ricochets. He straightened, howling for Bishop over the storm.

Bishop charged from his cover in the mountainside, letting loose with both barrels, shooting upward, burning the air.

The man shot back at the same time, flame from the pistols flaring wide, a slug opening Bishop's throat, spinning him backwards into a deep pit. He grabbed for a limb to brake himself. No use. He fell without screaming, hitting bottom with a head snap, the shotgun barrels smashing piles of jagged rock around him.

But it wasn't rock.

Bishop lay still, snow cooling his face, life seeping through the fingers of the left hand he'd clamped on his windpipe. He tried moving. What he was lying on moved with him—little bits and pieces, crunching under his weight. He turned his head barely an inch, and his eyes met the shattered half-face of a human skull.

Beyond it, another, and then still another. Empty eye sockets, half jaws, and shells of broken teeth were scattered among the snapped, hardened bones of thousands of skeletons piled atop each other. Bishop forced himself up, his bloody fingers smearing wet on the dried remains surrounding him.

All that created the mountain.

Not stone and earth, but body upon body. It was as if a mass grave erupted its corpses and stacked them miles high. Muscles, ribs, spines, arms, and legs of the dead formed its hills, crags, and ledges. What should have been granite was gristled flesh, the mountain's plants only tangles of rotting hair.

A patchwork of petrified skin made the steep walls of the pit. The stretched faces of men, all ages and types, were locked in agony, screaming silently.

Bishop's mind reeled, the stench burning his nose and eyes. He tried to whisper to God while managing to get beyond his knees, standing on bones and hardened flesh.

A slug hit him in the back, then two more tore each leg.

Blood sprayed, and he dropped again, his face beside the bodies of a young woman and a boy. They were curled together in an eternal embrace.

"Your family's been waiting, John. Just for you." The man with the Navy Sixes stood high on the rim of the pit, looking down, reloading. "I know you want to be reunited."

Without the sun's glare, Bishop could see his clothes were shades of red. His face, which he kept lowered was more distinct, but still curtained by ice and snow.

Bishop cradled the delicate bodies of his wife and son, protecting them as he heard the pistols cock. They crumbled to dust in his arms. The shots from above were a roar.

The water hitting Dr. John Bishop tasted of lye soap lumped in with chewed tobacco and spit-back. He rolled out of his bunk, coughing like hell. Sheriff Tucker stood by the cell door with an empty wash bucket, his flannels barely covering his whiskey belly. He pushed his bifocals up on his nose with a snort. "Christ on a crutch, you got to shut up!"

Bishop yanked the soaking wet dirty sheet off the bunk's hay-bag mattress. He coughed more gray water, slopping his beard, then settled on one knee, fighting for air. "Same dreams again."

"You ain't gettin' nothin' dry tonight! I've had prisoners mess the bed, piss the walls—"

"Clean up since?"

Tucker's voice got louder. "They've killed each other,

killed themselves, and none was more trouble than you!"

"My sincere apologies."

An arm sprang between the bars of the adjoining cell, locking Bishop in a choke hold. It was massive, covered with ape-like hair, and its owner stunk of sweet-jack rye from two nights before. "I'm a man what values his sleep!"

Tucker traded the bucket for a tarnished Colt pocket revolver and pointed it at the prisoner who was squeezing Bishop's windpipe through the bars. "Let him go, Harvey!"

Harvey kept Bishop locked. "Gonna shoot me? Make your sister a widow?"

"Best gift I could give her."

Bishop pulled at Harvey's huge arm with his one hand, but it was made of God-steel.

Harvey's laugh was like a mule braying. "A one-armed man! Can't do nothing!"

Tucker took a step to Harvey's cell, aiming the gun directly at the back of his head. "But I can. Let the man go, Harv, or Esther'll have a lonely Christmas."

Harvey relaxed his grip, dropping Bishop to the wet stone floor. "Hell, he's gonna hang anyway. What's the difference?"

"The difference is you're an inbred ass, and I'm the law. All right there, Bishop?"

Bishop worked some feeling back into his neck with his one hand. "I'll make it to the hanging."

"Don't you have no more of that stuff to keep you quiet?"

"Chloral hydrate."

Besides the bunk, the only other furniture in the cell was a three-legged stool where a slop-drenched Bible and a small amber bottle were placed. Bishop's cell was one of five, separated by a slab of waist-high iron plating and bars to the ceiling. The privy was a hole cut in the stone floor covered by a busted lid.

Unlike the rest of the town, the jail was sturdily built, something that didn't escape Bishop when he'd ridden into town five months ago. Surrounded by clapboard and false fronts, it was the only stone building on the main street. The only sure thing about Paradise, Colorado, was its bad temper.

Bishop had met a proper lady, and she'd called it, "The mule pie of Colorado."

He'd laughed at those words coming from her mouth, but that was before the robbery and the massacre. Before the blast that turned him inside out. Before being left to die. All the things that were a jumbled fog of memory.

Sheriff Tucker said, "Hey, I gotta ask again."

"I heard you." Bishop gave the empty bottle a shake. "All gone."

"That stuff got you through the nights, at least. Doc Benson claimed these dreams 'd stop in a week. He lit out, leaving you and your tortures behind. It's been months like this!"

"Longer than that for me."

Harvey bellowed, "That ain't no comfort for the rest of us, you screamin' like a virgin on her wedding night!"

Bishop said, "Seems to me that men and women scream the same way." He absently rubbed the stump of his right arm with his palm, his fingers tracing the elbow joint and the roiled flesh around it. He stopped himself when he almost clasped his missing right hand.

"Look it! Crazier than an outhouse rat! Scratchin' at an arm that ain't even there!"

"It's called phantom pain. You wouldn't understand."

"See, I know about real pain, the kind what sets your insides on fire. How 'bout feelin' something real for a change? Something for all them men you killed?"

"You or Tucker ask me that three times a day."

Bishop flopped on his bunk, tired of conversation and ready to try sleep again. Just *try*. Water squirted and bits of wet hay dropped from the mattress bag as he stretched out, eyes shut.

Harvey said, "So let's hear it."

"I guess it depends if they were trying to kill me. You know more about it than I do."

"I can see lots of people wanting you dead."

"Leave my prisoner alone." Tucker opened Harvey's cell door with a large brass turnkey. "You're sober enough. Get the hell home."

"But Esther said she didn't want to see me for a week."

"Can't blame her for that. Find a stall at the livery. It's no matter to me. And you borrowed my good Sears, Roebuck."

Harvey grabbed the rain slicker he'd been using as a pillow, then stepped around his brother-in-law, who was holding open the cell door with one hand, keeping the Colt in the other.

Harvey said, "You're coming for Sunday supper?"

Tucker wiped his spectacles on his sleeve. "We'll see. Now get on to the stalls, sleep with the horse pies."

"That suits me right to the ground. I can't abide to be around no half-a-man anyways."

Bishop regarded Harvey. "How do you feel about the boys who fought in the conflict?"

"What the hell's that supposed to mean?"

"I'm just trying to learn about you, Harvey."

Tucker stepped in front of his brother-in-law, jamming the pistol into his chest. "Out."

Bishop had his left arm behind his head. "I apologize again, Harvey."

"He's gone. Notice how much better it smells?" Tucker opened the door to Bishop's cell, the Colt still leveled. "We've been together a while, Doc."

Bishop's kept his eyes shut and didn't move.

Tucker continued. "Since the so-called massacre I mean. You're going down in the history books for that one. Train sailed off the tracks."

"All I know is what you told me."

"The newspapers."

"Them, too."

"You saved some lives that day, Doc, but you left a lot of blood 'n hair behind. That was some real killin' you did."

Bishop broke his words, trying to end it. "I—don't— remember."

Tucker said, "Not while you're awake. That's because you've gone crippled in your head."

"You're not going to let me sleep, are you?"

"Trying to help is all."

Bishop showed his impatience and sighed. "Tucker, I can't remember clear the last ten minutes, last week, or last month. But funny enough, I do remember a thing or two about medicine."

"Hell, I know you're the real deal. Your field kit's in the closet. I'm not saying I know more about what's wrong with you than you do, but see, I'm lookin' at you from the outside. Maybe that gives me something, huh?"

Bishop didn't answer.

Tucker pressed. "I've figured out a few things, like what's making you tick."

"I always like to hear from an educated man."

"Funny. It's usual for prisoners to look down their noses at the lawman. It's their nature. I'm surprised a doctor would run his mouth that way."

"I guess I can't do anything right today."

"Maybe you should give me a listen."

"I just want some sleep."

"Yeah. You're praying for it."

Bishop opened his eyes. He tilted his head to see Tucker standing over him, wearing a crooked kind of smile, the Colt an inch from his temple.

Tucker quick-touched Bishop with the gun. "Now, I don't have your fine learning, but you live long enough, you pick things up along the way. I can fix your problem."

"With that old .44?"

"I seen men break at Shiloh. Bawl like a newborn and never come back. See, mixed up in your head as you are, I don't think it's ever gonna leave ya alone."

"Probably not."

"You can't sort nothing out if you can't recall it."

"I can't call things up the way I could, but it seems I had a patient once, shot by his drunken wife. After that, he couldn't remember his own name." Bishop let it sink in. "The doc with no memory remembers the patient with no memory. That's what Harvey'd call outhouse crazy."

Tucker said, "Maybe he's right. What you went through was like the war a second time. Fighting off the robbers who blew the train off the track; helping those soldiers protecting that gold? Even when they were being shot to pieces, you were in there."

Bishop gave a moment before saying, "Killing a lot of men, I guess."

"That's what's doggin' you . . . because you was doing both. Being a doc and a killer." Tucker's voice stayed a hiss. "Can you live with that torture?"

"You claim they'll hang me as soon as the circuit judge rides in."

"Who knows when that'll be? Maybe months? You really want to go on like this? Hell, I wouldn't. Bein' no use to myself or anybody else. Doc, you know how bad it's gonna get."

Bishop smiled. "So, what's your thinking, Tucker? That maybe I won't get hung? That'd be a problem?"

"Not for me. Not really." The lawman dropped his voice to barely a whisper. "If you tried an escape, I could shoot you with cause. I'd do it right, too, and all your loco talk'd be over for sure. Now, that's peace, ain't it?"

Bishop shut his eyes again and gave a quiet laugh before he spoke. "Right now, that doesn't seem like such a bad idea, but I'll wait for the judge."

"And tell him you don't remember all the blood you spilled?" Tucker was only a step away from Bishop. Sucking in his gut, he suddenly took an official tone. "I was offering a real way out of your suffering, but if you ain't going to take it, let's look at it another way."

Bishop lay still, knowing what was next.

Tucker said, "The judge don't care if he kills you or if I do. It's the same sentence."

"Going to try this play again?" Bishop brought his right arm down to his side, measured his words. "Either I pay to end my intense suffering—"

"That smart mouth again. *That* you remember."

"Or I pay to get to trial."

Tucker said, "You've been a lot of bother, Doc, but I'm a good man. Merciful. You got a lot of them train robbers, but they still got away with a strongbox of cash. And what about that gold you got squirreled off someplace? How 'bout all of that?"

"You listen to too much barroom talk. I couldn't give God a dollar if he struck me with lightning." Bishop felt the barrel of the Colt against his temple again, the vibration of the hammer locking into place.

Tucker leaned in whisper-close. "You really want to go out a liar?"

Bishop didn't blink.

Tucker said, "Wait for the judge? Live with night terrors? Your business, but the only way that's gonna happen is if you pay to stop the pullin' of this trigger."

"We all pay, Tucker, one way or t' other."

Tucker's words edged like broken glass. "Smart mouth and damn stupid."

The balled fist of Bishop's left hand sledge-hammered Tucker just below the earlobe, pounding the bundle of nerves next to his jaw. The sheriff heaved over, stumbling away from the bunk, knees unsure.

Bishop jumped from the bunk. "My ending isn't coming from you!"

A spasm travelled down Tucker's arm, but the Colt stayed in his fingers. He tried to raise the gun, eyes refusing to focus. He blinked, tried again. His hand twitched, but pulled the trigger. A shot spit off the wall, before tearing into the wet Bible, thudding between the pages.

Bishop brought down his left arm again, a wide blow using all his shoulder strength. Tucker hit the floor hard, bifocal lens shattering, his face slopping into the mess he'd thrown from the wash bucket.

A bullwhip cracked.

The knotted leather snake wrapped around Bishop's neck, jerking him to the floor. He grabbed for the long tail as it snapped back, splitting the air. The whip came down across his eyes, then again on his chest, face, and arm. Sharp-edged leather sliced muscle deep, then peeled off.

Crack.

Bishop fought back with his left, shielding his eyes. The lash kept ripping, spattering his blood in a fine rain. He didn't see Sheriff Tucker stand or pick up his gun. He only felt the whip.

Crack.

Harvey said, "He ain't dropping!"

The barrel of Tucker's gun smashed the side of Bishop's head, washing his eyes red, the blow pounding him down.

Bishop heard one of them say, "Ain't nobody can take that much punishment. Nobody."

CHAPTER TWO
Blood on the Horn

Colby had gone by so many names he'd forgotten most of them. It was usually something he picked at random from the Bible and then mumbled to the trail boss, hotel clerk, or whoever. Folks never seemed to question him, but sometimes would mention that he had the same Christian first name as their pa or grandpa. The only problem was that he had to remember to answer when the name was called out.

Everything else, including who was the priority kill if there was more than one target, always came off like clockwork. But he had trouble with damn names. That was something to work on.

He was rolling his cigarette too loose, the makings sprinkling the tops of the new boots he'd scarred with a heated edge of a bowie. His hands refused to co-operate with the task, the paper tearing between his thumbs and fingers until he finally managed to patch together something that was close to a misshapen cigar, bulging in the middle, ragged tobacco peeking out from both ends.

Somewhere behind him, he could hear whiskey-snickers from a couple other rope hands, lighting their own smokes and shaking their heads at his incompetence.

He called out, "Any of you fellers spare a match?"

One of them, older, with a Winchester repeater resting across his lap, rode over, still having a joke, but trying to be good-natured. "Andy, I never seen nothing like you."

Andy! Why the hell did he think it was from the Bible? Colby took note of the name, tipping his hat and grinning wide.

Holding on to his laugh, Winchester handed him a match. "So, you're drawing wages?"

The poor excuse for a cigarette didn't want to be lit. Colby struggled until it finally flamed. He coughed, "Yes, sir. I surely am."

"Not wanting to offend, can I ask what for?"

"Same as you, I guess."

"Not the same as me, son. I'm on a special contract with Mr. Chisum." Winchester's voice was deep but quiet, commanding attention in the way he gave each word its proper measure.

Colby thought that if Winchester ever delivered a sermon, he'd listen to it. "Well, I'm here to take care nothin' happens that's not supposed to, sir."

"Make sure Chisum's cattle get to the railhead." Winchester motioned to the herd of cattle behind him, 1,944 at the supper count.

They were decent stock, not spongy but not muscle-bound either. Settling down for the night, a couple heifers were pushing each other, rubbing hair, but nothing serious. It was a good quality herd for a rancher who wanted to build something for himself. A starter.

Colby had actually thought about having a nice place, a little extra security. Something like what his folks had.

That notion had nothing to do with the job at hand, and he stopped it as soon as it entered his mind. *No imaginings* was his rule, so he wasn't listening when Winchester made another statement about the cattle and their value.

Colby's grin took up his entire face when he replied, purposefully stumbling over his words. "Yes, sir. That's as fine a bunch of that shorthorn breed, you know, that I ever seen."

"Durhams can fetch an all right dollar."

"That's a for sure, and I'll be keepin' a good watch on 'em."

"But what about those men yonder?" Winchester let the question hang, jerking a thumb toward the riders trolling the edge of the herd, listening for incomers and scooting back the strays. No muss, no fuss, just earning their pay.

Soon they would share the one low fire and take their grub quietly, with voices down, so the cattle would stay settled. It was the way professionals did it, and those men were all pros. It was the point Winchester was trying to make, but Colby already knew it. He'd been watching them closely, making note of who did what, and how.

And the guns they carried.

Winchester said, "I've known some of them since they were kids, and they've grown up to be damn handy"—

he looked back at Colby—"and all good with a gun. Good men."

Colby's strained grin had gone lopsided, and he kept nodding his head in agreement, even when it wasn't needed. "Yes sir, you can see it. That's why they're drawing top wages."

"You must have something on the ball, too, or you wouldn't be ridin' with us."

"Well, I surely want to do a good job. I'm eager."

Winchester drew out his words. "That's fine, but you're all elbows and thumbs. Seems like you should have more experience, given your age."

Colby inhaled deeply on his misshapen cigarette. "The other fellas been talkin'?"

"They're looking at you. So am I."

"I surely don't want to disappoint nobody."

"Then step up. Throw a rope or show yourself with a gun. You have to do something, son."

The twisted cigarette went out. Colby tossed it before opening his stained jacket to show a shirt that had been patched so many times it didn't deserve wearing and that he had no gun belt. By contrast, Winchester's shirt was fresh, and buttoned to his neck, his new hat held in place with a chinstrap.

Colby said, "I don't carry no gun. Maybe you can teach me? I admire that rifle."

"If you're serious, we can give it a try. But"—Winchester's eyebrows came together, forming a gray question mark over his sandpaper face—"if you can't shoot, how are you standing guard over anything? This isn't adding up for me, son."

"Actually, I misspoke."

Colby held up a hand to pause Winchester's next remark and took a gold pocket watch from his dirty jacket. The watch was polished diamond-clean, and he handled it delicately, snapping the engraved face cover open to note the time. "I make sure things go the way they're supposed to."

Winchester covered the hammer on the rifle with his palm, easing it back. "What in the Sam Hill does that mean?"

Colby held the watch, smiling at a cameo on the inside of the cover. It wasn't a silly grin, but something real and satisfied. He snapped it shut. "Swiss works. Always perfect. My meaning is, that you have a choice to not use that rifle, sir. I hope that's the choice you make."

Winchester crooked his elbow, settling the rifle on Colby when shouts from the other cowboys startled him.

They were loud cries, and one had some panic. "Whoa, Lordy, do you see that?"

Winchester turned his attention for a heartbeat.

That heartbeat was all Colby needed to slip the blade down his arm into his palm and launch it, bullet-fast and sure, burying itself completely into Winchester's chest. The blade had no handle, and plunged so deep, Winchester's body seemed to swallow it whole, the wound just a slit above his heart, spraying a geyser of red.

Colby had hit the artery he was aiming for. It was perfect. Surgical. Winchester looked down at the blood soaking his starched-white shirt, then back to Colby, wounded surprise in his eyes. He tried to crack off a shot.

It was only a grazing as Colby dove from his horse, rolled, and came back up to his feet in a single acrobatic motion, before yanking the rifle from Winchester's hands. There was no struggle; his fingers just let it slip away. The older man settled forward, clutching his chest. Colby pushed him out of the saddle with the rifle barrel and watched him tumble.

The sound of the body hitting the ground was a confirmation. Colby gave Winchester a few moments to see if he'd move beyond twitching. He didn't. That satisfied Colby.

The shouts of the cowboys trying to figure what the hell had happened and the sound of the cattle stirring rose together like orchestrated music. Colby felt the thundering under his feet and faced the wide slope of grass that led into the small Kansas valley to see the demons crossing it at full gallop, charging toward the herd.

Their horses were phosphorous white skeletons with bursts of flame rippling from their manes and tails. Cloaked and hooded in red, the Fire Riders numbered twenty. They rode in a tight military formation, almost shoulder to shoulder, out of the spring night. Half held torches high, with their rifles in saddle scabbards. The others rode with pistols in their free hand, keeping their reins tight with the other. Several brandished cavalry sabers.

Some cowboys broke wide, getting off their shots, while the rest kept the herd in check. Colby positioned the Winchester to his shoulder and took aim, shooting the cowboys from their horses as if he were knocking old cans off a fence post.

He had seen one show off his quick-draw, so he killed him before angling the rifle around and shooting an older fellow who kept his gun in the belt loop of his pants. The revolver was drawn, and he was trying to steady it, when Colby put one through his throat.

Colby had talked to him over morning coffee, learned about his grandkids and his reputation as a man who could kill six men with five shots. He'd gotten a kick out of the old man's bragging, so he hoped the cowboy hit the ground dead, not lingering.

The one who laughed at Colby the loudest?

He rode fast around the herd, drawing down and screaming at the rustlers, letting loose four rounds from a Henry rifle. He managed to hit one Rider in the leg and a horse in the rump. Colby cracked a slug into the laugher's chest, saw him lurch back in the saddle but still holding on, then fired again, taking him out through his left eye.

They'd been difficult shots, each one a flame with an echo that Colby didn't let die before shooting again. He made it all one clean action, one continuous sound, and then it was done. He felt satisfaction as the Fire Riders circled the cattle and began moving them off, with no one putting up a fight.

Colby touched the side of his collarbone where he'd been bullet-kissed. The tiny wound burned as if someone had slapped him with a hot spoon, but the pain of getting shot was nothing. What Colby hated was that a bullet wound of any kind was evidence that the job had gone sloppily.

This job had gone well.

He stayed his tall chestnut stallion, patted the sweat from the back of the animal's neck as a steer butted his way out of the herd and started to run. His cries were loud, getting louder. The other cattle stirred, brayed, began pawing the ground.

Colby angled his horse around, the rifle at his shoulder, just in case. A cloudless moon gifted him just enough light to watch it all over the sights of the Winchester.

The Fire Riders signaled each other to ride out for

a larger circle, giving the cattle their room, then moving ahead of the herd. Cloaks were stuffed into saddles and belts cinched tight to prevent excessive movement of their clothes, to prevent the cattle from spooking any more.

Eyes in the herd were wide, heads bowed to fight, and cries getting damn loud. Their weight and near panic could be felt as the cattle slammed into each other, ready to run for nothing.

One of the Riders, just a towheaded boy with his hood pushed back, galloped past Colby, charging for the running steer. With a good grip, the boy seemed part of his horse as he rode alongside the steer but not too close. He let his pinto and the shorthorn share movement before slipping his lasso over its head and pulling it easy. The steer bellowed, twisting at the rope.

The herd reacted to the cry. A few more started to break. The Fire Riders chased them down.

Colby stood in his stirrups, watching the boy lean from his saddle, stretching as far as he could to grab the steer's tail and bring it up toward his shoulders. He held it there, his skinny body straining, but legs locked around his horse.

The steer slowed, feeling the pressure on his tail. The kid pulled up, dropped from his saddle, brought the steer to a stop. He dug in his heels, tightening the lasso, and turned the huge animal around, leading it back to the herd.

The Riders had moved in front of the other cattle, slowing them enough to push them toward the trail break. The boy let the steer loose, and it fell in with the others.

Colby settled back in his saddle as the other cows and steers were brought into line. The boy showed the other Riders how to work them, make them move together.

A Fire Rider pulled up his white-skulled horse and spoke through his hood to Colby, his words catching in his throat. "We almost lost it, but you did it good for us."

"You were late."

"We're riding in, not coming on the Kansas Express."

Colby kept the rifle cradled in his arms. "I'm just saying that when there's a plan, I like to stick to it. I'm not inflexible, as you can see."

The Rider's voice was easy, the Eastern Europe bleeding through. "That old man was a dead shot with a rifle. He was a worry, I can tell you. But you got them all."

"I like a job done thoroughly. This is a good herd, and you got it without a fight, which was the point of my being here."

With the Fire Riders pushing them, the sound of the cattle moving out was solid in the air. The towhead was in the lead, guiding the herd with expertise.

Colby had to shout over the din. "That's a good boy, knows more about what he's doing than anybody."

"He's a kid. He is learning."

"Just an opinion." He held out his hand. "My money. The rest of my fee."

The Rider just looked at him from behind the red hood, his barrel chest straining against the matched tunic. There was no expression that could be judged, no sense of emotion in the eyes, so Colby angled the barrel of the rifle toward him.

The Fire Rider said, "You going to kill me?"

"Not part of the strategy, but if it needs to be altered, I can accommodate and get my fee from your superiors." Colby frowned. "Did you understand anything I just said?"

The Rider had a Peacemaker in his hand. "I can't never tell if you're an educated ass or just an ass." He took a stack of bills bound with paper bands from his saddlebag and tossed it.

Colby caught it with one hand, keeping the other on the rifle's trigger.

"You want I should stay while you count it?"

Colby slipped the cash into the pocket of his filthy disguise. "We'll be working together again. If it's short, we can settle our debts personally."

"You talk like that, but my face, you haven't seen it."

Colby said, "Not in person, but you have a wife— dark hair with blue eyes, which is very unusual—and two daughters. In Havalock County, isn't it? And you're Romanian?"

The Rider managed to spit through his hood, turn his horse, and run it to join the others as they herded the cattle across the small patch of grazing land, toward their new water and new brands.

Colby just shook his head in wonder at the quality of the people he was forced to sometimes work with. It almost wasn't worth the feel of the cash in his pocket. Almost.

He watched as the last of the Riders followed the herd and was lost in the night shadows. He dropped from his stallion and walked it to the small cook fire, poured himself half a cup of reboiled coffee, then topped it off with premium Evan Williams from a silver comfort flask.

He could still hear the cattle making their way over the hill, just a distant jumble of sounds. The stallion snorted in the night chill.

The fire was dying.

Colby looked at the cowboys scattered about the

camp, lying facedown, their lives spilled wet around them, their blood black in the moonlight. He lifted his cup of coffee and bourbon, toasting his targets, "Gentlemen, to a hard life lived well."

The voices were fragments, drifting through the barred window above Bishop's bed. He knew one of them was Tucker, but the other was someone younger, with a thick Louisiana accent, talking so fast his words swamped into each other without a pause in between. He kept repeating Bishop's name, but the rest was blather to him, as he fought himself awake. Bishop tried sitting up, but his right hand jerked him back. He'd been handcuffed to the iron frame of the bed.

Harvey laughed, his braying coming from someplace Bishop couldn't see. "How'd you like it? Can't open your big mouth now, can ya?"

Bishop hadn't been asleep. He'd been unconscious. Coming back was like putting together pieces of a broken mirror—sounds and faces not quite fitting, slivers missing. And the pain. The more Bishop was aware, the worse the pain hit him, but he wasn't going to slip back. He wasn't.

Harvey dangled the bullwhip on Bishop's swollen face, just letting the frayed tip rest on one of the wounds. "I started with the Cattleman's Crack to put you down, and then I used the Snake Killer. Just a little flick to bring the whip back, that's the trick. Supposed to take the head off a rattler. Must sting like hell."

Bishop managed, "It does."

"You're gonna have some scars."

"Already have some."

Harvey teased the end of the whip by Bishop's

purple . . . and shut . . . eyes. "Maybe you'll have, uh, bitchin' pains in your face," he brayed, "if you live that long."

Bishop twisted away, throwing a kick at Harvey. "You never dropped me with that whip."

Harvey punched Bishop in the chest with the whip handle. "Keep tryin' half-man, 'cause your time's coming."

"Kill a one-armed man while he's chained, maybe when I'm sleeping? Brave as hell."

Harvey slammed the edge of the bunk with one of his size twelves, knocking Bishop off, wrenching his left arm behind him, stretching the wrist that was anchored to the iron frame.

"I don't have to do nothing. That guy out there with Tucker? He just claimed the body of one of the men you and that squaw killed. Chaney? I dug him up, threw him in his wagon. He's a relative, and damnation, does he want to see you."

"I'm sure." Bishop stood, slowly turning to release his arm, almost popping his shoulder. The whip marks seemed joined as one blister across his face, the purple cuts splitting up his cheeks, eyes, and throat.

Harvey said, "Tucker won't let him in 'cause he might blow your damn head off."

"Want to save that for yourself?"

"Hell, it won't take that much to finish you."

"Harvey, there's nothing you can do. You'll never match what I've known."

Harvey coiled the bull whip. "You really askin' for more?"

Bishop's broken face came together in a go-to-hell smile.

* * *

Albert Tomlinson didn't fill up a quarter of Colby's hotel room doorway. He stood there clutching a leather satchel and waiting for permission to enter. His new suit hung too loose on his stooped shoulders and couldn't hide the single-shot Marlin Standard pistol in his inside pocket. The weight of the gun actually made him favor his left side a bit.

Colby, in a satin robe piped along the collar and sleeves, noted the outlined shape of the Marlin and guessed its make and model.

"You're quite a man with weapons, Mr. Colby."

"One of the reasons you hire me. Shut the door. The drafts in this place are this side of intolerable."

Albert shut the door, pressing his hand flat against its parquet inlay that was in keeping with the rest of the room. The furniture was new. A bookcase took up one wall and a personal-sized desk was built into it. The large bed was angled between a standing fireplace with scuttle and bed warmer and French doors that opened onto a small balcony overlooking the street. A pair of rocking chairs waited in the balcony's shade for whoever wanted to enjoy their comfort.

"Have you taken advantage of your balcony, yet?"

Colby said, "No reason to," as he took pressed pants and clean shirt from the closet and started to dress.

"It's paid for . . . at the maximum rate. Seems a shame to waste it."

Colby checked a loose button on his shirt, feeling no need to respond.

Albert said, "Me and my girls were making do in a prairie schooner, trying to get down Wyoming-way, for my new position and all. Ever travel like that? I think we found every piece of bad luck you could trip over, but finally made it."

"Congratulations on your tenacity."

Albert's eyes couldn't help but envy the shaving kit laid out on the dresser. An ivory-handled razor lay open on a fresh towel. Specialty lathered soaps were stacked neatly next to the washbowl, alongside a bottle of imported after-scent.

"A place like this would have been a fine break from the way we were getting along."

"You're working now, Tomlinson. Why not treat yourself?"

"I've never felt comfortable doing that."

"All business, yes?" Colby noted. "There's a tub behind that folding screen. I just used it. The bottom's still wet if you need to check, but the bed has more lumps than a swaybacked mule, so I'd ask for a partial refund." He tossed Albert the too-patched shirt caked with dust, sweat, and a little blood. "Put that in the stove."

Albert checked it for rips before stuffing it into the belly of the room stove.

Colby looked at him. "Thinking you could get more use out of it?"

"Not as a shirt. Maybe to patch something else."

"Thrift comes part and parcel with your work, but that's evidence I was the bumpkin who couldn't lasso a sleeping coonhound. An embarrassing guise, so we'll let it burn. But, it did win me this." Colby held up the Winchester, his fingers tracing the silver scrollwork around the stock and cheek piece. "That's a twenty-four-inch, heavy twisted barrel." He cocked the rifle. "Do you hear that perfection? The finest that Winchester makes, and this is even finer still, the '73. Owned by a gentleman of breeding. I wish he hadn't chosen to use it, but he had his job, and so did I."

Colby placed the rifle on the bed as if putting an infant down for its nap, then laid out a thick, rolled saddle blanket next to it. It was a Navajo pattern, fastened at both ends and the middle with buckled leather straps. The bed sagged under its weight.

Albert asked, "So, you didn't carry a gun with you on this job?"

"Questioning my methods?"

"No, we're very pleased. Just wondering why you take the chance."

Colby regarded him for a moment before unfastening the straps and unrolling the blanket, revealing his weapons cache. Four rifles of various make and caliber were fitted into special sleeves. Six pistols were arranged around them, held in place by small leather ties, and a pocket held ammunition. An assortment of knives lay flat along the blanket's edges. He looked at Albert. "What chance?"

Colby took the three throwing blades he hadn't used and put them back in their own pocket. "I have these made especially for jobs like yours. Very balanced, very effective. The edge sharper than a Japanese katana."

"I see. Very nice."

He heard Albert swallow and smiled. He slipped a long-barrel Buntline from its ties, and checked its action. "This beauty hasn't seen use in too long, which is never a good thing for a gun, and that leads to your question. In some cases, I don't carry because no one feels I'm a threat if I'm unarmed. I can always take a firearm from someone—they're all around me—but if they think I'm wandering around without . . . well, people are more inclined to write me off. That's my element of surprise."

"You definitely surprised the hell out of them. It's appreciated."

Albert opened the satchel and removed an envelope that was straining with contents. He held it out to Colby.

With a look, he said to drop it on the bed.

Albert did. "There is another job in the offing, but it's got to be done quickly. You'd have to leave right away."

Colby was wrapping his new prize Winchester in lightly oiled cloth. "It's always urgent."

"And as always, my employer would like to put you under yearly salary. It's rather generous."

Colby smiled at the way Albert's voice dropped when he spoke of salary. "I'm sure, but I prefer to continue on a situation-by-situation basis."

Albert took a second envelope from the satchel, this one long and narrow with an oval family portrait attached to it. Colby took the picture, studied it for a moment, his eyes fixed on the young couple and their son. The husband and wife were blond-headed, wearing their Sunday best. Her features were plain but better than his. Both had one hand on the shoulder of their blond son, who stood in front of them, smiling.

Colby turned the photograph facedown and said, "The child looks to be about ten. Isn't this the boy that rides for you?"

"If you're asking if he's a Fire Rider, yes."

"He worked last night. He's good, has good control. Better than the rest. Why are you giving him to me?"

"They stopped to water the herd and were set upon by John Chisum's men. The boy got himself captured."

"Do you want the Chisum men also or just the boy?"

"The amount in the envelope is the answer. They

were camped ten miles past the Little Fingers and moved on from there."

"That should be an easy track."

"Just so long as it's done quickly. Those are the instructions, and I've delivered them."

"And very precisely, too. In a case like this, I think a message needs sending. To discourage Mr. Chisum's men from trying this again." Colby pulled a rifle from its blanket sleeve and replaced it with the Winchester. He held up his new selection. "My choice would be the Colt's Dragoon revolving rifle. Do you agree?"

Albert had a pencil in his hand and wrote in a small ledger he'd produced from his inside jacket pocket. "Whatever you want, I'm sure will be appropriate."

"That ledger suits you better than the pistol."

"All business expenses are noted."

"What do you have me down as? What do you call me?"

"No name. Just the job—regulator."

Colby loaded the Dragoon. "God, that term's just a pretentious disguise. Enter what I am—an assassin. You pay me to take human life. I'm not ashamed."

The depot clerk they called Junior struggled to write as fast as the stranger was talking, but was losing the fight to age-failing eyes and ears. "Sorry, sir. You're gonna have to say again. From the top."

The stranger, finely dressed in tailored wool with a matching hat, and only the grime on his boots spoiling the image, leaned into the window and slowed his thick, New Orleans speech. "Whatever happens to that prisoner yonder, make sure to wire me straight away. Now, if he gets himself hung—"

"Well, they got him up for murder. Quite a few," Junior interrupted as he scribbled with swollen knuckles.

"If he gets himself hung in or out of his cell, or shot by anyone, or trampled by a runaway stallion, or struck by lightning, you wire me through Western Union, general. I'll check frequently during my travels. I'm fully aware of Doctor Bishop's situation, but must know immediately if they're any changes."

"Yes, sir, Mr. Chaney. I got it all."

"Actually, this might have been easier on you. My apologies." Virgil Chaney pressed an embossed business card and ten dollars into Junior's palm. "You should know there's a lot of fellas interested in Dr. Bishop. They have asked me to do them the same service." He nodded without changing expression and handed Junior a new fifty. "I trust this takes me to the front of the line?"

"Yes, sir."

Junior sneezed at the ripe perfume rising from the corpse slung on the back of Chaney's freshly groomed horse. "If you and your friend are off to Louisiana, we should box 'em up, straight away."

Virgil Chaney said, "Hardly a friend. He was my third cousin. He died at Dr. Bishop's one hand. We won't be taking the train, but I believe people will know we're approaching, especially if the wind is behind us."

Junior laughed like he should as Chaney climbed onto his horse, then took a fine handkerchief from his breast pocket with a flourish and tied it around his head, covering his mouth and nose. "Whatever happens to Doctor John Bishop?"

"I'll send the wire. First thing."

"Good man." Chaney tipped his hat with the silver band before turning his horse away from the Paradise rail station and riding the scant mile out of town. The corpse was lashed behind him.

Junior sneezed again.

Bent over his desk, a blood bruise from Bishop's fist mapping one side of his face. Tucker regarded three separate envelopes in front of him. Each one had different initials on it. From the cell, Bishop made a pained sound.

Tucker kicked his chair back "Goddamn, I don't want to hear nothing from you!"

"Hurting."

"You hurt 'cause you got a smart mouth and you're jackass stubborn! You gonna come across with that money you got hid?" Tucker waited for Bishop's answer, hand on his gun.

Finally Bishop answered. "No."

Tucker grabbed a bottle of whiskey from his desk, tore open the cell door, and poured the alcohol over the near-open wounds lashing Bishop's face, "Maybe a drink 'll make you feel better."

Bishop threw his head back as the whiskey soaked the cuts. Searing fire rolled him from the bed, dropping him to the cell floor, his left arm still chained.

Tucker said, "You ain't gonna get the best of me twice!"

Bishop managed a grin. "I can live with this, Tuck. I couldn't live with the infection that the whiskey just killed off. Thanks, Sheriff, you did me a real service."

CHAPTER THREE
Prophecy

Across a stretch of beauty more than four hundred miles away from Paradise, Colby was enjoying a morning ride, feeling the sun, and thinking of sending Albert Tomlinson a complimentary note. The bookkeeper's information about Chisum's men and the Three Fingers had been absolutely right. They'd made camp there, leaving a lot of sign behind. Colby knew it wasn't a matter of sloppiness. They worked for Chisum and assumed no one would be damn fool enough to follow or challenge, especially with a prisoner in tow.

He'd ridden up on the first campsite, ashes in plain sight, then tracked them for a few miles, their horses leaving a perfect trail in the soft earth of the riverbank they were edging. The trail made sense since this finger of the Arkansas River led directly to a railhead where they could board the train for New Mexico and then on to the big J.C. ranch in Roswell.

They were taking the back way, quiet, with a false sense of security. Colby always liked that. He'd once told an employer, "The easiest man to kill is one who's sure he's beaten the odds."

He stayed casual in the saddle, letting his stallion follow his nose. The Dragoon Revolving Rifle hung in a scabbard by his left leg, with the Navajo-blanket arsenal secured behind him. Just to be thorough, a new Smith & Wesson Schofield that had belonged to a big mouth was holstered on his hip. That was an enjoyable kill, and Colby liked the pistol for luck, if nothing else.

He found a shallow and crossed over to the other side, riding upward onto a small trail that gave him a good view of the river and the opposite shore. The air was pine-sweet, and the taste settled in his mouth like a drop of honey. His relaxation was total, even as the Chisum men came into view. Using a spyglass, he counted five cowboys with six pistols, and three rifles.

Another man in a tall felt hat and finely tailored long coat rode alongside the group, sometimes speaking to the older cowboy riding point. They exchanged a laugh the others didn't share. The man in the hat had a face as pink as an infant's, with no hint of hair on his head at all.

Colby noted the aberration, then swung the glass to the others.

The young Fire Rider rode in the middle of the group, hands hog-tied to his saddle horn, head bowed, and blond hair tacky with blood. Colby focused the small telescope, bringing in sharp focus. The boy had bruises around his eyes and a purple lash along his jaw where he'd taken a hell of a punch.

Colby pocketed the scope and urged his horse on.

Moving ahead to a small outcrop, he pulled up, hidden by a gathering of red maple trees. It was a perfect ambush point. Bedded with new grass, the trees provided cover and the river trail was a clear shot in either direction.

The Colt's Dragoon slipped easily from its scabbard. He wiped it down, humming as he looked around. The place would be perfect for him and his son to picnic one day. Maybe do a little fishing. Colby allowed himself the thought for a few beats, then cleared his mind as he took a crouching position behind the maples, the rifle flush against his shoulder.

He touched his neck where the bullet had kissed him. The quick shot of pain was small, but a reminder.

He narrowed his eyes at the Riders. The man in the felt hat was still riding close to the older cowboy.

Colby shifted his body, the weapon settling, feeling right. Completely comfortable. Somewhere above, a gathering of mountain plovers spoke in low music as he took aim, began his calculations for distance, and assigned a killing order.

The group rode into his bull's-eye range.

He watched as the man in the hat and the cowboy shook hands. He drew a breath, focused on the man's back, ready to shoot.

Someone shouted.

Colby's eyes shifted. The boy kicked at one of the flanking riders and took off running, his horse breaking for the woods along the river.

Colby followed the boy with the barrel sight and fired once, blowing a hole clear through him, throwing him hard from his saddle, hands still tied. The sound of the Dragoon was thunder, eating the boy's scream and not dying for miles.

The other cowboys opened up on what they could see—a blast of smoke from distant trees. They popped off shots in Colby's direction, the sound and the flash of their pistols moments apart. A slug tore into the maple trunk behind him as he leveled and shot one, two of the cowboys.

All in the head.

The slugs took them off their horses and delivered them to the riverbank. One spun in the air, landing face-first in the water, his blood swirling away pink. A cowboy with two pistols tried laying down a quick barrage. It was nothing but a nuisance as Colby hit him solidly between the eyes, leaving half to be buried.

Colby swung the Dragoon around as the older cowboy brought up a repeater. Colby took his face before he could get anything off, and his horse galloped away, the cowboy's body hanging in the stirrups.

The man in the felt hat was gone. Only a whisper of dust was left behind as he ran his chocolate mare away from the river, up a small logging trail, and into the woods.

Colby cracked the last rifle shot in his direction, the echo from his others still rolling along the hills. Nothing. No scream. Nothing. He jumped to his feet, tore the Smith & Wesson from its holster, and pulled the trigger four times, cutting into the trees that framed the logger's trail.

The shots were precise, aimed at movement between branches—the possible shadow of a rider. He waited for return fire or the sight of Felt Hat's mare running without a rider.

There was neither.

* * *

The kid charged from the train depot, the telegram wrinkling in his hands. He jumped from an old wagon tongue to a small pile of bricks, staying above Paradise's ankle-deep mud. Steering around a tethered mule, he ran past the prisoners' graveyard, then crossed himself before knocking on the sheriff's office door.

Tucker answered, his face looking like pounded beef. He gave the kid a dime for the telegram. "This is for swallowin' your tongue." He slammed the iron door and bolted it.

Still cuffed, Bishop was on his bunk, Bible out of reach, staring at nothing. He glanced when Tucker came to the cell with a bowl of soup from the night before. Bishop's nose and eyes were still whip-swollen purple, his teeth pushing against his lips, but the whiskey shower had helped.

"Gonna feed that to me?"

"You haven't had grub for almost two days. You're not gonna starve yourself in my jail. Sit up."

Bishop sat up, his only arm straining behind him. "I could use a spoon."

"You think so?" Tucker stood before him, holding the bowl of soup. "Cut off both your arms, and I wouldn't trust ya. Lean forward.

Bishop lowered his chin as Tucker lifted the bowl. "We both look like hell."

The soup was thick with old chicken fat, but went down.

Tucker took the bowl away and held out the telegram. "You're gonna have a visitor tomorrow. A woman. Maybe she's coming for all that money you're hiding?"

Bishop let it lie, then said, "Any chance for more soup?"

"Chow time's done."

Bishop didn't hear Tucker, didn't care about chow. He thought about the woman who was coming. Something flashed in his mind. A streak of lightning behind his eyes. A beautiful young woman on a painted horse, leathers torn, bloody tears on a proud face. Raging in Cheyenne, surrounded by twists of steel, blades of fire, and a pile of bullet-riddled bodies.

It was nightmare and memory colliding.

He struggled to remember something else, a memory of seeing something else . . . but it was lost as a rain of blood flooded his mind's eye.

Tucker said, "You look like you went someplace, Doc, but you didn't."

Bishop gave his cuffed hand a jerk. "You heard the man, Sheriff. Outhouse-rat crazy."

The steam whistle shrilled then sputtered into a coughing fit, thanks to a bullet hole in its brass. The old Baldwin Locomotive churned through the low Colorado hills, wood smoke pluming. It was not making good time, and the engineer had to announce its coming over and over.

In the only passenger car, Frank Farrow covered his ears, trying to find a comfortable spot on the hard bench seat. The whistle finished, and the car heaved, knocking his tall felt hat to the floor. He picked it up and set it on top of the suitcase resting beside him. Handling the case as if it were spun glass, he carefully adjusting its position.

Sitting directly across from him, the woman in starched gray that matched her manner was unaffected by the whistle or the rough ride. She kept her attention on a copy of *The Woman in White* by Wilkie Collins. It appeared she had an idea about herself, about her image, that was so precise, anything that forced her from it would probably make her shatter like Grandma's vanity mirror.

That was Farrow's first assumption about the woman . . . and it was wrong.

On the seat next to her was large squared birdcage with a domed top and draped in barkcloth. Without taking her eyes from the novel's pages, she reached into a purse, took out a small robin's egg wrapped in tissue, and held it next to a slit in the cloth.

Farrow didn't find her unattractive and leaned forward on his elbows, watching. A sharp-edged, black bill snatched the egg, then instantly retreated back into the cage.

Farrow said, "Is that a raven? If it's a crow, he's as big as a hoot owl."

"But it's not."

"Ravens. Very intelligent birds."

"I've found him to be so, yes."

"The eaters of the dead."

His last remark made Ophelia Wylde leave her book with annoyance, not moving her head. Her expression remained locked, even as she wondered about Farrow's complete lack of hair, which made him seem eerily faceless, except for his black eyes fixed on her.

The car jostled again, the tracks groaning under the train's weight. Farrow ran his forefinger across his upper lip as if a waxed mustache were growing. "If I were him, I'd think I'd rather by flying."

"Sir, are you accusing me of being cruel? I could open the cage door, and Eddie would remain inside. I don't impose myself on him."

"Not at all. I just know birds a little bit. I had a parrot for a time."

"Hardly the same thing."

"Parrots can be mean. Mine was. The raven's more docile, isn't he?"

Ophelia finally looked up. "Eddie can be provoked."

Farrow said, "I didn't mean to interrupt your reading, ma'am. My apologies."

Ophelia put her book aside. "I'm slightly irritated because you did mean to interrupt. You're curious about something, so go ahead and ask. Then I can return to my book."

Farrow gave himself a moment. "I heard you ask the conductor about our arrival in Paradise."

"And why is that your business?"

"That's my stop, too. I guarantee there aren't two more passengers on the next five trains with Paradise as their destination."

"I ask my question again."

Farrow shifted just enough to reveal the shoulder holster under his jacket, and the .38 revolver tucked in it. "It's just that there's very little in Paradise, nothing in fact. But I can't imagine we're both going there for the same reason."

"I would seriously doubt it."

"Or the same person."

Ophelia picked up her book. "You're being intrusive, sir."

"My name's Frank Farrow, ma'am. I work for the Chisum Cattle Company, and I'm familiar with you, Miss Wylde. Very. That raven's your calling card. You've achieved some fame for your abilities."

"And whatever you've achieved, is it infamous? I see the condition of your hat."

Farrow picked up the felt hat and put the tip of his finger through the bullet hole in the crown, before giving Ophelia a nod of surrender. "That was a close thing. I've worked both sides of the law, yes."

"And what side are you working now?" Before Farrow could respond, Ophelia continued. "Don't bother. I can—perceive—who you are, sir. I assure you that our reasons for visiting Paradise are entirely different."

"I've never met anyone before who'd ever summoned a ghost."

Ophelia's words were separated by moments. "That's . . . not . . . what . . . I . . . do."

Farrow let the train's voice take over—cars banging into each other, steel groaning, then settling as the track smoothed—then he said, "It would be a real humdinger of a coincidence if you were going to Paradise to see Dr. John Bishop. He's become notorious in his own right, hasn't he?"

Ophelia turned a page before finishing it, refusing to meet Farrow's look. She went to her purse for another robin's egg and held it in front of the cage. "*Sauvez-moi des idiots.*"

The egg was snatched.

"My French is poor, but certain words I do recognize. My apologies. I'm just a businessman with a curious nature."

Ophelia said, "No, you're not. I won't be manipulated by conversational cues and games, Mr. Farrow. Believe me, I know them all."

"Understood."

During the conversation, Farrow's hand rested on the suitcase next to him, palm down, making sure it was there. He shifted his attention out the window as the car swayed, passing the twisted remains of a derailment.

Soot smeared the glass like a fine, dry cloud, blurring his vision as if he were seeing tintypes of the ruins, specters of the train wreckage. Huge sections of the mail- and boxcars were blasted apart, partial roofs and doors scattered along the hillside, all scarred with bullet holes. Steel wheels, axles, and corroded iron lay by the tracks, rusting in giant heaps for scavengers to pick over and the weather to eat.

The train slowed into the curve before the Paradise depot, passing the gigantic, burned corpse of the locomotive lying on its side where it had jumped the tracks, its steam belly torn in half.

Dead and useless.

"God a-mighty, who could have survived that?" Farrow glanced at Ophelia for her response to the deliberate question he left hanging.

She gave away nothing. Head barely turned, she stole a look out her part of the window, but her eyes were fixed on the wreck as if she were sighting it down a long barrel. Then she turned back to her book, refusing the distraction.

The awful whistle got them out of their seats.

The train rolled into Paradise, almost overshooting the small station, wheels skidding across poorly repaired tracks. The engineer peered from the cab, swearing like hell as Farrow and Ophelia Wylde stepped from the only passenger car.

He helped her onto the platform, she holding the raven's cage high with one hand and a large carpetbag in the other. A burst of brake steam caught them both as the engine chugged, not waiting another minute before moving on to a better town.

Farrow said, "So, this is Paradise."

"Your irony is not biting."

Farrow did his best to block Ophelia from any more of the train's grime. She nodded and stepped around him, walking deliberately to the edge of the platform and the planking that crisscrossed Paradise's muddy streets. He stayed beside her, carrying his briefcase and offering his free hand, which she would not take.

Ophelia kept moving. "You must know, Mr. Farrow, that your manner is off-putting to me."

"Oh, I'm very aware. I bid you good afternoon." Farrow stepped back, made a grand gesture with his felt hat, and allowed Ophelia a considerable lead.

She maneuvered the planks toward the jail, the raven's cage leading the way. As she paused to take in the place, her back stiffened even more. Silently, she agreed with Farrow that Paradise was ill named.

The town was rotting from the streets up.

The scatter of buildings had been washed dirty brown by the swamping spring floods, the high waters soaking everything through before leaving behind piles of silt and filthy debris that fed the termites. The needed repairs were stacks of green lumber splitting apart, windows without glass, unfinished stairs, and never-shoveled walls of mud.

The livery was empty save for a buggy missing a wheel, but the small corral beside the depot had two played-out horses and one tall bay that kept head and tail high while walking the fence.

At the end of the main street, an old two-story was trying for resurrection as a couple of grunt-backs struggled to hang a double front door with a Chinese symbol for love in its center. The rest of the house was in dire need, but the symbol was fine stained glass. Paradise's only touch of opulence.

Ophelia glanced over her shoulder as one of the men swore at a hammer-busted finger. She recognized the stained-glass symbol, watched Farrow quickstep from the planking to the front porch of the place. A heavy girl in bodice and nightgown was on the balcony, sipping a cup of tea.

Marge leaned over the railing, spilling the tea. "Are you Mr. Farrow? They're waiting for you in the parlor."

Ophelia muttered, "So obvious," and added a phrase in French before continuing along the planking to the squat stone building that was the Paradise jail.

The raven squawked, "Nevermore!"

Farrow heard it and laughed as he went inside.

Wearing a velvet suit with a lace collared blouse, Soiled Dove led Farrow into the House of Pleasures parlor. He thought it less desperate than the rest of Paradise. Sheets shrouded moldy furniture and water-stained walls waited for paint, but a new pool table still in its crate took up the center of the room and several carpets were rolled into a corner. All that offered a bit of hope.

He was impressed with Dove, the way she moved in her clothes. Her valentine-shaped face with the know-ing smile, tight strawberry curls, and barely five feet of height, made her nymph-like. A knowing innocent.

An explosion of a voice turned Farrow around.

In his thirties with a broad chest and smile, Mayor O'Brien roared into the room. Sleeves rolled up, he held out a big hand for the shaking. "Mr. Farrow, this is a fine thing to meet you!"

Farrow held back. O'Brien's hand was streaked with blood from a badly cut thumb.

O'Brien jammed the thumb into his mouth. "Stings worse than a Sunday hangover. I'm not much of a carpenter."

"You're putting up the doors?"

O'Brien gestured for Farrow to sit in one of two satin chairs. "Well, somebody has to. And the girls are always busy." O'Brien guffawed as he took a seat.

Soiled Dove wrapped his bloody thumb with a hand-kerchief. "He's the nicest mayor I've ever known."

Farrow nodded. "I'm sure."

O'Brien said, "Honey, see about my private sour mash."

"Actually, a glass of port would go down better, if you have it."

Dove smiled. "I'll bring the whiskey and see what we can do about the wine." She gave the two men a little bob before pulling the parlor doors shut. They didn't hang straight, but she finally got them closed.

O'Brien said, "I have to work on those, too."

Farrow let his smirk play. "You're not what I expected."

"Sometimes a man has to roll up his sleeves." O'Brien opened a box of cigars. "So, working for Mr. John Chisum? Folks claim a lot of things, so I don't know if you have responsibility or you're mucking stalls. Either is fine with me." He offered a cigar.

Farrow declined with a wave of his hand, bringing a silver cigar case from his jacket, popping it open. "Wouldn't you enjoy something of a little more quality?"

"I'm satisfied with my own kind, thanks."

"You might want to improve your lot." Farrow set his suitcase on the covered couch and opened it with a small key on a chain. He stood back, his own cigar clenched in a Cheshire smile, revealing stacks of neatly bound bank notes, numbering thousands.

O'Brien said, "I'll hear your proposition."

* * *

Ophelia Wylde had stepped off the planking before reaching the jail, hiked up her dress, and walked around the low-slung building to a small patch of weeds in the back.

It was a place forgotten behind the jail, bordered on one side by a falling-down fence where the unclaimed murdered of Paradise found some kind of rest. A smattering of slapped-together crosses stood as markers. Numbers had been scrawled on them, but no names or dates.

Sheriff Tucker had that information in a little book, listing all the numbers and who they were. Also, who'd killed them or who they'd killed. It was simpler than keeping track of names or making new markers. If family wanted to claim number forty-six, all they had to do was dig him up.

Ophelia dropped her carpetbag, hung the cage on a bent nail sticking from a fence post, and lingered by a grave that had been freshly turned. She closed her eyes for a moment, shoulders lowering, the rigidity leaving her posture.

It was silent—no sound around her. Nothing.

The raven cried, snapping her eyes open, a wave of feeling bringing her body instantly to attention.

Watching the whole time from the small window in his cell, Harvey hacked as she took a pad of foolscap from the carpetbag and quickly drew on it with a piece of charcoal, her hand moving furiously.

Ophelia took the cage and stepped deliberately, passing Harvey's window. He spit, catching the hem of her dress. She took no notice and continued to the front door of the sheriff's office, each step a punch.

* * *

"You're drooling. It wouldn't matter if I wanted to buy your mother," Farrow said as he dropped the lid on the suitcase, then struck a match, relighting his Havana Robusto. He took a seat opposite O'Brien, drew deep to make a showing, ready for the mayor's immediate grovel. That's what he was used to.

O'Brien leaned forward on his large arms. "Don't be fooled by the sweat on my neck. You want results from me, present yourself and your business like a gentleman."

Soiled Dove entered with a glass of ink-dark red wine and a whiskey decanter. She silently poured.

Farrow said, "Sometimes you have to push to know who you're sitting with. My apologies."

O'Brien said, "Maybe."

Dove's eyes were on the case, even as she set out the drinks. "We didn't have any port, but this is a decent red from Williamsburg that I think should go down nicely."

Farrow couldn't hide his surprise.

Dove gave the men a smile and a little curtsey before leaving.

Farrow tasted the wine, approved.

O'Brien said, "If the cards cut right, she's going to do very well."

"I imagine some of the town ladies aren't welcoming that, but every business is important."

"Especially when you're trying to come back from the dead. That why you throw open that suitcase like you're dangling a carrot in front of a mule?"

"I meant no offense. I understand now." Farrow raised his glass. "To the mayor of Paradise! A man who knows how to do business."

Mayor O'Brien tipped some sour-mash into his glass. "You never know, do you?"

Ophelia was before Tucker, her body and manner thrust forward, the raven's cage on his desk. Harvey sprawled in an empty jail cell, running the whip through his hands, snickering.

She said, "You were given proper notice of my arrival. That prisoner has a right to visitors."

"I ain't saying you can't see him. Just tell me what it's all about."

"Private family matters."

Tucker held his bifocals like a monocle, squinting through the one unbroken lens. "But you ain't family. You're just some crone come buttin' in here, shrieking orders."

"If I violate the law, do you think the two of you could handle me?"

This last made Harvey bray, "You gonna try us?"

Ophelia said, "Doctor Bishop has a right to see me in his cell. You can inspect anything I give to him, monitor our visit."

"I don't think you're here to bust him out, but we'll check you out. Harvey'll be on guard. I got business, and you got fifteen minutes."

The raven made his voice heard.

Ophelia moved to stand by the cell door. "Doctor. Bishop, I am Miss Ophelia Wylde, and I've travelled to see you. Would you object if we visit?"

Bishop stood, the handcuff slapping the iron railing. His hair was combed, and his bloodstained shirt was buttoned to his neck. Trying not to grin because it pained too damn much, he grinned anyway, his whip-swollen face turning in on itself. "Just watching you these last five minutes has been a great pleasure, ma'am. I'd be honored to make your acquaintance."

Ophelia looked at Tucker. "Open it, then you can go to the bordello. That's correct, isn't it?"

Tucker swallowed his words. "No ma'am, it ain't." He made a show of rattling the keys before unlocking the door.

Ophelia stepped in as Harvey peered through the bars of the adjoining cell.

Harvey said, "Stinks in here, don't it?"

Bishop did his best to stand. "I'm sorry about these conditions."

"I've been in jails before." Ophelia turned to the sheriff. "A disabled man, compromised, and you have him chained like a wild animal?"

Tucker said, "Yep, and that's the way it's gonna stay. Fifteen minutes, Harvey!"

Eddie disagreed. "Nevermore!"

Ophelia took a few steps closer, smearing the fresh spots of blood on the cell floor with the toe of her shoe.

Harvey pressed his face against the bars, his tongue wagging. "That bird got a name?"

Ophelia stood quietly for a moment. "Eddie."

"Funny."

Bishop said, "Then why don't you two have a laugh?"

Harvey sauntered from the open cell, giving the bullwhip a loud crack. "Don't do nothing I wouldn't do, and that ain't much."

Ophelia looked at Bishop. "Another warning? You have these men on edge, Doctor."

Bishop said, "Harvey'll lean by the window, listening to every word. Then he'll repeat them wrong."

"That doesn't bother me a whit." Ophelia took another step, stopped. She felt something. Her arms stayed close to her side, but she allowed her fingers to part an invisible curtain, a small gesture she tried to obscure. Her voice broke just above a whisper. "Vóhkêhésoa told me there was black surrounding you, your aura."

"White Fox." Bishop mulled the name, was lost in it for a moment, then said, "She would know," before reaching out his right half-arm as if to shake hands. "Miss Wylde, you have me at a disadvantage."

"I've never felt anything like this. Violent death is all around you."

Bishop pulled on the cuff. "It's why I'm here. What do you mean, *you feel*?"

Ophelia said, "I'm here to offer you some relief." She took a letter from her purse. "This should serve."

Farrow emptied his glass, nodded toward the still-crated pool table in the middle of the parlor floor. "What's your game, Sheriff? Elimination? I prefer three-cushion, myself."

Tucker stood behind the mayor, waiting for the offer of his private stock. "Oh, I just hit a rack straight. Maybe wager a drink."

Farrow said, "I'd guess you win free drinks all night. Pool table, the ladies—this will be the place to be, provided the mayor gets all his work done."

O'Brien just smiled. "It's not easy. Take a drink, Tuck. Find a seat."

Farrow handed Tucker a cut Havana. "Not next to the suitcase."

The sheriff poured himself a shot and held the cigar as if it were solid gold.

Farrow said, "Those are Mr. Chisum's special imports."

O'Brien said, "Bring out Chisum's cigars or silver

coins dropped from his hind end, you're not getting anything up on us."

"Ran the bank here, didn't you Mr. Mayor? Until it failed?"

"By many acts of God. The railroad was supposed to bring business that it didn't, a couple good horse ranches were taken over and moved upstate. That hurt, but didn't kill us. We're strong people in this town, Mr. Farrow."

Farrow threw a glance at Tucker's damaged face. "That's very clear."

"We faced raiders—"

"Actually, you didn't." Farrow sipped his port.

O'Brien continued. "And flooding from the snow-melt up mountain damn near wiped us out."

"Damn near? You said you were dead."

"Coming back from the dead. Towns come back. We obviously have some value to you. What exactly is all that money supposed to buy?"

"Doctor John Bishop."

Tucker laughed. "Right after we hang him! I'll even let you keep the suit he wears!"

Farrow said, "His release."

O'Brien said, "There's no bail."

Tucker pulled some tobacco off the end of his tongue. "You know how many murder charges he's got on him? Hell, don't you know what happened here?"

"I read about it, saw the wreckage coming in."

"Them damn terrorists attacked that train, must of left fifty men dead before riding out!"

O'Brien said, "Except Bishop."

Farrow took a last sip. "But he wasn't with them. In

fact, he was about the only person in this dog-pile who fought back, isn't that so, Sheriff?"

Tucker shook his head, saying, "I wouldn't put it that way myself."

"That's how your deputy put it. He's down in Texas, speaks very highly of the good doctor, but not much else." Farrow brought his words in close. "Have you seen that shotgun rig? Seen him use it?"

Tucker said, "I've seen what happens when he does."

"Lots of dead men." O'Brien took his drink. "And when Bishop goes to trial, that means the hotel will be full up with reporters and rubbernecks. They'll all need a place to sleep and keep their horses and have a nice time. That's money to every business in town."

Farrow nodded. "Including this one. Anything else?"

O'Brien said, "The charges have already been filed. To reverse these plans won't be easy. Or popular."

Farrow asked, "All of these issues are solvable?"

"Dr. Bishop is no common outlaw, but there's a lot to consider."

"We've made all considerations."

Tucker drew in the taste of the fine leaf, let the smoke dance around his nose, but his mouth was dry, his heart racing as he rubbed a gold coin between his fingers.

O'Brien said, "You can't put a price on justice."

"Justice like letting John Bishop swing for fighting your fight?"

"I have to think of the town of Paradise, not just one prisoner." O'Brien finished the bourbon in his glass. "I'm trying to build something here."

Farrow regarded O'Brien. "A responsible elected official. It's nice to meet you, sir."

* * *

Eddie's "Nevermore" scraped the air as Bishop read the letter for the last time. Ophelia stood in her spot near him, but keeping a few steps away so she could observe. The darkness of his soul shadow had left her genuinely rattled, but she wasn't going to show any more emotion than she already had. That was a mistake.

He held out the letter to her. "I can't fold it."

Ophelia manipulated it back into an envelope and put it on the upended table with the leg that had been shot off. "I watched your eyes. You couldn't read everything she wrote."

Bishop said, "Half was in Cheyenne. I could read it once, but now I can't make heads or tails. My memory's spotted, at best."

"But you remember her, and her given name. Also, that she's considered beautiful."

"Yes, I remember."

"And your wife and son? Fox gave me details."

Bishop's voice was low. "That will never leave me."

"What about the rest? Soldier's disease?"

"Concussion from a grenade. The town doc sewed up my head then took off."

"I don't wonder. A very poor job, indeed."

Bishop pained through a swollen smile. "This is all new. This, I remember pretty well."

Ophelia said, "When you heard you had a visitor, you thought it was going to be Fox."

"The sheriff wouldn't uncuff me, so I got Harvey to comb my hair and button up my shirt."

"I'm sorry to disappoint."

Bishop said, "Miss Wylde, you delivered the letter. I appreciate it, and I'll try to read it again, but do you understand I'm a man they want to hang? All I know about what I've done is what they tell me. Maybe that's a strange kind of blessing."

"You may not recall a man named Chester Pardee. He was a ne'er-do-well who died in a gunfight against you. He had a link to your past."

Bishop said quietly, "I did fight Chester . . ."

"You killed him. His family asked me to bring them comfort, and I could do very little, given the kind of man he was. It's better you disposed of him. My journey took me to White Fox, who was with you, and now here."

"You get paid to follow the dead?"

"To assist the grieving, the troubled." Ophelia unbuttoned her sleeve and rolled it up to show a bracelet with four interwoven beaded strands joined together by a silver and turquoise clasp. "From White Fox, for helping you. I've never had anything so fine. That's an inherited skill. I believe her father is a gunsmith? Didn't he fashion your bizarre shotgun that's now so infamous?"

Bishop nodded. "Probably so."

"White Claw is also a thief and killer. She told me." Ophelia rolled down her sleeve to hide the bit of vanity. "Don't let your medical training reject what I have to say. I've found men in your profession can be very closed off."

"Nevermore!" screeched from Eddie's cage.

Bishop said, "I'll try. I want Fox to get what she paid for."

Ophelia let his words settle. "Dr. Bishop, what do you know about otherworldly phenomena?"

Bishop's swollen expression said it first. "Not much now, and damn little when I had my complete memory."

"You don't believe the dead have any influence on the living? You've left a lot of dead men behind."

Bishop jerked at his chain and angled his head toward the small window above his bunk. "Those are the graves of men I shot. Tucker can give you the names. I don't remember them."

Ophelia said, "They remember, and they've told me about it."

Harvey's bray erupted just outside the cell window. He glanced in with an all-crooked-teeth smile. "You buyin' this horse manure, Doc?"

Ophelia said to him, "We still have nine minutes . . . if you can tell time." To Bishop, she said, "You're not that much of a fool, are you?"

"Not like Harvey, no."

Ophelia moved closer to Bishop, tentatively placing her hand at the end of his left arm. It flexed, as if it were all there.

Ophelia said, "You can't explain that feeling, but it's real."

"There's a reason the body acts the way it does."

"And there are reasons the spirit behaves the way it does. Doctor, I was a charlatan who became a believer. I've used every trick in the book, sometimes to give someone a little hope, sometimes to bleed a fool dry. I know intimately the difference between what's fake and what's not. I walked in here and never felt anything so bleak in my life. If I was more romantic, I'd say you were an Angel of Death."

"You do know how to sell it, madam."

"When someone has an epiphany, they want to share it."

Bishop said, "But I'm just a man waiting to be condemned. Or so they tell me. Lot of prisoners in this country in the same fix, I imagine."

"But I wasn't sent to any of them. Are you saying you don't have nightmares?"

"You've earned your bracelet."

"I want you to see something before I go." Ophelia reached into her bag and removed a rolled sheet of paper. She opened it, holding it up so he could see her sketch of a man at the bottom of a deep pit with another man standing above him, aiming a gun.

"I drew this minutes before I walked in here . . . after standing at those graves. What does this mean to you?"

Bishop regarded the sketch but couldn't bring forth any words.

She said, "The only way your torture ends is when you kill a dead man."

"No, I think my torture ends when they hang me."

Ophelia was planted before him, holding out the drawing as a challenge. "Your quest was revenge against those who wronged you the most. Some are buried fifty feet from here. Is Beaudine the name?" Her words echoed.

Bishop said, "Tucker knows who's out there. He has the names."

"Beaudine."

Bishop coughed when Ophelia repeated the name. He thought he tasted blood in the back of his throat, erupting from an injury. His face numbed as if being covered with snow. He felt a sudden rush of cold. A picture of a man standing over him with an ax appeared in his mind.

He could feel both of his arms and sensed being held down.

Coming from somewhere was the sound of his wife and son . . . screaming. It was distant, like birds calling in far-off trees. The feelings and images lasted only a few heartbeats . . . like a slash of heat lightning.

Quickly, Bishop was back in his cell.

Ophelia locked into his eyes. "I knew that would stir you. I learned that name standing by those graves, and it took you someplace, didn't it? You remembered?"

"Amnesia turns the brain upside down and shakes it. Everything's displaced."

"That sounds like a doctor explaining to a patient."

It hurt like hell, but he had to smile. "I suppose I still am a doctor. Someplace."

Ophelia said, "And an avenger, right? This specter you're dreaming of is the worst of the lot. He wronged you more than anyone. I don't know who it is, the messages weren't clear, but you will confront him, and that'll be your peace."

Bishop said, "You give me all this nonsense as if I was getting out of here."

"I'm just giving you the messages I receive."

The light in the parlor had dimmed with the afternoon. A streak of sunlight focused on Farrow as he lifted the shelf out of the suitcase, revealing a compartment underneath containing two cloth sacks. His Cheshire grin returned. "Go ahead, Sheriff."

Tucker grabbed the two, tearing into one with stubby fingers. He almost burst out, but kept his voice low as he turned to O'Brien. "God a'mighty, I never seen so much money."

O'Brien said, "I have."

Tucker emptied one of the sacks of gold coins into his hands, dropping several on the floor. He grabbed for them as O'Brien watched.

"You get everything here, if you choose it." Farrow closed the case and locked it. "That's a hell of a lot for the two of you or enough for Paradise to get on its feet again. And, I might be able to arrange for a cattle shipment or two to work through your depot."

Tucker said, "It'd be a damn great thing for the town. You can't say that ain't true."

Farrow's smile was constant. "And it means you don't have to build a gallows, Mr. Mayor."

O'Brien stood. "What the hell makes this man so valuable?"

Farrow shook his head. "You only have to know that he is."

O'Brien looked at Tucker thumbing the stack of bills, loving the feel, and soaking in the deep perfume of new money. The sheriff couldn't hide his grin or pathetic giggle.

O'Brien studied his drink, thinking about a different sheriff.

Farrow said, "Gentlemen, we're in a house where everything's for sale. I need an answer."

Bishop brought up his cuffed hand as far as it would go to extend a courtesy to Ophelia. "Honestly, I think you've been playing a cruel game, madam, but I'm still obliged for the letter."

Ophelia didn't shake. She rolled up the sketch, placed it in Bishop's left hand, and let each word carry its weight. "Trust the dead."

Tucker slipped off the planking, and sank deep into the mud. "Maybe we could put some damn sidewalks in on Main Street. That'd be a nice change!" He freed himself with O'Brien and Farrow's help.

The mayor said, "Don't spend what's not yours, Tuck."

"The money's yours, the prisoner's mine." Farrow said, "If Bishop did that to your face, you must be awful glad to be rid of him."

"He looks worse." Tuck shook slop from his boots. "These are from Sears, Roebuck, and only a month old!"

O'Brien said, "Why does Bishop look worse? What have you been up to?"

"Doing my damn job."

Farrow was the first to reach the sheriff's office door. "Doing his job in an interesting way. Even allowing a carnival humbug to see your prisoner."

"What?"

"Want to have your fortune told, Mr. Mayor? She might even do it for free."

Tucker reached around to unlock the cell. "I didn't know who the hell she was!"

O'Brien said, "Why bring this up, Mr. Farrow? Sounds like you're trying to talk your way out of our agreement."

"Just the opposite. I want you to see how our deal solves many problems, including incompetence."

Harvey's nose was inches away from Eddie's beak as he squinted into the raven's cage, its cover pulled back. "Go on, be smart again, you sumbitch."

Eddie tilted his head, blinked twice at Harvey.

Out of Bishop's cell, Ophelia recovered the cage. "I've never before seen a man challenge a bird to a contest of wills and have the bird win."

Harvey frowned. "That little bastard's nothin' but a smart-ass!"

"Well, smarter than some."

Bishop laughed from his cell, which brought Harvey to the bars. His hand went to the coiled bullwhip that dangled from one of his belt loops. "You still think hangin' later saves you from pain now? You ain't learned your lesson?"

Tucker moved to Harvey. "Back out of there, Harvey."

Harvey said, "You want to hear what they was talkin' about? These two are crazy!"

Tucker elbowed him out of the way as he opened the cell door. Farrow tipped his felt hat with the bullet hole towards Ophelia.

Bishop said, "More visitors? Is this my lucky day or my worst?"

Farrow said, "I think you'll be celebrating this date for years, Doctor. You're a free man. Get that chain off him."

Bishop brought his arm up, pulling the cuff out straight as Tucker went to him, keys jangling. "Going to have Harvey take me out back, Tuck?"

"It's no joke, Doc." Tucker unlocked the cuff, then stepped back. He touched the side of his face. "I ain't even bringing charges."

Harvey filled the jail. "What the hell, Tuck?"

Bishop stood up straight for the first time in weeks, his legs searing, but the pain was good, giving him relief as he walked it off. Tucker didn't go for his gun, and the door to the cell stayed wide open.

Farrow said, "Doctor, arrangements for you have already been made."

Bishop still didn't move toward the door. He looked to Ophelia for a clue of some kind. She nodded, not breaking a smile, but satisfied. She held the raven's cage high, stepped around the group of men, and walked out the front door.

Farrow watched her go. To Bishop, he said with a grin, "I'm sure she predicted this would happen, so let's not make her a liar."

Bishop leaped to the window and looked out between the bars. Ophelia walked steadily on the planking, stepping around the slightest hint of mud on her way to the station.

He called out to her, but she had no interest in looking back.

CHAPTER FOUR
Related by Blood

My only son,

First, let me wish you the happiest of birthdays, and say that I hope this letter reaches you in time. It is hard for me to believe that it was thirteen years ago that I held you in my arms and couldn't imagine what a fine young man you'd grow into. I can only add how sorry I am that I won't be able to join you, but please take your classmates for a party celebration on your father, leaving behind a little bit for yourself.

Work continues, with jobs being plentiful, for which I'm thankful. It is dull and offers little reward beyond the money which affords us your schooling in England, giving you the best possible education.

I am planning for a great Christmas holiday for us both, perhaps with me making the trip to you, rather than you coming here. I can't think of a better Christmas than to be in London with my son, but

*that is months away. Your current job is to have the
happiest of birthdays.*

> *Devotedly,*
> *Your father*

Colby finished with a little swirl below the r *in* father, *as
was his habit, and then made an ink slash through it in the
style of John Hancock's signature. He blotted the letter, then
placed two hundred dollars in its center and folded it into
thirds before putting it into an envelope and sealing it with the
wax from a red candle burning next to him.*

*The wax dripped, and he pressed his signet ring into it, let-
ting it cool before turning the envelope over and addressing it
to his only son. When he was done, he blew out the candle,
turned in his chair by the small ornate desk, and enjoyed the
embers in the hotel fireplace, burning warm and orange, as he
thought about the preparations for his next kill.*

John Bishop sat up in bed, the sheets bundled around
him, and said, "Be still now, we're saying grace."

The woman's hand was on Bishop's chest, and she
whispered, "What? Are you okay?"

Bishop looked to the doorway, but there was nothing
there but an empty blue shadow. He rubbed his eyes
with his left palm. "I'm sorry I woke you."

"You were dreaming."

He lay back in the large bed. "Better than most I
have lately."

"Tell me."

"Go to sleep."

"If you say it out loud, you'll feel better."

He knew she was right. His voice was quiet, as if de-
scribing distant music: "It was my family, eating dinner,

and my boy kicking the leg of the table while we said grace. It seemed very real."

The woman's voice was warm out of the dark. "Because it was. Now you can find your way back to sleep."

Bishop shut his eyes, the voices of his family still echoing.

CHAPTER FIVE
Hired Guns

The house detective had knocked on the hotel room door four times, the last, a pounding of force. There was no answer, although he could hear the guest moving around inside.

"Mr. Andrew Barmuster, I'm with the hotel. Open the door, sir. There's a matter of a large bill that needs settling." The detective took enough time to draw a .38-caliber pistol from his jacket before using his passkey on the lock. The lock clicked. He thumbed the hammer back before turning the doorknob, his sweaty finger almost slipping.

The parquet door swung open into empty and quiet.

He stayed in the doorway, searching the room with the pistol barrel. "Mr. Barmuster, I know you're here, so better to show yourself. I am armed."

No response. The detective inched his way in. The bed was neatly made and packed bags stood at its foot.

The flames in the fireplace had burned down to a glow. The air smelled warm.

He tried again. "Sir, you haven't paid your bill. You're trespassing. I have the legal authority to arrest you, but that doesn't have to happen. Please show yourself, and let's get this settled."

He took a few more steps past the dresser and opened the closet door with his foot. Empty. He backed away, turning from the closet toward the bed, when he stopped, catching a glimpse of a figure on the balcony. It was a man standing against the far railing, masked by the curtains hanging in the balcony doorway, moving with the evening breeze.

Colby said, "Don't turn, not even an inch."

"What—"

Before the detective could get out another syllable, the knife had flown from the balcony, across the room, and sunk into his shoulder, cutting to the bone. He dropped in a rain of blood and pain, the pistol clattering into the washbasin.

Colby moved to the detective. He watched him twist on the floor, holding his shanks to his chest, rocking back and forth, smearing himself on the Persian rug.

He yelled, "Lord on fire, I wasn't going to kill you, Barmuster!"

Colby knelt next to him. "No, I'd never give you the chance, but I had to prove something to myself. You were a great help." He packed a damp washcloth around the blade and the wound, soaking up the blood. "Really, thanks very much."

"Where's my gun? I'll come back proper!"

"It's soaking wet, and coming back at me would be a mistake. Now, because you'll get medical attention you're not going to die. I'll leave the money for it."

The detective squeezed his eyes closed and took an enormous breath. "Barmuster, if you've got money, what the hell are you doing this for?"

Colby said, "You wouldn't understand, but recently I was not able to do my job as well as I would like, and I was afraid I was losing my abilities. Putting that knife into your shoulder, from that distance and in that exact spot, with your body in the position it was in, half-turned away? That wasn't easy, friend, but I did it. Clean. You've given me back my confidence, and I thank you."

"This was my first day on the job. I can't lose it. . . ."

"You need to bite on this." Colby forced a hairbrush handle between the detective's teeth before pulling the knife from his shoulder with one fierce yank. The meat tore, but it was out. The detective choke-screamed, the sound lost behind his tongue, then rolled onto his side, unconscious.

Colby placed a hundred and fifty dollars in silver on the dresser, picked up his bags, and stepped around the detective curled on the floor and spreading red. "Burmuster? I didn't remember I'd used that." He walked from the room, leaving the door slightly open so the desk clerk and bellman could make their discovery.

The detective screamed.

"The last time you saw me, I was something you'd find in the shed with my legs open."

"I wouldn't say that."

"You don't have to, 'cause I just did." Soiled Dove had carefully shaved off Bishop's scraggle of a beard. Her fingers dug into the earthen jar, gathering the yellow salve, and then travelled across the lashed wounds on his face.

"That Indian you was with? She left this for Kate, so she's the one who's really helping you, not me."

"The day we got the weapons." Bishop felt the cool, as the salve found its way into the lacerations on his cheeks, nose, and chin, then settled there. "I'm surprised you remembered."

"Because I was too dumb or had laudanum pouring out my ears?" Dove pulled the handle on the side of the barber chair, angling it toward her, bringing Bishop back flat, his head slightly raised on the cushioned rest. "I was just dirty feet and a nightgown."

She stepped back to look at him then dabbed a tiny welt with the last bit on her index finger. "Even with this, you're still a good-looking man, just not put together right."

"That's pretty much how I feel." He tilted his eyes to her. "How did you ever end up in Paradise?"

Soiled Dove put the jar on an upended crate next to the bed and wiped her hands on a towel. "Widow Kate's is the best house in two states. You've been there, and you all talked about big plans to open new houses from here to California."

"That's gone out of my memory."

"Do you remember you made a deal to kill Major Beaudine?"

Bishop regarded her for a beat then said, "I remember enough of Beaudine."

"Well, you did it. Word was they buried him in pieces. As soon as Kate heard, she started making her moves with lots of money at stake. I told her I was ready to take charge, open the new places. It don't look it, but big things are going to happen in this town. We just wanted the first taste."

"No more dirty feet."

"No, sir." Soiled Dove curtsied. "The trick to movin' up is not to let 'em catch you listening."

The chair sat Bishop up. "So, you're going to be quite the madam."

"Of five new houses, and no hog ranches neither. The best you'll ever visit. I'm training Large Marge. She'll do all right."

"Well, I love the chair."

"There was only one thing my daddy loved more than getting his hair cut. This is the master's suite. You're the first guest."

The room was L-shaped, wrapping around the second floor of the house, and as unfinished as the rest. The upholstered barber chair and the Victorian bed with carved headboard were the room. As in the rest of the house, the rugs were rolled up and the walls were bare.

Bishop wanted to swim in the huge bed but settled for six hours of sleep with no nightmares before Soiled Dove and Large Marge woke him with coffee and comfort.

He was cleaned, pressed, and his face doctored. "This has been a fine stay, and I'm genuinely honored to be the first."

"Don't worry. Your name won't go on the wall. Mr. Farrow really put out, though."

Bishop looked at Dove. "Did you know I'd be getting out of jail?"

Dove's response was a smile.

Large Marge, spilling from a different pair of pajamas with pink bows on her hips and breasts, and dancing across her backside, walked in carrying a red hood in one hand and the double-barreled shotgun rig in the other. "All for you, Doc!"

Marge could barely lift the rig, and Dove grabbed it from her stubby fingers. Marge tossed the hood on the bed, and Dove put the gun rig beside it, arranging the straps and bandolier not to tangle. On the pillows were a hat and a folded duster.

Marge said, "That hood's from them Fiery Riders. Anyway, you're supposed to take a good long look at it and tell that Mr. Farrow everything you know."

"That's still not much. Now."

Instead of the hood, Bishop picked up the hat, a new Stetson the color of dried blood.

Soiled Dove said, "It suits you."

Farrow was at the door before Bishop could try it on. "Get him in the rig."

Bishop held his elbow joint steady, as Soiled Dove fit the prosthetic cup over the corrupted end of his right arm. She was cautious, sliding it up the arm. Bishop twisted it to make it fit. The lining of the cup was soft deerskin, a fine woman's touch. He thought of that as the inside of the cup formfitted around the hard tissue of his amputation. He made the adjustments, a few small twists, so the shotgun that protruded from the cup hung straight.

He leaned forward "The straps go across the shoulders, then tighten."

Dove didn't speak, just pulled the straps over his shoulders. He grunted in pain, and she stopped.

"It's all right. I think there should be a little pain as part of this." He put his left arm through the opposite strap.

She tightened them by fastening both sides to a small

hook like a belt buckle that hung in the middle of his back.

Bishop used his left hand to snug the silver chain attached to the shotgun's double triggers, then Dove looped it through the rig's straps and brought it all the way across his back to his left side, where it was anchored.

He stood and brought his right arm up slowly. The gun felt heavy as he moved his body, favoring his right side, getting used to the weight and the way the weapon moved.

Soiled Dove held out a box of .12-gauge shells. "Do you want to or should I?"

The sun was dipping as they walked the uneven planking from Soiled Dove's to the train platform, Farrow in his tall felt hat with the bullet hole, Bishop wearing the black duster and Stetson that shielded his eyes and healing face.

The shotgun rig was now his right arm. Conscious of its weight and how it made him move, he was learning the weapon again.

The double barrels were barely visible below the cuff of his duster sleeve. A slit was sewn into it where his forearm would be, so the rig could be broken, reloaded. The special bandolier, with six shells, was tied high, almost to his shoulder.

Farrow said, "How do you feel, wearing that again?"

Bishop moved his shoulders, let the gun shift positions and react to him. "It's been a while, Mr. Farrow. I'll get used to it."

"You and Chisum share a common enemy."

"So you keep telling me."

"You're going to be in the front lines. You've got to sight down on the right people, don't you agree?"

"Just point me, and I'm supposed to shoot?"

"We saved you from the hangman, Doctor. I think that gives us a little bit of sway on your targets, don't you?"

"I'm not a hired gun."

"Half-gun?" Farrow smirked at his cleverness.

Bishop said, "How old were you when you got the fever?"

Farrow stopped, tipped his hat. "Nine. Lost every bit of hair I had. You think you're a doctor. With that special rig, I can't figure exactly what the hell you are, but my job's to deliver you to Chisum."

"Don't worry. I'm getting on the train."

"Instead of being cuffed up in a jail cell?"

"Damn right about that."

Farrow had the red hood in his hands, poking his fingers through the eyeholes. "Cowards and killers. Am I right?"

"You keep waving that thing at me like a verónica in front of a bull."

"Maybe you'll remember putting a dozen Fire Riders in the ground? Didn't one of them toss the grenade that scrambled everything?"

"That's what they say. You're a thorough man."

Farrow patted Bishop on the shoulder, pulled his hand away at the feel of the gun straps. "You'll know your enemies again. They're Mr. Chisum's, too."

Junior cracked his swollen knuckles before turning up the oil lamp on his small high desk by the ticket window. Arthritis in his neck fought him as he looked over his shoulder, watching Bishop and Farrow move onto the depot platform.

Hollis, a cowpoke with gravel for skin, sat on a barrel behind Junior, slicing an apple with a wide blade. "You see 'em? I see 'em."

Junior's head bobbed as he spoke, his neck paining him. "Yes, yes. I ain't blind or deaf! Fetch his horse. The train'll be here in ten minutes."

"So you pray. Gonna send a wire to that dude?"

"Fetch it!"

Hollis said, "You told me to remind you is all." Arms dangling, he walked out the back door toward the corral.

Junior shuffled dog-eared train schedules, old mail stained with rings from his coffee cup, and threats from a freighting company, before finding Chaney's embossed card VIRGIL LOUIS CHANEY. WORKS OF LITERARY DISTINCTION. PARIS, CHICAGO, NEW ORLEANS.

Junior took a pencil from his pocket, ran the lead across his tongue, and then set down his message for Chaney, double-checking with the Morse manual for every word. He cracked his knuckles again before tapping the brass telegraph key.

The gate to the corral beside the depot creaked open, its bottom slagging through the mud. Hollis walked Bishop's tall bay onto the loading platform. He was followed by a breed wearing a hat slouched low over his head, his braids tied behind his neck with a piece of beaded leather. Hollis wasn't wearing a gun. The breed wore two under a dirty fringed jacket.

Farrow said, "Your horse and the rest of your things will be on the train."

"Like I said, you're a thorough man." Bishop went to the bay, stroked his mane, patted his withers. The horse was clean, newly brushed. It nickered softly, angling its head toward him and instinctively nudging his left arm.

Hollis fed him the last bit of his apple. "You can see who he belongs to. I been seeing after him."

"Until I was hanged?"

Hollis dropped his face and scraped the wooden platform with his toe. "Guess that was the deal, yeah."

"No worries. Thanks for the work."

Hollis looked up. "You're the one with that special gun?"

Harvey snapped his whip at nothing, cutting the light in the air as he stepped onto the platform with giant, long-legged strides. "Hell's-a-fire, yeah, he's the one! And that gun sure is special. It can kill one man and save another from a hanging!"

Bishop turned to Harvey. "You're not coming near my horse with that whip."

"Didn't even cross my mind, because I got you." Harvey beat the air again, the bay recoiling at the crack.

Bishop handed off the reins to Hollis before facing Harvey, the shotgun coming up automatically, snapping into place. It was a quick move that surprised Bishop. Instinct was taking over.

Harvey's grin trembled. "Want to try me, Doc? I ain't got a gun like you. Don't need one. I beat you down once."

"No, I was cold-cocked. Funny what you remember."

"Don't matter. Without that rig, you're nothing. Maybe this fella should give me all kinds of money." Harvey barked to Farrow, "How 'bout it? I'm a better man. Got two strong arms. Why don't ya give me a job with Mr. Chisum? Hell, you don't even have to buy me out of jail."

Farrow said, "You're good with that whip, Harvey. I'll pass the word on to Chisum, so you can go on home."

"I got rights to be anywheres I want to be, and I want

to say good-bye to my buddy, Shotgun. Make sure he gets on that train without a problem."

Bishop tilted his body just a bit, bringing the barrel of the rig above his waist, locking it for firing. "I don't like that moniker, but today, maybe it fits."

"That special gun is the only way you can beat me. Ain't that right half-man?"

Bishop said, "Harvey, this doesn't have to go any further. In about ten minutes, you'll never see me again."

"Half-a-man, and money falls out of the sky for you. Gun down a dozen men, and there's no rope. Doesn't seem fair, do it?"

Bishop said, "I've got my debts."

Harvey stepped closer. "That some kind of answer?"

"What do you want?"

Harvey shook the coiled whip in his fist like it was a warrior's spear. "I beat you to hell, and you still came back for more. The sheriff saved your ass, but he's not here, and these folks would like a look-see at a man what refuses to die."

Bishop shook his head. "That ain't me by a long shot."

"I deserve to watch you crawl."

"Your reputation as a man to be feared is safe with me."

Harvey let the bullwhip unfurl, the end hitting the ground as he brought back his elbow to snap it hard. "Lower that shotgun, I'll lose the whip, and we'll go. See what you really got." He shouted, "How about it? Our famous prisoner, the shotgun killer, in a fair fight for once?"

Used to Harvey's mouth, the few loungers around the depot watched without saying a word. Hollis and the breed walked Bishop's horse to the loading dock, not looking back.

Mayor O'Brien stood on the balcony of Dove's house, Large Marge beside him, sipping more of her tea. They didn't call out, just watched and waited.

Farrow said, "You can't waste time with this fool. You have a job waiting and have to be in shape to do it."

The shotgun unlocked, reverting to its position straight by Bishop's side. He took the few steps to where Harvey was standing.

Harvey held out the whip then let it fall. He smiled. "Take it off."

Every bruise and cut on Bishop's face burned, but he ate the pain, met Harvey's stare. "I don't have to lose the gun. I've got no need for it."

Harvey's next word was a gut-pulled scream as Bishop's heel smashed into his knee, tearing it sideways beneath the skin. Doubled over, Harvey tumbled to the platform. Tears and more screams covered his face.

"That's what half-a-man can do, Harvey." Bishop turned and walked down the platform to where his horse was standing.

Farrow stayed with him as Harvey's voice colored the air, his crying and curses all anyone could hear until the distant whistle of the incoming train wiped them out.

CHAPTER SIX
Hell Travellin'

Colby stood at the counter of the Butterfield Line station as the clerk updated the stage runs on a mounted chalkboard. He was precise in his writing, crossing the sevens in the European style. Colby checked the update against his own watch, approved, then presented his letter.

The address made the clerk ask, "Blackheath?"

"Yes, it's seven miles—"

"Actually, nearly eight *kilometers* beyond London, last stop of the railway." Colby's surprise gave him half a step back.

The clerk said, "I gauge London to be ten cents over five dollars. I'll have to confirm for Blackheath." He thumbed the postage rate book.

Colby was impressed and didn't hide it. Out of targeting habit, he sized up the other travelers in the small but clean waiting room.

A roughneck snored loudly in the corner, his hat

pulled down. while a young fellow in new jacket and collar read a newspaper, despite the honking. Two older women took up the bench on the opposite side, speaking in strained whispers. They wore all-over gray. Colby assumed them sisters, but he was more interested in the young fellow and the Colt nickel-plated pistol he'd holstered in the top of his boot.

"Five dollars and seventy cents."

Colby faced the clerk, who repeated himself. Colby handed him one carefully folded bill and exact change. "How long for delivery? My son's birthday is soon. That's his card."

"Four weeks at the outside. The Royal Mail's very reliable."

"That's been my experience, as well."

The young fellow crossed his legs, pulling at his trouser cuff to hide the pistol grip.

Colby watched without looking at him then said to the clerk, "Where do you hail from?"

"Iowa. The Continent is what you dream about between stage runs."

"Dreams are what keep a man motivated." Colby moved to the waiting area and sat next to the young man holding the newspaper too close to his face. Smiling at his slight tremor and the drops of sweat that had fallen from his forehead, dotting the newsprint, Colby said to him, "Hot?"

The young fellow thin-smiled his "yes."

"I find it rather cool and pleasant. You should take some water. You might be coming down with something."

The scream in Bishop's ears was actually metal pounding metal as the train picked up speed, rounding the curve that led away from Paradise. He stood on the small grate between the coach and the boxcar, the coupling inches away, the tracks underneath passing faster and faster, and the rushing cool night air feeling pretty good.

The cars bucked and heaved, but he kept steady, his left arm crossed, holding the shotgun in place. The tracks jolted him, the iron chains holding the cars yelling under the strain, but he didn't move. He was fixed.

And then the destroyed locomotive was there.

It was blue in the random streaks of moonlight breaking the clouds, turning it into a huge, eerie death monument beside the tracks. Bishop kept between the cars, trying to lose himself in the blasted iron and fire-twisted steel of the train wreckage, to bring back some kind of memory. Trying to find something.

The cars picked up speed.

Bishop held on. There were flashes. Bodies tossed by explosions. Young soldiers torn by a Gatling gun. Riders charging to the slaughter. It was a chaos of thought that lasted less than seconds and brought him no closer to filling the lost stretches of his memory.

The cars were moving faster.

The train roared onto a straightaway through a mountain pass, then eased. Bishop opened his eyes. Memories were still jagged pieces, but at that moment they weren't weighing him down.

The taste and smell of the rotting sweet of Tucker's jail cell was gone from the back of his throat, replaced by the cold rush coming down from the mountain. He watched the landscape pass, the profile of the Rockies and the coyotes jumping at the whistle, their shapes darting for the trees.

The boxcar's access door banged open and Bishop stepped from the coupling. Peering in, he saw his bay secured between hitch posts in a stall at the shadowed far end.

"*Vé'ho'évo'ha.*"

The door slammed heavy behind him, Hollis and Breed blocking it. Breed had two revolvers. Hollis had a wide-blade that he shifted from left to right.

"Still taking care of my horse?"

Hollis smirked. "You know what Tuck said? That you had the craziest goddamned mouth of any prisoner he'd ever seen. Even when you was gettin' whooped."

Bishop backed up a few inches, taking in the movement of the two men, watching Breed more than Hollis. "You and the sheriff talked."

"Tuck yaks about everything, special about how crazy you is. Who were you talkin' to out there?"

"Ghosts. Now what?"

"You're crazy . . . and worth money. Dead, you're worth money. Half-dead, a little more."

Bishop said, "I came in to check on the bay. We can leave it at that. The door isn't locked."

Hollis froze. Breed made a move, the gun in his left aimed at Bishop's chest, his right aimed at his head. It was a juggling act.

Bishop stayed with Hollis. "Okay. You want to do this, tell me what it's about. How much?"

"Between me and the man what wants you bleeding."

Bishop nodded to the Breed, and Hollis said, "Not him! He's Mex and Comanche. Got no money and nothin' to say."

"Unlike you."

"Crazy, crazy mouth." Hollis let the blade settle in one hand. "Do you even get what's happening here?"

"Yes. Do you?"

The rig snapped into place and fired, blasting Breed off his feet before his next breath. Bishop had aimed low, tearing through the meat of Breed's left leg.

Breed gritted his teeth, fingers clamped on the wound, blood and flesh mushing through them, but not allowing himself a sound.

The bay bucked against its stall.

Hollis backed into a corner, slashing, the blade jabbing at nothing. Pure panic filled his eyes.

Bishop brought the rig up an inch, arm straight and locked. Smoke had cleared from the first barrel. The second was ready. "He's going to die if he doesn't get to a doctor. If you know about me, you know I can help."

Hollis slashed. "Tuck said you was too crazy to doctor no more!"

Then slashed again, with a giggle.

Bishop blocked it with the shotgun barrel. "You're a damn fool if you don't see I'm giving you and your buddy a chance."

Hollis looked to Breed coughing up blood then back to Bishop. He turned the blade, making a show. "So— what's *your* offer?"

"You keep living. Who's coming for me?"

Hollis said, "But if you ain't dead or dying, then I will be. That's what they said, and I'm stickin' to that."

"That knife's nothing. Around your feet? That's your friend's life. You're losing your chance, boy."

Hollis took a step out of the blood pool, wiping the soles of his boots on his pant leg. "But—they're payin' out a lot, and you can't match it."

"I can better it." Bishop's voice stayed low, train thunder behind it. His movements extended the rig, shifting automatically, the barrel pointing directly at

Hollis's face. "You can die right now or maybe you live and they never find you. You've got ten seconds."

Hollis said, "A second ago you were a doc. Now the bastard comes out. Goes with that fancy gun."

"Who put up the bounty?"

The answer was a stammer. "A-an a-army of f-folks. Some of 'em d-dead. We've got to bring you back with your guts spilt, so they can watch you die. Or your head, make sure you're gone. I-I could've sure used that m-money." Hollis squeezed his eyes tight, waiting for the second barrel.

The bay whinnied and bucked, busting the silence, fighting its ropes. The rest happened in moments. Breed brought up a pistol, throwing back the hammer. Bishop turned, fired, the second blast spreading Breed across the floor and walls. The train whistle shrilled.

Hollis charged the side door and yanked it wide open.

Bishop shucked two shells and reloaded. He half-stepped, calling out to Hollis, who dove from the car into the darkness. His jump missed, and he rag-dolled into a tree, bone and branches snapping together—not even giving him time to scream.

The whistle yelled as Bishop hung in the open door to see Hollis's body by the tracks. Bent almost in half, his chin between his shoulder blades, the cowpoke was left behind, getting farther and farther away as the train rounded the next curves.

Hollis was gone, dead by choice.

Bishop dragged over what was left of Breed, letting him fall from the car before straining to shut the door with his one hand.

The bay kicked at its stall, splitting lumber, crying out. Bishop moved to his horse, its head thrashing.

Dodging its jaw, he reached out to run his hand along
its neck, gently scratching and repeating *Nahotse* over
and over. The Cheyenne word had come to him out of
the dark. As he said it, the bay's muscles stilled, its heart
stopped pounding.

Bishop's did, too.

He stayed for a few miles before walking back to
his car.

The coach was empty. A single lamp at either end
cast a dim, yellow glow over the seats. Slumping next to
a window, he wondered if Chisum had bought every
ticket. He pulled the shade, put his feet up and hat
down, and tried for some peace.

"These are yours, Doctor."

"Sure as hell, you shouldn't call me that." Bishop
turned in his seat, the shotgun automatically leveled.

Farrow took a step back, grinning. Bishop lowered
the rig, locked it.

Farrow said, "Whoa. My fault. That's not how you
approach an armed man."

Bishop nodded at the joke as Farrow put a black
leather field medical kit and a volume of Edgar Allan
Poe next to him.

"I don't know what all was in that bag. Tucker probably helped himself, but you've still got a lot of instruments. Some I can't imagine what you use them for."

Bishop opened the kit with his left hand and looked
inside for the first time in months. He picked up a
muscle clamp and manipulated it. "I—I know."

"Hope I don't find out. I admire the gold initials."

Bishop regarded the Lt. Bishop on the side in raised

gold, most of which had flaked away, fracturing him. "That was my wife's idea."

"The Poe stories belong to her?"

"Somebody else."

The red-hooded riders charged through the Laramie Mountain pass, keeping themselves ten across as they gained on the Butterfield Coach.

The coach driver cracked the reins on the six-up, and the horses broke fire on the new road, pulling ahead, legs in perfect sync, sweat pouring from their backs. Next to him, a bearded man with a scattergun turned himself around on the seat, taking count of how many red hoods were coming for them.

Driver pushed down a small grade, then brought the horses up hard, the stagecoach swerving, but turning sure as they reached the new road. They jolted from the grade onto the road, the passengers calling out as he pushed the horses for all their speed.

Beard waited for a Rider to get close, and got off one shot before his chest and back exploded. Driver wiped blood from his eyes as Beard fell, hitting the road, coach wheels crushing his legs.

The Fire Riders bore down.

A Fire Rider ran his stallion up close to the coach team, hair rubbing hair, leaping from his horse to one of the leaders. The driver snapped his whip at him, biting nothing but red hood. Fire grabbed the lines and pulled back, slowing the team. The others caught up as the coach rumbled down, the horses winded, their mouths foaming.

Fire swung off the leader as one of his men tossed him a bayoneted Springfield rifle. He caught it and trained the barrel and knife on the driver, who'd jumped from his seat with his hands up and Beard's blood drying on his face.

Fire's voice was accent-thick, but loud enough through his hood. "This is all for you, to stand and deliver!"

Two more Riders opened the coach, hauling the sisters out first, letting them tumble with the tiniest of screams. The snoring roughneck was next, arms high, followed by the young fellow with the gun in his boot.

Colby came out last, hands raised, taking deliberate time. "I don't know about the ladies' purses"—he helped them to their feet—"but if you want real money, I'd suggest you're looking in the wrong place."

Fire pushed the bayonet against Colby's chest just enough. "Maybe I slit your stomach. Maybe you swallowed a fortune in gold when you saw us riding up."

Colby never lowered his arms, but nodded toward the young man. "You might check him. He has a new Colt in his boot, nickel-plated, possibly never been fired. He won't draw it because he was going to rob the strongbox with the help of the driver."

The young fellow tangled his feet, falling against the coach brake. "That's some dirty wash, mister! You don't know me!"

The other Riders formed a sloppy circle around the coach—demons on skeleton mounts, not uttering a word, holding repeating rifles and polished sabers.

Colby said to young fellow, "You've been perspiring and trembling since we left the way station, and had plenty of time to bring out that pistol before they stopped us."

Snoring said, "That don't prove nothing except he's a coward. Me, I ain't got no gun."

Colby acknowledged that with a nod. "But I don't hear our driver contradicting me."

Fire swung the rifle around to the driver, who said, "We better let it go, Henry."

"Why'd you open your goddamned mouth? They didn't know what the hell—"

The rifle shot blew apart young man's cheek. He fell, eyes open, hand twitching around the Colt Lightning he'd pulled. The sisters cried louder as Fire brought the bayonet flush with the bottom of the driver's jaw, the tip slicing the skin.

"How much did you take, the money?"

The driver's head was back, his eyes toward the sky. "About fifteen thousand in scrip and gold."

"Give me only ten. Count it out."

Driver said, "I don't get this."

"Do as you been instructed."

Fire pulled the bayonet away as the driver snatched the bank deposit bag he'd stashed under the boot.

Handing it over, he inched back, smearing the trace of blood from his throat. "You better figure it out. I don't want no mistakes."

The driver counted out the money. "You rob the line, we take a cut, cross territories, pay the toll. That's the new law. You savvy that much?"

Driver said, "Understood."

Fire nodded, and a rope whipped around the driver's neck, jerking him to the ground. All guns stayed on the passengers as two riders stuffed a bandana deep into the driver's mouth and lashed his hands and feet tight.

They held him down, and Fire knotted the line to one of the team, unhooked the traces, then fired a shot by the horse's ear. It bolted, dragging the driver, screams choked, across the flats.

Fire watched for a moment, turned to the passengers, and said, "Now he understands good," before smashing Colby in the jaw with the stock of the rifle, spinning him down.

"Get on a horse, nelly son of bitch! The way you're dressed, somebody pays something for you!"

Colby stayed on his knees, holding his face. "Will you allow me my luggage?"

"Get it. Maybe pay for that, too!"

Colby pulled himself to his feet, holding on to the side of the coach. He pointed to one small valise and the Navajo blanket stuffed with his arsenal.

A hooded rider grabbed them both and secured them behind a saddle. "Mother Mary's tears, this is heavier than my son! Silver or gold?"

Colby hauled himself into the stirrups, his face numbing. "Hardly."

Fire said, "I'll find out myself. Don't get no ideas. That horse does what I want only." He pointed to the young fellow in the pool of black-red soaking the sand. "He's dead. You're not. Take that to church."

The sisters held each other, and Snoring stayed on his heels as Fire swatted Colby's horse. It started a run, following the straight road. Fire took off, keeping a few steps behind, his rifle casually aimed at the back of Colby's skull.

The other Riders held, then turned out their circle and followed, pushing their "ghost horses" to gallop for the foothills.

The funeral director held his nose with two fingers as the autopsy surgeon cut away the gunnysack shroud. There'd been leakage, and the fabric had fused with the corpse's skin, which tore with the sack. A small metal tray at the dead man's feet caught the runoff.

Keeping both hands buried in his overcoat pockets, Virgil Chaney stood by the display coffins as the surgeon worked.

The surgeon threw out words. "You told me your cousin was shot."

"Indeed he was, by a special double-barreled model."

The surgeon stepped from the corpse and dipped his hands in a bowl of antiseptic. "It must have been very special, because this man was stabbed to death."

"That's not what I was given to understand."

"Hold your nose, then look for yourself. He's been rag-tagged back together, but those are stab wounds in his chest, not gunshots, and certainly nothing with a shotgun. Maybe your killer had two weapons, but your cousin met his end from a knife."

Chaney stepped from around the coffins, taking a small, black camera from one of his pockets.

The funeral director broke a grin. "That's one of those super cameras? Sub-miniature? I've heard of them, but never saw one in person a-fore."

Chaney focused the lens on the body "Then today is lucky for you, isn't it?"

The surgeon said, "I understood only Army spies were allowed those."

"I'm a new kind of spy . . . for *Harper's Weekly*." Chaney snapped the picture, took out the small, dry negative plate, and slipped it into a protective envelope. "I understand he was seen with a young Cheyenne maiden of some temper. He met his end in a hotel room she and the shotgun-man occupied."

The surgeon laughed and poured a tumbler of gin. "Lots of people end up on this table for that reason. I don't know who did the killing or who had their pants down, but nobody used a gun. Now, what about his disposition?"

Coughing from the odor, the funeral director piped in with a voice that was two cats fighting. "Should we select a coffin and make plans for an immediate service?"

Chaney said, "That odorous bag was appropriate for my cousin. Put him back in and deposit him in the nearest well."

The surgeon said, "Up to you, but I always think people deserve a decent burial, even if they didn't have a decent life."

Chaney was already at the door. "I'll make sure to quote you."

The tall man with the lean mustached face and dark suit was in a freight wagon, checking his watch and the ammunition stores stacked behind him, when the train pulled into the Lincoln County station. He didn't get down from his seat, but waited for Farrow and Bishop to step from the single coach among the boxcars.

Farrow blinked at the New Mexico sun and the heavy smell of the stock pens. They walked to the wagon, while behind them hundreds of head of cattle were loaded onto the train from a large corral. Manure dust and shed hair thickened the air.

Farrow blew his nose. "Really stings."

Bishop said, "It's the business of your boss."

"Yours, too. That blood on your coat, from last night? That's your badge of honor."

Bishop adjusted the brim of his hat, catching the shadow. "There was no honor involved."

"Just survival. You and Lincoln County are going to fit together fine."

At the wagon, the man holding the reins said, "You Bishop? You're with me."

Bishop looked to Farrow. "So, this is where I earn my freedom?"

"Everything costs, Doc. I'll take care of your traps."

Bishop climbed aboard the wagon, keeping the shotgun flush with his side. "You're from the Chisum spread?"

"I work for him like everybody else around here. Name's Pat Garrett. Welcome to the war." He snapped the reins, and the team quickly stepped around the drive that circled the train station before leading out across miles and miles of Chisum country.

CHAPTER SEVEN
Battlefield

The range had no end. Grass-thick land washed beyond the horizon and then beyond that. Pat Garrett pointed out graves of sheep herders caught stealing water and reminded Bishop just how much influence great cattle barons like John Chisum had on the bright future of the new healed United States. "This was wild country, not safe for anybody. Mr. Chisum's changed that. Need the water? Just ask. Some grazing time? Same thing. Follow the rules, Mr. Chisum's law, you'll have no problems."

Bishop said, "That's a hell of a speech."

"And believe every word. I was a lawbreaker once. I came around."

"For money."

Garrett said, "Man decides about his future. That's why you're here, ain't it?"

Bishop adjusted the rig by his side, but couldn't get comfortable.

The wagon bucked as Garrett took it off the road and onto a trail leading to a small flat between grassy hills. Bishop heard gunfire echo as they got closer. Shots in scattered volleys were followed by cannon-like reports.

Garrett said, "The enemy's hid. We're just trying to flush 'em out." He brought the wagon over a small rise so Bishop could take it in. The enemy position was an old adobe with a collapsing thatched roof and small corral. A sleepover for cowboys moving herds. A dead man hung on one of the corral rails, two exit wounds in his back, his hands clenching a rifle, eyes filmy and open.

The shooting had stopped for reloading. A thin layer of gun smoke lingered over the Chisum men who'd been killed in the last hour.

Garrett angled the wagon behind a flurry of blooming Yellow Bells that offered cover. The distance to the hut was about sixty yards, with no-man's-land in between.

Bishop stood, looking for movement among the dead. "You got a lot a men out here?"

Garrett said, "Maybe eight left. We know there's two, probably more, in the cabin."

"Four for each."

"How many don't count for much if they're well-heeled."

A rifle barrel parted the shutters of one of the hut's two windows, resting on the sill before letting loose. It was rapid fire, followed by more from another rifle right beside it. Never stopping. Chisum men were hit bloody and hard. Spun around by slugs, then hurled aside by their force, their bodies were torn to nothing.

Eyes were punched by bullets when men raised up from behind logs and boulders, trying to return fire. Another shooter let loose from behind the adobe. Slugs ripped the brush, the cover, ricocheting off the rims of the wagon wheels. The horses bucked, kicking the wagon back.

Garrett pulled Bishop to the ground, gave him a signal to wait. They grabbed the team's harness, held them steady.

Gun thunder from Chisum men in the tall grass powdered holes in the adobe, chewing windows and doors. The dead one by the corral was hit by strays, the impact lifting him off the fence and dropping him.

The shutters slammed shut.

Garrett kept low at the back of the wagon. "Better not of hit the horses. That's a good team." He threw open the gun and ammo boxes, looking to Bishop. "You're in it now. Hadn't you better load that thing?"

Bishop's voice flattened out. "I'm ready."

Rifles laid down fire as the Chisum men ran in from gullies and trees, bullets chasing them. One old boy rolled down a slope, came up, put two hopeful shots into the adobe, then tried for cover. "That'll burn 'em!"

A slug from the hut tore through half the old boy's rib cage, a second pushed his voice out the back of his neck.

Others made it to the Yellow Bells.

Worn and bloody, they were all cowboys laying somewhere between sixteen and sixty. Sporting old-trail faces and busted knuckles, some were using guns for the first time in years. They grabbed water and ammunition, filling canteens, cartridge belts, and Winchester repeaters.

Bishop handed a cup to one of the boys, a man in his thick-cut forties, lying on the ground, coughing blood.

Thick Cut drank, then doused his face. "Feels cool."

Bishop said, "You best forget about this fight."

"That ain't why Chisum's payin' me."

Another said, "He ain't payin' enough for this."

Garrett looked at the bunch. "Everybody in that cabin must be hit."

A cowboy spit. "Yeah? They're still shootin' us to pieces!"

Maynard, whose nose had been creased by a bull's hoof, broke through the brush, shouldering a wounded man. He carried a big-bore .76 in his free hand, dumped the unconscious cowboy by the wagon with the other.

"Damn fool tried to go around the corral where that one sum'bitch is hid out. Took a pepper ball in the leg."

Garrett's question was "What about the one who shot him?"

Maynard said, "Back inside, waitin' for me to blow his head off. And I'll oblige him."

Random shots ripped from the adobe. Maynard returned fire without a target, letting loose. "Eat that, ya pecker-licking bastards." He cracked off his rifle until it hammered empty. He dropped to one knee, still cussing.

An old cowhand said, "You sure as hell got 'em runnin' scared, Maynard."

Garrett said to Bishop, "Tell me if we're gonna have to bury this one."

Thick Cut said, "You talkin' about me, Garrett?"

Bishop checked Thick Cut's eyes, opening his lids with his left thumb, then mopped the bullet wound with a handkerchief. "Who's down there anyway?"

The echo from the last volley was still rolling as Maynard grabbed some fresh shells, cocked them into his Winchester. "Goddamn fence-cutters—"

"And all goddamn good shots," the old cowhand interrupted.

"Workin' for them wormy bastards in the red hoods!" Maynard looked to Bishop. "And he wouldn'ta been shot, except Garrett had to fetch you!"

"You got way too much mouth."

The voice was a woman's and full of Missouri. She crouched next to Thick Cut, both hands tight above the bullet wound, squeezing. Small in her denims, with auburn hair framing a round, almost pale face. Freckles across her nose, and green eyes gave her color.

Bishop said, "Good. Use all your strength," before wrapping his belt around the cowboy's leg in the exact spot where Rose had clamped it, slowing the bleeding from the blown-apart artery. She deftly switched hands from the leg to the end of the belt, pulling it tighter before looping it off.

Garrett reloaded his pistol and said to Bishop, "Guess you're the field medic, too."

The cowboy's eyes rolled back and his breathing shallowed. More gunfire came from the adobe. Bishop instinctively shielded his patient. Maynard and Garrett cracked off rounds from behind the brush, swearing to send somebody to hell. Anybody. Every bullet from Maynard's .76 was a stick of dynamite, killing the adobe. Packed mud, hay, and wood, blasted.

Two other Chisum men boiled the air with Winchesters, laying fire at targets they couldn't make out.

Everyone held up, waiting for screams. Something.

Then, return blasts came from behind the shutters through a tear in the roof and pinned them down.

Maynard spit. "Them cutters a damn army? We're gettin' it from everywhere!"

Rose said, "I spied them first, and there's three in that adobe! Only three!"

"One's dead, and we're still outgunned!"

Bishop said, "This man's dead, too, if we don't get him out of here." He and Rose gathered Thick Cut's legs, one of Chisum's men got under his shoulders, and hefted him into the wagon bed.

Chisum's man said, "Sure hope he pulls through. I like his coffee."

Rose said, "I can get him out the back road."

Bishop elevated the torn leg with an ammo box, settling his body. Thick Cut's head rested on a folded blanket, when a bullet hard-jerked him to one side. The slug tore through his right temple and blew out his left before splintering one of the wagon's wooden slats.

All guns turned.

The Fire Rider was charging from a small hill, coming in from behind the Chisum position, firing a Spencer Springfield, taking another cowboy dead off his feet.

Garrett steadied and shot twice at the Rider's horse, ripping through its neck, crashing it forward.

The horse screamed.

Rifle flying, the Rider lurched from the saddle, tumbling with the animal, then hitting the ground face-first, almost killed. The horse lay heaving, legs chopping and body twisting, a red geyser from its throat misting everything around it.

Rose stood by the wagon, took aim through the Yellow Bells, and fired her Colt .45 clean, giving the stallion peace.

The Chisum guns were dead-on the Rider as he rolled onto his back, pulling at his hood to breathe.

Garrett ordered, "Hold fire! We want him alive!"

The Fire Rider managed to get to his feet.

Garrett kept his gun trained, his voice low to Bishop. "If I have to shoot, think you can put him back together, at least so he can talk?"

"Aim for his legs." The barrels of Bishop's rig unlocked with a move of his shoulders, but they stayed angled toward the ground as he called out, "I know you're hurting, but try and come toward us!"

Garrett yelled, "Hands up, fingers spread!"

The Rider took a shaking step, then stumbled. He was more than fifty feet away from the Chisum guns, bloody and moaning into the grass.

"Don't go to him."

Bishop was halfway up. "He'll not make it."

Garrett said, "Or he's luring you out. I don't need that." He yelled to the Rider, "Show your face! Surrender, and we'll come for you, this man's a doctor!"

Garrett's words were cut by two shots pumped into the Rider's chest, blowing out his back. Shots ripped the Yellow Bells and the wagon. Sniper fire. Garrett dove under the wagon, scanning the ridge, shooting at a glint he thought was a rifle barrel.

A couple of Chisum men ran from the cover of the brush, firing wild at the adobe hut, before diving for an old water ditch. Slugs punched their throats, sending them tumbling then landing . . . dead.

The shutters on the hut were wide open. The gunmen inside sprayed the area with rifle and pistol rounds. Maynard's warrior cry was above the sound of the guns as he bull-charged the adobe, pumping shots from his Winchester .76. His war whoop and the rifle fire were constant.

A bullet through his cheek spun Maynard off his feet. Another shot, blowing out his shoulder, dropped him.

Garrett and Rose opened up with their rifles as Bishop ran to get where Maynard was lying. Darting from side to side, then coming low around the side of the corral, Bishop had the rig at waist level, the hammers back, and the trigger line slacking.

Maynard's face was slick with blood. Bishop turned him over. Still alive. Shots ripped. Bishop whirled, his duster flaring, the rig coming up, snapping into place. A slug blew through Maynard's boot. He cried out. Bishop moved, tightening the trigger lines with his shoulders.

Ducking, he got to the adobe, the shotgun shoulder-high, barrels extended, and locked. He pressed against the wall. A rifle flamed from the window right above his head.

He sprang up, blasting the shutters apart, tearing the gunman in half.

Bishop dropped, pressed tight against the wall again, then saw Garrett throw a signal. He waited a few heart-beats, then pulled the second trigger to almost firing, straining against the trigger.

A second gunman jerked open the front door, level-ing rifle and pistol. Bishop fired, blowing shot through his chest.

Bishop snapped the breech, shucked the shells, brought two down from the bandolier. An automatic motion. He swung around as a Fire Rider charged from the other side of the corral.

The Rider in red, a rifle slung across his back, leaped his horse over the rail fence, and drew a Peacemaker out of a holster. Bishop pulled both triggers, sending him flying out of his stirrups as if God's fist had punched him.

The Rider landed dead, his hood filling with blood like a water bag.

Bishop fixed on the corpse for a moment, fragments of memory bombarding him—other riders in hoods and robes; men he'd killed with the rig; a slaughter along a stretch of railroad tracks; and a grenade exploding beneath him.

For that instant, he felt the blast again.

He looked away from the dead rider, the flashes vanishing as quickly as they'd come. Around him, the rolling echoes of the guns were fading, and the natural quiet of the place was replacing them.

Victory or surrender, the silence after a battle was always the same. Bishop had heard it too many times, but there was something else.

Chisum men began coming down from their positions behind rocks and gullies, limping, shouldering each other.

Their voices, cries of the wounded, grew louder, striking Bishop's ears. He snapped the gun to his side, the rig no longer a physical and mental extension of him, but something separate. Focus came back to his eyes as he knelt by Maynard, checking his pulse.

Pat Garrett was standing beside him. "You're quite a medic . . . with one hell of a gun. How about him?"

"Steady. He's made of tough stuff. Stupid, but tough."

"That one by the corral was sniping," Garrett said. "That's why we're losing this thing. We got three of theirs, and we're burying, what? Eight? Ten?"

"You'd know better than me. They're scattered all over this battlefield."

"Battlefield." Garrett made his point. "Now you're seeing the light, Doc."

Bishop didn't respond. He just stood, not acknowledging the smoke still drifting from the double-barreled weapon at his right as Rose brought up the wagon to load the dying and the dead.

CHAPTER EIGHT
Blood Ties

The purple on the trimmed woodwork of the master's suite had dripped into a twist of color that wriggled to the floor. Mayor O'Brien carefully wiped the paint, keeping away from the wallpaper he'd just smoothed.

Sheriff Tucker reclined in the barber chair near the bed, adjusting his neck as Soiled Dove made the last, short strokes with the straight razor, lopping the stubborn hair under his chin. "I thought the whole point of that money was so you could put down the paintbrush and worry about runnin' the town."

O'Brien said, "This is running the town, Tuck. Giving a new business every advantage."

Soiled Dove wiped the razor clean on a towel. "And we appreciate it."

Tucker smiled. "I know you do, darlin'."

O'Brien dabbed a bit of purple on the baseboard. "So where are the bodies?"

Tuck said, "They were a few miles down the tracks. I just had 'em put in the old icehouse."

"Without ice."

"I know it's busted down, but they both got family that'll want 'em buried. Been kind of cool lately, so it'll be a day or two before they go ripe. Got any of that rosewater, darlin'?"

Dove took a small bottle of scent, sprinkled it on a warm towel, and wrapped Tuck's face. He settled back, giving a quiet groan.

O'Brien stood. "How do you explain what happened, Tuck?"

Tucker shrugged, the warm towel hiding his expression. "Them two both got records. Hollis never was any good, and Breed just did three years for robbery, so it ain't nobody's surprise that they turned up shot."

With Tucker unaware, O'Brien moved to the barber chair, standing right beside it. "There's quite a price on Doctor Bishop. We've got the chance to really set this town up, but we can't have any muddy water, Tuck."

Tucker smiled. "Let him out, and take 'em down."

O'Brien whipped the towel off Tucker's face and spun him around. Catching the chair with his foot, the mayor leaned into him. "Do you understand what I'm getting at?"

"Yeah, yeah. I get it."

"Then say it."

Tuck looked at Dove, whose face was a mask, then back to O'Brien. "None of this can come back on us."

The mayor nodded, reached into the toolbox beside the paint cans on the floor, and took out a stack of hundreds wrapped in a paper band.

"That's more of Farrow's new money, ain't it?"

"No, it's yours. Twenty-five hundred." He dropped the stack of bills onto Tucker's lap.

The sheriff eyed the cash, but didn't pick it up. "You've been real good about cuttin' me in, and I appreciate all of it."

Soiled Dove said, "It's not a gift."

Tuck toweled his face again. "I get it, I do, but I've never really pulled the trigger on no one. Not to kill 'em. I talk big, but Man of Peace was my campaign slogan when I ran for sheriff, remember?"

O'Brien said, "And this is about keeping *our* peace."

Harvey was stretched out on the bunk in his cell at Paradise jail, his leg splinted with two pieces of thin pine, a lash of heavy rope keeping it straight. He took a long pull from a bottle of Don Sauza, letting it burn his mouth before swallowing. His complaints started as soon as he saw Tucker by the cell door. "You gonna kick me out again, Tuck?"

"You're fine, you're fine."

"'Cause I'll want paying."

Tucker kept his eyes to the floor. "No, Harv. You did good."

Harvey drank again. "Damn right I did." He sniffed the air. "Aunt Petunia's ass, where have you been? Don't tell me. I know. Rosewater perfume! See, I can't do them things now 'cause of this busted leg."

"You want one of the girls to come down, see you? I'll pay."

"I don't feel like doin' nothing, and that's your fault, too. I always play the fool, Tuck, but when you give me the high sign to get the whip, teach one of these birds a lesson, I'm on it."

"You've been a real help, Harv. I haven't always been a good brother-in-law. I know that. I think Esther's real lucky to have you."

Harvey regarded Tucker. "That mean you're going to get me a real doc to fix my knee?"

"We're going to take care of that."

Harvey sat up, holding the makeshift contraption that was setting his leg. "Hell, if that one-armed son of a bitch hadn't busted me up, I'd say get him!"

Tucker moved to Harvey, settled on the small stool next to his bed. "That'd be kind of a funny deal, since the doc busted you in the first place."

"That's what I said."

"How bad are you hurting?"

Harvey got the last swallow, then smashed the bottle against the cell bars. "I need another, is what! Or something stronger. I been shot more than once, so I don't know why this pains so bad."

Tucker said, "I know it pains. I tried to make a deal with Bishop when he was suffering with the terrors, trying to give him a little relief."

"Hell, that man's crazy, and you let him out!"

"You know why."

"Yeah, cash from that Farrow that I ain't seein' none of. I sent them two after him, and they come back dead, so I don't get none of that bounty, neither."

Tucker slipped the pistol from the belt loop near his back, keeping it down as he spoke. "I know it ain't fair, Harv, but we'll get this straightened out."

Harvey said, "I'm tired of waitin' for you to do right by me, Tuck. I'm tired of gettin' beat down for ya, delivering your messages, and gettin' into fights that you don't want to mess with." He lay back on the bed. "I got nothing because you give me nothing. When my leg heals, I'll ride on. Let you tend your own patch."

"What about money . . . and Esther?"

Harvey ran his fingers through his beard, had a little snort of a laugh. "Hell, she'll be glad to see me gone. You've said it a thousand times. I figure you're smart enough to dip into your cash, keep me satisfied, till I figure out the rest. Maybe find Bishop myself, collect that bounty." Harvey grabbed his leg, rocking forward on the bunk. "Goddamn a mule, my leg's burning."

Tuck took the money stack from his shirt pocket and handed it to Harvey.

Harvey held the money with both hands, then looked at his brother-in-law.

Tuck said, "It ain't like you don't deserve it."

"There was a time when I really did try to be a good husband." Harvey's hands stayed wrapped around the stack even after the bullet from Tucker's gun took off the back of his head.

Colby's jaw was still stinging from the rifle blow, but he didn't let that distort the beauty of the Wyoming countryside stretched out before him. The grass was a lyrical wash of green and blue, one color giving way to the other as the tall blades bent with the breeze.

In the distance, a herd of buffalo grazed, some taking water at the edge of a small stream. Colby rode easy, having a deep drink of the day and his surroundings before saying to Fire riding next him, "We're always thinking of money. Makes us forget the treasures right in front of us. The great creation."

Fire scowled. "What the hell are you going on about?"

Colby angled a little closer, he and Fire only a foot or

so apart, their animals snorting at each other. He slipped the Uberti 1875 from the snap-pocket inside his jacket.

His voice was clear, cheerful. "Take off your hood or I'll put a bullet in your spine in an exact spot that won't kill you, but will set you on fire. You'll be begging me to put one in your brain. And then I won't."

Fire glanced over his shoulder at the other hooded riders coming up from behind. A couple exchanged words, hands on guns, and then one shouted, "Everything all right?"

Colby said, "They can't help you. They're not good enough."

Fire called out, "Yah, it's all fine." His voice was an Eastern European bark, spitting out his words like they were plug nickels stuffing his mouth.

Colby said, "Well done." He motioned to Fire's head. "Hood."

Fire pulled it off, revealing a shaved head.

He was older than Colby expected, and fatter, with a face that was a mush of huge, drunken leftovers—bulbous nose, veins mapping cheeks, and a thick neck. He didn't speak. Just sucked his teeth, keeping everything to himself.

Colby said, "I can barely understand you when you wear that thing, and as we're currently working for the same man, it's right to finally know your face. Let them know, too." He gestured with the pistol. "Do it."

Fire turned and waved to the men in hoods riding behind them. They shrugged. Some returned it.

Colby said, "That's good. Friendly."

"You're full of jack-sass."

"And you're not garbled anymore. They call you Hunk, correct? For Hunkie."

"Name's Bogdan."

"Your father's a coal miner. Your brothers, too."

"You threw insults about my family's honor, threatened them."

Colby said, "During the last cattle raid, you were argumentative. I actually wanted to kill you. After striking me today, well, I just want to be very clear about where we stand."

"You think I'm to take this?"

Colby went through the files in his mind. "You've had blight for two years and are about to lose your farm. Your wife, Frieda, where will she go? And your two boys? Want me to tell you their birthdays?"

Hunk said, "You don't got to prove it."

"It's my business to know as much as I can about the people I work with. It can be a little confusing when everyone's wearing a hood."

Colby gave a friendly wave to the Fire Riders while keeping the gun aimed at Hunk. None of them made a move. "The one on the speckled pony? With the little finger missing? Claims he lost it in a gunfight? His wife chopped it off when he forgot their anniversary."

Hunk said, "Okay. So you know much. Then you know they're not going to like it, me riding in like this."

"The charade worked. The coach passengers think I was abducted, and we're far enough along we can drop the pretense. You're just no longer in charge."

"Yah, I see the damn gun. Very fancy."

"And it cost me. You understand why I can't allow myself to be seen in a compromised position, led by you?"

"You don't want the big bosses to think you're sucking hind teat."

"Very good." Colby turned again in his saddle and called out to the Riders behind. "Gentlemen, do you mind if Hunk steps down, and I take charge?"

The response was mumbled through the red hoods covering their faces.

One Rider managed, "Long as money's waitin' when we get back!"

"Excellent!" Colby turned back around and said to Hunk, "You're still scout, leading us in, but I'm in command. Don't worry, you don't have to salute."

Hunk said nothing, his tall horse keeping pace along the grassy trail toward Rawlins. Colby rode alongside, holding the gun on him, enjoying the day, and whistling a beautiful tune.

CHAPTER NINE
Bleeding Soldiers

Seeing the dust from the wagons and men rising in the distance, Farrow brought two horses to the cross-roads leading to the Chisum Ranch. Rose was driving the team, with Bishop in the back of the open wagon tending Maynard and several cowboys that had been rough-bandaged and were still blood-wet.

She angled through a steep turn, heeling the wagon and making the horses run close to the edge of the road. The wheels jumped. Farrow signaled for her to stop. She pulled up, the pair snorting, a dry fog of dust settling.

"What the hell, Farrow? We've got to get these men inside so Doctor Bishop can tend them!"

"Take 'em to town. Bishop's wanted in the big house."

Bishop said, "These men are . . . my patients."

"An hour ago you didn't know them. They work for Mr. Chisum. They'll see his doctor in Lincoln. You're needed elsewhere. Don't make me insist."

Bishop said to Rose, "Don't waste any more time on this. Get going." He dropped from the back.

Rose slit the air with the whip, ripping the team off at top speed.

Farrow presented the reins to Bishop's bay. "He made the trip in fine shape."

Bishop mounted up as a convoy of Chisum men approached, Garrett leading them. Some were walking-wounded and others rode, leading horses soaked in foamy sweat, dead men tethered to them. A bottle of milky tequila was passed among bloody hands.

Garrett slowed to Farrow. "Here to offer comfort, Farrow? They're all on the payroll. They deserve something."

"The worst-off are on their way to Lincoln."

Bishop said, "The worst are head down on those saddles."

"The men have chuck waiting for them by the bunk-house."

"You're a hell of an errand boy."

Farrow looked to Garrett. "I do my job, which includes extending Mr. Chisum's hospitality to you for dinner. Doctor Bishop's accepted. Should I tell the boss of this ranch you have other plans?"

Garrett was taken aback. "No, I'm obliged. Let me make sure this bunch is taken care of."

Bishop said. "I can help."

Farrow said, "Mr. Chisum wants you now, Doctor. Garrett's perfectly capable. He'll join us later."

Garrett said, "It's all right, Doc. You earned a good meal."

Bishop looked back toward the men. "There's a lot of dead and injured." He brought the shotgun across his lap. "Mr. Chisum and I are going to have some real words over this . . . dinner."

Farrow said, "Fine with me. I eat in the kitchen."

The washbasin was a new model with a built-in pump and porcelain catch-bowl. Bishop leaned against it, pulling his shirt off over the shotgun rig.

Claude Ray knocked, then opened the water closet door just as Bishop freed his sleeve. Balancing himself on one leg and a willow peg, he held a clean shirt in one hand and a shot of Suits Kentucky Bourbon in the other. He was just over the hump of twenty, and didn't look like he shaved his blond fuzz more than once a month. "Mr. Chisum's compliments."

Bishop took the drink. "Unhook me in back? That buckle?"

Claude Ray loosened the straps as Bishop pulled the double barrels away from his half-arm, the skin around the elbow joint raw and bloody from the shotgun's kick.

"If you don't mind my saying, that's quite a contraption."

"It has its uses." Bishop rinsed the raw joint, then dabbed the arm with a towel while noting Claude Ray's leg. "Right above the knee. How'd you lose it?"

Claude Ray opened the rig's side breech and examined the back straps. "Dustup down by the Pecos, but Mr. Chisum didn't toss me out after they cut me down. Let me rest up here and paid for the surgery."

Bishop reached for the clean shirt. "Your boss sounds like a hell of a man."

Claude Ray put the rig beside the washbasin. "That's

his starched button-down you're putting on, and that was his whiskey."

John Simpson Chisum stood formally by the tall-backed chair made from dark wood, one hand in his pocket, nodding as Bishop entered the large dining room with the domed ceiling.

Bishop paused to take in the man he'd heard so much about—surprisingly slight of build, a thin face, set jaw, and weary eyes. Bishop knew the look. Wars won, battles lost. Years had left deep marks on the cattle baron who sported precisely cut clothes, a mustache, and iron behind his eyes.

Chisum welcomed his guest, the Tennessee in his voice intact. "Doctor Bishop, I can't tell you how pleased I am that you're joining me in more ways than one."

Bishop, in Chisum's collared shirt with the empty right sleeve pinned back, held the shotgun rig in his left. "Mr. Chisum, there were a few minutes today when I thought I'd never be sitting down for a meal again."

"I offer congratulations on your victory. Also, apologies."

"Taking down those men isn't what I expected my first afternoon."

"Why don't you lay your weapon over there?" Chisum gestured to a dry sink against the farthest wall. A beautiful piece, it was in keeping with the rest of the room and the perfect place to display an array of imported liquors, custom cigars, and other vanities of a Big Auger.

Bishop was caught by the large oil painting immediately above the sink deft in its detail of the Tennessee

Twin Rivers campaign. The surviving soldiers wore red-soaked rags, their uniforms unrecognizable, standing among a litter of dead comrades from both armies. An engraved plate on the gold-leaf frame identified the battle.

Chisum said, "The artist captured the horrors, didn't he?"

Bishop's stare was fixed on the dead. "From what I recall, and what I saw today. Thanks to you."

"This isn't how I wanted us to start. Again, your specialty gun can rest right there."

Bishop put down the rig. "Were you at Twin Rivers?"

"I wasn't, but I'm Tennessee-born. Lost family and friends. I was making sure our boys had plenty to eat and praying the conflict would end."

"I'm sure you did all right."

Chisum's correction was measured. "Trading Confederate scrip for cattle, trying to get rid of that money before the surrender? I would've done better to feed the cash to the herd."

"That bad?"

"End of the war, family gone, debts I couldn't pay and no way to settle. No animals. and no kin. Dead broke like everybody else and their grandpa."

"Everybody else doesn't own half of New Mexico."

"We both know that's not true. I got new beef contracts only when the army was whole again. Lots of struggle till then, trying to build something." Chisum nodded toward another art piece. "The painting near the window? Now, that's a fine piece of work."

Bishop moved to the beautiful depiction of branding time during a New Mexican winter, all shaded blues and white.

"Even got the jingle-bob of the ears. Every piece around this room is like a different part of my life, from the war till now," Chisum said, looking over to Pat Garrett standing in the entranceway, waiting to be formally brought to the table.

Garrett had brushed his suit, kept his hat in his hands. "It's a real tribute to Mr. Chisum."

"Call them records of what we've accomplished so far. All are the work of American artists. I don't need a European to show me my own country. Patrick, please sit at the place next to me."

Bishop said, "There's a lot of room on these walls."

Garrett took his seat as two maids and Claude Ray set out calabacitas, beans, and fruit.

"Room for what happens next, Doctor. I'm hoping you'll be there to see it. Please sit."

Bishop's place was on the other side of Chisum, opposite Garrett. The maids, all high cheekbones and beautifully proud, poured wine. The younger topped Bishop's glass, casting a glance with fierce eyes. He met them.

There was a lightning strike of White Fox . . . battling her enemies.

Chisum's voice pierced Bishop's memory. "That skirmish wasn't the best way to be introduced to life here in Lincoln."

"Excuse me, Mr. Chisum, but . . . bullcrap. You got me to see your war up close, believing I'd throw in with you if I survived."

Garrett drank his wine, silently proud that Bishop was using his words. Claude Ray set out the rack of roasted pork.

Chisum started carving. "You've got the wrong idea of me, Doctor. I'm not that calculating. I don't play with anyone's life. My men or yours."

Bishop said, "That's good to know. And I survived."

"We want to find a way to stop these raids, get back

to business. No more blood. I've been in this fight before."

Claude Ray limped back to the kitchen, balancing on his one leg, almost losing the dish, and then catching it.

Garrett said, "He got pecosed."

"I don't appreciate that, Patrick," Chisum said, then offered corunda to Bishop. "The frontline of the last cattle war was the Pecos River. That's where Claude Ray got ambushed. Anybody got shot, the boys called it 'getting pecosed.' If you'd been with us, maybe he'd still have his leg."

"Mr. Chisum, these last forty-eight hours have been all kinds of hell. You paid a lot for me to be at this table. It's time to speak plainly."

Chisum regarded Bishop. "I'm losing men and stock every week, and frankly, I can't afford either. We're down to bones and scraps, and the damnable Fire Riders are the reason."

Bishop said, "Your scraps are enviable."

Chisum was settled against his high-back chair. "I intend to hold on to what I've got left. The Fire Riders aren't taking any more from me."

Bishop said, "Farrow claimed we shared a common enemy."

"You disagree?"

Bishop chose his words. "I have . . . suffered . . . at their hands."

"And did real damage back. I know about your injuries, even the ones we can't see. How much of your battle in Paradise do you remember?"

"Not as much as you'd like."

Chisum took a drink. "I have a plan, and I want you

to be a part of it. That's very important to me. Patrick, you're going to be leading this."

Bishop said, "My own wars haven't gone as well as yours."

Garrett said, "You're a sure man with that double barrel, and you saved some lives today."

"I had help from a young lady who earned more than her share of your gratitude. All the men did. They bled for it."

Chisum said. "My men are treated well."

"The ones that live?"

Garrett said, "All of 'em. And Rose is taken care of. No worries."

Chisum said, "Doctor, you're making your points, but I need your medical expertise and that special rig. You're a hell of a combination."

Bishop regarded Chisum. "You said I might have a choice."

"I already gave it to you, and you chose dinner instead of a noose. Good, sound thinking."

Garrett snorted a laugh as Chisum continued. "You're here, and I'm offering the opportunity to finish what you started. You won't be going it alone."

Bishop said, "I'd have your private army backing me?"

"Just my men. Think of them any way you want. I want the Fire Riders, so do you. Why not throw in? Help win this war against the red hoods, wipe out the scourge. You'll be riding out rich and with peace of mind. What's all that worth to you?"

"I have a lot of blood on me. So do you."

Chisum didn't push back. "When the time comes, I'll have to settle with my Maker. I know that. As for *your* death sentence, the good people of Paradise are a forgiving lot. You're no killer to them now. You're an infamous character who spent time in their jail."

Garrett said, "Stroll back into that town, they'd buy you drinks all night."

Chisum said, "You can win us this fight, Doctor Bishop."

"I'm just one man, Mr. Chisum, and not a whole one, but what's left isn't for sale."

Chisum said, "You haven't taken any money from me. In fact, you're the only one who hasn't."

"My soul's intact, even if the rest of me isn't—"

"A man who underestimates himself makes a terrible mistake. As far as I'm concerned, you're the most important person for a thousand miles."

"Because we want death for the same people?"

Chisum said, "Let's say we both have unfinished business. Partnerships have started on a lot less."

"No." Bishop looked toward the shotgun rig just feet away, the barrels pointed at him. "I told Farrow I wasn't a hired gun."

John Chisum said, "Not a hired gun. An ally."

The little blond girl pushed the feet of the hanging corpse, giggling as it swayed. It had been on the turret for days, birds pecking at the head and hands, pulling his shirt, pants, and flesh to pieces. His shoes were gone, and his feet were coal-black from the blood gathered in his soles, the toes curled back into nothing.

The girl's hair was stiff as old wheat, and she maneuvered it away from her eyes, snorting through a pug nose that took up too much of her face. She said to the dead man, "See, this is what happens when you don't play by the rules," then gave the body another push.

The rope holding it groaned, and the knot slipped, dropping it a foot. She jumped back just as she heard her father's voice.

Albert Tomlinson, a bookkeeping ledger in one hand and a small lantern in the other, called out to his daughter. "May Flowers! Leave that dead one alone, and send these boys out with a song!"

May Flowers defiantly nudged the body one more time. before singing. Her angelic voice carried delicately across the open yard where riders in red were mounting up. Two of them checked the repeaters in their saddle slings, shouldered them, and listened.

"Yes, we'll gather at the river, the beautiful, the beautiful river; gather with the saints at the river, that flows by the throne of God."

A rider with few teeth pulled his hood down, adjusting its fit, before grabbing a torch from an oil barrel and lighting it. He fell in with the two who'd checked their rifles, and they looked back at the perfect voice with the bulbous eyes and snout nose.

She was still singing: *"On the margin of the river, washing up its silver spray; We will talk and worship ever, all the happy golden day."*

The three rode out the gates, the smoking yellow torch, cutting the midnight dark.

"Gather with the saints at the river, that flows by the throne of God."

Albert moved behind his daughter, easing her away from the dead man hanging, letting May Flowers's voice follow the riders as the torch became a lightning bug, dancing for a moment, then gone.

* * *

Colby's horse stayed true, following the slight curve of the trail. It was a forgotten stretch across the Wyoming flat, and he envied the animal's night vision, keeping around gopher holes, and just enough ahead of the riders behind them, so he could have a good shot at each.

Just in case, he figured the order, as he always did to stay sharp. He didn't have to turn around to know who was where. He could feel it. Hunk was out front, with the others following two across. They all had their hands casual on their guns, and one had a bowie knife in his belt for show.

Hunk came up alongside Colby. "You ain't losing me."

"Just getting the lay of the land. You'd say so if I was riding in the wrong direction, correct?"

Hunk kept his head down. "Got nothing to say about nothing."

Colby saw the ball of fire in the distance, moving toward them at a full gallop. "Gentlemen, hold up."

The men heeled, standing in their saddles to see the three Fire Riders charging out of the dark, becoming more distinct. They moved from blurs of motion, to shapes of red, to men in hoods and flowing tunics. The one holding the torch rode point, those with the repeating rifles flanking him. They came up too fast, heeling their horses to one side, avoiding collision.

The Rider with few teeth and the torch barked, "Where the Sam Hill is his blindfold?"

Hunk looked up, but Colby answered. "There's been a change in command, so no blindfold needed."

Torch nodded to the rifles on either side. "There's a right way to bring a man in, and this ain't it."

The Uberti pistol was in Colby's hand, leveled between the eyes of Torch's red hood. "Before you try anything, understand I'll put two in those with the rifles before your gun's raised. Your horse is skittish, so he'll bolt, and then I'll put one between your shoulders before finishing with the headshot. I thought you should know the sequence of events."

Torch said, "Snap my fingers, and these rifles—"

"You'll have a bullet through your eye before your thumb hits your forefinger. We take money from the same man. That doesn't put us at the same skill level."

"You're all the chin music, ain't ya?"

Colby said, "Think of this. Bring me in as a corpse, you'll have a great deal to answer for. I do the same for you, I don't think I'll have too big a problem. Now, how do you want to proceed?"

Torch's horse pawed at the ground as he knuckled the reins, looking at the men behind Colby to see their move. Nothing.

Colby said, "They just want to get paid. The fact is, Hunk knows the way in, so we don't need an escort. Just your light."

Torch back-stepped his horse. "I know how to follow orders!"

"Good. You can say I used guile to trick Hunk. And you."

"Guile? What the hell's that?"

Colby said, "You'll all be properly educated, I promise."

Torch angled his pinto around, quick-spurring it into a run. The flame was kept high, orange sparks spitting, leaving a trail behind. Colby and his band followed. Those with the rifles broke to either side.

Colby nodded to each. "Don't worry, Hunk. If anyone's reprimanded, it'll be me. You won't lose your status."

Hunk finally raised his head. "Think I don't know, but I do. Think you're too smart, but you're not. *Te voi ucide— o zi.*"

"*Nu ai nici un secret.*"

Hunk nodded, appreciating that Colby had spoken to him in his own language, assuring him they had no secrets between them. Colby sped his horse slightly ahead, and began to whistle.

The porch was wide, running the length of Chisum's house. He stood at the freshly painted railing, drawing on a briar pipe, keeping watch on John Bishop and Pat Garrett walking to a bunkhouse. Bishop carried his shotgun rig, and Garrett an unopened bottle of Chisum's best bourbon. Garrett had a hand on Bishop's shoulder, exchanging low tones.

Farrow stood with Chisum without a sound or a glance, eyeing the conversation neither of them could hear. "Garrett sealing the deal?"

"I doubt anything Patrick or I say has much impact on Dr. Bishop. He's a man of his own mind."

"Yeah, what he remembers."

"He's always to be treated with respect."

"I've spent my time with him." Farrow took a glass from a small table, checked it for spots before pouring water from a flowered pitcher. "He's the key to these raids. If he rides out and gets captured or killed, your men won't be responsible."

"You mean my hands will be clean?" Chisum checked the pipe bowl, tamped the tobacco. "Never happen. Not now, not anymore. Good or ill, my brand's on everything."

"Do you want me to take the next step or not? Your choice."

Chisum relit the pipe. "Damn right it is."

"There was a strategy. That's what I've been following. You want to change up?"

"Meeting Dr. Bishop has given me pause, that's all. It's called having a conscience."

Farrow wetted his throat before saying, "Mr. Chisum, you want to head off defeat, offer your enemy something they'll never get otherwise. Don't you? You're risking everything you've got."

"Speaking to me like I'm a fool is a serious mistake." Chisum watched the smoke rise and vanish as the night settled on the miles he owned. A zone-tailed hawk screamed, its voice carrying over the flats. "That's a victory cry; he's got his prey."

Farrow said, "I've done my job, said my piece, earned my pay."

"No, you haven't."

The towers of the prison were falling-down silhouettes to Colby; ruined, sloping giants against a night sky. Torch signaled approach, someone inside the prison responded, firing a shot.

The front gates parted.

Colby's horse threw back its head, sidestepping as a

gunman with a shaved head sprung from a hidey-hole by the stallion's legs, like a striking rattler. Colby brought the chestnut around, holding it tight. The animal bit at the air, but didn't buck. Didn't panic.

Shaved Head threw aside the Shoshone blanket that had hidden him under the sand and climbed on behind the last Fire Rider passing, the rifle anchored on his hip.

Colby said to him, "Welcome aboard."

The prison gates were fully opened. Heavy canvas, painted to look like stone, hung over one door, trapping the light of the cook fires and oil lamps inside.

Torch charged through, followed by the convoy of Colby, Hunk, and the rest. Shaved Head dropped off the back of the horse, helped close the gates, and threw the huge bolt.

Colby took his horse to the middle of the old prison yard. The others went to a stable hidden behind another canvas painted like ruins from a fire. Just to the side of the camouflage were a short-barreled Bulldog Gatling gun, tripod, and ammo.

Colby slipped the Uberti back into his jacket, taking in the place and its mask. The surrounding walls were ten men high, laced with a mile of rusty-tooth barbed wire. Sections of the wall had been blown apart by massive explosions, leaving twisted iron supports and mounds of shattered concrete behind.

The ruptures were filled with crates of bullet brass and slab lead, the rubble hiding a new forge for making ammunition. A bullet maker was working, pumping air for the furnace, melting lead, and pouring ten slugs at a time into molds.

He gave Colby a toothless grin. "Aye, a friendly cuss. Can't shoot worth a grandma's turd, but loves making bullets." Reg Smythe extended a giant hand in greeting. "Mr. Colby, I presume."

"You presume correctly." Colby noted everything about Smythe seemed overgrown—thick red hair, thick English tongue, gin-blossomed face on a head cut from granite.

Smythe said, "You're the one what changed up the rules on us. I *was* Sergeant Smythe, now just Reg." Smythe's squeeze numbed Colby's fingers before he got his hand back, worked the blood back into it.

Colby asked, "So, Bogdan made his report?"

"That damn name's too hard to spit! He don't work that fast. Besides, he can't write. Hunkie told me you took over. Not a problem here, mate."

Colby said, "I won't abide second-rate treatment."

A stable hand took Colby's horse and walked it to a newly built structure with a tented exercise paddock on one side of the yard.

Colby said, "Quite a place."

Smythe looked up. "Been here more than twenty-five years . . . as a sergeant of the guard, not behind the bars."

Colby judged the man to be well over six feet tall, but he was almost doubled over, his legs dangling useless as he leaned on two heavy crutches. Dead weight.

"And not always a cripple."

"Where did you take the bullet?"

Smythe balanced himself on the crutches topped with stuffed leather. He moved forward with his arms and then pulled himself to them, like a dog dragging broken legs. Colby stayed alongside.

"Run-in with an old prisoner. Now, he's not walking the earth, and I am. Almost. But I never question the

Lord's providence. Build an empire, you pay the price. Am I right Mr. Colby?"

"Indeed, Mr. Smythe." Colby noted an area bordered off as a target range, men challenging each other with long-staffs. They were crude skull crushers, but learning. More canvas, shredded into strips with brush and branches sewn on, hung from wire stretched between posts, hiding the training from the outside. "Breeden's Rangers?"

Smythe drew his crutches up, smiled. "You're good. The only unit to make proper use of camouflage in the conflicts, but that's not my thinking. I sold Dev Bishop an old trick of Blackbeard's—take a shipwreck, outfit it with the newest guns and men ready for attack. Lying on its side, no one suspects nothing . . . until it's too late."

"How long have you wanted to try that?"

"Since I was a lad about ten when me dad told me the tale."

"I thought I heard the sea coast in your voice. This prison's quite the shipwreck."

Smythe's laugh was burned into the back of his throat. "Biggest ever. Everything's got to be protected. These men are going to be a true army. Not yet, but soon."

Cases of cavalry rifles were stacked open, gun sections wrapped and tied. A couple Fire Riders assembled the weapons, set them on wooden racks next to the firing range. Perfect assembly line.

Colby said, "Ah, the new carbines. Devlin took my suggestion."

"Lifting them from a troop train was hell's own job, but your thoughts do not fall on deaf ears, here, boy-o. Now, if we can learn that idjit to make the ammunition for 'em, we'd be rolling in clover." Smythe took himself a few feet closer to the entrance of the cells. Like the rest, the stone building was smoke-scarred, with shattered windows and a hole in the roof. But it was all paint and lumber fooling the eye.

He made a sweeping motion with a crutch. "More than a hundred stationed here, most taking the old cells, but they want for nothing. We've got med wagons, good horses, good food, decent whiskey. Better than anything else they've known."

Colby saw the crazy quilt of Riders' faces.

Smythe said, "Ex-slaves, coolies from the railroads, Swedes from the mining camps, Dagos and Jews run out of the waterfronts."

"Different without their hoods, yes?"

"Nope, the same. They all thought they were going to get a chance out West, and got cheated out of it. That's how Dev rounded them up." Smythe's grin broke his face in half. "We've got the men spoiling for a fight, an arsenal of over five hundred weapons, including a Gatling, mines, and grenades. That's something to brag on."

"All perfectly camouflaged. From the outside, just a place for coyotes to hump." Colby said, "You could take an entire town."

"Or a bloody state. Dev Bishop'll lay it out for you."

Colby nodded toward the hanging corpse.

Smythe said, "A renegade who didn't share our vision. He's past ripe and should probably come down, but still a good reminder."

Colby said, "What about him? Indispensable, too?" He nodded toward Hunk, who was taking a glass of store-bought rye at a mess table, watching a couple kids wash the white skeleton paint from the horses, scrubbing them down.

Smythe looked to him, then back to Colby and shrugged. "He turned in his cash like he was supposed to, and you're here. Does his job okay."

"But not with a standard of excellence."

Colby slipped a blade from his blanket of weapons, fitting it in his palm perfectly as he moved across the yard. He brought it down fast, slicing Hunk's ear cleanly from his head.

The ear dropped to the ground, and Hunk followed it, screaming. "*Fiul dacă o căţea!*"

Colby walked easily back to Smythe, wiping the blade clean, folding the ear into his monogrammed handkerchief.

Smythe said, "Now, that's a Cheshire grin," then barked, "Get him taken care of!"

Colby said, "He struck me, which was a mistake, but he can still hear to take orders. I was precise."

Fire Riders pulled Hunk away, dragging him to the med tent in the corner of the yard. Hunk tossed them aside like rats in the well bucket, but more tackled him. Brought him down. One Rider calmed him with two whacks of an ax handle. The doc had a drink then started sewing him up.

Smythe slapped Colby on the back. "Right. You've had your treat for the evening."

"My head's clearer. When do I see your Mr. Bishop, the one with both his arms?"

Smythe spit a laugh, dragged to the cells. "Tomorrow. We're waiting for a word from a man inside."

Hunk's voice was blasting from the med tent, "*Am de gând să te omoare, banditule!*"

Colby said, "Never been called a bastard in Romanian before. I was afraid my language skills were getting rusty, but Hunk's given me some good practice."

"Get some sleep, mate."

"Oh, like a baby."

The room was at the end of a narrow passage that laced the top tier of the prison's main structure. Colby followed it to the last door, marked FILE ROOM, and went in, shouldering his Navajo-wrapped arsenal.

He put the arsenal at the foot of the small bed that still had some spring and didn't seem ticky. Wooden cabinets, labeled PRISONER DEATHS, and ATTEMPTED ESCAPES had been pushed to the walls, making room for a small table with a pitcher, bowl, and towel.

Colby daubed the last few hours out of his eyes with the moist towel, before opening the file folder that had been left resting on his pillow. The first page was a wedding photo of John and Amaryllis Bishop, each one smiling wider than the other. The sepia had begun to turn and was spotting the image with brown, like dried blood sprayed across the bride's dress.

Colby daubed his eyes again, thinking aloud. "The good doctor with two arms."

Rose loosened the wrappings over Maynard's wounds, the blood on the sterilized cotton having dried in a starry pattern and stuck to the gauze bandage around it. Bishop moved the cotton several inches, centering it on the wounds. "Keep the pressure on the bleeding point, there."

Maynard looked up at Bishop, sniffed agreement. "I've had it worse. Think they hit slugs that were already inside me." He let his eyes drift before snoring.

Chisum's other men lay stretched out on their bunks, bandages around arms and chests. Legs elevated, a head completely wrapped. The ones who were awake got a few shots as Garrett went from bed to bed, pouring Chisum's bourbon.

Rose said, "This feel like an infirmary to you, Doc?"

Bishop straightened. "One of the better ones. Chisum's doctor did a good job."

"He said the same thing about you."

"Make sure they tend to their dressings, but that's good stitching. He layered the wounds." He said to the room, "You're all going to heal up just fine." He looked back at Rose. "And you're a good nurse."

Still in her denims and bloodstained shirt, she bobbed her thanks, then laughed. "I didn't have much choice."

Garrett said, "What about your supper?"

One of Chisum's older men grabbed coffee from the stove, poured her a cup. "She ain't had time to eat, been too busy helpin' us! Garrett, you sit at the big table now, tell me how many we're gonna bury before this mess is done. I served the Union, came on to Chisum's to cowpunch, that's it."

"Hell if I know," Garrett passed the cup to Rose. "That's why Doctor Bishop's with us. Help with the peace."

The old fellow said, "Can't come too soon for me. I don't like getting shot."

Bishop moved to the bed where the shotgun rig, a blanket, and some necessaries had been put. "Still not sure what I'm supposed to do."

"That don't sound like much of a promise."

Garrett said, "He's with us."

Bishop held back his answer for a beat.

Rose stepped in, "Let the man get some rest. Hell, we could all use it."

The old fella said, "I just need me some more Chisum bourbon."

Rose smiled. "That, too."

Bishop started for the back door, all eyes on him. Garrett almost made a move, but poured shots instead, holding the bottle to the light before tipping it, a holdover from his bartending days. He saved the heel of the bottle for himself and drank, watching Rose follow Bishop into the dark, dutifully carrying his medical bag.

"Hurricane's Mr. Chisum's top horse." Linus brought the chestnut out from the end stall. She was more than twelve hands high, with perfect ears and a white diamond between her eyes.

Farrow pointed to a scrolled saddle hanging in the tack room.

Linus tied Hurricane. "He never said nothing about his best horse or one of his best saddles."

Farrow crowned his felt hat with the side of his hand. "I'm on a special mission for Mr. Chisum. It'll be just fine."

Linus laid a clean blanket across Hurricane's back. "It ain't that I don't trust what you're saying, Mr. Farrow, but lots of smiths tried for this job."

Farrow slid fifty neatly folded dollars into the pocket of Linus's leather apron. "I've got a ways to go tonight."

Linus smiled. "And you're just now out of the barn."

Farrow took out a silver money clip straining with bills and held it out.

Linus glanced. "You can travel without cash?"

"There's something waiting for me on the other end." Farrow's hand didn't move.

Linus secured the saddle straps on Hurricane and grabbed the clip without another word.

Bishop found a place beyond the light-throw from the bunkhouses, and laid out his blanket. He set the shotgun rig in some grass and settled.

Rose put the med bag next to him. "They think you're heading for the barn. Don't get up." She sat, tucking her knees against her chest. "Just so you know, if you did take off, I wouldn't blame you."

"That doesn't go for the others. Especially Garrett."

"He's working his way up. Mr. Chisum found him. He was a stick man behind a bar. Now he's eating at the big table, with you. You didn't work your way up around here. You didn't have to."

Bishop said, "Chisum bought me out of a jail cell."

"We know all about it. You're all they could talk about for the last week."

"You know why?"

Rose looked at him. "Because you're the shotgun man. The avenger. You're in the papers. They think that'll scare off folks who want to raid our cattle."

"I'd never think of myself that way, and Chisum knows it."

"Mr. Chisum has a way of turning things in his direction."

"That what happened with you?"

Rose picked up a piece of grass, chewed before voicing her thoughts. "I've been around since the Pecos. Things happen, you stick to what you're good at. I know horses and cattle, and can shoot all right."

"That doesn't mean you're caught up in someone else's land war."

"Actually, it does." Rose watched Bishop untangle the straps of the rig, lay them straight on the blanket, then said, "Today gives us some history, so I'm going to be a little forward."

Bishop folded his sleeve around his half-arm. "I think I was, a little, so be my guest."

"I know something's going to bring you into this fight all the way. I ain't sure what it is, but you've got skin in this game."

"That might not be the right way to put it."

Rose laughed. "All right. See, you wouldn't guess from the way I present myself, but my woman's intuition is pretty good."

"You present yourself just fine."

Rose whistled through the blade of grass then tossed it. "Really? Don't want to bunk inside? That wind over the flats can bite."

"I've had a lot of inside lately. This'll suit me."

Rose stood, dusting her britches. "You know what's best for you."

Bishop stood too, offering his hand. They turned as the man in the tall hat rode full-out for the main gate. They watched Farrow and Hurricane for a few moments, fast-moving shapes outlined by moonlight, then Rose walked toward the collection of barns and service houses. Bishop lay back on the blanket, finally getting some peace behind his eyes.

CHAPTER TEN
Plans for Dying

The skull shattered with John Bishop's hard landing, teeth erupting from its jaw, falling back on him like rain as he hit the bottom of the pit. He rolled to one side, feeling the mountain of bone and shreds of hardened flesh powder under his weight, shifting like a sinkhole of sand, giving way. Swallowing.

His wife and son were beside him on the pile, just brittle remains—tufts of hair, eyeless sockets, faces locked in silent screams.

He heard the sound of pistols cocking, and instinctively tried to protect his family, cradling them as bullets ripped him from above. Slugs tore his back and neck, a geyser of blood spraying Amaryllis's dried skin.

He brought the shotgun rig, slick with his own blood, up from his side and fired both barrels at the figure dressed in a flame-crimson robe. Looking down at him from the edge of the pit, he held a smoking gun in each hand. The shotgun blasts hit the figure in the chest, but didn't kill. Somehow, he stood.

Strong. Ignoring the massive wound, taking a step closer to the edge.

Letting Bishop see his face.

See himself . . . John Bishop . . . dressed as a Fire Rider.

He curtained his eyes with his palm, denying what he'd just seen, and sat up. Taking two shells from the bandolier, he slid them into the rig as his stronger self stood above him. With two good arms and two good hands, the image looked down into the death pit, defying one-armed Doctor Bishop to do something.

A blast from the shotgun was meaningless.

Bishop wrist-snapped the rig closed and lurched forward, trying to aim over the piles of bones to blow away the man with his face.

Just destroy the face.

Bishop's mirror image steadied his pistols and said, "You're where you should be, Johnny. Dead. With your family. Actually, you're obliged to me."

Bishop made the move to pull both triggers.

The barrel flames and the roar of the pistols came first, slug-punching Bishop backwards, deeper into the pit, more bullets hitting him as he fell.

Falling, he managed to pull the triggers, firing into the darkness. Into nothing.

Still falling.

"They killed 'em all!"

The voice barely made it through. Vibrations from the gravel wagon kicked Bishop in the head, waking him, bolting him to his feet. He cleared his eyes of the dream as the driver ran the horse team hard toward the gravel turnaround in front of Chisum's house.

He yelled again. The alarm bell rang.

Men and riders broke from the bunkhouses, pulling on jackets and boots, shouting to each other to meet the wagon. A few had torches, streaking the sky before the sun broke.

Bishop called out, "Garrett!"

Pat Garrett slowed his horse and tossed him a canteen. "Get the sleep out of your throat. Chisum will want you to see this."

"What's going on?"

Garrett threw away the word: "Massacre."

Rose ran from the small hut behind the barn, Claude Ray limping beside her, trying to hold her back. He grabbed for her arms, a piece of her blouse. She twisted off, leaping onto the back of the wagon as it jack-tailed to a stop.

Garrett and Bishop rode up just as Rose yanked back the canvas covering the bodies, twisted on top of each other. She pushed an old man's corpse aside to find what was left of the towheaded kid who knew how to ride and rope.

Bishop was down from Garrett's horse when Rose screamed.

It came from someplace deep inside as she tumbled to the ground, spitting up air and coffee. She jumped on the first empty horse she could grab and broke it into a run toward the hills.

John Chisum stepped onto the porch, buttoning his shirt as the other men crowded about the heap of bodies in the wagon. Above it all, the younger maid watched from Chisum's bedroom window, the curtains breezing around her as she brushed her hair. And listened.

Chisum demanded, "Where'd you find them?"

The wagon driver already had a flask in his hands. "One of the Arkansas fingers, scattered on the river-bank. Animals got to a few, but I knew 'em by their clothes. Didn't look to me that none even got to draw a weapon."

Bishop turned the bodies over. Half-faces were frozen in surprise, with a bullet hole just above or below an eye socket. The backs of their heads were nothing but hair matted over gaping exit wounds.

Garrett said, "Army sniper. I'd lay money. That's not chicken shooting."

Chisum said, "We captured one of the Fire Riders, and they killed their own rather than have him talk. Just a boy."

Claude Ray hung on the side of the gravel wagon, looking down at what'd been left of Rose's nephew. "Rose kept hoping he'd make it back, maybe stay on. She prayed for it. Really prayed."

Chisum said, "These are the kind we're dealing with, Dr. Bishop."

Bishop was thinking of his son. "I know."

"Get them buried, and place a marker so Rose can find him when she comes back."

Claude Ray said, "She's not safe out there alone."

Bishop said, "Let her ride it out."

"Sound advice." Chisum moved to the railing, leaning forward. "I want every man—"

"You ask some of these men to mount a horse, their wounds will open, they'll be dead in an hour," Bishop interrupted. "They shouldn't even be out of bed."

Leaning on a rifle butt, Maynard said, "I got business to finish with these bastards, and I'm gonna finish it!"

Chisum said, "Only the able-bodied will have a part

in our response, so get yourselves ready. Maynard, I wouldn't try to stop you. What about you, Doctor? Are you included in this?"

Bishop looked back at his bedroll, with shotgun rig and medical bag beside it, then to the bodies. "I am."

The young maid watched the men scramble before turning from the open window, and picking up her dress from the floor beside Chisum's bed. She stepped into it, ready to serve breakfast.

The blood on Colby's handkerchief was darker than before, and there was more of it. He seized again, gulping air, then spit tar-red across his own monogram when someone pounded on his door.

He didn't have a chance to answer before a little girl, strings of black hair over a mean face, pushed the door open with her foot. Her head was too large, and one shoulder was weighted by an oversized carpet purse. She lurched into the room, wobbling a tray with one glass of buttermilk and a single piece of dry toast. "This is your'n. My arm's going."

Colby took the tray, and April Showers moved to the bed where his Navajo cache was unrolled, and all the weapons laid out. He put his breakfast on top of one of the cabinets, watching her.

She seemed to sniff at the blanket before touching the leather-pocketed corners that held sets of custom-made knives. She played their edges with her fingertips then looked up at him. "That's all you want for breakfast?"

Colby wiped a string of blood from the corner of his mouth, drank the stomach-soothing buttermilk. "It's more than sufficient."

"I don't know what that means. I swept this room

out three times 'cause Mr. Bishop said it weren't clean enough for you."

"You did a fine job. Thank you."

The little girl examined the rest of the armory—the barrels of the rifles and pistols wrapped and cushioned, the ammunition, telescopic sights, special attachments beside them. She picked up a Colt short with a customized Beretta barrel. "You use all these guns?"

Colby unwrapped April from the pistol. "Not all at once."

"You don't have to talk at me like I don't know nothing. My dad's Tomlinson. You're the special killer."

Colby froze his smile and didn't answer. "I saw a little blond girl last night. Your sister?"

"Yeah. Not even a year older, so we got to do our birthdays on the same day. That's a cheat."

"She can sing."

"Like a dying frog. I'm better. Much."

"You'll have to favor me with a concert sometime."

April Showers squinted at Colby, trying to figure. "You got all them special guns and knives, but you talk like an old lady. Don't make sense."

Colby finished the buttermilk. "Your father, where is he this morning?"

"I ain't supposed to take you there. You're to see Mr. Bishop. Your eyes is yellow like my cat's, right before she died."

They'd moved into the hallway. Holding his new target file, Colby pulled the door behind him. "No key for the lock, but I'm positive everyone here is trustworthy."

"There's that lady talk again."

April Showers was already down the small, stone access way that led from the old prison offices to the cells, the too-big purse swaying from her shoulder. She slipped the knife she'd stolen from Colby's cache into a pocket. "You got something else besides them guns? Money? Or maybe pretty earrings you took off somebody's grandma?"

"You ask interesting questions."

"And you special-kill people."

Colby let the echo of their voices drop off against the stone, but didn't respond.

She said, "Everyone here's a thief, and they all shot somebody, or done some stabbing. Not as much as you, but they got their own business, so don't pay no attention to me. That's how come I know everything about this place."

"I think not paying attention to you is a vital mistake."

"I do what I want, except when I got the heavy lungs. See this here?" April opened the purse, took out a celluloid breathing mask attached to a small, leathered box by a length of rubber tubing. She held it over her face. "Keep it filled with ice. Makes me take air when I can't."

"I've never seen anything like it."

She took the mask off, wrinkled her snout. "Crazy doctor with one arm made it, and give it to me. He didn't even know me, but that's what he did. I'll always recall that."

Colby said, "Sounds like a grown-up worth knowing."

"I heard you. Ought to get him to make you one."

The access way turned into an open landing where fire-damaged paintings of the previous wardens galleried the walls. Traces of black powder and soot laced the about-to-collapse ceiling.

"These here are the men what kept everybody prisoner in this hellhole."

"You know, my son doesn't use language like that."

Beyond the portraits was a heavily armored door that she hit with tiny fists. "Then he ain't in the real world." She hit the door again. "Fancy don't mean nothing. The last warden put all this up to fool everybody. It's all about foolin' people so you can pull it off behind their backs."

Colby said "How old are you, truly?"

"Don't get no ideas." April kicked the door twice and a bolt was thrown from the opposite side.

Hunk's punch was hard. He pulled back, then landed his knuckles into the shaved man's jaw again, like firing two rapid shots from a revolver.

Colby judged from the blood spray across Shaved Head's skull that he'd already taken at least three hits, maybe four. Hunk half-stepped back, lowered himself, then laid into Shaved's side, his ribs snapping beneath the skin.

April Showers squeezed Colby's arm with excitement. Shaved Head collapsed, begging for mercy as his knees folded together.

But no one could hear his voice over the cheers and hoots of the Fire Riders in the arena that was the prison's old common area. Two tiers of cells stacked like iron cages were built in a semicircle with a catwalk running their length and iron stairs joining them. Fire-twisted, but with crude repairs, they were now barracks, not jail cells.

In the center of the commons were the old wooden chow tables and a whipping post from the War. The Riders stood on the tables, rifle and grenade crates, surrounding Hunk and Shaved Head, thundering with each punch. Laying bets on the survivor.

Smythe crutched himself through the crowd, his voice topping everything. "All right, ladies, you're missing the point! This is training. It's not Saturday night at the bloody Palladium!"

Hunk was about to make another move, but Smythe put up his hand. "In the cells! Drag-ass down here for a lesson!"

Colby looked up to the second tier of the block and watched Riders peel out of the bunks in their cells, putting down guitars and letters, wandering down from the catwalks and old guard stations. They'd afforded themselves some creature comforts, all stolen, making each cell their own. One watched from his rocking chair, enjoying a pipe.

April Showers pushed around Colby, perching on top of the whipping post as Smythe shouted, "A man what steals from his own brigade is no man! Not under my command!"

The crowd circle tightened.

Hunk wrapped one hand with a thin, metal cord used to secure ship's canvas to decking, then looked to Smythe, who gave the nod. Two Riders lifted Shaved Head by the shoulders, and Hunk held up his chin, before pulverizing his jaw with the wrapped fist.

Hunk looked directly at Colby when he hammered the blow, then another, pulping Shaved Head's face to nothing.

Smythe said, "All right, a little too far, but you'll remember this—when you steal, it's for the brigade! Kill? For the brigade! Got it, boy-o?"

Shaved Head rolled over onto his back, eyes blistered shut, teeth tearing through his lower lip, grabbing that last gulp of air, and then—done.

April shrieked, the crowd cheered again, a few singing

Romania's anthem "*Hora Unirii*." Hunk grabbed a towel to dry himself off, careful around his missing ear.

April tried to sing along, but couldn't. "I don't know them words."

Hunk never broke his look at Colby.

"You really do keep yourself in check. I'd heard that."

Colby turned to see Devlin Bishop standing behind him, sporting a pressed shirt, pants, and manner.

Dev took Colby's hand to shake it, guiding him away from the crowd, as Shaved Head was dragged off, leaving a wide smear of blood across the floor. Others got out of the way of the corpse and settled their bets.

Smythe barked, "School's out, ladies! Time to pay up!"

Dev said, "Little reminders like this are important for the men. Keeps them on their toes."

"He rode in with us, seemed like a decent enough sentry. How much did he appropriate?"

"Does it matter?"

Colby said, "I get it. It's the act, not the amount."

Dev smiled. "I'm going to recall that."

Hunk threw his towel, and April Showers caught it, the smell stinging her eyes. She pulled the mask from her purse, covered her mouth and nose, and turned the crank on the small device, letting the cool, new oxygen fill her, while fixing her eyes on Colby and Dev Bishop.

Colby held up the target file. "This made for interesting reading."

Dev said, "As long as you can do something about it. Watch yourself."

Colby quickstepped to one side as a trapdoor lifted from a section of stone floor in front of him. Dev grabbed hold of an iron ring attached to the door and hefted it back. The telegraph operator scrambled the last of the steps from the solitary cells below.

Dev held out his hand. "The information?"

The operator held out a length of yellow telegraph tape, eyes blinking in the morning light. "Yes, sir, with date and time, just like you said."

Colby asked, "Good news from the belly of the beast?"

Dev Bishop regarded him. "It's why you're here."

April Showers watched as Colby and Bishop vanished behind an always-locked door on the far side of the old cellblock, with Smythe hauling himself after. She touched the stolen knife in her pocket and smiled under her oxygen mask.

John Bishop ran his hand down the bay's neck, stroking its length as he walked him from a stall. The horse was rested, well-tended.

Outside the corral, Bishop threw a leg over his back and pulled himself up with his left arm. Chisum men lined up by the ammo shed next to the stables, getting new stores of ammunition and extra guns.

Maynard stood unsteadily at the end of the line, his wounds wetting his bandages, but loosing a war whoop when Chisum and Garrett rode up.

Chisum said, "Men, I'm damn proud of each of you. You don't have to worry about your families or your pay. I'm doubling it."

A cowhand said, "My salary goes to my wife and kids. That's why I'm doing this."

The crowd agreed and Maynard broke through. "Hell, I'm doing this to get another crack at those red-hoods!"

Chisum said, "I guarantee you'll get both! Dr. Bishop,

would you take a ride? Let me show you what we're fighting for, and how we'll win."

Bishop angled over to Chisum, who led his men away from the ranch.

The grassland was an open stretch, protected on all sides by sloping hills creating a small valley. Four hundred head of Angus cattle were scattered between the hills, either grazing easy on sweetgrass or settled by the small bent of a running stream. Cowboys with rifles poised rode the loose edge of the herd.

With Garrett and Bishop beside him, Chisum heeled his horse to a crest above the valley. The horse stepped too close to some brush hiding a flock of prairie chickens, and the birds broke wild, cawing loudly as they flew away.

Two cowboys heard the noise, looked up from their position at the far end of the grazing basin, saw the three men on the hilltop, and went rifle-to-shoulder before Chisum signaled them with a wave of his hat.

Chisum said, "Right now they'd take a shot at anybody riding up."

Garrett said, "They're better than that, sir, but they're damn nervous."

Chisum lit his briar pipe. "With good reason. That's prime stock, birthed, raised and nurtured here. My stock, my sea of grass."

Bishop said, "It's a beautiful picture."

Blue smoke drifted from Chisum's mouth as he spoke. "Except for some scrub herds, about all I have left. Patrick, you've a map in your saddlebag."

Garrett unfolded the map onto his lap. It detailed the

Goodnight-Loving cattle trails from Texas to Montana, and had eleven red slashes scattered over three states.

Chisum said, "Each mark means men and stock lost to the Fire Riders. Men buried, cattle stolen."

Bishop leaned from his horse to look. "How much has it cost you?"

"Well over a million dollars, Doctor. But my men?" Chisum pointed to the cowboys, "Just working for wages, but I know the name of everyone that died and take care of their families."

Bishop said, "They can't fight a trained army."

"I won't dignify those terrorists by calling them an army, but you're dead right. Cowhands don't stand a chance."

Garrett said, "Before we move out, Mr. Chisum, why not request a cavalry escort? You've got the contract for the government beef. When the Riders attack, the soldiers can mow 'em down. Job's done."

Chisum said, "Fire Riders have spies, Patrick. One word leaves this ranch, and they'll know what we're doing before we do. See a patrol, and the Riders'll never come close until the soldiers move on. Then they'll wipe us out. We've got to go it alone." He nodded to Bishop. "That's how the good doctor took them on."

Bishop said, "You keep saying that. I barely got through it alive."

"But you did, and left a pile of their dead behind." Chisum put another match to his pipe. "We're forcing the enemy's hand by moving those four hundred up the northern trail to a cow town set off the main. Called Myrtle."

Garrett said, "Beg pardon, sir, but why're we headed to Myrtle? It's little more than a hole for a dog to pee in. Why not push into Colorado?"

"Because it is just a hole, and it'll lure the bastards in. They'll think we're just stopping over."

Bishop said, "You're sure the Riders will try?"

Chisum took the briar from his mouth and tamped the bowl. "I trust history. They've been targeting my smaller herds with less men. They leave no survivors and take every animal."

Garrett said, "And they've always come in at night."

Chisum said, "It's two days on the trail, but you've got to reach Myrtle by sunrise to give yourselves a full day to set up for a raid. Let them think we're drinking, whoring, and sleeping. Anything but ready."

Garrett half-agreed with him, "They'll get a surprise . . . I hope."

"Patrick, it's your reconnaissance, your decisions on who goes where. You've got the pen, a barn, and hotel for cover."

"There are a couple new men, supposed to be pretty handy, taking the place of the ones we lost."

Chisum said, "Mr. Tunstall's volunteered a few guns as well. " He turned to Bishop. "They're going to hit us hard, and anything you can tell Patrick will help bring our victory. Defeat's not an option."

Bishop said, "My old captain used to say the same thing before every battle, and he lost a few. I know you've got a lot at stake, but so do we all."

Chisum's eyes were back on the spread before them. "We've got to make this a safe country again."

Bishop's half-arm jerked in its sleeve. "You're welcome to anything I can remember, as long as we all agree I'm here on my own business."

"You're riding out with us, Doctor. That's all that matters." Chisum turned his horse and started down the slope to the herd.

Garrett watched the cattleman break toward his animals before sidling to Bishop. "You were on the fence last night. What changed?"

"You put any stock in dreams, Garrett?"

"You mean what the Navvies and Cheyenne preach?"

Bishop gave it a moment, then nodded. "Something like that."

"Can't speak for anyone else"—Garrett turned his horse—"but I'm not a damn fool."

Devlin Bishop sat at the warden's high desk. A large chart behind him showed the Fire Rider raids across three states, each one marked in red. Smythe got himself into a chair, pulling his legs out of the way for Colby.

Dev opened the target file. "Mr. Colby, everything's here that you need?"

"More. I'd seen most of the newspaper stuff before. Your brother's a rather famous man."

Smythe snorted. "That's the damned wrong thing to say, boy-o."

Dev said, "You're not wrong, Mr. Colby. John's gained some infamy, that's for true."

"You tried to have him killed and failed. His revenge quest has captured a certain, shall we say, public spirit? The man with the .12-gauge arm, perfect for the penny dreadfuls."

"If you're going for some kind of laugh here, I'm not getting it."

Colby said, "I just want you to understand that special circumstances like your brother require special compensation."

Dev was smiling. "Hell, I knew that before you did."

A quiet tapping on the door brought Tomlinson in, his steps not making a sound. He placed a sheaf of papers on the desk, straightened them, then inched away, folding his hands together.

Dev nodded. "You know Mr. Tomlinson."

Colby extended a hand to shake with a flourish. "Indeed I do. Still favor the Marlin Standard? I've also had the distinct experience of meeting your young daughters."

Smythe killed the laugh up from his belly.

Dev tapped the folder. "Mr. Tomlinson calls this your retainer. There might be a lot of work coming up, and I don't want to have to chase you down."

"I've always made myself available when I can."

"Always with a new price. Instead, you're going to be regular pay, maybe not as high as you'd like, but steady."

Dev stood, revealing a bullet hole in the center of the chair. He poked it with his index finger. "You know it's the only time I've ever purposely taken a life? Slug passed right through Warden Hog. He didn't even blink. I knew, if I was going to sit here, I'd have to claim it as my own."

Colby said, "A coup?"

Smythe said, "You ain't far off, boy-o."

Dev sat on the edge of the desk, arms folded, looking down at Colby. "I was in solitary for four years with a man who knew history. My schooling's spotty, but I can listen. He taught me what the ones he called 'Empire Builders' did. In Rome, Greece, places like that. When he wasn't fever-crazy, he made a lot of sense."

Smythe said, "In the Indian Nation, all the way to California, there's almost no law. There aren't enough men to back it up."

Dev looked at the map. "The law will come with the

people, but if we're there first, they'll have to pay to be safe, to not be robbed. To stay alive."

Smythe said, "Oh, and they will."

Colby said, "That's a fine, old business practice. You learned a lot from your cellmate. I'd say you're well on your way."

"Right now's the time to figure out if you're going to be a part of it."

Tomlinson added a meek, "It does offer security, Mr. Colby."

Colby picked up the contract. "I haven't said no, but I do have a condition. Payments aren't to be made to me, but put in a trust account for my son. When that's arranged, we'll visit this again."

Dev looked to Tomlinson. "Get it done." To Colby he asked, "Well?"

"You have a time and place?"

"My brother will be riding with a herd of Chisum cattle up the northern trail to a small depot. Mr. Chisum's been a great source of income for us."

Smythe said, "Aye, but you can only hit a man so many times, then you ruin him for the future."

Colby said, "Protecting future investments. That's wise."

"Chisum and I came to terms."

"He turns your brother over, and you allow him to get back to his cattle business?"

Dev retook the warden's chair. "Forget turn over. My brother's got my blood in his eye. He needs putting down."

Smythe said, "Aye, the mad-dog kill."

Dev handed the target file back to Colby, who flipped to the last pages, stopping at a fading, glued-together photograph of the Bishop brothers. John, about ten, his brother a few years older, standing together, with hair and collars slicked, and grinning wide. Dev's hand was on John's shoulder, which is where the photograph had been cut in half.

"My father had that done, figuring it would please our mother. She's the one who cut it, but Pa sent me that piece during my last stretch."

"When you were condemned to death?"

Dev frowned. "I changed them plans."

"And so you did. In the next days, we'll right the family wrongs. Are the descriptions of the special shotgun accurate?"

Smythe said, "That came from me. I saw it up close and lived to tell the tale."

"It'll make a fine addition to my collection."

The buffalo hide had just enough give for the shears to cut through. It was an older piece, curling at the edges, but Linus worked through them, cutting it into a triangle, then fastening it to a pony-sized bridle strap.

He looked up from his craft at John Bishop, who was leaning against the workbench, affixing springs to either side of the shotgun support pieces.

Linus said, "I did the best I could to curl that wire tight. You sure those are small enough?"

Bishop screwed the springs down between the metal sections that bent at his elbow and supported the gun barrels along the arm extension, making a shock absorber. He gave the left side one last turn. "Fine job."

"That should take up some of that kick."

"And kick it does, like a blind Missouri mule."

Linus laughed, holding up the buffalo hide. "This'll

go around your elbow so you can brace it without plowing backwards whenever you shoot."

"You're good at what you do, Linus."

"I don't get to work on things like this. Usually, I'm just shoeing the horses, the few we got left anyway. I'm not bellyaching"—Linus held up the completed elbow brace—"but this was a hill to climb. I like to test what I can do."

"You did right well."

"A fix up isn't the same as starting from scratch. The man who made this rig knew what he was about."

Bishop gave it a moment, then said, "Yes, he knew about weapons." He steadied himself as the blacksmith secured the shotgun rig's straps across his shoulders. Bishop adjusted the gun's soft-lined arm-cup around his right elbow joint, finding comfort, as Linus threaded the chain from the triggers to the small silver ring that anchored it to his left side.

Linus said, "Give it some slack."

Bishop held out his arm as if being fitted for a Sunday suit, and Linus cut two links from the chain, then used pliers to twist it back together. Bishop lowered his arm, the trigger line pulling exactly as it was supposed to.

Linus slipped the elbow pad onto Bishop's arm, then fastened the small strap. "Between this pad and those springs, that mule kick should be a kiss in the dark."

Bishop stepped away from the table, cocking his arm, the shotgun snapping into place.

Linus stood back to admire the whole apparatus. "That's quite a rig, and now it's Mr. Chisum's."

Bishop shook his head. "No matter what happens on this drive, what I'm doing isn't for sale."

"Glad to hear it. He's a good man, but he owns

everything. I'd like to breathe somebody's else's air for a while, but I know I probably never will."

Bishop slipped on his shirt.

Linus helped with the buttons. "You do need two hands, Doc."

Bishop studied Linus's face. "Who's the Apache, your mother or your father?"

Linus handed Bishop his beaver pelt bandolier. "My mother is Jicarilla. Chisum lets her have her own place two miles down the road. Most take me for Mex."

Bishop took the bandolier lace in his teeth, tied it off like a bandage with his left, before filling it with shells. "Reach my medical bag."

From the bag on the workbench, Linus took out a folded sheet of paper laying on top of the instruments.

Bishop slipped the last shotgun shells into the bandolier sleeve, nodded at the paper. "Can you make that? I figured it out this morning, but my writing's pure chicken scratch."

Linus laid the paper flat and smiled. "No worries. I'm schooled to read." He studied the drawing and the dimensions on the page. "Uh-huh. I can do this, and it'll be a good job, too."

"No doubt."

Linus regarded the plans. "Doc, that gun, that was your idea? Like this here?"

"It was in my mind, and I got the right man to build it. He had two hands."

"Funny. We're rigging you with this double-barrel, then you give me this to build. You're really two different kinds, ain't you?"

Bishop said, "Like being half Apache?"

Linus didn't disagree.

Bishop brought his shoulders together. He felt the

chain working in concert with the straps, become taut, and set to pull the triggers. All in one motion.

Linus inched the medical bag toward him. "Doc, looks like you're all set."

Colby had a bolt-action rifle in his hand when the fire erupted again in the back of his throat, choking him. He grabbed hold of the foot of the bed, spit bloody strings into the washbasin, gulped water from a pitcher, then spit again.

"Try this here." April Showers held out her breathing mask.

Colby took it, placing it on his face as he'd seen her do. She cranked the small handle on the device, circulating cool, oxygenated air through the rubber tubing to the mask, easing the coughing. He lay the rifle on the bed and sat at its foot, holding the mask over his mouth and nose as the little girl continued working the machine.

"Helps a lot, don't it? You don't have to say nothing, because you can't. I know."

A moment later, Colby wiped the corners of his mouth with his stained handkerchief, gulping his words. "You came just in time. You're right. That's a marvelous thing."

"Yeah, works good for me. I wanted to see what kind of gun you was going to take."

Colby stood. "Child, the less you know, the better." He splashed water on his face.

"You people always say things like that, like I ain't old enough. I saw the beating. And didn't I just save your hide?"

"Not exactly."

Colby dried his face, the spell over. He was tall and intimidating as he regarded the little girl with the disastrous face. "You're not the type I normally do business with, but I'll trade you. Five minutes on your machine, for the knife you took this morning."

April squinted, wrinkled her snout. "Won't tell nobody I got it?"

"If you don't reveal that I needed that mask."

April shrugged. "Not sure what that means, but I'll keep your secret, if I get to keep the blade."

Colby said, "Just use it with discretion."

Linus turned the iron plating in the coal scuttle with a pair of long tongs, heating the tip of the iron, then pounding the end to a thin, flat point. He cooled it in a metal wash kettle full of water.

Steam rose as Chisum rode into the stable and got down from his horse. "Did you see Dr. Bishop?"

Linus put the thin, iron plate back in the scuttle, heating the tip to refine its shape, then took the horse's reins. "Yes, sir. The doctor's ready for the drive."

"Good." Chisum glanced into the largest stall. "Where's Hurricane?"

Linus relieved the horse of its saddle. "Mr. Farrow's still got him."

"Let me know when they return. That's a fine horse, though. Fine ride."

"He's one of yours."

Chisum stepped out of the stable's back door, walking to the house, where the young maid waited for him by the kitchen. He didn't say a word, but placed his hand on her belly before going inside.

* * *

Blinded again by tears, Rose pushed through her rage, keeping her horse running full-out. The animal broke hard through the tall grass, finding the road to the Lincoln train station, and followed it by instinct.

They came in fast, and she twisted the reins, pulling the mare back. Her eyes were soaking, but she hadn't intended to end up there. Rose wanted someplace else. A clearing. The edge of a brook. But it is where the horse had brought her. Stopping short. Snorting.

"It's all right," she said, patting his neck. She rode along the trail from the road to the loading platform, before pulling up. Two men from the ranch loaded a coffin from a wagon to a boxcar. A name was written on the coffin lid in chalk, and she recognized it as one of those killed in the massacre the day before.

Rose turned the horse toward a stretch of grass on the other side of the street, swung off the mare without hitching it, and settled on a park bench that had been dedicated to John Chisum by the town council. Arms tight across herself, Rose rocked back and forth, saying something only she could hear.

Hurricane nickered, and Rose looked up. Chisum's best mount was tethered to the only rail across the street. She stood and walked to the horse.

Farrow watched through the window of the small café directly opposite the train station. Rose ran her hands across Hurricane's back, finding the Chisum brand before kissing him on the nose. His lips curled back, and she fed him an apple core she had in her shirt pocket.

Virgil Chaney was at the small table, too, as were a sarsaparilla, still foaming, a short whiskey, and three boxes of Havana cigars. He examined the contents of an envelope, counting the money inside. Satisfied with the total, he looked at Farrow, who was still staring into the street.

"Something's truly captured your attention."

Farrow said without turning his head, "Just a minor annoyance outside."

"Worth a picture?"

"Hardly."

Chaney held the envelope just out of reach. "You're guaranteeing that Bishop's riding out with Chisum's men?"

Farrow faced him. "I've been working to make this happen for months. He's going. All the directions, everything I gave you, are accurate."

Chaney handed over the cash, smoothed his lapels. "You do very well for yourself, Mr. Farrow."

Farrow slipped it in his jacket without looking inside. "You know, I actually like Dr. Bishop, but his death has presented a number of opportunities."

While tapping the camera case on the chair next to him, Chaney said, "I don't want to kill him per se, but it's imperative that I witness it."

Farrow looked back into the street to see that Rose had ridden off then turned to Chaney. "And you will. Just don't forget to give proper attention to the entire event. The massacre will be newsworthy."

"Sir, above all else, I am a journalist."

CHAPTER ELEVEN
Riding Hurt

"That thing won't go off, will it?"

Bishop was on the edge of a low-slung cot, the shot-gun locked by his side, as he checked Maynard's dressing. "Not if I don't want it to. One of you put some antiseptic on this cotton, will you?"

A cowhand with a bandage swathing half his face dripped pine tar syrup onto the cotton ball Bishop was holding. He wiped the dried blood from Maynard's stitching and the swelling around it. "Wrap it again, but tighter this time. He needs the pressure."

Maynard bent forward, pain gut-punching him as the cowhand relaced the bandage. Bishop put his supplies back into the med kit and tossed a roll of gauze to an injured drover on a far bed, who caught it.

Maynard winced. "You say I can't go on this drive, that Chisum won't allow it. But that'd be a damn fool thing to do. I been in on this war since the start."

"Oh, going to see it through?"

"I don't know what your stake is"—Maynard shifted, pain from the gun wound slicing him—"but I don't leave no fight unfinished."

Bishop snapped the med kit shut. "What if I said you weren't in any condition to finish it?"

"Then I'd kill ya."

A cowboy said, "Hell, Maynard, you wouldn't even be here except the doctor dragged your worthless ass out of that field!"

Maynard said to the cowboys in the bunkhouse, "I know he done a good thing, but now he's got to do another by not gettin' in my way!"

Bishop stood, the rest of the house watching from beds and corners, waiting for the shotgun to snap upward, taking a firing stance. It stayed locked. "A lot of these men need time to heal, but I can't truly stop anybody."

Maynard grinned. "Especially me?"

"I wouldn't even try. You're strong as an ox, twice as stupid. A few hours on a horse, and those stitches start coming apart? You might be in for a surprise."

"If I'm on that horse, I'll take care of the rest."

Rose's kiss was brief, just brushing Claude Ray's cheek, before she opened the corral gate and brought out her brown and white stallion. He supported himself on the fence, watching her tie down her bedroll and a Winchester scabbard.

She had washed and changed clothes, but seemed more exhausted than before, her eyes and mouth permanently down.

Claude Ray said, "Honey, this is all going to be taken care of, but you've been real lucky, so far. Those fence-cutters? You could have gotten really hurt."

Rose checked her mount's new shoes, and Claude Ray tried again. "We owe Mr. Chisum, but this ain't like it was before. How many did we lose yesterday? You won't have a third of the men we had at the Pecos."

He took a step on his peg, grabbing hold of a fence post. "I don't want you to end up like me . . . or worse. That'd kill us both. Mr. Chisum's a good man. He'll understand."

Two cowboys jumped the rail fence, slipped ropes over their horses, and brought them out of the corral.

One of them said, "Claude, I wish I was stayin' here with you, keepin' the frying pan hot!"

Claude Ray let it go. He said to Rose, "We'll figure another way to pay Mr. Chisum for his kindness."

Rose pulled herself into the saddle and looked down at Claude Ray looking up at her.

He said, "I know you're hurting."

She put a hand on his cheek before falling in with the other riders.

"Paradise, you know it?"

Dev Bishop and Tomlinson were in the prison yard as the Fire Riders packed gear and horses, putting on tunics and sheathing blades to their belts. Dev checked an army carbine and handed it off while Tomlinson referred to his notebook, looking up his PARADISE entry.

"I've not been to that part of Colorado, but we've transferred over fifty thousand dollars to their bank. I'm unclear as to the nature of this investment."

"You're meeting a woman who calls herself Widow Kate. Can't miss her. Round as a fat mule's ass, lives in a wheelchair. She's behind this deal."

Tomlinson said, "I'll put her, and it, under a magnifying glass."

"Check her plans, verify the money she's kicking in. If it's real, the whole town could be ours. When you're back, the drive'll be over. We'll have a fine herd to add to the stores and maybe Paradise, too."

Tomlinson said, "And the question of your brother will have been answered."

Dev looked to Tomlinson. "You've a way of saying things without saying them, bookkeeper." He started across to the camouflaged ammo cache. "It edges me."

Hunk was beside the break in the outer wall where the hand bombs and dynamite were stored behind a painted canvas. He hefted a ten-count crate of Adams grenades onto the back of a pack mule and lashed it secure.

Dev said, "Don't be blowing holes in that cattle. It's supposed to be fine breed stock."

"These are for the Chisum men. I know what to do."

"I know. You're commanding this, Hunk."

Hunk cocked his hat to one side, away from his missing ear and the stitches that had sewed his wound together. "So, maybe I'm worth more than my fists?"

Dev nodded. "More . . . or you wouldn't be riding for me."

"Then what about the dandy man?"

"He bushwhacked you."

"Never again."

"He's on his own special business. Let him do his work. You take care of Chisum's men and the herd."

Hunk knotted the line tying the crate. "Oh yes. The easy part."

Dev said, "Spill the right blood, show everyone they'd be damn fools to go against us, and you'll never have to worry about anything. Ever."

Hunk took Dev's hands, smothering them with his

own. "No blood on these"—he dropped them—"but I have family, and they need taking care of."

Dev took a cigar from his shirt pocket, cut and lit it. "Bogdan, that's why I want you for this. You're a man who knows how to make a right choice."

It was the first time Dev had called Hunk by his proper name.

Hunk extended one of his paws. "I have gratitude. *Sunt recunoscător.*"

At the Chisum ranch, John Bishop put gun oil, a clean rag, and two boxes of .12-gauge shells into his medical kit before tucking it into his saddlebag. He got onto the bay, his long coat draping, hat pulled down, double-barreled rig in place.

Claude Ray limped to him, peg leg dragging, waving an arm. "Doctor Bishop, this is your business. My wife's not right-headed. She shouldn't be going, but grief won't let her stay."

Bishop said, "I'll try to turn her around." He gathered the reins in his left hand. "You should see Linus."

Claude Ray glanced at the blacksmith shop, turned back to say something else to Bishop, but he was gone.

In the prison yard, the Fire Riders brought their horses to the center, tightening saddles and cinches.

By the weapons stores, Colby worked with Toothless, finishing the prep of his special ammunition. Toothless fit a lead slug into a casing held in the bullet vise before Colby pressed the side of a Chinese dragon dagger into the soft lead, then quickly pulled it back, the pattern of the knife's tail perfectly dividing the tip of the bullet into small sections.

Toothless cackled like hell and brought out more slugs he'd poured from a mold, fitting them into the brass he'd laid out.

Dev watched the procedure. "Doesn't the slug flatten when it hits the chest?"

Colby patterned another slug. "On the contrary. These are high-velocity rounds, so the tip splits apart after it enters the target, then moves through the insides, stirring them." He made a circular motion with his hands. "Like a cook with a good stew. Much better than shrapnel."

"Whatever you say"—Dev examined a completed bullet—"as long as you've got what you need for the job."

Colby took a piece of ice from a small bowl. "I'm very satisfied." He put it in his mouth like a chaw of tobacco, cooling his throat.

GOOD FRIEND CHISUM I HAVE SENT
ALONG SOME OF MY BEST MEN TO ASSIST
IN YOUR MISSION. IT IS UNFORTUNATE
THAT WE FIND OURSELVES HAVING TO
RECLAIM OUR LANDS AND BUSINESSES
FROM THESE MARAUDERS BUT IT MUST
BE DONE AND I HAVE EVERY FAITH IN
MR GARRETT TO ACCOMPLISH THIS. I
AM GUILTY WITH REGRET THAT AGE
PREVENTS ME FROM RIDING ALONGSIDE
BUT I WOULD ONLY BE A HINDRANCE.
I WISH YOU ALL GODSPEED. KNOW THAT
ALL I HAVE IS AT YOUR DISPOSAL.

SINCERELY HENRY TUNSTALL.

Chisum was on the crest, reading the wire a final time, then pocketing it, and watching the drovers start the herd out of the valley toward the northern trail. The cattle were obedient, with a few stragglers easily shooed back into line.

He loved to watch the movement from the back of the herd to the front—the wave of motion and muscles under hair as the animals followed each other to the next place for water and the place for camp after that.

Chisum missed the sound, the dust, the coffee. Missed being a part of it.

Pat Garrett rode up. "Those jingle-bobs will fetch a great price!"

"That's not what they're supposed to fetch."

Garrett dropped his voice. "I know that, Mr. Chisum. And the men know it, too."

"Who's riding"

Garrett pointed out the crew. "I picked our fellas who're best with a rifle to put them around the town. Maynard's still bandaged up, but he can fight. Rose insisted, and she's a better shot than most. And him." He nodded to a young man in a sombrero, taking a wide turn around the back of the herd, getting between a couple strays and the stream. "Name's McCarty. He's one of Mr. Tunstall's. They say he's too quick to shoot, but that might be a good thing."

"Remember the time when only the trail boss needed to carry a gun? Man put a rifle on his saddle if he wanted something special for chuck. Now, we have to ride out with enough guns to face a band of Commancheros."

Garrett said, "These are violent times."

Chisum stayed on his men and cattle. "Patrick, this drive's to end the war, so we can get back to business."

"It's what we all want, sir."

"Back to business, Patrick." Chisum let his words settle, then added, "Just don't be foolhardy."

"I'll do what's best, sir."

Chisum looked back to Garrett, who tipped his hat and rode down to the moving herd. Something weighing him down, the cattleman climbed onto his horse slowly as Bishop brought the bay to the vantage point and stopped.

Bishop said, "Well, Farrow told me you always get what you pay for."

Chisum eyed the bandolier, the leather-gloved left hand, and the shotgun, steady in the special sling hanging from Bishop's saddle so it would rest parallel to his leg. "As much a warrior as any I've seen coming across the flats."

Bishop said, "Still a one-armed man, Mr. Chisum."

"You're facing down our enemies, Doctor." Chisum wasn't looking at Bishop when he said, "I wish you all the luck."

"I never had much of that. Just strange chances."

Smythe had put on his best double-breasted jacket and had polished his shoes even though his dead legs would drag them through the slop of the prison yard. He crutched his way down the stairs from the gallery of wardens to where his men had brought their horses into formation.

He pulled himself to the weapons rack as Riders took the last of the carbines without chatter, only purpose. They nodded and pulled on their red hoods. The horses stirred and there was the rattle of tack as the men took their mounts, but no other sound.

No jokes, no passing of whiskey.

Dev Bishop faced the yard and Riders from the gates, standing on several blocks of stacked granite like it was a pulpit. He acknowledged Smythe, then raised a hand.

Tomlinson, flanked by his snouted daughters, leaned between them. "Sing."

"Rolling home, rolling home; rolling home across the sea, rolling home to dear ol' England, rolling home, fair land to thee."

Smythe watched Dev drop his hand, signaling the Riders to move out. In his fire-red tunic, Hunk rode point, holding his right hand to the temple just above his missing ear in the European style of salute. He sliced the air as he rode past Dev. Colby followed two horses back, his select arsenal secured behind his saddle.

The other riders, horses freshly painted as skeletal demons, all rode with formality, respecting their mission training. Rifles, specially made battle axes, and long swords hung from belts and saddle sheaths.

In perfect union with the movements of the troop, the girls' voices lifted the sea shanty Smythe had chosen. *A troop.* That's how he saw them. He straightened himself on the crutches to stand tall, beyond his useless legs. The nerves were dead, but he wasn't. His troop was ready for battle, and if he couldn't feel anything below his hips, he could feel pride.

Tethered to the last rider and weighted with grenades, the pack mule was the last to clear the gates, just as the girls sang their final note. April Showers threw a quick punch at her yellow-haired sister. Tomlinson yanked them apart.

Smythe called out, "Girls, you did me proud!"

Dev moved across the yard as other men stowed horses, stolen rifles, and supplies.

Smythe nodded a greeting. "You stood inspection. Did everyone pass muster?"

"They're not ragtag anymore. Your doing, Sergeant."

Smythe crutched himself along as Dev walked. "If Chisum delivers your brother, then you've broken him. Every cattleman in the territory will be running scared when they read about it. That's one hell of a thing, boy-o."

"When you'd come down to the tombs and beat me so I couldn't eat for a week, ever think it would end up like this?"

"Things can change." Smythe stopped, slashing a line in the dirt with the tip of his crutch. "That's the way I used to think. You crossed a line I wouldn't, which is how come you were a prisoner and I was the sergeant of the guards." He dragged himself across the line, his feet erasing it.

Dev said, "And now you've crossed it?"

"It never truly existed. We were always of the same stripe. We just wore different clothes," Smythe said. "Sometimes a uniform's nothing but a clean rag. It took me a while to come to that."

Dev said, "Major Beaudine told me that a man's only measure is the loyalty he inspires."

"See, you didn't leave me on that mountain with a bullet in my back. That's why I'm still here." Smythe put his crutches forward, pulled himself along. "I'm glad that lunatic died screaming, but he wasn't wrong."

The kneecap was plated tin that Linus had hammered around a section of fence post, rounding it out in Chisum's stable. He'd cut according to Bishop's plans, hinging it, then fastening iron struts on either

side that curved to an ankle as a leg would. The base
was a thin piece of iron Linus had forged to a length
matching Claude Ray's foot.

"The doc wanted you to have something better than
that damn peg you're always dragging." Linus held out
the artificial limb, but Claude Ray made no move,
staying by the stable entrance.

"Linus, that's really something. Probably too good
for me, but I'll wait till my wife comes back before
trying it."

"You don't want to surprise her?"

Claude Ray said, "Rose was there when they outfitted
me with this piece of pine. I want her here for this, too."

Linus worked the knee's smooth motion. "You could
take her dancing."

Bishop stayed back, trailing the Angus herd as they
spread out across acres of scrubbed grassland. Pat
Garrett peeled to the side, giving signals to the outriders who were threading their way around, keeping
the cattle moving toward a cut in the hills that led to the
northern Colorado trail.

Bishop watched Maynard struggle in his saddle,
shifting his pain, while the new kid in the sombrero
rode the length of the herd, back and forth, whistling
and yee-hawing the cattle's pace.

Rose rode drag behind them all, the animals kicking
up a moving curtain of dust and hair to ride through.
She pulled her kerchief up to her nose as Bishop moved
up beside. The bay stayed perfectly in step with Rose's
stallion, keeping Bishop close enough to hear over the
sounds of the drive.

"Break now, you'll be back at the ranch in time for lunch."

Rose leaned from her saddle, swatted a straggling cow behind the shoulders to get it to catch up with the others. "That sounds like Claude Ray talking."

"I told him I'd try."

"I figured you'd understand my doing this better than anyone."

Bishop said, "You're not facing one man. This is a tactic to bring down an attack."

Rose didn't look at Bishop, but the animals and cowboys in front of her. "I know what I'm riding into. I've done it before."

"Brave as anyone I've ever seen, Rose, but you've got a husband. I'm alone. That's the difference."

Rose pulled her kerchief. "It wasn't my nephew they killed. It was my baby boy . . . from before Claude Ray. They killed my son. I never—" She broke from Bishop, then rode to catch up with the herd.

CHAPTER TWELVE
Assassins

"Sure tastes like Colorado, don't it?"

A Fire Rider, hood bunched up, licked coffee from his thick mustache then poured himself a little more from the fire by the chuck wagon. The other riders were scattered about the orchard. Another small campfire burning at the far end showed rows of apple trees and inky silhouettes of the horses nibbling at them. The moon was large and low, with a light spring snow dancing in front of it.

Mustache drank again, melting the snowflakes that had been caught below his nose. He turned to Colby. "Don't know what you're missing. This is damn good coffee."

Colby was sitting by a small kerosene lamp, making notes in the Bishop shotgun file. There were scribbled surmises about the rig's black powder grain, figuring something heavier given the amount of buckshot dug from the Riders already killed. He made a column of numbers of possible extra shells Bishop carried, figuring how fast he'd run out of ammo, and the rig's original make, in case he'd faced it before.

He made another notation, then finally said, "I'm glad you're enjoying it." His finger pressed the bullet wound on his neck, the quick sting of pain keeping him focused as he wrote.

"You know we got orders not to talk to you, to leave you to your own patch?"

Colby glanced up at the figure that was blocking his light. "And you're disobeying those instructions. Why?"

"Find out what makes you so special. Maybe I'd like to improve myself."

"I doubt that, and I doubt this."

Mustache backed on his heels as Colby stood and walked toward the chuck. He called out to Colby's back, "Walking away? That's a grievous insult."

Colby took a closer look at the last piece of peach pie and checked the night's bean pot that was hanging over a flame. "You're trying to start something, but I can't imagine why. You're not insulted. You're finding an excuse. We all have our work, so let's leave it at that."

Mustache said, "How much you getting paid for yours?"

Colby stayed by the chuck wagon and called out to the riders who were just beyond the firelight, their red tunics browning in the shadows. "Bogdan! You're supposed to be in command here. Are you going to take control of this?"

Hunk stood, backed by a line of Riders. Two had drawn pistols, the others were waiting, fingers tapping guns and knives hanging from their belts.

Hunk said, "These men are my command. Mr. Bishop said you were on your own."

Mustache's face was suddenly close to Colby. "You ain't part of this raid."

Colby was steady. "I don't owe an explanation, but I'll say I have a special mission. My own raid, if it makes you feel better."

"Special? With them rifles?"

Colby said, "Bogdan, you should stop this man."

"He said you was on your own. You said it, too." Mustache kept pressing forward, chest out, his chin a locked challenge. "This 'special mission' sounds kind of piddling. Hell, I'd bet real money I could do your work better than you, make that 'special' pay. I don't think Mr. Bishop cares who pulls the triggers tomorrow, ain't that so, Hunk?"

Hunk stayed put. "He just wants the job done. What we trained for."

"Your training seems to ebb and flow. I was very impressed with our exit this morning, but not so much by your actions now. You seem determined to challenge me." Colby had moved to the back of the chuck wagon, sorting through the salt, ground pepper, and tins of spices. He palmed a small can, popping the lid with his thumb. He kept his back to Mustache, feeling him advance.

Mustache said, "Well, that clears the road, don't it?"

The powdered mustard flew from Colby's hand as he turned, a splash of yellow directly into Mustache's eyes. He yelled, tumbled back, and Colby shot him in the chest three times with a small-caliber Smith & Wesson he had in his belt.

It happened so fast, the echo of Mustache's voice and the roar of the gunshots faded against the distant hills at the same time. Mixing there, then dying in the rocks.

The light spring snow dusted Mustache's face on top of the mustard, slopping it into a yellow mask. The coffee cup never left his hand. Colby tucked the pistol behind his back again and took a few steps away from the corpse as the other Riders came in for a closer look.

One said, "damn fool," and another laughed in the back of his throat.

Colby said, "Gentlemen, I apologize. We have our separate missions and upbringing, but this should never have happened."

The Rider who'd choked out a laugh said, "Hell, this raid don't depend on that jackass."

"What say you, Hunk? Was this some sort of last-minute test before the battle?" Colby pulled his watch chain from the small pocket on his vest and displayed Hunk's ear that he'd threaded onto it. It had started to shrivel, but kept its shape. He gave it a little twirl, saying, "*Eşti un măgar.*"

Standing in front of a fire now, Hunk didn't answer the insult, just watched as Colby put his trophy back in his pocket. Finally he barked to the others, "We all got much work to do! Someone check the horses, make sure none have bolted."

Colby stepped over the body, settled by his lamp, opened the Bishop file again, and continued his notes.

John Bishop held the *Police Gazette* at an angle, catching a bit of light from the Chisum chuck fire to see the pen and ink rendering. The double barrels were blasting at the same time, tearing through the guts of two finely dressed men, while two more lay on the bank floor in pools of black blood. His teeth were a wide grimace, his one hand locked in an angry fist. Just behind him, what looked like a widow woman was on her knees, praying.

"Too many teeth, and I think they've got me a little short." On a blanket, resting against his saddle, the rig off his arm and beside him, he flipped through the penny dreadful with his left hand, not giving further reaction to what he saw.

McCarty shifted from one leg to the other, formally holding his sombrero, but not concealing his excitement. "Kept that magazine for better than a year. Always wanted to see the rig in person, see if it was true."

"Am I robbing the bank or protecting it?"

"It don't matter, does it? They wrote it up."

Bishop said, "They surely did."

"Well, can I? Look at the rig?" McCarty's words were breathless, and Bishop gave him permission with a look.

McCarty picked up the shotgun, handling it as if it were made of spun glass and antique gold. His smile split his face as he opened the side-breech, looked down the barrels, and checked the tightness of the triggers. He whistled. "How fast are you with this thing?"

"I've learned."

McCarty used both hands to lower the gun back onto the blanket, careful not to tangle the shoulder straps and trigger lines. "I'm good with a Colt, feels natural in my hand; most folks can't see it leave my holster. But that double barrel, well, the way it's rigged, it's really a part of you."

After consideration, Bishop said, "It is. Now."

McCarty's voice dropped. "How's that feel? To be . . . the same as the gun?"

"Not like this." Bishop tapped the page, then handed back the *Police Gazette*, its cover screaming SHOTGUN— THE TERROR OF THE WEST! by Virgil Everett Chaney.

Pat Garrett came down from the edge of the pine woods where the herd was tucked for the night. He was riding a hammerhead roan a good two hands taller than anyone else's so he could look down on his men, even if they were saddling a good horse. He eyed McCarty from his saddle. "This one bothering you, Doctor?"

Bishop said, "No, we've been having an interesting talk."

McCarty frowned. "You don't have to be on me, Garrett. We all know why I'm here."

Garrett said, "And you're gonna have a chance to prove your reputation real soon. Need you thinking clear. Get some rest."

McCarty threw Garrett a defiant salute and a quick laugh, then reached to shake Bishop's empty right sleeve. He quickly switched to his left and said, "A lefty. It was nice to meet you, sir. Honor to be riding with you." He got on his horse and rode to where a few drovers were catching sleep or coffee.

Garrett dropped, pulling a bottle of bourbon from his saddle with him. In one motion, it was open and being poured into a shot glass with initials PJG engraved across it. He handed it to Bishop. "Gave it to myself for my birthday. A little something fine."

Bishop listened to the herd, watched the hired guns roll dice by the fire or practice their technique. They were flickers in the night, drawn in streaks of orange from the flames. One was spinning a Winchester from his hip then firing on an empty chamber. McCarty was laughing, showing off his lightning-quick draw.

Bishop handed Garrett the empty glass. "They can't wait."

"Hired guns always want to show off."

"Like shavetail troopers."

"They're getting extra pay, and know this isn't just about moving the cattle."

Bishop nodded toward Maynard a hundred yards away, slumped in his saddle, snoring loudly. His horse stood eating at some tall, wet grass.

Garrett said, "He's earning his wages for sure."

"Those bandages are filthy. Damn fool won't let me clean him up."

"Nobody ever accused Maynard of having any sense." Garrett poured a shot for himself. "So tell me, Doctor, how'd you take on so many of the Fire Riders?"

Bishop talked to the sky, trying to put things in order. "I didn't know they existed until I was in the middle of a fight. I was tracking the men who killed my son, and they came down on us."

"The red demons, right?"

"That's what they looked like that first time."

"How many did you put down?"

Bishop frowned. "I-I don't recall."

"Then the train?"

"Later, but yes, then the train."

"That's what impressed the crap out of Chisum."

"I try to remember. It's still broken pieces, but you're right when you called it war with them. Attack, pull back, attack again in a new way. Battle skills."

Garrett drank his own shot. "Like the cavalry or Crazy Horse?"

"Either."

"You didn't let go of any of this with Chisum."

"He's not riding into anything."

Garrett studied the empty shot glass. "That's why he's got us."

"I recall they used dynamite on the tracks. And a Gatling on the troopers. Those sounds stayed with me."

"The Riders used grenades, too?"

Bishop looked to Garrett. "So they tell me. That, I don't remember so clearly. Maybe I still have half a one in my skull."

Garrett laughed. "Not a surprise."

"Now let me ask you a question. What am I doing here? Why did Chisum go to all this trouble, instead of letting me hang?"

"You saying you're sorry you didn't?"

"I'm saying I don't know what I bring to this fight"—Bishop lifted the rig—"other than this, and I doubt that's worth all the money he's paid out."

Garrett said, "Chisum was having you ride in, come hell or high water."

"That much was always clear. Are you supposed to keep me alive?"

Garrett corked the bottle and stood. "Doc, I'm worried about keeping myself alive."

"Get back to Chisum's big table?"

"My intention is to be a regular guest."

Bishop said, "You're an honest man, Patrick. I appreciate that."

"I've got a few moves figured for us, but if this fight busts open, you might be on your own."

"That suits me to the ground."

Garrett took the reins of his horse, ready to lead it

away. "I know you got some thoughts on Rose. Frankly, I don't need a dead woman on my hands."

Rose's voice carried from the edge of the woods. "You want to know about Rose, why don't you ask Rose?"

Garrett brought the hammerhead around as she walked from the pines, hitching her belt.

"The Doc's got nothing to say. This is on me. And no matter what's ailing me"—she made a jerking motion with her whole body toward the boys by the fire—"I'm still as good a shot as any of these you got." Rose looked to Bishop. "Well?"

John Bishop stayed lying against his saddle, his only hand on the shotgun rig, and said to Garrett, "We're both here on personal business. Rose is looking out for herself, and I don't doubt her marksmanship."

Garrett said, "As long as she does what I need her to when this thing starts."

Rose said, "I'm standing here, right?"

Pat Garrett rode off.

Rose cast a look down at Bishop, who had pulled the shotgun closer to him and tilted his hat down. His voice came from under its shadow. "See how you feel in the morning. Give yourself that much judgment."

It was the mandibles that Farrow saw first—the large jaws, ghostly white, with the fanged canine teeth, moving in and out of the tree line. Then breaking. Running.

Farrow's horse twisted against the reins, the skeletons roaring out of the dark, surrounding him. The painted ribs, spines, and legs of the horses glowed in the moonlight.

He drew a Colt as the Fire Riders closed their circle

around him. "I've never seen you done up like this. Must scare the hell out of the farmers and rubes."

"It does good with everyone." Hunk broke the circle, bringing his skulled stallion next to Farrow's own. Hunk's face was uncovered. He handed Farrow a small parcel.

Farrow said, "So, you're the deliveryman?"

"I command. They do what I order."

Farrow threw looks around him as the Riders brought their horses two steps closer. Dead-eyed stares came at him from their hoods. He could see shouldered rifles and blades.

One Rider bled the air with a Prussian saber before turning its polished edge toward Farrow's throat and holding it there.

Farrow said, "Well, by fire or the sword, eh?"

Hunk said, "What's your meaning by that? Answer quick!"

Farrow watched the saber. "Just the motto of another group I work for."

Hunk put his words into pieces. "You . . . double . . . the . . . deals?"

Farrow said, "That's why I'm paid."

Hunk's large hand almost covered the Smith & Wesson it held, the barrel seeming like an extra finger.

The parcel went into Farrow's jacket, his hand glancing the pistol he had holstered, but he judged the situation, and simply raised his arms in surrender. Farrow never lost his tight-lipped smile of advantage.

Hunk chuckled. "You look a damn fool."

Aimed directly at Farrow were guns of all type and blades that were less than a foot away. He said, "Absolutely no offense intended. I'm here to take you into Myrtle."

"What time the Chisum men coming?"

"That's been worked out. I won't tell you wrong."

Hunk eased the gun back to his belt, which signaled the others to raise their weapons. The saber remained.

"What time?" he asked again.

"We figure around noon."

The saber went back into its sheath. No one said another word.

Farrow brought down his arms.

The evening dusting had picked up, and Farrow turned his collar against the snow as he started out of the camp. The hooded Riders on painted-fleshless horses followed.

CHAPTER THIRTEEN
The Bleeding Ground

The storm came through a jagged break between two Rocky peaks, a natural wind tunnel turning raindrops into skin-slicing needles. It was a half hour past sunrise, but the rolling clouds darkened the sky like midnight.

Bishop stayed the trail with the bay, duster buttoned to his throat, the rig slinged. Sharp rain soaked him, but he felt good. Ready. He'd slept with no nightmares, no slashes of memory.

The others, sporting rubber slicks and pulled-up bandanas, kept the cattle moving with the storm beating their backs. McCarty, sombrero tilted back, not caring, waved to Bishop, locking his arm at the elbow imitating the double-barrel. He hooted a laugh before running his horse along the trail's edge to the front of the herd.

Maynard followed, struggling to keep pace, fighting

his wounds. His bald-faced mare drifted close to a bull that knocked them both away. He lurched in the saddle.

Garrett charged up from behind, swatting the bull with a coil of rope, water spitting off its hide. "You said you were up to this! Getting these to town isn't even half of what we're supposed to do!"

Maynard was pale, sweating in the cold. "Don't doubt I got some fight in me!"

Garrett said, "I'd bust your jaw in half if I didn't need every man."

The rain was coming in buckets as Garrett angled off on his tall horse, not letting Maynard throw another excuse.

Bishop stood in his stirrups and called to Maynard over the storm, "Let me check you out!"

Maynard didn't turn around, just fought to stay mounted.

Rose rode up on her brown and white from half a mile back, having kept her distance for the night. Beside Bishop, her eyes were fixed on the cattle and hired guns, water pouring from the brim of her hat. She said about Maynard, "I guess some folks just can't accept help."

"Garrett thinks we'll hit Myrtle in an hour."

"Good, that's good."

They rode for a bit, then she said, "Look, I don't want to hear nothing about my time to turn back."

Bishop said, "Some folks just can't accept help."

"You're on a vendetta for your family, just like I am for mine!"

"Don't make comparisons."

Rose finally looked at him. "When somebody you

love is killed, why does it seem that another killing is the only thing makes you feel better?"

"Fact is, it doesn't."

"Then what are you riding for?"

Bishop let the rain answer.

Colby organized his ammunition in neat rows within easy reach, along with two pistols, and a polished stiletto. When he was satisfied with the arrangement, he opened a hinged cedar box and admired the new Fiedler telescopic sight resting in its velvet lining.

He secured the scope to a Winchester 1875 Single Shot with a jeweler's screwdriver from a set in his vest. Hunk's ear dangled on a gold chain from the vest pocket like a watch fob. He slipped bundled sheets under his knees for comfort, then brought the rifle to his shoulder. Setting his elbow on the windowsill, he adjusted the precision eyepiece on a twenty-cent coin lying in the muddy street below until it came into sharp focus.

Bishop, Garrett, McCarty, and Rose had all taken up the side of the trail to ride ahead of the cattle, their horses deep in the slop. With Myrtle less than half a mile away, Garrett raised his hand to slow the herd.

Garrett said to Rose, "You and McCarty are at the back."

Thunder tidal-waved over the hills, with another jag of lighting. The cattle felt the sound in their spines, smelled the lightning burning the wet air.

McCarty threw a look at the herd. Stirring. Uneasy.

Batting each other, locking horns. He said, "I don't blame 'em. Scares the hell out of me, too, when God gets angry."

"They're ready to run."

Garrett said to Rose, "Keep them back. I'll tell you when."

McCarty poured out the water trapped in his sombrero, then tied it under his chin. "That sounded like an order, Mr. Garrett. And you know what? I'm gonna do her!"

McCarty galloped off. Rose's eyes, frustrated and dark, locked on Bishop, and she was about to say something, but whipped her horse around, riding after the sombrero.

Maynard cut between some broad-shouldered albinos, almost colliding with Rose. He was gripping his chest. "I'm ridin' in the cow crap. You pushin' me off this fight?"

From his higher position, Garrett looked down on him when he said, "The Doc and I take stock of the situation—"

"Take stock?"

"That's right. Then you'll obey orders like everybody else. Might just keep you alive."

"Keep favoring that one-armed son of a bitch, and you're the one's dyin'!" Maynard struggled his horse around, before taking it through a small break in the storm-bent trees leading away from the trail.

"Good riddance." Garrett lit a short-rolled cigarette, then said to Bishop, "So how many times have you ridden into hell on purpose?"

Bishop drew the rig. "I think you've been reading the penny dreadfuls, Garrett. It's not like that." He moved

his shoulders, taking up the slack of the trigger lines
that ran up his sleeve to the rig's brace.

"You son of a bitch." Garrett laughed under the
thunder as the two rode the last minutes toward Myrtle.

The side of Hunk's head still bled when he crooked
his neck the wrong way. He was in the corner shadows,
cramped against a mildewed hay bale, holding balled
linen to the wound. The riders with him kept their
horses and voices down.

One whispered, "Hunk, can you lend me an ear?"

Some nervous laughs spewed from the others.

Hunk daubed drying black blood from the stitches
where his ear used to be, thinking of stabbing the *tâmpit*
with the big mouth. "You've had your joking. Be ready
to attack."

One of the men was holding a sword. "You're a
foreigner. I carried this when I was with Bloody Bill
Anderson. I know how to send a message."

Hunk said, "You're not the one in charge here. Just
be ready to follow."

The rider kept the blade poised, making a short,
chopping motion like he was cutting off a head.

The heavy rain curtained the wood and iron junk
piled at the foot of what was Myrtle's main street. The
roof of an old caboose and a blasted-apart potbelly
stove were stacked along with empty flour barrels and
railroad trash, giving perfect cover.

Bishop and Garrett brought their horses in close.

Garrett leaned out of his saddle, taking in the town. "Same old hellhole."

Bishop thought Garrett wrong. Myrtle wasn't a hellhole, it was a T-shaped corpse, silent and rotting. Just a few buildings stood around an old cattle pen attached to a twisted rail spur where a dilapidated freight car, front wheels missing, had been left for dead years before. Lean-tos and shredded army tents, roughly patched together for prosties, took up the rest of the street that ended in a small crossway.

A ragged and empty two-story dry goods emporium stood at its center. A shattered window on the second floor was being beaten by the storm, its curtains blowing out from the inside.

Bishop took the bay a few steps from the junk pile for a better view. Nobody walked into the street for a looksee of the strangers bringing in a herd. The only sound was the rain overflowing gutters and water troughs.

Not even a dog barked.

"We've got targets on our backs."

Garrett said, "Hell, yes."

The air had the taste of ashes and felt hot in the storm.

Bishop snapped the rig into a firing position from his hip, throwing beads of water off the barrels. "I'd just gotten my medic stripes, and we'd crossed into North Carolina, an open field, corn stacked in huge piles across it. We couldn't see the enemy, but we knew. They sent us in anyway."

"How many were killed?"

"More than half the company."

Garrett shook his head. "That, you remember."

"In pieces."

"We sure as hell don't have a company backing us."

On Garrett's last word, glass dropped from the broken window on the second floor of the dry goods emporium at the end of Myrtle's main street.

There was the silhouette of a rifle.

The water blowing around the window frame hazed Colby's aim. He wiped the telescopic sight and his eyes, then tried fixing on his target again. He sensed Bishop and Garrett behind their cover, knew if he had even half-an-inch break right or left, he could put a bullet in a skull, reload, and finish before the first target hit the ground. Making two shots count was a test of reflexes that Colby enjoyed, and there was great satisfaction when it worked.

He also wanted to see the travel pattern of the special bullets he'd fashioned and the impact of the slugs creased with the knife blade. All things a professional considered.

But there was no clean shot through the rain. Yet.

Rose and McCarty were behind the last of the herd, a couple leather bags with wagging tongues. Another low roar of thunder scattered a pair of shorthorn bulls, and Rose watched as hired guns threw lassos, stopping the running cattle and pulling them in.

They looked at Myrtle just ahead of them, but were handling the animals easy, like they were told.

She called out to the gunman who was shoving the bulls back into the herd. "You're riding too close! They're already spooked!"

"Chisum claimed a special job! There ain't nothing special about this crap!"

Rose had her revolver in hand, under her rain slicker. "I'm working, same as you."

"Except I know what to do proper with a Colt Six." The hired gun rode off.

McCarty said to Rose, "Forget that cow pie. Garrett told you what's what?"

"You've got his fool orders. I'll follow mine."

Chaney stood in the doorway of the emporium's second-floor room where Colby was positioned at the broken window with his rifle. "They're showing caution about coming in," the reporter said, then checked the exposure on his small camera. "A picture before the slaughter of Chisum's men and then one after, to shock and amaze."

Colby quick-aimed a Derringer Four-shot Pepperbox at Chaney's face.

"I have an arrangement with Mr. Farrow."

Colby remained silent.

"Your employer wants the world to know how dangerous his group is. I'll tell the tale, and you do what you do, Mr. Colby."

Colby leaned forward, bringing the Derringer closer.

Chaney nodded. "I look forward to photographing John Bishop's corpse." He bowed slightly, giving it a flourish before shutting the door behind him.

A cough ripping him, Colby dropped the Pepperbox, then cupped his hands, caught some cold rain blowing in, and splashed his face. He spit blood into a handkerchief before aiming the Winchester at the rotting pile of wood and railroad iron at the end of the street . . . focusing on a target he couldn't yet see.

* * *

The bay and hammerhead were moving antsy, but Bishop and Garrett kept them reined tight, using the junk pile as a shield against the storm. Staying hidden.

Garrett said, "Break, and we'll be slaughtered faster than pigs at Easter."

"Lay some cover. I can get behind those old tents, work my way up, take care of the sniper in the window."

"Got that feeling like in Carolina?"

Bishop agreed with a look, and Garrett continued. "We don't know how many Fire Riders are lying in there. Chisum sure as hell waltzed us into it."

"It's what we signed on for." Bishop leaned forward in the saddle, ready to try. "I'm still on my own business. If I go in, they'll come right for me. I'll do what damage I can, but it'll give you all a fighting chance, maybe close in on them from the back."

Garrett said, "You're no use as a dead legend, Doc. Who do you distrust more? The Fire Riders or Mr. Chisum?"

Bishop's shoulders were rolling, tightening the shotgun lines, the weapon aimed from his hip. "It's an even split."

"How do I fare?" Garrett brought up his fine Colt with the scrolled barrel and fired three shots into the storm. The sky reacted with a hot spiderweb of lightning that lit up everything for miles.

That was Colby's cue.

He fired just to the left of the Colt's barrel flame, estimating the location of his target's head behind the junk pile. The slug tore into the old caboose roof first, the lead splitting into threes as it was meant to, then out the other side, creasing Garrett's hat.

Garrett swung the hammerhead around as Colby's second shot sparked off a busted coupling hitch inches from Bishop's temple.

Slivers from the ricochet sliced Bishop's face. He smeared the blood with his fingers, and Garrett grabbed the shotgun, holding him back. The bay twisted, pawing at the ground. Garrett nodded down the trail, water sloshing over the brim of his hat.

Bishop looked.

The herd was stampeding through the rain, legs pounding full-out, bulls and cows spread out across the trail, moving like hell.

Roaring toward Myrtle.

Hunk took the shooting as the signal. The battle cry "*Luaţi-le în iad!*" erupted from him as he leaped his horse from the old freight car. Fire Riders jumped alongside him, clearing the doors, and onto Myrtle's main street. Red tunics flapped like demon wings, their painted horses rain-smeared white, making them ghosts.

They hit the deep mud running, guns and sabers drawn. The storm exploded, blowing a hole in the sky above them.

Thunder roared.

On the trail, Rose and McCarty ran the herd from behind, shooting over them, whistling and screaming. The cattle charged faster. Heads down, horns slicing wet hair and rawhide, and eyes bloody-wide as they stampeded Main Street, ripping through the corral on one side, tents and outbuildings on the other.

Charging the Fire Riders.

Wild, the cattle plowed into men and horses, sharp horns piercing flesh, stallions screaming and bucking, throwing their riders. The red hoods scrambled, mud and soaked tunics weighing them down, as they shot at the herd before being trampled. Arms snapped and ribs powdered. Broken hands held on to destroyed rifles and bent-in-half swords.

Horses cut the air with ghost-painted legs, flailing wild, before falling back, bellies gored by longhorns, crushing riders tangled in their stirrups.

Lightning crashed.

A pair of Riders took their horses behind a rail fence, firing at two Chisum men riding alongside the cattle. They hit them both, sending them spinning off their saddles before being crushed under the stampede.

Quick screams sounded, then blood erupted.

From behind the junk pile, Garrett shot one Fire Rider in the head, and Bishop blasted a hole in the other's chest. The cattle busted down the corral fence, running in panic and dragging the corpses with them.

Hunk jumped his horse over the bodies of his fallen men, making it to the barn near the rail spur. The walls of the barn shook as the cattle smashed them from outside, the planks buckling. Hunk ran to a back stall and untied the mule with the case of grenades on its back.

In the street, a Chisum gun rode in fast, staying wide of the cattle as they trampled the last of the corral, splintering it. He pulled a repeater from a scabbard, lever-cocking it in one motion, not seeing what was behind him.

Bishop spied the outline of the Winchester taking aim from the emporium. He swung the bay around, firing a warning blast. The Chisum gun didn't heed and the sniper's bullet blew out his throat.

Bishop watched him fall. He snapped the rig to his shoulder and pulled the reins on the bay as the gunman hit the ground.

Bishop broke from his cover.

In the window, Colby slammed home another shell, aimed, and found Bishop galloping for the stampede. He wanted a clean head shot, but Bishop threw himself to one side of his saddle, keeping the rig low, circling around the running cattle, using them for cover.

Colby swallowed the blood backing into his mouth and fired anyway, the slug hitting another Chisum man square in the chest, picking him up, and dumping him on the street.

Decent kill.

He loaded again as Bishop rode out of his sighting. Thunder roared again.

Rose and McCarty kept the cattle running, pushing them from behind to keep pulverizing Myrtle.

McCarty said, "You're doin' fine, miss! Just keep one hand on your gun." He saluted Rose, then ran his horse behind the junk pile where Garrett was positioned with a rifle. McCarty dropped from his horse and stayed down, waiting for the enemy charge, grinning as he checked his pistols. He howled a laugh. "You didn't think you were gonna keep me with the cow asses, did ya?"

He popped shots from behind the old potbellied stove, shooting the Fire Riders who rode around the boxcar to the rail spur, trying to escape the stampede. Hard targets.

"That's nine." He looked at Garrett. "That's the ninth son of a bitch I ever killed!"

Garrett's words were flat. "It's good you're keeping count."

McCarty fired again, wounding the Rider. "Hell, Garrett, ain't this why I'm here?"

Bullets from the Riders splayed around them, and McCarty and Garrett dropped back from the junk heap, letting the Riders come around the side of the destroyed corral. Garrett shot two, sending one heaving into the slop, the other opening up with a pair of pistols, angry at being hit, and swearing like hell.

McCarty killed him between the eyes, the red hood splitting with the slug, revealing the Rider's surprise. McCarty whistled at his own shot. "Ten. Ten men. Who can lay claim to that?"

Garrett kept up the rifle fire. "Just give cover!"

Bishop charged into the battle, coming up on the other side of the running herd, the shotgun braced against his shoulder infantry-style, ready to drop and shoot.

Suddenly, the ground shook.

The first Adams grenade landed in front of two Chisum men, blowing them sideways off their horses, animals landing on top of them. The rain turned the yellow heat of the explosion white, bloody mud bursting with it.

Panicked blind by the blast, the cattle were running in all directions, trampling the dead, tearing into men and the last standing buildings.

Bishop's horse veered at the grenade's impact, almost losing footing in the rainy slop. He kept the reins sure, and the bay responded. Leaning forward, close to the horse, Bishop plowed through the deep mud.

No slowing down. Almost there.

The next grenade hit a Chisum rider from behind, the force tumbling his horse forward at a full gallop, neck twisting into the ground. The rider landed hard, his arm snapping. He tried standing. A sniper's shot put him down, landing him next to his thrashing horse. Pat Garrett fired the shot that mercy-killed the animal.

In the window, Colby reloaded, seeing Bishop dodging the stampede, then tearing through the blowing smoke from the grenades.

Lightning struck. With cattle scattering around him, Bishop leaped the bay to the small trail running parallel to the main street. Hidden by the old tents and lean-tos, it was the walkway for hookers and railroad men to get in and out, and too narrow for a horse and rider.

Taking cover, he rolled from the saddle and forced the bay down to the ground between the tents in a single motion. Coming up with the rig snapping out directly before him, barrels aimed, he shot at the Fire Riders riding against the Chisum men.

He caught one in the chest, turned, and fired again, tearing another off his horse at the knees.

Bishop's head pounded, a wash of blood filling his eyes from inside, casting everything he saw with a red shimmer. He was "seeing blind," reflexes faster than before, senses sharper. No hesitations. Instant.

Beyond instinct, beyond the adrenaline of combat, he'd transformed into something else, Bishop was finally the weapon.

Colby watched the Fire Riders go down, admiring Bishop's speed and deadly aim—nothing random, no counting on the spread of the buckshot. He calculated

Bishop's position from the tilted direction of the last blast and fired from the window.

The slug danced an inch from Bishop's head as he dove. Springing the rig's breech, he reloaded then snapped it shut. Automatic. Bishop let fire go, spreading another Fire Rider with buckshot, dropping him into the stampede. The cattle were still running. Onto the side streets they ran, pulverizing storefronts and men, their cries and the thunderstorm the same.

Dodging to a new cover position, Bishop loosed first one barrel and the next, blasting rider after rider. Dead off the saddle, the bodies fell as he shot another before the first hit the ground. He grabbed the second box of shells from his saddle, filled the bandolier and both barrels.

The Rider with the Bloody Bill sword dove from his horse into the tent canvas, and came up firing, pistol in one hand, saber in the other. Bishop blew his arm off at the elbow, the sword spinning away, then finished him with the second barrel.

He breached, reloaded, and aimed for his next targets, trigger lines set across his shoulders. He fired again before running the length of the street, using the cattle for cover. He dropped to the ground opposite Hunk's position in the barn door.

Hunk pulled the strap on another Adams grenade and hurled it, the blast tearing open the junk pile, ripping jags of iron and wood shrapnel through the storm.

McCarty and Garrett were foxholed behind the junk pile, debris slicing above them. The explosion sent their horses running. Garrett came up and opened fire on the hotel room window, cracking off a series of shots.

Colby ducked against the window frame, Garrett's slugs punching the walls around him. Another spasm choked his throat. His hands were shaking as he grabbed a handful of shells, loaded, and fired at a distant Chisum rider. He watched him drop and felt better. Spitting the acid from his mouth, he loaded and scanned for Bishop.

Colby said to no one, "You are mine."

Hidden by the far corner of the emporium, Bishop was facing the barn and out of Colby's sight. The last of the cattle were slamming each other, still crying, but slowing.

The thunder was rolling off.

At the end of the trail, the last of the cattle were running into Myrtle while the storm travelled back toward the mountains. Their horses throwing mud, two Fire Riders rode down hard from a cross street and trapped Rose along the edge of the main trail. Their horses blocked her as she tried bringing her brown and white stallion around. They jammed her ribs and then her back with rifles as she turned. For a moment, a rifle barrel brushed the edge of her jaw, and she felt the sight.

One Rider, blood streaming from the edge of his mouth onto his hood and tunic, managed, "Chisum let you do this? Get yourself killed for this flapdoodle?"

Rose said, "What about you? Earning your pay?"

The Rider pulled off his soaking-wet hood and ran one hand across his bleeding sandpaper face. "Sorry, lady, but you work for Chisum. I got to show something for today other than some missing teeth."

At the barn door, Hunk yanked the strap, setting the fuse on the next grenade. He leaned out, reeling his arm back to throw toward the junk heap where Garrett and McCarty were laying rifle-fire cover.

Bishop triggered, tearing open Hunk's knee, folding him. The grenade rolled from his hand, the fuse sizzling inside its iron globe.

Bishop saw a break between the cattle and ran from his spot. Slipping. Dodging.

Colby fired, hitting a shorthorn cutting in front of Bishop, colliding against other cattle and bringing one down. Howling screams and bloody chaos continued.

Colby shucked the spent cartridge.

Slammed by the animal, Bishop rolled toward the barn, scrambled to his feet, and grabbed the Adams from a deep hoofprint. He hurled it with his left hand toward the second-floor window.

Colby reloaded.

Hunk yelled a warning.

The grenade spun in the air, leaving a tail of smoke and coming into focus as Colby pressed his eye against the telescopic sight.

Rose didn't move as the Rider raised the rifle to point at her heart. She eyed the rifle but stayed even in her tone. No panic. "Did you ever ride with a young boy? Great with a rope? You should know, since you killed him so he wouldn't talk about your raids."

"I don't know what the hell you're talking about."

Near the emporium the grenade exploded, hammering their horses. They reared, Rose and the Rider fighting to stay on.

Rose's pistol blew apart her rain slicker, catching the Rider in the chest. She turned, and fired again, clipping the second one's shoulder. Red sprayed from his side as he whipped his horse toward the small cut off the trail.

Rose stayed fast behind him, even as the first Rider was lying on the trail, counting his heartbeats and feeling the cold wet of the ground where he knew he'd be buried. His eyes were locked open to the light fall of rain.

The injured Rider pushed his horse, cutting through the trees, the water in the branches above drenching him. One arm blood-coated and useless, he jerked his horse too far to one side, slamming himself into a branch.

Almost on top of him, Rose pulled the stallion back, bringing up her pistol, when he used his good arm to hurl his Winchester, the weapon spinning. She ducked, the rifle breaking against a knotted trunk behind her. He lurched his animal down the rest of the cut, pushing to the open clearing on the other side of the trees.

Rose and the stallion stayed tight around the tall pines, leaping a large tangle of roots. Finally breaking from the woods, they came out onto a field of tall grass that had been flattened by the storm. Cattle that had found their way to the spot were calm and grazing. A few nudged each other, and some were lying down in the cool wet grass, tending to their own.

The injured Rider was there, catching air, his hood off. He was about thirty, his anonymous face softer than his partner's. His mouth sagged open with pain as if he were silently screaming. He looked up as Rose came to him, the pistol protruding through the blast hole in her rain slicker. "How many times you gonna shoot me?"

"Did you know a boy who rode with you?"

Not hearing the question, the Rider continued. "Look,

you all beat us down good, looks like. I don't know how many are alive, but you can tell that to Chisum."

Rose stopped her horse less than ten feet from the Rider and looked beyond him to see Maynard sprawled in the field; a bullet in his face had taken off his nose and part of his cheek. She pointed at Maynard. "I rode with him."

The rider looked, then tried to get on the good side of the conversation. "I'm truly sorry. I didn't kill him, but I know how that is, loyalty and such."

"He was a jackass."

"I'm sorry about that, too."

"You work with somebody, it counts. That's how come I can tell you knew my nephew—a boy with sunny hair, better with a rope than anybody's business. Tell me about the raids you did together."

The rider's bloody arm was drooping, but his words were coming faster. "I heard you ask a-fore, I don't know nothing either. I don't. There's a lot of us he could've been with."

"All you getting rich, stealing cattle? Robbing banks? That's why you killed him, so he couldn't tell the law it was you?"

"I swear on Mary's virgin eyes, I never killed no one. Never robbed no bank. I did okay with cattle, but if you don't shoot, I'll take myself home and never stray again."

Rose said, "That money, that's what my nephew dreamed over. All he could make rustling. Like you. You knew him, I know you did. You filled his head with those bad notions, got him killed."

The Fire Rider was wishing he had a gun, anything, when he said, "I—I'm married."

Rose ignored it. "Just a boy. Got himself killed riding with you damnable red hoods."

Before he could beg, Rose sensed something behind her. She kept her gun trained, but turned in her saddle and saw a man on Hurricane crossing the field at a quick trot.

She was about to call out when Farrow shot her.

CHAPTER FOURTEEN
Wounded

The ammo in the bandolier was spent.

Bishop dug into his pockets. Nothing. He breached the rig, pulling the dead shell from the right barrel, then checked the live round on the left. He shut the shotgun as quietly as possible, muffling its locking with his palm, and setting its position straight from the waist . . . to gut-shoot.

He had one heavy-grain shell, and no idea who or how many he'd be facing when he reached the top of the stairs that led to the emporium's second floor.

Blood still washed across his eyes, turning his vision hellish. He was on the top step when his strength erupted again, kicking open the door to the room in the corner, tearing it off its hinges. He stepped inside.

The window had been blown apart by the Adams grenade.

Scorched by the blast, the frame and wall plaster were lying in the middle of the floor. Colby's special ammunition was scattered. One bullet had been driven into the door like an arrow by the Adams's force, splitting the wood.

The only signs of Colby were the spatter on the wall about the height of his shoulder—if he was in his sniping position when the grenade blew—and one of his monogrammed handkerchiefs, also bloodstained, dangling from a jag of broken glass.

The last of the storm was soaking the room.

Bishop backed out, turned into the hallway, triggerlines drawn tight from his elbow, when the white-hot flash blinded him.

Minutes before, Chaney had mounted the Stockwell camera on a small tripod of his own making and positioned it at the end of the second-floor hallway. His ears were still ringing from the grenade, and he kept shaking his head to clear them. He poured the mix of magnesium powder onto the flash tray, then pressed himself against a wall, squatting on his haunches out of sight.

He'd seen Bishop in the street below, and tried for a picture of him walking toward the emporium, shotgun raised, with Hunk lying a few feet away, screaming over his bleeding leg, but the rain was still falling. Focusing his spy camera through the old windows was difficult. The image could have been mushed into a gray fog so he'd switched to the Stockwell, sure it would give him what he wanted.

His index finger was on the flash powder igniter, thumb on a cable to the camera's shutter release as Bishop was a blur of motion, kicking open the door to Colby's room, charging in.

Chaney held his breath. "*God, to damn that—*" He never finished.

The magnesium flash filled the hallway with hot

light, and the barrel flame from the shotgun exploded at the same time, blowing apart the camera, lens, and bellows. Buckshot ripped the wall and sent the tripod spinning as Chaney ducked, still feeling the heat from the flash pan. Screaming out in pain, he clamped his hands over his blood-wet face.

Pat Garrett's boots sunk ankle-deep as he moved around the litter of corpses on Myrtle's main street, checking faces for his own men. Every step was a chore as the mud tried trapping him, holding him in place as he bent over each body for identification. He used his rifle as a crutch to pull his long legs free of the slop and get to the next.

He kept his collar turned against the easy rain that was washing the blood from the dead men and animals before forming rivulets that snaked down the street, emptying into deep puddles of reddish brown.

With a whistle, McCarty leaped over a puddle, then helped Garrett turn a body that had been pressed deep into the street by the weight of a fallen horse.

Garrett wiped away inches-thick mess from the face. "This is one of the guns who came with you."

"Jim something. Good man, decent with a carbine, but slow."

"He took it between the shoulders."

McCarty said, "Mr. Tunstall thought highly of him, but I got more of those red hoods than he did."

Garrett straightened up. "I wonder if the sniper's keeping count, too."

"Then he knows he lost, don't he?"

Garrett freed himself and found a solid patch next to another sprawled corpse clutching a Colt long barrel.

It was a Fire Rider, his side opened by a shotgun blast. There were more, at least twenty, lying among the remains of the cattle-smashed storefronts and fences. Some were recognizable, others weren't.

Garrett took the Colt from the dead Rider, checking its action and saying to McCarty, "You shoot well under any circumstance."

McCarty was standing by a horse that was nudging the twisted body of its dead Fire Rider with its nose. "Hell, I wasn't the one who got those down by the barn and all them coming from that railcar." He stroked the horse neck to withers, its demonic disguise smearing off on his fingers. "The doc doesn't like being a legend, but after this crazy fight? I don't think he's got any choice. This'll be another fancy cover."

Garrett used the rifle butt to pry the body of a fat Fire Rider from the wet. "Maybe you'll get lucky and they'll write about you, too."

McCarty couldn't help his grin. "Here's to hoping."

Garrett turned the fat rider over and pulled off his hood—an outlaw. His nose was beaten flat, giving him a pig's snout. "I know this one, even shot him once, raiding cattle. Did you get him this time or was it me?"

"I shot that hog at least once!" The voice was one of Garrett's men, riding in from behind the shorn tents and wreckage.

Flanked by a few others, all were torn, tired, and bloody, but they'd made it through the skirmish. The battle relief played on their faces as one lit a cigarette then passed it along.

The first rider said, "Thank ol' Jesus there's more of us standing then there is them. We earned our pay, but it was that shotgun made the difference."

* * *

Chaney was sloppy deadweight, making no effort to walk, as Bishop hauled him down the back steps of the emporium, half carrying him on his shoulder like a bulging flour sack.

They reached the bottom of the stairs, with Chaney muttering, "You slaughtered me," over and over, the dried blood on his face cracking as he spoke.

Bishop hefted his one good arm, adjusting Chaney's weight, and kept moving, not saying a word or looking at him.

A heavy piece of the windowsill, blown apart by the grenade, crashed to the ground, just missing them, as Bishop carried Chaney around the side of the emporium to the front of the barn, then let him crumple into the mud.

Chaney said, "I'm the one making you famous, and you slaughtered me . . ."

Not yet was Bishop's thought, but his mouth stayed clenched, taking in the litter of corpses that began at the barn and stretched the length of Main Street. Fire Riders, clutching guns and sabers, were nothing but sacks of flesh wrapped in red shrouds that had once been their robes and hoods. Useless.

And John Bishop was the reason why.

Any empathy he'd felt once was gone. He wasn't allowing himself that reflective moment over fallen enemies anymore. It was pointless. They were dead. He wasn't.

Metal scuttled at Bishop's feet.

He turned, bringing his boot down hard, pinning Hunk's hand to the barn floor, his fingers clenched around another Adams grenade. Hunk hadn't pulled the primer pin strap, and Bishop pressed with his heel, cracking a bone.

Hunk grabbed his blown-apart knee, spitting out, "*O să te omor, fiu de căţea!*"

Deaf to Hunk and Chaney's crying, Bishop picked up the Adams, judging its weight in his palm and how the iron globe helped balance the double barrels that were his right side. He held the grenade out before him. The weapon felt natural, the way a scalpel had felt the first time he held one as a medical student. Different times, and now, a different place in his mind.

There was movement in the distance.

Bishop looked past the end of Main Street at the horse galloping up-trail toward him. Perfect movement with head down, but no rider. Still shimmering red and running fast.

Rose's stallion broke past the junk heap, leaping over a bomb crater, and landing in the center of the street. The horse was slowing stride on its own as McCarty took a jump to grab hold of the bridle, then eased it to a stop by the corral's shattered fence.

The brown and white stood among the dead, Rose's saddle tilted to one side, a stirrup broken, and blood smeared across the horn and seat.

The wet smell of the sheep's wool broadened Colby's nose as he lay in the tangle of barbed wire. A few ewes nuzzled him as he struggled to sit up, metal jags digging at him through his clothes.

The impact of the grenade had propelled a piece of wood into his shoulder, but he'd managed to keep his rifle, and to stumble down the back stairs of the emporium, through the smoky fire of the explosion.

He didn't remember finding his horse or riding away from Myrtle along a back trail with the shotgun blasts and the screams of the Fire Riders echoing behind him. Finally losing consciousness, he'd fallen from his saddle.

He'd never ridden away from an assigned target before. Those thoughts were cut in half by a hot jolt as his eyes rolled back, catching a flash of his own rifle pointed directly at his face, before he lost consciousness for the second time.

She came into his view, and the wash of blood that John Bishop saw through started breaking apart like water beading against polished leather. He angled the bay from the cut in the trees to the slope of grass where Rose was lying.

Gunshot and bleeding.

She was on her side about twenty feet from Maynard's body, and quite still. With every step closer, Bishop's vision cleared, the pounding between his temples vanishing, allowing the sounds around him to enter.

He pulled up his horse, closed his eyes tight, then opened them. The sky had lost the last tint of his blood to become the blue-gray after a storm. Streaks of sunlight showed Chisum's cattle grazing along a high ridge.

Bishop could feel each breath completely filling his lungs as he dropped from the bay and pulled his field medical kit from a saddlebag. Running to her, he jangled it open with his left hand, his voice with him again as he called out, "Rose."

He repeated her name louder and louder, but she didn't stir.

Other riders were coming in. McCarty was on the

brown and white, with Garrett the last to clear the tree
line on his tall hammerhead. Chaney and Hunk shared
a Fire Rider horse tethered to Garrett's saddle, both of
them with hands tied and fresh wounds.

Chaney mumbled to anyone and the ground, "Slaughter of the innocents . . ."

Garrett said, "Write it down, Chaney."

Bishop was kneeling, the shotgun locked straight at
his side. He had two fingers beneath Rose's jaw, checking
her pulse.

McCarty said, "I think I know what you're doing, but
never seen it done that way before." He got down from
his horse.

"Don't tell me she's dead, Doc."

"I can't, because she isn't. Get a bedroll."

McCarty took a blanket from behind his saddle and
spread it on the wet grass while Bishop laid out bandages, antiseptic, and the wooden case for his surgical
equipment. He flipped the latch, thumb-popped the
lid, revealing the polished knives and instruments in
their velvet-lined casket. He chose the proper scalpels
with instant precision. Bishop's moves with his med kit
were as instinct-sure as breaching and firing the double
barrel.

His instructions were clear. "Rose first, then the
Rider, then Chaney's mouth. Garrett, get that slick off
her. McCarty, take the bottle of carbolic, that one in the
middle, and soak some linen."

Garrett pulled the rain slicker over her head, the
rubber sticking to her bullet wound. He freed it carefully, then tossed it aside, as Bishop cleaned the wound
with antiseptic.

"Turn her."

McCarty and Garrett put Rose on her back as Bishop

cut around her shirt, pulling away the bloody cloth to see if the bullet had torn deeper, done any worse damage. A medium-caliber slug had entered clean on her left side, just below the rib cage.

Bishop angled her to examine the exit wound. There wasn't any. A slash of flesh bubbled in the center of a black and purple bruise that spread along Rose's hip, exactly where the bullet had lodged itself.

McCarty said, "You're really gonna operate on her now?"

Bishop turned to the instrument case, taking a "bleeder" scalpel, opening the razor-styled blade from its wooden handle with quick motion. "I'm going to patch her, so you can get her to a proper doctor."

Garrett held her in position, halfway on her side. "Chisum's doc is probably the best for two states, but Rose thinks it's you."

"Right now, she doesn't have much choice," Bishop said as he swirled the bleeder in carbolic before slicing across the purple bruising. The blade glanced the edge of the embedded slug. "Just skidded under the surface." With blood erupting around the scalpel, he peeled back the skin.

McCarty sopped the blood with linen.

Bishop dropped the bleeder and grabbed bullet-extracting forceps. "Ever think about medicine?"

McCarty was wincing, looking away. "I'm smart enough to know I ain't got the brains for it."

Garrett said, "You've seen a hell of a lot worse than this."

McCarty still wouldn't look. "Yeah, but not with women."

Bishop used the small porcelain scoop on the end of the instrument, pressing it against a plane of raw muscle under the slug before gently rolling the lead out of the wound crater. "She's lucky. It didn't break apart."

Chaney called from his horse, "Is that what you do, Doctor? Shoot them, then sew them up? Create your own patients?"

Bishop laid the extractor aside. "Maybe you should write it that way."

Garrett held a curved suturing needle that Bishop threaded with carbolic catgut. He took the needle, saying, "Except, I didn't shoot her."

Hunk yelled, "No, me you shot! *Bastard nebun!*"

Bishop said, "You're next," while lacing Rose's wound, bringing the tissues together as Garrett cleaned around it, following the perfect stitching. One-handed, Bishop took the sutures through the sides of the wound, pulling it closed with just enough strength, before tying it off and cutting it. It wasn't the work of a field butcher, but fine surgery.

Garrett said, "And you say you can't remember a damn thing."

Bishop rubbed his eyes, his vision still clear. "She'll need something clean."

McCarty got some new denim from his saddlebag as Garrett and Bishop finished her bandaging. "So, what do you tell Chisum?" Bishop asked.

"That we fought the battle, lost some good men and a quarter of the herd, but wiped out some Fire Riders." Garrett slipped one of Rose's arms through McCarty's clean shirt. "And Rose is still alive."

Bishop said, "Get her to a doctor before sunset."

McCarty finished the buttoning. "Mr. Tunstall said something about Chisum paying out a victory bonus." He turned, waving his sombrero toward the Chisum men who were rounding up the herd and gathering them along the far hillside. "Hell, if anybody ever earned any victory money, we're it. Miss Rose, too."

Hunk let a word drop. "Wrong."

Garrett stood. "You said something, Hunkie?"

Hunk met Garrett's stare. "You're wrong. About the victory. Wrong."

McCarty said, "Hey, I counted the dead, ya gut-eater! We both did. There's a hell of a lot more of yours than ours lying back there."

"You don't know what has happened today. It was *afacere*—a deal. Worked out." Hunk bent forward, holding his knee with bloody fingers. "We're all fools."

Garrett took a step, but Bishop moved beyond him instantly, pulling Hunk off the saddle and dumping him on the field—like tossing a rag doll. The huge man landed hard, before Bishop planted a foot on his chest, pinning him down.

"Are you talking about the massacre? That?"

"I won't be killed by you—!"

"What was worked out? What did you mean?"

"*Dumnezeu*—!"

Bishop smashed the edge of the double barrel against Hunk's knee. He screamed. Bishop's one hand went around the thick throat, squeezing Hunk's voice to whispered curses. "*Prostii!*"

"I can help that knee"—Bishop kept his left hand on Hunk and raised the rig again—"or crush it. Use the bone saw from my kit or put it back together. Understand?

Hunk nodded.

"Choose."

Hunk spoke after Bishop released his throat. "Don't . . . don't take my legs. Doctor."

"Tell me what you meant. What deal?"

Hunk connected with Bishop's eyes, saw something red-shadowed and dark filling them. "It was set for us. We knew when you would be there. That's why we were waiting."

Garrett said, "To steal Chisum's cattle, but we beat you down with them, instead."

Hunk bent his head back, sucking in moist air. "Not just the cattle! I was told to leave you hanging, like butchered. Let this Chaney take pictures to show everyone to fear us, so they'll pay up."

McCarty spit. "Didn't work out that way, did it?"

Hunk said, "You were more clever as fighters than we thought. But, you were to lie down when we attacked. Not fight so hard, and let us have the doctor."

Bishop took Hunk's windpipe again. "Why? Why did you think that?"

Straining to tears, Hunk swung one of his giant hands and gripped Bishop's shoulder, trying to break him off. Bishop squeezed harder with his left. Muscles steeled, he raised the shotgun like a club.

Hunk finally let go, and his words poured out as Bishop allowed him air again. "Farrow. He told us. He led us into the town, gave all the information."

Garrett said, "There's an honest-to-God son of a bitch."

Bishop said, "Farrow always works for somebody. Who wanted me? Chisum?"

"You are dead now, what do you care?"

"You're right. I am dead." Bishop jammed a knee into Hunk's chest, pressing his entire weight against him, pressure-choking. "Who wanted me!?"

"*Neică*—brother. Your brother. He did all this."

* * *

Colby felt the barbed wire biting as he was coming to, swimming back from a deep, painful sleep. The jags were in different places now, not that accidental tangle when he was caught in the fence, but at his wrists. Coils across his chest bound him to a sheep-shearing chair.

The boy with patchy beard and worn overalls checked the ties holding Colby in place, daubing his fresh blood as if he was catching random drips from a freshly painted fence. Satisfied, he took a step back, watching Colby's eyes struggle open.

He drew a cup of water from a rain barrel and threw it into Colby's face, then filled it again and held it to let him drink. The water cooled the acid in Colby's throat. Lambs in a side pen bleated, poking their snouts through wooden slats as if trying for a better look.

The boy said, "My father always splashed his face as he was coming back from a bout. From that barrel, in fact. You seemed to be in need."

"I'm definitely not drunk."

The boy stood in front of Colby as if he were on sentry duty, speaking as if afraid of mispronunciation. "I found you tangled in our fence, and you didn't move. You hadn't died, so, it must be drink. I know a thing about drink. I found all your guns, so I know you came for me, mean my family harm."

Colby pulled on his wrists bound by the barbed wire to the chair's sloping back, designed to keep the sheep comfortable and in place while being shorn. With each pull, the wire cut deeper, bringing him sharper focus. He said, "No, I didn't. What's your thinking, son?"

The boy held up the watch chain with Hunk's ear dangling. "This isn't what a Christian man of no harm wears. You are an assassin, working for the cattlemen. We got sheep, so you are to kill us. That's easier to figure on than *a-b-c*."

Damp lamb's wool was the air, and Colby could see two-blade shears hanging on the wall, large tubs for boiling, and bales of fleece stacked around the barn. Ten sheep stalls, open on one side, allowed the stock to wander as they pleased.

That didn't escape Colby's sense of humor. "It pleases me that the lambs have their freedom." He twisted on the rotating seat of the shearing chair, loosening the wire holding him there. Back and forth. The razor barbs sliced cloth and skin, almost to muscle, but started to give. "You treat them better than you're treating me."

The boy said, "They can be trusted. My father had another regulator tied to that shearing chair for three days. When he was awake, he spoke of his work. I know your reasons for being on our ranch."

Colby settled. "You're wrong as you can be, son, about why I'm here."

The boy moved to Colby's weapons. "That's not what I see."

"I understand, son. I do." Colby worked his wrists and ankles. "May I have some more water? Wouldn't it be soul-proper to give me some?"

The boy took the cup and filled it. He was skinny, with a long reach, and kept as much distance as he could as he put it to Colby's lips.

Colby drank, his body turned slightly in the shearing chair, his arms stretched behind him, bent at the elbows. "Thank you, son. I'm sure you're a fine provider."

The boy lowered the cup. "I have learned from my father—"

Colby head butted the boy, then smashed him with a raised knee, catching his chin as he fell onto him. He scissored both legs, bound at the ankle, on either side of the boy's neck, clamping him tight.

It had taken seconds. As the boy struggled, his arms waving, Colby called out, "I know you're there. You can come out. It's all right. Don't be afraid."

Lambs cried as the dumpling worked his way over the edge of their stall, tumbling to the floor. His eyes were as big as his four year-old face, and he wiped his tears on the sleeve of a nightshirt.

The boy got out, "Jacob, run for the house!"

Colby asked the child, "Your brother? Do you want to help him? Bring me those shears."

Jacob stood frozen, tears running down his cheeks.

Colby growled out, "Jacob, if you want the bad dream to be over, bring me the shears right behind you. Can you reach?"

Rose slumped unconscious in the saddle as McCarty swung onto the brown and white. Wrapping his arms around her waist to sit her straight and steady, he laced the reins through his right hand.

Garrett placed her feet in the stirrups, adjusting them sure, before pulling a small sack from the inside pocket of his long coat. There was the rattle of gold coins as he tossed it to McCarty, who caught it with his left.

"Your victory pay. From Mr. Chisum."

"You could've kept it hid. I'm obliged to you, Garrett." McCarty called out to Hunk, "I told you, gut-eater!"

Hunk snorted as Bishop turned the handle on a brass Petit's tourniquet.

Drawing the strap slightly tighter above Hunk's freshly bandaged knee, Bishop said, "Hold it."

Hunk took the handle.

Bishop slipped a finger between the strap and the

side of Hunk's leg. "It's slacking. This is a field piece. We need something to hold the pressure more exactly. I don't want you to lose that leg."

Hunk smirked. "Oh, yes, I'm sure of that."

"Just hold it."

As Bishop started packing his field kit, Hunk said, "So what to do? I save my own leg, while you ride me to an execution? Do it here. Easier."

Bishop shook his head. "Not here."

Garrett placed a hand on Bishop's shoulder, then held up the victory pay. Bishop glanced, but didn't move for the money, just put the rest of his instruments in the kit.

Garrett said, "You surely earned it, Doc."

"Chisum's got nothing to do with me anymore."

"Hell, we all know that. You didn't take a dime, but he wanted you to have something to help after, if you made it out alive. Maybe for your next war."

Chaney was adjusting the wrap of gauze across his cheek. "That's more compensation than I'll ever see for my pain."

Garrett said, "Mr. Chaney, I've known fellas cut themselves shaving who were in worse shape."

Bishop took the sack, slapped two gold pieces into Chaney's hand. "For your camera."

Chaney was defiant. "I have another."

"I know." Bishop turned to Garrett to return the gold, but he was walking for his horse.

Without turning around, he said, "You made the right choice, Doc. Take the money. Help yourself. God knows the men calling the shots have plenty."

Bishop stored the money and medical kit in his saddle-bags, before throwing a leg up and saying to Garrett, "You've got my patient. Get her home."

"We'll do it. Hope you get home, too."

Hunk yelled from the back of the horse he was sharing with Chaney, "Garrett! I'm your prisoner, you need to take me to a doctor, then to Chisum!"

Garrett was on his horse. "Not my prisoner, and you've already got a doctor."

"But this one tried to kill me!"

McCarty brought the brown and white around, keeping Rose secure with his arm, cradling her. "If the doc wanted you dead, you'd already be buried."

Chaney held his hand against his bandaged face as if he was going to break into pieces. "I intend to quote you, Mr. McCarty."

McCarty howled, "Get my name right!"

The outriders started moving the cattle herd from the far hills, heading them back toward the trail slow and easy.

McCarty, holding Rose, broke the pace. He could feel her struggled breathing against him and urged the brown and white. The horse moved steady and fast, getting ahead of the herd, and following the trail to the next town.

In a moment, they were through the trees. Bishop approved. Rose's chances were good.

Pat Garrett tipped his hat, which Bishop returned, before locking the rig from his waist, and looping the tether line from Chaney and Hunk's horse to his own saddle.

Chaney said, "I won't be buried next to this immigrant."

Hunk said, "I wonder how you're looking with a grenade in your mouth."

Bishop looked to Hunk. "Just keep pressure on that leg."

* * *

The shears were too big for Jacob's hands as he tried closing the blades through the barbed wire, only to have them slip sideways or clatter to the barn floor.

Colby kept Jacob's brother trapped, his knees locked around his neck, ready to snap it with a single twist of his body. His voice was soft. "Try again, son. This is magic. If you set me free, your brother goes free. Just cut the little wire, that's all."

Jacob wedged the blade around the wire knot, trying to get a grip, the shears slipping away from his stubby fingers. Finally, the edge of the blades cut one of the wire ties, pulling the barbs back from Colby's wrist.

"Look at that. Your brother's almost free. Just like magic. Try again."

Jacob jammed the shears under the wire for the last time, catching a piece of wire between the blades, then squeezing it with all his tiny strength. Wires popped apart, and Jacob fell backwards against a sheep stall.

He was sobbing as Colby brought his arms from around the shearing chair, sitting up and releasing his brother. The older boy sagged to the floor, his brother throwing himself around his neck.

Cutting and pulling, Colby unwrapped the coil from around his chest. "Boys, I'm going to need some help for the next few days. You have to take me in."

Jacob held on tight, as his brother said, "You can't be in the house. Father won't allow it. Best ride on, sir."

"You're a strong boy." Colby freed his ankles. "I would say your father is gone, or—"

"He'll be back in the winter," the older boy said, cutting Colby off. "He'll be back before Christmas."

Colby stood, his clothes soaking from the barbed

punctures across his body, and the large tear in his shoulder. He managed a step, steadying himself on the edge of the sheep stall. "I'll be gone long before then. Help me inside."

Bishop stood among the bodies of three Fire Riders, the dried mud plastering their red tunics with spatters of gray, hoods pulled away from buried faces. He was holding the Bloody Bill saber, broken off and jagged just above the haft. The shotgun rig was poised on his right side.

Chaney was in front of the ruins of the emporium, adjusting the lens on his miniature camera as far as he could. The short glass near-rounded the image, taking in Bishop, the dead men, and beside them, Hunk, with his hands tied and leg bandaged.

Chaney held the camera steady. What he was seeing was distorted, but true. Bishop kept still until Chaney said, "All right. You wanted to send a message, Doctor. This will surely be it."

Bishop said, "You're the one who sends the messages. I'm sure you'll give the story a lot of special touches when you write it."

"I'll invent very little this time."

"You can probably take the bandage off in a week, but keep your face clean. Avoid infection."

"Doctor, you still haven't made reference to who I am or my family's history with you, which is rather colorful."

Bishop said, "I've known who you are since Paradise. Somebody told me your cousin's name is on the list of men I've killed."

"It's quite a lot of names."

"My burden. He was the gambler?"

"A poor one."

Bishop nodded. "He certainly used poor judgment. Are you looking to settle?"

Chaney flourished. "Not now. There's too much reporting about you I have to do. That's my priority above personal concerns. And . . . I choose not to be shot by you twice in one day."

Bishop turned to Hunk, who was still mounted, and slipped the broken saber under the tourniquet strap, turning the handle halfway. "That should work. Give your hand a rest."

The handle steadied the pressure, allowing the proper amount of blood flow to the damaged knee.

Hunk nodded. "It's . . . it's better. Feels better."

Bishop knelt by one of the dead Riders, a shotgun poking out from beneath his blood-sticky tunic. He wrenched the weapon away, opened it, and took out two unfired .12-gauge shells, then found half a dozen more in a side pocket. He slipped six in his bandolier, loaded the rig, then hung a small canvas sack containing the last of the Adams grenades off his saddle horn.

Hunk said, "That Chaney's taking another picture."

"I hope he gets a good one."

"They won't like you taking ammunition from their dead."

Bishop climbed onto the bay, the newly loaded rig angled at Hunk. "Seems appropriate to me."

Hunk said, "So, I'm the prisoner. Now what?"

"Death, probably. But Hell first."

Chaney fitted the last small negative plate into the camera and steadied himself on a piece of the emporium balcony laying in the street. The battle hadn't gone the way he was told, but what had happened he could sell all over the world.

He waited, thinking how sure he'd been that Bishop would go for the killing shot and finish him off, but had doctored his face instead. Then, insisted that he take photographs.

Bishop was bringing his horse around, and Chaney had the miniature camera solid in both hands, his thumb holding the shutter open long enough to balance the muted daylight, long enough for the tiny negative to capture a battleground littered with enemy dead and Bishop riding away from it, a Fire Rider prisoner tethered behind him.

The shutter clicked.

CHAPTER FIFTEEN
Resurrections

Sheriff Tucker rested the Henry rifle on top of the cremation urn and sighted. He was close, maybe ten feet away, but wanted to see the bullet enter, enjoy its exit, and the aftermath. That thought made him smile.

He kept the rifle aimed at the oversized, green-lacquered coffin, a gold-inlaid dragon coiling around it twice before the head and tail met on the highly polished lid. The dragon's eyes were red jewels that shone in the broken bits of light coming in from the shuttered windows of the workshop.

The voice seemed to come from the dragon. "Just how damn stupid are you, runt?"

Half-hidden by the huge coffin, sitting up like a corpse reacting to a formaldehyde gas bubble in its stomach, a man rose. Dead-thin, with crude stitches joining his forehead and hairline, a souvenir of a scalping, the outlaw looked to have been killed years before.

But there he was, lighting a cigar and paying little attention to Sheriff Tucker or his threats.

Scalped Outlaw said, "Wave that Henry around all you want, but I'm not doing a goddamned thing until I see the boss man."

Albert Tomlinson leaned against the ticket agent's window of the Paradise train depot, reaching for a stack of telegraph messages that he could see had his name across the top as RECEIVER.

"That's the way to ruin your suit!" Junior heaved his words as he shuffled in through the back door from the stables, dragging a canvas mail sack behind him. He got himself to a stool and held on. "That's wet paint on the window. Put on not ten minutes ago. I'm surprised at you, Mr. Tomlinson."

Tomlinson instantly yanked back his arm, then pulled his glasses down his nose, peering through the bottom lens of the bifocals, examining his jacket for stains. He brushed at his tweeds, picking off a bit of tacky paint. "You have a number of urgent communications for me."

Junior's wooden teeth got in the way of his words. "I was going to send a boy. Any problem getting anythin' from me since you been here?"

Tomlinson spotted another smear of blue. "No, your work has been satisfactory, so far."

"You bet it has. The mail should interest you."

"The package to my daughters?"

Junior said, "Already sent." He fished into the sack and handed Tomlinson a rolled newspaper before moving to the telegraph desk and sorting through the messages with shaking arthritic hands. His habit was to lick his thumb, separating each telegram at its edge, then pulling it from the pile. Tomlinson had three.

Junior handed over the telegrams. "Sorry about your jacket, but we're getting a fancy do-over, too."

Tomlinson put the telegrams in his side pocket without reading them. He stayed with the newspaper, turning its pages.

Junior pointed to an article. "My good friend wrote that piece. Know what happened in our jail, don't you? Right across the way? That Shotgun Bishop was here. Now he's killin' like it's open season."

Tomlinson didn't answer. He walked from the ticket window, around the side of the station, following the newly built planked sidewalk. He didn't look away from the article, purposely shutting out the activity and rising noise around him.

Up and down the street, crews were painting storefronts, replacing windows and doors, hauling away piles of flood debris in flat wagons. Even the graveyard next to the jail had been mowed and its fence whitewashed.

Music leaked from a couple joints, the sound of the morning pianos scraping each other before mixing with the work voices in the street—shouted greetings and orders and the constant sounds of hammers and saws.

What wasn't being built was reopened. Paradise was full of railroad men, cowboys, and laborers staying over for a night or a week, but all for sure leaving their pay behind.

Tomlinson quickly avoided two workmen hauling a chuck-a-luck table into an unfinished saloon. Some old boys hung out by the front door, waiting for it to be set up.

One of the workmen stumbled, catching Tomlinson's attention. "That table's worth more than your house. I'll be back to check installation. These . . . gentlemen . . . are anxious to play."

One old boy belched out, "The Sheriff'll lose more cash than all of us put together! That dumb son of a bitch couldn't find luck if it bit him sittin' down!"

There was more hacking laughter until Tucker busted the jaw of the laugher with the butt of the Henry rifle, swung around, and slammed another in the gut, dropping him to the sidewalk.

It had happened so fast, Tomlinson didn't even have time to turn around. The gamblers were sprawled around his feet, yelling and cursing. The laugher spit a tooth and some pink.

"Those are potential customers, Sheriff."

Tucker casually wiped his glasses on his sleeve. "This little lesson in respect won't stop them from betting their pockets. Your problem's across the street."

They waited for a liquor-heavy wagon to pass before crossing to the coffin maker's.

"How long was John Bishop in your jailhouse?"

"At least a month, till Chisum bailed him out. You know all this . . . or you ought."

"It was a missed opportunity. You should have killed him when you had the chance."

"I just do what the money tells me."

They were standing beneath a sign that read YOUR VESSELS TO HEAVEN—$19.95

Tucker said, "You're in charge. Have at it."

Tomlinson entered the front room of the coffin maker's shop where the finished models were set out. A few were made of rosewood, metal handles at the feet and head, but most were painted pasteboard, with a place for a name on the lid, and PARADISE scrolled alongside so the insects would know where you ended, broke.

Tomlinson had Tucker cock the rifle deliberately for the sound, but made him follow behind two steps as he strode into the workshop. Months before, that would have been unthinkable, but the bookkeeper's mild nature had been replaced by a sense of authority over the men whose salaries he was controlling. The curved posture was gone, his words carrying quiet force. He told the dark of the room, "I'm paying you. This stoppage is unacceptable."

A ring of smoke drifted from behind the opulent green-lacquered coffin, before the scalped outlaw sat up. He at the smoke and said, "You're sounding like a yard boss I had, or an overseer. I never paid neither of them no never mind. Get ready to open your pockets, boss man."

Scalped Outlaw grabbed a sledgehammer and rolled away from the coffin. The barrel of Tucker's rifle followed him as he went to the back of the workshop and swung the hammer from his shoulder, smashing a corner wall. Three heavy swings broke through the planking, revealing an open tunnel behind. Scalped Outlaw pounded with the sledge and kicked the pieces away until a man could pass through.

Tomlinson said, "We know about the tunnel."

"That's an access way to the old gold mine, vein lasted all of a month. I worked it, with an outhouse-crazy Sioux who gave me this haircut." Scalped Outlaw jutted his head toward Tomlinson and Tucker, who had the rifle pointed directly at his skull.

Tucker provided some information. "That's when this place was actually supposed to be a paradise. You can't tell me nothing."

"Yes, the very reason I hired you and gave you plans as to what was needed. There's no secret here. I *hired* you." Tomlinson emphasized the word to remind Scalped Outlaw of his position.

"If there ain't no secret, why's the runt pointing that Henry at me?"

Tucker said, "Try *runt* one more time."

Tomlinson put a hand on Tucker's shoulder. "The sheriff's here because there's a disruptive employee making threats."

Scalped Outlaw held the sledge with both hands, ready to swing as Tomlinson moved to the smashed wall and peered into the tunnel.

It was thick with spiderwebs and the dust of rot. Globed oil lamps, smashed and hanging loose, had once been attached to wooden crossbeams supporting the tunnel's opening, but a little deeper, the timbers were piled together with rubble from the falling-in sides and an unsupported roof.

Tomlinson said, "Follow the plans."

"Want me to crawl in, shore that up, and build another entrance? I'll need extra men. Drag in some of the teamsters who're spending time in the pleasure houses, double my pay, and give me a taste. You might get what you want."

"A taste of what?"

"The gold you're pulling out of there. Half of every dollar sounds about fair. And that, I want in writing."

Tucker said, "Like you can read."

"Good enough. That tells me you're serious about this."

Tomlinson wanted to see how far it would go. "Or?"

Scalped Outlaw said, "These things collapse all the time. Would probably take a lot of your new street with it." He leaned back next to the casket, taking a deep drag on his cigar. "Keep the runt away from me or I'll hump him dead with that rifle."

Tomlinson watched Tucker for a beat, the purple tinge around his ears spreading with his anger. "Get him ready for work." He walked back out into the sunlight and traffic.

Tucker smashed the outlaw quickly in the neck with the rifle barrel, choking the smoke in his throat. Scalped Outlaw heaved onto the floor.

Tucker shouted, "Suck on it! Like your mama and the field hands. C'mon!"

Scalped Outlaw opened his lips, but not his teeth.

Tucker smashed again, parting his jaws, and shoving the barrel of the Henry into the side of his mouth. "This is what a runt does. You're going to get in there and start building, while they work out the details of your contract. Do it, or I'll blow a hole in your cheek, or take it a step further than your Sioux friend. Ever seen a tongue split? How you think you'll talk after that?" He took a deep breath. "Ready for work?"

Scalped Outlaw nodded, the gun barrel knocking into his teeth.

Tucker pulled back the Henry. "Only one rule in Paradise—respect the man with the badge."

The girl held up large, udder-shaped breasts, so Widow Kate could see the two symbols tattooed just beneath them.

Kate was trying to lean forward, eyes squinted, her own stomach blocking her, but read, "*Feng kuang*. That means *crazy*." She brought her wheelchair back a few turns, letting the girl tuck herself back into the bodice that was barely holding her together, her pale-white curves fighting any restraint.

Soiled Dove, in a finely appointed purple dress and dangling earrings, kept an arm around the girl, gently stroking her shoulder and lifting her chin so her eyes would meet Kate's when she spoke.

Kate said, "You worked in San Francisco. Got that mark for killing a customer."

"Yes, ma'am." The girl looked to Dove, then said, "He couldn't be pleased, and I'd tried for sure. He broke some of my personal things. A turtle comb and a hand mirror. I used one of the pieces to protect myself."

"It's good you told me."

The girl lowered her chin again as Kate wheeled behind a massive desk that had once belonged to the captain of the Pacific ship *Siberia*. She didn't look up, waiting for Kate's verdict. Dove's touch never left her shoulder.

Kate ran her hands across the plush fabric of dragons carved into the chair's armrests and drummed her fingers as her Chinese cook silently set out a luncheon tray.

The cook retreated on bound feet, and Kate still hadn't said a word. She shifted her massive weight in the wheelchair, its upholstered back automatically adjusting for her comfort with a quick clicking of small gears. It was an elaborate mechanism, but elegant and imposing. Perfect for her.

Soiled Dove said, "I was thinking of the new house."

With swollen fingers, Kate picked up a ceramic spoon shaped like a duck and dipped it into a bowl of bird's nest soup. Holding the spoon was a chore. Bringing it to her mouth, even more of an effort. She swallowed. "You won't be working here in this house. I have a new house just down the street, and I need one like you there. I've had difficult johnnies in the past, but there'll be nothing like them in my places, so forget about that tattoo."

The girl glanced up with her eyes. "Yes, ma'am."

"Dove will tell you what I expect in your behavior."

Dove whispered in the girl's ear, "No worries," before opening the office door and letting her out.

Tomlinson was standing in the hallway. She shut the door on him, turning to Kate. "You'll want me here for this, won't you?"

"Why?"

"This is about our future . . . business."

"Tell Mr. Tomlinson to wait a few minutes, then he may knock."

Soiled Dove seemed frozen in her spot, unblinking, as Kate sipped some more soup and read the newspaper that had been laid out neatly next to her luncheon tray.

Dove said, "I've another ten girls coming in this week. Do you want to see each? Or I can find them spots."

Kate adjusted the light of the ornate jade lamp on her desk to look closer at the photographs of John Bishop standing among a mountain of dead Fire Riders. "Do what I ask."

Soiled Dove stepped out of the office, shutting the door behind her.

Kate gave herself a moment, fixed on Bishop. "Oh, Goddamn you, Doctor," she said with a shake of the head that was disbelief and admiration together.

She was counting the bodies, her finger making a dent in the newspaper as she spotted each one, when Tomlinson's knock came three times. She took another spoonful of soup before allowing him entrance.

He wasn't fully in the room when she said, "So what happens now?"

"I'm not understanding the question."

Kate rolled quickly to where he was standing, his hands in his pockets in near-rude defiance. "Your new demeanor doesn't suit you . . . or me."

"I just solved a labor problem."

"It's an insult to imagine I'm not completely aware of everything that happens in Paradise. I'm not worried about the backs needed for work. I'm talking about money."

Tomlinson's shoulders were curving inward. "Well, ask again. Just be specific."

Kate said, "John Bishop killed a cadre of your riders, and not for the first time—"

"I've seen the photographs, read the exaggerations."

"He's a hero in these papers that show him with one of yours as a prisoner, which means he'll take the war right to you."

Tomlinson said, "I don't disagree with a thing said."

Kate pushed herself a few feet closer to Tomlinson, making him take a stumbled step back as she stubbed a short finger into his chest. "I want to know about the money. Are the deposits going to be there? You've had a setback, but I'm making Paradise new again."

Tomlinson said, "I know what we invested in. I approved it."

"You can do that from a shallow grave?"

Tomlinson's voice dropped, his confidence draining out in front of Kate. "I'd ask that you control your famous temper."

Kate's eyes narrowed in the round folds of her face, making them almost disappear: "I know Dr. John

Bishop . . . well. He's done me a good turn before, and I repaid in kind."

"Me as well."

"Would you like to see my scars?"

Tomlinson said, "Bishop truly helped my youngest daughter. He was kind."

"Think that makes a difference? You work for his brother, and he'll put down anyone who stands between him and that killing. It's what tears him apart, what drives him. I *know* this man."

"But, we have an army."

"Nothing but targets."

"That's foolish thinking. We have an organization spread across the Southwest to control all outlawry."

Kate snorted. "That's a hell of a term."

"That's why you came to us. To build our town."

"My town."

"Correction. Our investment."

Kate said, "Partial, and maybe your best one. You'd do well to remember who set this all in motion."

"You and your fleshpots are to be admired, ma'am." Tomlinson held out the three telegrams. "Devlin Bishop is authorizing another hundred thousand dollars. He believes in your *City of Paid-for Sin*, and these . . . family issues . . . won't stop business. I won't allow it."

Kate said, "I doubt it will make any difference. Paradise is my dream, and I expect to die here, even have a coffin built just for me."

"Yes, I believe I've seen it. Stylish."

"I expect to have one death. John Bishop's had a dozen. So far."

Tomlinson said, "You're taking that trash too seriously."

"You won't stop him, sir. If I had the Texas Rangers,

the army, and John Bishop coming for me, I'd worry about Bishop." Kate rolled back to her desk and took a small opium pipe from an ivory box, which also held the penny dreadful with Bishop on the cover. "What the hell. If anything does happen to your Fire Riders, I can't swing a dead cat without hitting someone who wants in on this."

She dropped a small bead into the bowl as Tomlinson said, "You won't need anyone else. If I drank, I'd say we should toast to a . . . secure partnership."

Kate lit the pipe and drew it in deep, then stabbed a finger at the photograph of all the dead Riders and said, "I can't do that, because you, sir, are not secured."

The creek was rain-swollen, water running fast and just reaching the belly of Bishop's horse. He glanced over to see Hunk, feet dangling in the current about an inch, his wrists loosely bound, but the rigged tourniquet holding.

They reached the other shore, which was the edge of a carpet of sweetgrass that stretched open for miles toward the Rockies, the creek weaving alongside. Bishop swung off his saddle, keeping the rig against his shoulder and letting the bay drink as he freed the knot that tethered Hunk's horse to his own.

Hunk, who hadn't said a word for more than twenty miles, managed to say, "Set the horse free, because now you're to kill me?"

"Get down off there. I want to check that knee."

Hunk sat up straight, bringing his one good leg around, and balling his massive fists in case Bishop pulled him from the saddle again.

"You need help." Bishop offered a shoulder and Hunk took it.

Bishop attended to the knee, cleaning and adding another stitch. Hunk jolted back when Bishop touched some swelling on the outer side of the leg. He gave Hunk a piece of leather to bite on as he tweezed a last fragment of buckshot from the edge of the tissue.

"When you get shot, often it's not loss of blood that kills. It's the germs on the bullet. The infection does it."

Hunk spit out the leather. "Still, your gun."

"You're damn lucky to be alive anyway, with that ear."

"We don't have a good doctor."

"Where?"

"Nowhere." Hunk shook his head. "He's what they called a field butcher. You know what that is?"

"It means he's done a lot of amputations. So have I."

"But not this time."

Bishop said, "You have information I need. I don't even know if a one-armed man can perform an amputation. I mean, do it clean. That's a funny problem, isn't it?"

Hunk chose his words carefully. "Yes. Funny."

Bishop daubed the stitches before rewrapping the leg. "I might have to do you, the way they did me. Do you know what happened to my arm?"

Hunk was holding the handle of the saber with the two inches of broken blade. "They would read about you at the fort. Everything."

Bishop took the saber, twisted the blade through the tourniquet strap, and turned it, keeping it taut.

Hunk said, "I don't understand you. Are you going to kill me or not?"

"Gangrene might still do it for me. If I lose patience

or think you're used up, I might." He started for the creek. "Or maybe I'll get you back to your wife and kids."

Hunk said, "That won't happen."

Bishop dropped on the bank, splashed water into his eyes with his one palm. He kept it there, feeling the cool of the water, but the double barrels were swivel-aimed from his hip, always on Hunk. "When you die is up to you. Twenty years from now . . . or twenty minutes."

Hunk's face was locked.

Bishop said, "My brother. You're taking me to him. You said the 'fort.'"

"You still don't even know everyone that you're fighting . . . or what."

"You'll show me or that leg will pain you till you're begging me to take it off."

"There are two men in you. Fighting all the time, I think."

Bishop said, "Then you have good reason to be afraid."

Linus pumped the bellows of the smith's furnace, heating the coals, before edging in the new horseshoe. He drew the air for extra heat, then turned the shoe, the iron-black giving way to molten yellow. He had the iron on the anvil, hammering it around the horn, forcing a turn, when Claude Ray came to the open door, watching him work to the center of the shoe, hot sparks flailing.

Claude Ray stepped into the stable. "New ones for Hurricane?"

"I imagine Mr. Chisum will want all new after we get her washed down."

Claude Ray hung on the side of the workbench, the

artificial leg Bishop had designed for him, right where
it had always been since Linus built it. Linus turned the
hot iron, heating the other quarter as Claude picked up
the prosthetic, working the knee back and forth.

Linus said, "You ready for that now?"

"You did real good, fine work."

Linus punched the shoe's nail holes, sweat washing
his face and arms. "Chisum showed us Garrett's message. Rose has been to the doc and is coming back to
you to heal herself up." He dropped the shoe in the
cooling bucket. "She really went through the storm, so
maybe it'd be nice if there was a different man waiting
for her at home."

Coming up the Chisum road, the brown and white
stallion walked easy, protecting Rose and her injury as
she sat up straight in the saddle on her own. Garrett was
alongside on his hammerhead, keeping in step, keeping an eye.

Behind them, McCarty and the outriders broke off,
riding across the open stretch beyond the stables and
corral. McCarty whistled before galloping toward the
pasture where the remaining herd was being gathered.

John Chisum was on the porch, the maids and staff
milling around him. There was excited chatter, but he
stood alone by the railing, waiting for Rose and Garrett
to get to his lawn before taking the front steps and
meeting them with an outstretched hand.

Garrett got off his horse before Linus and a stable
boy led it off. Chisum eyed the animal, patted its neck,
and then said to Garrett, "Where's Farrow?"

"He's gone, Mr. Chisum, along with your prize horse.
That's after he tried to get us all killed and shot Rose.

But we're here . . . and most of your men and most of the herd."

"Don't misunderstand me, Patrick." Chisum took hold of Rose's horse and helped her down. "You don't know how glad I am that you're back safe."

Rose said, "Me too, sir. I got some back. I did that."

"So I heard." Chisum helped Rose into the arms of the youngest maid, her belly swollen by weeks. The maid shouldered Rose toward the main house, the other maids coming up to briefly hug her.

Garrett said, "This shouldn't be a victory dance, Mr. Chisum. There's a lot dead left in Myrtle. We beat the Fire Riders, but we're told that wasn't the plan, that Farrow had something else in mind."

Chisum said, "I don't know a damn thing about that, but there was a . . . negotiation."

Garrett's laugh was ironic and someplace deep. "There always is."

The Chisum cowboys brought their horses in, got handshakes and slaps on the back.

Chisum tipped his hat to them, shook a few hands, then said to Garrett, "They wanted Dr. Bishop. You knew that straightaway."

"Uh-huh. So did he, but couldn't figure why."

Somebody handed Garrett a glass of whiskey. "But, they got him all right."

Chisum coughed. "Dead?"

"Hardly."

"Where is he now?"

"Tending to his own business. He brought down the most of the red hoods, and I gave him his money." Garrett finished the glass. "Mr. Chisum, I'm saying it out loud—they were waiting. We were set up not to win this, but we did. Maybe it's about time you declared yourself."

Chisum said, "You're on the side of right. You have no worries on that score. What about Tunstall's guns?"

"McCarty made a good show of himself."

"John will be glad to hear it."

Garrett said, "You spent a hell of a lot on Bishop, maybe to give him up. But most of us are here because of what he did. His fight. As I see it, this battle makes all debts to you paid in full." There was a threat under Garrett's words and his forward leaning stance with his gun.

Chisum let them both pass. "I'm damn proud of you, Patrick. You're an asset to this ranch, and I hope to see you tonight at dinner. In the chair next to mine."

Garrett held out his glass. It was refilled.

The youngest maid helped Rose almost to the porch steps before they stopped. Rose whispered something to herself as she saw Claude Ray by the corral gate. In a new pressed suit, he was standing on two legs. He was holding a small gathering of violets in one hand, hanging on to a fence rail with the other.

Words didn't happen as he let go of the fence and started toward his wife. Taking an unsteady step, the prosthetic snapped into place. Stiff. Trying, he waved to Rose then took another step. Better each time, but he fought for balance.

Rose went to Claude, almost catching him, her own wounds burning. They got hold of each other with both arms and wrapped tightly. The flowers dropped from his hand, scattering at their feet.

Claude Ray didn't break and held Rose tighter. "Not dancing, but close."

* * *

Bishop pushed the bay fast along the field of tall grass, Hunk's horse keeping the tether between them straining. A nye of pheasants broke from the grass, splitting in two directions, darting away. Bishop aimed from the saddle and fired both barrels, bringing down three birds. He slowed the bay, then cut into the grass to pick up the kill and hang them from his saddle.

They were good shots, and the pheasants weren't buckshot-chewed.

Hunk said, "Good to see that thing can kill something other than men."

Bishop was actually smiling. "Enemies."

Hurricane reared back, legs kicking wild as a rope went around Farrow's chest and another went around his neck before he was hurled from the saddle. His chin hit the ground, head snapping back as two Fire Riders lashed his ankles tight. Farrow rolled to one side, squirming against his bonds, his Sears Roebuck vest and jacket caked with mud, dust, and someone else's blood.

A Rider pulled a rag from the water trough and stuffed it into Farrow's mouth, killing his screams.

Smythe was at the prison gates, jabbing at Farrow with the end of one of his crutches. "That was supposed to be our victory, mate. Splashed all over, to scare anyone who might come up against us. You said you had it worked out, but you didn't, did you? If you'd done it right, you wouldn't be in the spot you're in now, right? Aren't I right?"

The rope was tossed over a butcher's gallows and Farrow was pulled into the air by his ankles. He swung back and forth.

Smythe pulled the rag from his mouth, sloppy water following. "Am I right? You corked it up."

Farrow's eyes were closed tight. "This is making me sick! I can't be upside down!"

"You won't be for long."

"I got Chisum's trust and did what I was supposed to do!"

"Saying it don't make it so, mate."

"How could I know Chisum's men would fight like that? Or the Shotgun would take you all on? You wanted a massacre!"

Smythe said, "Yes, we did."

"I did my damn part!"

Smythe stopped the swinging with his crutch as hooded Riders gathered around, breaking from the mess table and passing a bottle hand-to-hand. Some had torches. All had guns and blades. Farrow cried out over all their murmurs and accusations.

Newspaper pages blew across the yard—Bishop and the Fire Riders scattered everywhere.

Dev Bishop broke through the crowd of his own men to look Farrow in the eye as he hung like a hog for butchering. He put a hand on Farrow's chest, holding him steady. "You let that photographer take pictures of my men. And my brother. And their bodies. Even after the fight, you could have stopped that. The photographer was your man, but you ran off. It looked like Gettysburg—my men dead and everybody seeing."

Smythe said, "Oh, big mistake, mate."

Farrow coughed out, "But everyone's still afraid of you, your raids."

Dev said, "Not as long as they see my brother defeating us." He looked to one of the Riders, who was holding a machete.

Smythe said, "Opening that throat will tell a story."

Farrow's eyes were wide with panic. Dev squeezed his arm, reassuring him, "This is a failure from a man who's a coward, not a traitor. Different kind of punishment."

Bubbles frothed from Farrow's nose, the tears rolling back into his eyes. "That's right! I'm no traitor. That's why I came back here. To show you. I work for you."

Dev threw a look, and Smythe shoved the rag back into Farrow's mouth, tickling his throat to choking.

Dev turned and walked away as the first shots hit Farrow's body, followed by a volley of others emptying their pistols into the hanging target. The rag erupted from Farrow's mouth, his body spinning in place with every bullet strike. The last ones hit the ropes, and Farrow dropped to the ground, shredded.

Smythe looked to Dev, then said to the men, "He gets buried proper."

Dev was holding Hurricane by the bridle. "This is a damn fine animal. One of the best I've ever seen."

Smythe said, "Then it wasn't a total loss. That's one of Chisum's best, and you took it from him."

Dev didn't have a word back. Just pulled himself onto Hurricane.

Smythe stood before him, leaning on his crutches. "We're not letting this defeat stand, Dev. We've still got Colby and all these fightin' men. I don't think your brother's crazy or fool enough to take us all on. That's bloody suicide."

Dev snapped the reins, and Smythe twisted out of the way of the horse. Hurricane cleared the prison gates, moving fast and perfect into the Wyoming night.

Smythe gestured with his crutch toward Farrow's still-tied body. "I don't want that stinking rat here! Burn him!"

* * *

Bishop said, "The fort, which direction?"

"It's dark. How can I say which way? Or anything. I am confused by America." Hunk turned the pheasant on its skewer and took another bite. His hands were still tied, but he managed.

Bishop sat nearby, his meal finished, his eyes fixed on the open dark around them. "You're running out of time with me."

"You can't remember nothing?"

"Tell me what I want to know."

Hunk said, "You sound like a town policeman. Police or sheriff, that's the only thing in this country that's the same. Since I got here, everywhere I go, someone talks a different talk, different language. No wonder you can't understand each other. I'm from two countries, so worse for me."

Bishop was sitting up, his attention somewhere else. "How can it be two?"

"Born in Bucharest, but joined Russian Navy. *Docher*— stevedore. You know this? My term ended and I had choice of Rumania or here. My wife and I went to Virginia, and I dug coal."

Bishop was listening to something far off drifting toward him. He set the gun hammers. "Why didn't you stay?"

"Private mine, did well. Workers all Rumanian, some Poles. Fire Riders kept raiding the shipments. They were taking our money anyway, so I joined. Lots of trash, the others. Like me, they came from other places, trying to find money to stay here."

Bishop stepped toward Hunk, drawing his knife. "Is that why the loyalty?"

Hunk followed the blade with his eyes. "I don't have

nothing better than them, and now, I'm prisoner. So, everything's much worse than ever."

Bishop was hearing something in the dark, whispers he couldn't make out. No animal calls or low whistles. Words. He hooked the edge of the knife between Hunk's wrists. "Think they would rescue you?"

"Your brother said I was a leader."

Bishop yanked the knife upwards, cutting the bonds. "So, you think you're worth something to him."

"Now I run, and you can shoot me?" Hunk's words were still hanging, when the Fire Rider charged out of the dark, billowing red and laying pistol fire.

It was all of one motion, Bishop and Hunk diving out of the way of slugs tearing around them, punching a canteen and ricocheting. The Rider turned close on his horse and charged back, ready to empty another six.

Bishop dropped to a knee, and shot upwards, the blast slamming the Rider sideways, his body hanging in the saddle, the horse still running into the dark.

The second Rider leaped from the shadows on the other side of the fire, slashing Hunk with a cavalry saber, a revolver in his other hand, shooting wild.

The bay and Hunk's horse tore away from the shots. Bishop turned, fired a barrel with his shoulders, sending the Rider falling forward, the legs of his tall horse buckling. Horse and Rider slammed to the ground, the Rider diving away. He sprang up, bringing up his gun and opening fire.

Bishop hit him with the second barrel, blowing out his chest. The horse scrambled, and ran. Bishop brought down two more shells from the bandolier, loaded and closed the breech. The barrels swung around from his hip, locking into place as he turned.

Hunk was on his feet, turning in one spot and

holding a knife in front of him. His eyes darted from one side to the other, looking for movement. This was the Fire raiding pattern he knew and had used himself. Attack, pull back, and attack. Keep the target guessing.

Bishop was by the low fire, searching, the rig set.

Hunk faced the dark just beyond the light. He knew a third rider was going to come in from behind. Could feel it in the silence. No whispering. No signal.

Instantly there, the Rider came running in fast, using a Winchester repeater, slugs tearing. Hunk leaped forward, grabbing the animal around the neck, his feet dragging as the horse ran, the Rider pounding at him with the butt of the rifle.

Hunk's massive hands locked around the horse just behind his head. His arms coming together, he pulled it down, slowing its run until it folded to the ground.

The Rider jumped from his saddle, kicking away from the horse and grabbing his rifle. On his feet, he cocked it, firing one shot.

Bishop opened both barrels on the Rider's chest, rocketing him backwards, the repeater firing into the sky.

The campfire was done, the last bits of orange dying. In darkness—not even stars—Bishop and Hunk took to the ground. The Rider's horse bolted to its feet, ran toward a black void, and was gone.

Bishops whispered, "How many do you think they sent for you?"

Hunk was catching his breath. "I don't know. The one with the sword, that was my friend, also from Bucharest."

Bishop said, "Call out."

"What?"

"Maybe some more of your friends are around."

Hunk tried to see Bishop's face, but the dark was total. He was a shape against miles of blackness.

Bishop's disconnected voice was flat. "I'm still giving you a choice. They won't."

Hunk finally spoke. "*Acest lucru este Bogdan! Cine este acolo?*"

An Ozark voice yelled back. "Hunk, you know I don't understand that loco crap of your'n!"

Bishop asked, "Who is it talking?"

"It's Ellis." Hunk called out, "Grudge Ellis! Everybody dead?"

"Yes, they all are. What about the shotgun man?"

Hunk felt Bishop's hand on his arm and said, "Shot and crawling away to die."

Ellis called back, "What about you?"

"I'm hurt."

Ellis said, "I'm coming in and I'd appreciate you not trying nothing." He lit a torch, let it flame, and held it before him as he crossed the field to the small flat where Hunk and Bishop had made their cook fire. He carried a Navy and kicked at the body of one of the Fire Riders with a hole blown through him.

Hunk was down, leaning on his good knee, still holding the knife, when Ellis pointed the pistol at him. "I'm real sorry about this, Hunk. We been trailing you since Myrtle, thought we'd get more of Chisum's men, but, you know, we didn't want no other fight right away. So we rested up."

Hunk said, "Until tonight."

"Well, we got our work to do. And you know you can't come back with us. Mr. Bishop and that Tomlinson don't allow that."

Hunk stood. "Yes, when you're gone, you are gone."

"That's right. You should've been dead already, but

I guess you got some cat in you. Turn around? Make it easier on both of us, probably."

Hunk stepped away from the torch, his arms folded across his chest. But he didn't lower his head or close his eyes. He just stood, waiting for the shot.

Finally, there was a sound. A gurgling.

Hunk turned to see Ellis drop to his knees, the cavalry saber protruding from his chest. The torch rolled out of his hands, and the weight of the pistol took his other arm to the ground, followed by his chin. Ellis's eyes were wide and wondering. They stayed open.

Bishop was standing behind Ellis, the rig down at his side, his hand slick and red with the blood from Ellis's back. He looked down at the body, the blade run through it, then to Hunk, who was holding the torch above him, throwing out a full circle of orange light.

Bishop said, "Are you going to tell me what I want to know? Show me?"

Hunk peered at Bishop. "Your eyes—"

"You're a Fire Rider, You want to be with them, be with all the others?"

"You save me, then kill me."

Bishop said, "I warned you." He moved his shoulder, and the shotgun sprang from the elbow, settling at his right hip, trigger lines ready. His expression was a mask as he favored his left side for a moment, shifting his body so the shotgun compensated, rising half an inch for a perfect kill shot.

"Time is now up. You decided. You're of no use."

CHAPTER SIXTEEN
Séotä'e

From "The Angel of Death Strikes Without Mercy—Again!" by Virgil Demetrius Chaney:

> Neither prayers nor bullets will ever stop him! Doctor John Bishop, who lost his family at the hands of filthy curs, now brandishes a double-barreled shotgun made of God's steel, meting out bloody justice to all those who wrongly cross his path.
>
> The latest scene of slaughter and justice was a small cattle town of the peaceful kind, where families live and grow in a Christian manner. That peace was shattered by the arrival of the demonic force known throughout the Southwest as Fire Riders, who invaded the town for their own evil purposes, only to be thwarted by Doctor Bishop, also

known as "Shotgun" or "The Angel of
Death."

Acting alone, Shotgun brought his own
style of justice to over one hundred
demons, sending them to their maker by
way of a fiery hell, spit from the end of
his two-barreled arm extension. I was
there, witnessing it all and taking the
photographs before you, at great and
distressing risk to my own life and safety.

Try as I might, I could never turn away
from the sordid, bloody end of these
devils, much as I wanted to. They are a
prime example to all lawbreakers as to
what to expect when you draw yourselves
against Shotgun.

But we, as citizens, must always ask the
ultimate question—is this man a true
spirit of justice, meting out bloody ends to
those that deserve it, or a wanton,
dangerous, criminal who belongs dancing
at the end of a strong rope? We, the
citizens of this great land, deserve to sleep
peacefully and secure.

Retired Army Captain DuPont Creed
of Del Norte, Colorado has called Dr.
Bishop "a mad dog, who needs to be put
down with all force."

Hero or insane killer who slaughters at
will? Those questions and more will be
answered in future issues.

The man with three chins said, "You really ain't got
nothin' here I want. On the counter, I mean."

White Fox turned the newspaper over to see the
photographs as the man examined the buffalo hides.

He ran his fingers through the short hair, laying out and checking the thickened skin on the planked door between two salt barrels. He was making a show of his expertise even though his eyes were rolling from Fox's shoulders to her ankles, then back again.

She had her hair tied back, revealing the perfect planes of her face, but not allowing any kind of vanity. Her leathers were loose and absent of any Cheyenne markings, and she kept a black duster draped around her shoulders. She was almost lost in it, with the collar up past her ears and the right sleeve pinned to the side.

"They're calling you *Séotä'e* because you're coming and going like a ghost. Nobody never sees you no more." The man with three chins waddled around the trading post, one hip grinding as he knocked at some hanging beaver pelts and pottery with a cane that was actually an old wagon wheel spoke. "Now, don't start that *nomáhtsé'héó'o* stuff with me. I savvy, know it means *thief*, but I can't give you no real money. This is trade. I'll allow two dollars apiece for them buffalo, and that's a fair bargain. And don't put on no high manners to make me think different."

Fox looked up, her fierce eyes peering over the clothes. "No, you cheat."

"I'd put myself against any post this side of Red River. I don't give short weight or hold back blankets when the snows come. I don't live big on your backs." Three Chins hoped for a reaction, but she gave him nothing. "Fine. Be a damn statue, but there ain't no more buffalo need, so I ain't giving you more credit than two dollars. You used to be kinder to me, would smile."

White Fox folded the newspaper, the photographs seeming to hurt her, and put it neatly in the outer pocket of the duster. All very deliberate and with purpose.

Three Chins watched. "I got that for you. Like I done all them magazines and everythin' else about that Shotgun. You want to know so much about him, it's like he was kin." He looked away before asking, "Is he kin to you?"

She said, "No."

"That's good." He moved closer, brushed the edge of the duster with the wagon spoke "You got yourself so wrapped up, I can hardly see nothing of you anymore. You shouldn't hide like that."

"Not hiding." She put her hand on top of his and guided it to the counter. "Three dollars, trade."

All three chins worked his smile. "You got yourself five hides. Now that's only fifteen." He strained behind the counter, retrieving a small boxed cavalry medical kit from behind the barrels then wiping dust off it with his elbow. "This is all you wanted last time, too. You doctoring?"

Fox looked at him. "We have the need."

"You get your medicine when the army says so. They find out I've been trading out these kits, they'd have me in stocks for ten years. That's a hell of risk, but I'd take it . . . for my wife."

She kept her hand on top of his, moving it gently. "You have one in town."

The old woman with the long knife rocked in her chair by the front of the trading post, watching White Fox put the Cheyenne war club back in her belt as she moved to her horse, put the medical kit in a deerskin sack that she slung across her back, then unhitched her painted mare.

The old woman smiled all gums and never stopped her chair or whittling.

Three Chins stood by the door, holding his swollen

hand. He shouted, "That's the second time you've busted my knuckles. There won't be no third. You ain't welcome here no more. Tell Dull Knife and the rest it's your fault they can't do no business!"

Fox turned to Three Chins. "You have a cooler. Put your hand there."

"I don't need no words from you. Here!" Three Chins hurled a stack of penny dreadfuls, newspaper clips, and flyers out the door, a strong Montana wind carrying them. "Them's all about Shotgun! That one by your feet? Somebody's even put up ten thousand dollars for his killing!"

Fox picked up the bounty notice as Chins said, "You savvy that? Ten thousand dollars! I'd like to see you go after that money. Get yourself shot in half!"

Three Chins looked to the old woman who'd carved the snout of a timber wolf out of sugar maple. "Grandma, you got nothing to do with this." He slammed the door, throwing the wooden bolt from inside.

The old woman kept carving. "He never was worth nothing, honey."

White Fox thanked her with a look, mounted the painted pony, and rode for the North Moccasin foothills, the Shotgun leaflets still scattering.

Hunk's hands were free and his knee felt better. He adjusted the blood flow from the tourniquet as Bishop had showed him. He manipulated the saber handle, looked up, and saw the barrels of the shotgun rig leveled on him, even as Bishop was turned, talking to the man standing by the gated fence.

They were on the first part of the Del Norte Toll Road, leading into the mining town, then the Blue

Mountains. Bishop paid for their passing and was asking some questions of the toll taker, who answered with waving hands and pointing.

Hunk watched, still captive, but not a prisoner . . . because *prisoners* were worth something. He thought about the men he'd been chosen to lead—or at least, friends he'd ridden with—and how they all wanted him dead. Because of what they thought he knew.

That bit made Hunk laugh to himself as he regarded his massive, powerful hands. His only true worth. He'd torn off his red tunic and wore a dead friend's coat with a large, bloodstained rip made by a cavalry sword. That made him laugh, too.

The toll taker was excited to see "that shotgun" in person and opened the gate. Bishop nodded his thanks and brought his horse around. He and Hunk rode through at the same time, the shotgun aimed at Hunk. Bishop's eyes were fixed on the road leading to the distant town ahead. He was keeping his own pace, his own thoughts, not having said a word since they'd fought the Fire Riders at their campsite the night before.

The horses were fed and watered, the afternoon bright, and for Hunk, the Colorado sky as open as he could want. Everything around them, the road and the miles of yellow-green to the mountains, was hopeful.

The rig stayed steadily on him. Bishop could take him out with the slightest gesture of his body. If Hunk broke his horse into a run, he wouldn't make it.

He said, "I told you where your brother was."

"You did. Finally."

"The prison in Rawlins."

Bishop adjusted his shoulders, moving the rig with both barrels directly at Hunk's face. "Nothing decent there. You said you didn't even know how many men were there."

"I said it changes."

"And you didn't know where my brother does his business."

"They never let me up there. They wanted me out riding."

Bishop said, "They led you to slaughter."

Hunk said, "I know they want me dead, so I'll take you to the fortress, but we're going deeper into Colorado now."

"Other business first."

"Where we are going, is it to kill someone? Of course. What else?"

Bishop turned to Hunk. His eyes had cleared the blood wash from the night before, but his face was still a mask. "It's to see someone who wants to kill me."

Colby held the Smith & Wesson Rimfire by its small wooden handle, thinking of the first time he'd ever used such a weapon.

The boy who had bound him to the sheep shearing chair was standing not five feet away. He was several years younger than Colby's youngest kill, and the thought of targeting a boy so close in age to his own son gave him pause. He didn't like to think himself capable of that, even as a moneyed assignment.

The thought shattered as quickly as it had come to him. "Simon, take this."

Colby gently positioned Simon's fingers around the Rimfire's handle, then lowered the boy's arm, letting the gun hang. "Feel the weight first, get used to that against your wrist, yes? That's what you have to get used to, and then bring it up."

Simon lifted the weapon. "It's not that heavy. I thought a pistol would be more difficult to handle."

Colby said, "It's still too big for your brother."

Simon wasn't sure if he should smile at the remark. He looked at Jacob, who was sitting by one of the fence posts, giggling. His nose wrinkled as a lamb flopped onto its belly in front of him, wiggling for attention.

Simon was trying to imagine his body and manner stiff. "Any gun is too big for his hands. I hope that always will be."

"Is that what your father would want?"

Simon cracked off a shot, not hitting a well bucket on a tree stump. The lamb bleated and ran away at the noise. Colby helped Simon steady his hand, before a harsh cough turned him away. He covered his mouth with a monogrammed handkerchief, spotting it with blood.

"Mr. Colby?"

"I'm fine. You're the one who must do the work." He mopped moisture from around his eyes, caught a breath. "It takes time to know how to shoot properly."

"I would never touch a handgun if there was drink available. Never. It is important to me that you know that."

Colby put a hand on Simon's shoulder, patting his starched shirt. "You're a responsible young man. I'm leaving this pistol and some cartridges with you. I want you to practice, though."

Simon lowered the gun again, then raised it to position. "Mr. Colby, this is not how I assumed things would go between us."

"If a stranger came onto my property, and I doubted

him, and had that chair? I'd do the same. Very creative. But I only fell into your fence."

"Yes, sir. I understand that now."

"And I never was here to do you any harm."

"Yes, sir. I understand that, as well."

Colby shucked the one round fire and loaded the pistol's revolving cylinder. "I've slept, am healed well enough, bandaged up, and had some decent stew. Making sure you can defend your home seemed like an appropriate way to pay back your hospitality before riding on."

"It's appreciated."

He handed Simon the gun. "But if I was here for the wrong reasons, you need to know how to handle a proper weapon."

"Did you teach all of this to your son?"

Colby dabbed his bloody mouth. "No, his life doesn't require it."

"My father would say he was fortunate. It's not easy to be here, to protect this place."

"Now, that's a steady hand. Good. Your father's going to be very proud when he returns."

Simon turned again to his brother. "Jacob, check the stalls. See about the water."

The four-year-old wobbled for the barn, a few lambs tagging behind him. He slipped in the wet grass, came up laughing. Simon waited for his brother to reach the open side of the barn and start crawling through the slat fence before turning to Colby. "My father is gone. Not coming back. Jacob doesn't know."

"Run off by the cattlemen?"

"No sir. He drowned in the Little Colorado. He was helping build the ferry down by the river crossing and was caught under the boat. I asked if it might have been drink, and the ferryman wouldn't say, but I feel sure."

Colby turned Simon to him, looking directly into his wide eyes. "Son, I have to cross the river, to find the bad man I've been tracking."

"Yes, sir, I know. We found some of your papers over by the fence you knocked down. Do you recall that?"

Colby allowed a smile. "I do, indeed."

Simon held up the pistol. "We never had a near crossing before. My father would have to ride a full day out of his way to find a shallow. This crossing would be his gift to you for helping my brother and myself."

"This will be a fine help, son."

"He's an outlaw, the one you're after?"

Colby said, "The man obeys only his own laws. So, I'd say that qualifies."

"You considered your answer carefully, like a teacher. And he only has one arm, yes?"

Simon straightened his white shirt, checked his collar button as if centering himself before raising the pistol to the position Colby had shown him. He fired three shots. One of them sent the bucket spinning away.

CHAPTER SEVENTEEN
The Blind Dead

He claimed everyone called him Old Chaw. His legs had been amputated at the waist. He'd strapped wooden blocks to his hands with oil-stained belt leather and planted them on the floor in front of him, leap-frogging forward using his arms and shoulders. His Union tunic was worn to tatters, the coattails ragged to nothing after dragging behind him for years, but the gold sergeant's stripes on his sleeves shone like they'd just been stitched on with new thread.

Chaw said, "The crazy bastard's out back." He moved faster than most men walked, half-rolling around corners, then jumping three steps ahead.

Bishop followed him into the rooming house, and Hunk walked stiff kneed beside him.

Set off from Del Norte's central street and flanked by stock pens and loading platforms, the house had been a day lodge for teamsters. As Del Norte grew, businesses pushed in other directions, forgetting that side of town and the men living there. Now it was a place for soldiers who'd run out their pensions and their road.

Everything about it, even under a clear sky, had surrendered.

Chaw stopped at the kitchen door barely on its hinges and looked up at Bishop. "Where'd you lose your arm? My legs are somewhere at Chickamauga."

"Mine was after the war."

"After? It's still goin' on, ain't it?"

As Bishop held open the kitchen door with the rig, Chaw said, "You didn't lose nothing. You traded up!"

They moved inside, a pot of sour coffee boiling over on a rusting two-burner. In the rest of the kitchen were pots with week-old beans, stale bread by the sink pump, and a sack of grits crawling with bugs.

Chaw pulled a wrinkled tie from his pocket and held it out to Hunk. "Captain Creed puts a high regard on respect and dressing proper."

Hunk said, "Bishop knows this man. I don't."

"He tell you he was blinded? But he'd still value that tie."

Hunk tied the tie as Chaw forwarded himself to the back door on his arms. "Where the hell you hail from, anyway?"

The steps leading from the kitchen porch to the small yard next to the alleyway were missing the bottom two. Old Chaw made the jump, landing on the soft grass next to the pile of dirt from the open grave.

"I asked for all things, that I might enjoy life; I was given life, that I might enjoy all things." It was a young voice, but commanding, and continued as Bishop and Hunk stepped into the yard. "I got nothing that I asked for, but everything I hoped for."

They took a place next to four old men in army

uniforms, standing around an open hole dug near the side fence. A body, wrapped in a moldy blanket and pieces of a battle standard, had been dumped there like so much old washing.

The old men used rosewater to cover the smell of bottom-turned whiskey and their dirty uniforms, but the sweet just made it worse. The four mourners were of different ranks—one sported a Confederate long coat—but all looked spiritually caved in.

Hector Hayward paused his reading, looking up from the prayer book as the Reb set Old Chaw on an apple crate, to make him the same height as everyone else.

Hector saw the shotgun and his eyes went to the rig first, then to Bishop and Hunk. He tried not to react, but failed, losing his place on the page. Finding it, he continued. "Almost despite myself, my unspoken prayers were answered. I am among all men most richly blessed." He closed the book, regarded the military men hanging on to each other, knowing what should come next.

Old Chaw said, "It ain't right if we don't fire no salute. Owner don't allow no firearms, says we're too old to handle 'em."

The Reb took a cap and ball from his long coat and held it up with whiskey-shot hands. Chaw grabbed the pistol and looked to Bishop.

Bishop said, "I didn't come here for this."

"Then why the hell are you here?"

Hector said, "Doctor, would it really put you out to do something for a dead man?"

Bishop cocked the shotgun rig and stepped back. Extending his arm, he fired the first barrel into the sky, then the second.

A murder of crows broke from a tree, and there were shouts from someplace across the back alley. The mourners began filling in the hole with flat spades.

Chaw said to Bishop, "Ain't none of this legal. You better git before the constable comes around. Tussling with you would be the biggest thing he ever done."

Hector was already up the steps, the kitchen door clack-slamming behind him. He stood by the attic door-way, pressing close to the raw-brick wall, bracing a Union service revolver with both hands, and aiming for a head shot to the next person in.

The door was an old rug nailed to the top of the frame. Hector watched it move as it was pushed aside. There was a shadow. Closing his eyes, he locked the hammer with his thumb before the gun was knocked clean across the room by the shotgun barrel.

The pistol landed without going off.

"Nice weapon." Bishop stepped in, followed by Hunk, who angled himself sideways, ducking the ceiling beams and dragging his injured leg.

Hector shrugged. "It was Captain Creed's. The one he lost in the river. I fished it out for him a year ago."

Bishop picked up the gun. "Hector, why'd you think you needed this?"

"I got pretty scared when I saw you, sir. You weren't . . . expected."

"I wasn't expecting the captain to be dead, but you sure as hell made me feel welcome."

"It's just . . . your reputation now. It's quite some-thing."

"So now you're afraid of me?"

Bishop tossed the pistol onto one of two small beds in a windowless corner. "You never were before."

Around the beds were scattered copies of the *Police Gazette*, some old newspapers, a portable field telegraph with wires dangling from it. Patched trousers and two shirts hung on a line. All of which Hector was packing.

Bishop picked up a beat-to-hell saddlebag and handed it off. "Don't let me stop you, son."

Hector's hair was darker and he was three inches taller than the last time Bishop had seen him but he still moved like a schoolboy unsure at the blackboard. Hector reached for one of the clean shirts as if he'd be shot in the back.

Hunk tore it from the line. "You had a gun on us, boy. Act like it."

Bishop said to Hunk, "You wouldn't know from the greeting, but this young man saved my life."

Hector put the shirt in the bag. "When we found you by the tracks, that was more blood than I could stand. I was sure you'd be dead by morning."

"The doc told me it was you who took me in."

"I figured I owed it." Hector moved about the room, never turning his back, snatching up his belongings. "That Miss White Fox, she got me out of those woods, and the Captain, well, he didn't want to see you die from the Fire Riders, not after they put us out."

"You helped me so Creed could come back and kill me himself?"

"That was in his mind, yes sir."

Hunk laughed. "Boy, you were with the Riders?"

Hector's eyes locked on the bloody bandages around Hunk's arm and chest, the corrupted leg outstretched. Hunk seemed monstrous to the boy as he dropped himself onto a bench, examining an empty vodka bottle that had rolled across the floor. "Why, yes sir. I surely was there with them. In that prison and everything."

Hunk pulled the cork.

"A mule skinner gave that to the captain in trade for his army sheath. We traded off almost everything he had."

Bishop kicked the stack of papers and digest magazines. "I'd think after you talked to the newspapers, you wouldn't need money."

"Well, they don't pay much. When they'd write about you, the captain had me read it out loud and figure something else to say. I'd telegraph it in. I learned to use that key pretty good." He put the portable telegraph kit next to his other belongings. "Is that why you're here? What we said in the papers?"

"It's how I found you." Bishop adjusted the rig to lay against his shoulder. "I'm here to settle accounts."

Hector stopped bundling his clothes and bit his lower lip. "Sir?"

"I'm going to Rawlins. You've been inside."

"Yes, sir?"

Bishop said, "I told you, I'm settling accounts. With my brother. I need someone who knows that prison."

Hector's stammer returned. "Y-yes, I've been inside. A-a-and so have you. You visited your brother. H-he told the story . . . often . . . many times."

Hunk said, "Your talk is worse than mine, boy."

Bishop said, "You saw me when I was near dead."

Hector's words were barely there. "I can't never forget it."

"That's my problem. I have forgotten. That grenade took a lot from me, son. Some things I just don't remember. I've got to know what I'm walking into."

Hector swallowed hard. "What about this gentleman? You've got the boots, that red stripe. You're a Fire Rider, sir?"

Hunk raised the empty bottle in a mock toast as Bishop said, "He came after you did, doesn't know all the secrets of that place. You crawled all through it. Said so in one of the Penny Dreadfuls."

"Yes, sir. I—I said those words. That story paid us the most." Hector put a hand into his saddlebag, finding a small cotton pouch. "Doctor, I owed the captain. He took care of me, and I promised I'd see him buried. It wasn't the best, but it was with his friends. I did it."

He pulled a pair of blue-paper sunglasses from the pouch and held them out. "He hated you so bad for needing these, being blind. He figured a way to kill you and get your brother to take us in."

Bishop said, "You have reason to help me."

Hector drew himself in, finally standing straight. "I listened to revenge talk for years. I don't want to hear nothing like that no more."

"I'm not saying it's right. It just is."

Hector gathered up the things from the bed and filled the rest of the bags. "You remember Mr. Fuller? He's in Oregon with his family, offered me a job working timber. Or maybe I'll go Virginia way. Find a good school. Everybody I'm around, since before I was a shaver, is shot and broken. I'm sick of it. There's a lot more going on in this country than folks killing each other."

Hunk said, "That boy, going to try for president?"

Hector looked to Bishop. "Don't you just want to be a doctor, again?"

Bishop took a step toward Hector, the rig still in

place, his words measured, even and quiet. "I'm settling accounts."

"You figure on me riding in, so you can get killed? And me with you?"

Hector pulled down the washing line. "No, sir." He looked to the pistol lying on the bed, then to Bishop. "If you're going to kill me, let's get it done."

"Hector, all I want from you is some information. I'm on my own business, and you're not part of it."

"They're having a town meeting just down the street in an hour. Forming a vigilante group to protect us against any more Fire Rider raids. If they knew who I'd been with, they'd hang me. This gentleman, too."

"You claimed to know secrets."

Hector buckled the saddlebags. "There's explosives buried all along the outside walls and in some old tunnels. If Mr. Bishop hasn't used it, it's still there."

Hunk said, "I never heard of nothing like that."

"There's tunnels all through the prison. Some your brother had built, others been there forever."

"These tunnels, he hid money there?"

Hector said, "Maybe. The captain, he gave me a book on mapmaking so I could study up. I figure I can draw it out for you."

Bishop said, "Do it. Please."

Hector sat at the small table, tearing the back page from the prayer book, and using a flat-lead pencil to sketch a diagram of the prison fortress. His lines were precise.

Hunk watched, then approved with a belch. "The yard has one side that's nothing but guns."

"That's different from before." Hector made the adjustment. "You're not riding with them anymore, sir?"

"Not no more."

Hector indicated the locations of a tunnel running the circumference of the main cell block and a series of false walls on the upper floors—places where he used to hide. "I don't know about now, but one day I found some guns, and cases of ammunition in a couple old closets. They said the guards would sell them out of the back to the Indians, but I don't know what's left, if anything."

He handed the map to Bishop. "When you get inside, Doctor . . . well, I wish you both luck. Honest and true."

They walked outside to a stable. With canvas topping nailed down to one side, it was barely a shed.

Hector took a saddle with hand-tooled scrolling and Creed's insignia and cinched it to a solid, well-built mare. "When we sold the captain's horse, I think that's when he started dying. But I'd never let him lose the saddle."

Bishop said, "I was always sorry about his eyes."

"Now I know it was his own fault, for not taking care. But I couldn't never tell him."

"Hector, I wanted to settle accounts with you and the captain. No matter why, you didn't leave me for dead." Bishop handed him the sack of Chisum gold. "It'll help you get where you're going."

Hector took the sack, almost dropping it because of the weight. He didn't look inside, putting it directly into his saddlebag. "I'm thanking you, Doctor. Feels like quite a bit."

"I thought you and the captain deserved something."

"Maybe I should stay and get the captain reburied proper, not planted like a potato the way his buddies did it."

Bishop shook his head. "You said you were leaving. That's best."

Hector pulled himself onto the horse, then slipped on Captain Creed's sunglasses and looked to Bishop. His eyes were blue-masked discs. "The captain would have hated that I read from the *Confederate Prayer Book*, but I couldn't find our Union one."

"You did fine, son."

"I meant it when I said good luck."

Bishop watched the young man take his horse with Captain Creed's saddle down the alley and around the stock pens. He let him ride out of sight before stepping from the stables to where Hunk was waiting with their mounts.

Hunk said, "Think I'd be running out?"

Bishop got on the bay. "No, now you've got your own reasons for going back."

"That's a truth. Besides, I don't get far with this knee. Rawlins, now? We could do it in two days."

"Not without weapons." Bishop angled himself, and the rig adjusted with barrels down close to his knee, then locked for the long ride. He brought the bay around to one of the side streets.

The ferryman cranked on the rope that secured the flatboat to the other shore, pulling it closer to the other side of the river, a calm offshoot of the Colorado that split into smaller rushes of water along a wooded bank.

Colby stood by the ferry railing, his horse tied and his arsenal blanket-wrapped behind the saddle. He watched a kingfisher dive, miss, and fly off. "Those boys told me their father helped you with the building of the dock."

"I'm just the ferryman."

Colby was watching a bird arcing toward the trees. "And a fine one, too. You know everyone on the other side of the river? A little beyond the trees? Ever heard of a crazy white man, lives by himself making guns and bombs? Kills the Indians, then dances with the corpses?"

The line was taut, the ferryman cranking it through, taking them to the shore half a foot at a time and giving no heed to a word Colby was saying.

Colby pressed. "That's quite a legend, if it's true. Is it?"

"I'm just the ferryman, mister."

The kingfisher dove again, snapping up a minnow just under the surface.

"That's one of the largest of the species I've ever encountered. I envy you, my friend. You see and hear all kinds."

The ferryman stepped to open the bow railing, pulling it aside for Colby and his horse to get onto the bank. "How much money you got?"

The Fire Riders were two over the saddle, one of them shot in the face and the other with two bullets in the chest. Their horses were tied together and being led by a Rider with a wild gray beard, who'd been shot in the shoulder.

Hurricane was at the water trough, April Showers brushing him down, gently singing "The Little Old Cabin in the Lane."

Dev Bishop stood by, arms folded, smiling. "He likes you, girl." He turned at the screams in the yard.

Smythe crutched his way toward Gray Beard dropping from his red-spattered horse.

"They wouldn't buckle. None of 'em." Gray Beard said, shaking off his tunic. "I never been shot before."

Smythe said, "You did better than them, boy-o. What happened?"

Dev patted the little girl's shoulder before making his way to the middle of the yard as other Riders gathered round.

Gray Beard said, "We stopped a freight wagon on the old coach road, told them to give up part of their load to cross through, and they opened up on us." He swung his arm in circles, trying to find some comfort. "Sweet Mary's backside, this hurts."

Dev said, "Did you get anything out of them?"

"Just these two dead. And Phil, he owed me five dollars."

Smythe said, "Get to the medic. Take care of yourself."

Gray Beard started walking to the medical tent beyond the gunsmith. "This ain't supposed to happen. Folks are too afraid to go against us. These boys weren't afraid of jack."

Dev frowned. "We can't have this."

Smythe said, "Paradise is almost done. Just the way we want it, and run right. That'll be more money than any of the bloody hijackings."

Dev said, "Not if people think nothing happens if they don't pay." He raised a hand, catching the eye of an eager Rider, a kid with a Winchester.

Three shots were cracked off as one, and Gray Beard was done. Hurricane stirred at the sound, but May kept brushing, kept singing.

Smythe said to Dev as Riders picked up the body, "These men aren't the problem, right? Jesus, we're killing off more of our own than anyone!"

"He failed. There's been too much of that." Dev went to Hurricane, took a brush, and ran it over the horse's back and sides.

May was still humming and smiling.

Smythe said, "It's your brother, boy-o. They're making everyone defiant, taking their cue from him. 'The dead man who came back to life.' To wipe us out!"

Dev kept combing. "Are you quoting?"

Smythe nodded. "The *Police Gazette*. He's got the cover again."

CHAPTER EIGHTEEN
Three Talons

The woods along the slope were dense, the thickest pine branches overlapping each other from tree to tree, forming a dark green barricade. Moisture in the air mixed with that bit of cool drifting from the running creek a few yards away. All that should have let Bishop sit back in his saddle and take it in.

It was a natural calming place.

But Bishop lurched forward, keeping the bay very deliberately along the small cleared trail. He stopped once without speaking, then continued on. Hunk was nearly alongside. If he slowed, Bishop did as well, keeping the shotgun rig ever present within Hunk's eyesight.

Hunk said, "You're riding like we're going into the worst battle. I don't see it."

The trap sprung, the first pine crashed across the trail in front of them. Blocked, the horses chopped back. Bishop and Hunk tried for a run, but a trip wire snapped, propelling large pine branches from either side of the cut into their chests with cannonball force. Both men were knocked from their saddles.

Hunk crashed onto his jaw, then his knee, the pain bolting him. Bishop landed on his back, a huge boot pinning both barrels of the shotgun against the ground. A hand clamped instantly around his throat. The fingers were slippery with blood.

"Let's go, dead man."

Bishop knew the voice and brought up his knee, pounding into some bulging kidneys and forcing the bloody fingers to let go. He rolled away and sprang to his feet, slamming the shotgun up under the bearded chin of Noah Crawford.

Crawford yowled. "Jesus, Doc, if I had any teeth, you woulda knocked 'em all out!"

Bishop said, "Show me where you're cut."

Crawford pulled back the deer hide to run his hand along the rolling folds of his scarred belly, trying to find the knife wound. Blood had already soaked through his Union suit, but the injury was invisible to him.

"It was along in here. Mealy bastard used one of my own against me."

Bishop said, "Move your stomach."

Crawford used both knotty hands to hold up the flesh. "Knife I was making for years, recognized the handle. Goes in real smooth, fine edge. Whoever you stick don't know he's dead till he drops. Sold a lot of those."

Bishop traced small red streaks to a deep slice in Crawford's abdomen, the skin folding in on itself. "That's a good incision. Might as well have had you in an operating theater."

Crawford took the knife from a pocket, his blood drying on the long blade. "Told ya it was a good edge.

He knows what he's doing, and he's got the deadeye for both of ya."

Bishop said to Hunk, "Get my kit."

Crawford stopped Hunk from the horses with a bloody hand as large as a grizzly's paw. "I'll take care of myself."

Bishop was settled by a rusting steel grave marker, the last in a small row among four others in the clearing of the pine woods just down the trail from Crawford's dugout. The wet grass around the DR. JOHN BISHOP marker was tall, curling against the name.

Crawford said to him, "Sorry you ain't down there for real?"

"Yeah, most days I am." Bishop stood, his left hand on his marker, the shotgun rig automatically shifting into place with his movement.

Crawford nodded to the rig. "Still workin' fine. I hear the tales, take pride in that gun. It was a good job I done."

Hunk, bandaged fists clenched, stood into Crawford, thinking of a move. "Why you attack us?"

The mountain man was actually larger than Hunk, and looked down at him. Swathed in animal hides stitched together like an insane quilt, he wore a dead man's boots with blades cobbled to the toes and bearskin half-gloves on hands that were also clenched into fists.

Bishop answered the question. "If you'd reached my place, he'd have popped you off like turkeys in a run."

Crawford's beard was a thick tangle, crusted around the eyes, and didn't move when he spoke. "I don't know who you are, friend"—he shoved Hunk back—"but getting me riled is a big mistake."

Bishop said, "He's with me, Noah. That's enough."

"For now." Crawford dropped his paw. "That Colby wanted to know when you'd be along, then stuck me to see what I'd give up. Clamped my mouth. He said didn't matter; you'd be here sometime. Was real cocky about that, too. Left the blade in, said something about 'preparing.' Didn't care if I knew his name, thought I crawled away to die."

Bishop said, "You see a sniper's rifle?"

"Hell, he's got an arsenal with him." The voice burst through the hair again, pointing to an oak that had been split by lightning. "There's four bottles of bug juice Crows left to appease me. Bring one."

Bishop said, "So, you're still called Vóhpóóhe?"

"I'll always be White Claw. Among other things."

Hunk knelt by the split tree, finding the bottles and some leatherwork and necklaces of hanging bear's teeth all tucked into the trunk's scorched openings. He took a bottle, pocketed a necklace. "The Indians, they set all this out for you?

"So I'll leave 'em alone." Crawford grabbed the bottle and splashed some white whiskey on the wound. He took a deep breath at the searing pain. "That'll wake up your guts for sure!"

Bishop said, "Where was the claw when you got stuck?"

"On the kitchen table next to my coffee. A jackass mistake. He got me from behind while I was feeding the horses. Took a good Colt Lightning off me, too. I'm gettin' that gun back. How much ammo you got on you?"

"The bandolier's it. I was counting on you." Bishop went to the one grave set off from the rest. A wooden cross with a name long weathered away marked it, but its dirt was freshly turned. "I recall reading about a coffin full of weapons."

"What the hell you talking about, *recall*?"

Bishop said, "He could have a Gatling gun down there, and I know you got traps and gun stashes everywhere."

"Better take a drink 'cause you're damn out of luck. Business been draggin' for a year. There's nothing in that grave but an empty box."

Hunk stiff-walked to the bay and took the canvas sack with the Adams grenades from the saddle. "We have these two."

Crawford said, "You allowed them damn things to clank around like that? Could've lost a good horse."

Bishop said, "That's what we've got."

Crawford said, "I watched him set up in the trees behind the corral. Wait till the sun drops, and we'll Crow-pounce. Close in, hang his insides like the warriors do it."

"If he said he was prepared, he means it." Bishop's words were quiet. "He wants to face me down. You don't have to get between that."

Crawford took one of his giant steps to the graves, stepping to the other side of the markers. "Doc, we've got history, and both hate this bastard. Being stabbed don't bother me, but don't be actin' high-toned about it. Supper'll taste a lot better knowin' he's bled out." He turned to Hunk. "I take it you're in on this, since you're riding together."

"I'm Shotgun's prisoner."

Crawford snorted. "I'll be a fiddler's bitch!"

"I want this Colby guy, too." Hunk touched the stitching on the side of his head where his ear used to be.

"He did that? There ain't a whole man between the three of us!"

Bishop was sitting next to his own marker, taking a small pull from the bottle. "Awful stuff. I've been spending a lot of time around graves lately."

With a chuckle, Crawford grabbed the liquor back. "Yeah, what's that tell you?"

The sun had just vanished behind the treetops, down to the horizon, when Bishop walked toward the dugout from the small side trail cutting the edge of the woods. The night birds were starting their song and the horses in the corral, stolen from a pony express depot, stirred along the high fence, nudging each other.

The weapon lines were tight across his shoulders, the anchor chain biting his skin and drawing on the triggers as he moved a few steps closer to the whitewashed dugout wall decorated with Cheyenne symbols and a large painting of five metal talons dripping red letters that formed the word *Vóhpóóhe*. He stopped, the mechanics of the rig clicking into place and bringing it to elbow height.

There were footsteps. A leg dragging.

Bishop got clear, moving to the corral, then stopping at a pool of Crawford's blood by the fence.

Hunk took position by a corner of the building. They didn't exchange looks as he threw the Adams grenade toward the woods. Spinning, the interior fuse burned down.

The pine trees blew apart at the middle, tops falling forward, crashing into more trees as pulverized wood spread into the air. The first gunshots came from beside the explosion as if the shooting was from the burst of heat.

Bishop fired into the pines, blasting through the brown fog of wood and smoke at a target he could only guess was there. More shots rang out. He turned, bringing the rig up from his waist, holding it straight out to follow movement through the trees. A shadow. Something.

He fired the second barrel, and ran low for the dugout, breached, and reloaded, the echo of the grenade explosion still coughing through the woods. He waited until it faded. Silence. Then he heard a sound like bones breaking before two blasted-in-half trees crashed into each other, hitting the ground.

Shots tore from the far side of the woods at that moment, random gun flames in the dark.

Bishop shot at the position, then held, watching as Crawford sprang up from behind the corral's water trough, pulling the ribbon on the last grenade, and hurling it with all his force.

Fire burst with the second Adams, eating the tops of the pines, twisting them into the air upon detonation. Straight gunfire pumped from a corner of the woods at the same time, the slugs tearing into the corral fence. The horses charged out. They broke the rails, leaped, and ran as Bishop reloaded. He moved to the edge of the woods, dodging the horses and hunting for the target.

The rig adjusted itself, coming up to a middle-firing position as instinct made Bishop turn, pulling back on the trigger lines. Still turning, he saw Colby step from the shadows aside the house.

With two pistols raised, he fired the Remington Double Derringer first, then the Schofield. The slugs pounded Bishop's chest, knocking him down. Colby kept with the Schofield, every shot an explosion of force from the pistol.

The last horse jumped the corral fence, running from the sound, smoke, and fire.

Bishop lay on his back, duster torn by bullets, his left arm still twitching.

Colby moved to him, both pistols still aimed. "You were a hard kill, sir. I know your history well, but I confess I regret not knowing *you*, because I have a thousand questions—"

The first barrel blew through Colby's chest, sending him spiraling backwards as Bishop sat up and fired again, throwing him against a fence post before he dropped to the ground.

Bishop made it to his feet as Hunk moved to Colby and knelt by him. Colby's eyes were wide, fearful. Both pistols were still tangled in his fingers. Hunk gently took the guns, then clamped one massive hand over Colby's mouth and nose while looking down at the watch chain with his ear dangling.

Crawford whistled, then threw the long-bladed knife, which Hunk caught with his free hand. He tucked the blade behind Colby's ear and started to cut.

Colby's eyes were even wider as he recognized Hunk, and the realization of his last moment dawned. Then he went slack.

Hunk looked down at him like he was about to spit. "That's what I wanted, so he'd know it was me taking his last breath."

Crawford said, "You going to finish the job? Looks like he had a piece of you for a souvenir."

"Not important now."

"Doc?"

Bishop nodded, opening his duster and revealing a slab of thick buffalo hide across his chest. Slugs from the two guns were splattered flat against it. He pulled off the hide with his left hand and let the steel grave marker he was wearing behind it fall to the ground.

The dark was the dark, even after the bag was pulled from Chaney's head, and the bandages unwrapped from his eyes. He could feel someone pulling on the dressing of his facial wounds. "That's me, damn it! I'm already deeply scarred."

Chaney sat with his back against a cold stone wall, wanting his sight to adjust to the room and the shadows moving in front of him. Red tunics, ghosts of color, as they hovered in the two pitch-black doorways on the other side of the subcellar.

Chaney could see a bit more, taste the damp as he spoke. "Would one of you untie my hands? You're obviously in total control. Where would I run to?"

Startling him, Dev Bishop's voice came from behind Chaney. He stepped in front of him, holding a bellows camera. "Nowhere, so you'd best settle in."

"Settle in for how long, Mr. Bishop?"

Dev liked the recognition. "As long as it takes for you to write ten of those stories."

"I had no idea you appreciated my work."

"I don't. You're not telling things right."

"Oh, you want me to extol the virtues of your Fire Riders, rather than condemn? Not an easy task, sir, considering."

Dev had moved closer. "Smart aleck. I don't need help recruiting. They're lined up out the door. This is about you showing the world more than a stack of bodies and making a false hero out of the man with the shotgun."

"Not my choice."

Dev slapped Chaney's bandages. "Did we do that to your face?"

Chaney jerked his head back. "Your brother, Mr. Bishop, shot me. And killed one of my family."

Dev was considering his words under a laugh. "I see. So you're a coward, and that's why you write what you do."

"My editors claim that our readers admire your brother for, what they see as, standing up."

"Against?"

"Well . . . against your supposed aggression." Chaney quickly added, "Their words, not mine."

Even closer, Chaney felt Dev's words against his face. "Then you'll knock him down. Make your people understand that the worst thing they can do is favor him. You'll write about that and about tyrants like Chisum, who think they can own anything they lay eyes on. You do that?"

Chaney said, "Oh, yes. Yes, I can."

"The territory I control is open. Anybody can do anything they want as long as we're in for a piece."

"Just a tax."

"That's right, and we're a hell of a lot more fair than the Washington pettifoggers. No blood has to be spilled. Just follow the rules."

"That goes for myself, as well?"

Dev hauled Chaney to his feet, then handed him the camera as the hooded riders stepped from the deepest shadows, all with battle knives. "More for you, amigo, than anybody."

CHAPTER NINETEEN

Warriors

The ladle had been shoved into the coals under the soup pot, heating the handle to bending before Crawford slapped the hot metal against his knife wound, searing the flesh closed. He held it, belly hair burning back, skin sizzling until Bishop yanked it from his hands.

Tossing it aside, Bishop said, "It smells like that, it's cauterized."

Crawford roared, "That's how we doctor around here!"

Bishop snapped the shotgun rig from his elbow. "And I'm the one's crazy as a suck-egg mule?"

Crawford smeared the wound with a mound of bear grease then buttoned his long flannels. "You're the one wants to take on a whole goddamned army, not me."

"How're your ribs?"

"Two, maybe a third, broken."

"Bastard wasn't kiddin' with that Schofield. I know you saved me, Noah."

"But that ain't gonna be all, is it?"

"No."

Hunk said, "You got Apache here?" On the other side of the dugout, he was sitting on the edge of a rope bed covered in finely tanned hides, admiring the razored edge of a War Hawk Club.

Crawford said, "That's Comanche. Born to the fight, every one of 'em. A Commanch come at ya? You're pissin' and prayin' at the same time." He picked up the five-talon iron claw from the kitchen table and fit it over his right hand. "I was good with this, and that Commanch was the one pissin'!"

"How many you killed?" Hunk swiped the air with the blade.

"Raiding party come in here, grab some horses, and try for my damn head!" Crawford said. "His brothers took off, chasing my best stock, left him on his own to kill me."

Bishop said, "Always a mistake."

Crawford nodded. "That Commanch damn near got me. That war club was sticking out of my neck . . . but damn near don't count, do it? I laid his guts out so he could watch himself die. That's what scares 'em into the afterlife."

Hunk said, "Where is he, this Comanche?"

"I left him strung up for a while, to keep White Claw's legend going, then buried him down creek way someplace." Crawford moved to Hunk and opened his arms, showing the spears, shields, and axes hanging on the surrounding walls.

Hunk said, "These are all from men you killed?"

"Every damn one of 'em has blood on it, and not just mine."

Hunk looked up at a mural that covered the curved ceiling above the bed. Tribal warriors charged across the sky with shields and lances, their horses breaking through the clouds to Heaven. The flicker of the one candle by the bed gave the mural life, its shadows making the horses run, the braves cry out.

"All of those warriors riding there, you fought them?"

"Fought 'em all, and killed about half. My daughter painted it, to remind me that Indians ride to Heaven and I ain't going to be so lucky."

"Okay, White Claw." Bishop opened Hector's plans of the prison, laid them out on the kitchen table made from a tree stump. "Look at this. See what we need."

Crawford said, "That paper's for your ass. I was the first to sell army horses to them Riders. Gutted two who tried to short me, then they was good customers, bought regular."

Bishop said, "But you've never been in the fortress."

"It don't matter. See, they ain't gonna come at you one at a time, like that cocky bastard."

Hunk said, "There's more than a hundred at the prison."

"So how you gonna kill who you want to kill?" Crawford turned, punching at nothing with the steel talons. "You got that gun rig, but you need something that'll really bring blood to the claw."

Bishop regarded Crawford, then said, "The wagon by the shed."

It looked to have been an old dairy wagon, with a full-sized cooler that was painted dark red and yellow. Its sides were fringed in gold and purple, and large tassels dangled from the front and back. The door to the cooler had been replaced with stable half-doors for someone to lean out of, smiling. Light blue, it was secured with a heavy throw-bolt. The only other openings were circular air vents on either side of the cooler, repainted to look like a woman's mouth blowing kisses.

The driver's bench had been divided into two seats, with a special gun turret coming up between the legs of anyone riding shotgun.

Crawford said, "Pullin' a gun or pullin' your pecker, this is the wagon for ya." He held an oil lamp high, throwing dim yellow around them.

Bishop unbolted the split doors and peered inside to find a bed frame, mold-eaten mattress, dirty sheets, and pieces of a broken chamber pot.

Crawford said, "Fella who owned it, called it Rolling Temptations. Only had his wife working, but he did okay, until he got himself killed, and she retired."

Hunk swung himself into the turret seat. "We can shoot from here, maybe five minutes before we're dead."

Bishop said, "That's not where I'm going to be." He checked the screwed hinges on the split door before climbing into the cooler. His foot plunged through the flimsy wooden floor, the rotten planks splitting in half, revealing a false bottom underneath.

A raccoon scrambled out.

Crawford said, "He smuggled a lot of guns, some whiskey. If the laws stuck their nose in, he had his wife shoot 'em from the bed when they opened the back. Or he let 'em get their pants off, then shot 'em. Good customer, though."

Bishop shook his foot loose. "How're you fixed for powder, Noah?"

Crawford lowered the lamp, eyes narrowing. "Well-fixed, as usual."

Bishop dropped from the back. "We'll make some

cuts from the inside, pull the bolts holding the cooler, then pack the floor with powder."

"Lotta work. How long you been figurin' on this?"

Bishop snapped the breech on the rig and pulled the spent shells. "And I'm going to need some ammo."

With Bishop and Crawford pushing, Hunk pulled the wagon, backing it from the side of the dugout and over to the overhang where Crawford did his gun and smith work. He dropped the wagon's falling tongue and stepped into the work area, taking in the rows of calibrated barrel extensions, specially cut shoulder stocks, and pistol grips. Trigger and safety mechanisms were precisely laid out on two large workbenches, with fine tools beside them.

Crawford allowed himself a laugh. "Not what you figured from White Claw, huh?"

Hunk admired the pieces of a Winchester Repeater that were being refitted.

Crawford said, "Everyone claims the '73, but they ain't seen what I've done. They'll drop from heart attacks soon as they hear the cock."

"A clock maker in my village, his shop was looking like this."

"The doc's rig is the best thing I ever done."

Bishop came around the wagon, unhooking the trigger lines from the shotgun rig, letting them slacken, then bringing up his arm so that the double-barrel was in front of Crawford. "Now you've got to do better."

Crawford spit heavily and released the harness, pulling the rig from the amputated arm. The cup had rubbed the skin raw. He placed the rig on the workbench next to a box of .12-gauge brass casings.

Bishop turned to Hunk. "Pull out the floor from the back. Save the scraps."

Crawford put a can of black powder on the bench next to the casings. "Okay, Doc. We'll draw some blood, then show 'em some fire."

Hunk yanked out the flooring, tossing out the bed and the sheets as Bishop worked one-handed, knocking the bolts from the inside of the cooler with a hammer, then loosely setting them again. He took the screws from the door hinges, replacing them with wooden pegs as Hunk piled more trash from the back of the wagon.

Bishop said, "Add to the scrap pile all the metal bits you can find, then bundle it all in the old sheets."

Hunk said, "I was in a cave-in once. Most men I ever seen die. My boss got his head knocked in two, which was okay. You work this out, set off these bombs, we'll have a cave-in there, too."

Crawford packed old, reinforced ammo boxes with four scoops of black powder from a barrel, tamping, then closing and sealing each tight for pressure. Filling the false bottom, he laid the boxes side by side with a fuse connecting them, and then covered it all with a rolled canvas. He picked up several clay jugs of kerosene, putting them atop the canvassed boxes, along with the bundles of scrap wood, old gun parts, and metal shavings.

His face and beard crusting, Crawford smiled. "Blood on the claw."

Bishop set the kerosene and bundles, into the wagon, tucking them into corners of the floor or nestled between the walls and ceiling. Small nails held the bundles in place, and the jugs were tied in place.

Hunk worked underneath, hammering a wedge

between the iron plates, giving just enough room to pull the fuse to the black powder out from inside, then tie it off. He wiped grit from his eyes. "You got some more powder? One box, packed tight."

Crawford handed him the box. "What was that word you called me?"

Hunk tied the box under the driver's bench and secured it on either side with scraps of wood. "*Nemernic.* It means to you are the ass of a mule."

Crawford worked on the shotgun rig, adjusting the trigger tension. "I'll have to recall that one."

Hunk stood up, looked to Bishop. "We're taking a lot of Riders with us. Maybe all."

"That's the point. Don't forget Colby."

Crawford said, "Hell, I'm letting the wolves have that high-toned prick. Be disrespected like that? That'd really boil his shirt."

Bishop flattened his words. "We need him. He rides in back."

"You're the doctor. I'm just a goddamned gunsmith."

"Who has everything." Bishop held up a glass bowl of magnesium chips. "This stuff almost blinded me. You know how to finish this. I'm going to round up the horses."

Crawford poured out a powder mixture through a small funnel into the brass shell casings and said to Hunk, "He's going to get his war."

"When we fought, I saw his eyes, bloodred, and he killed everything. Then he was doctor again, fixed my leg. This time, I think he fights until he dies."

Crawford sealed the shells and loaded the rig. "So the doc's finally a warrior."

Hunk said, "I just hope your daughter's right about them getting to Heaven, for my own sake."

"Too late to worry about that, but I ain't gonna be denied my pleasures in the here and now."

Crawford pulled the claw over his right hand and marched to the corral, with Hunk following. He jammed the five talons into the back of Colby's body, deep between his shoulders. Hefting him up, he dragged him to the wagon. "Wish he could feel this, but does me some good."

Hunk gathered Colby's feet and lifted, dumping him into the back of the cooler. He settled, dead weight, on top of the tarped explosives.

Crawford bolted the half-doors. "That necklace from the tree, keep it."

"I took for my wife. I want to send her something before . . . before we do this."

Crawford shook the metal talons clean. "It's Cheyenne. She'll like it."

The rusting steel grave marker settled into the soft ground quickly with Bishop leaning on it, pressing down. He backed up a step, seeing his crooked marker between White Fox and her mother. His name had been destroyed by Colby's bullet strikes, but that felt appropriate to him.

The sun was rising off the near Colorado peaks. The morning felt fresh, the clearing better than it had the night before. The bay and the stolen horses were in sight, drinking from the small stream that followed the woods.

"It was your reputation brought that bastard here. Told me he'd read every word printed about you, even something in French. Cocky bastard."

Bishop didn't turn at Crawford's voice, just stood in front of his own empty grave.

Crawford said, "I put up them markers so folks would think you dead, get you a little peace. But you wouldn't have it, would you?"

"I tried."

"Crazier than a suck-egg mule!"

"The bloodier the legend, the more fear in the heart of my enemies. Isn't that what you told me?"

Crawford got down from his horse, carrying the shotgun rig and bandolier. "Sounds about right."

"I never said a word to those papers. They came up with everything. I'd never put your daughter into it."

"You took care of her, Doc. That's how come I helped you this time. That prisoner says you got the blood eyes. I know what that is, 'cause it happened to me."

"A blood vessel breaks under pressure."

Crawford said, "That's a doc's way of figuring things 'cause then you don't have to think about becoming something else."

Bishop was someplace else. "It's not that."

Crawford crouched by the marker with ARCHISHA—MOTHER AND WIFE—SHE LIVES ALWAYS scrolled across it and pulled away some new weeds around it. "She couldn't take it. Hung herself instead of living with a wild killer. That ain't gonna happen to my daughter, not ending up here beside her mother."

Bishop said, "You got no worries, Noah."

"Hell, she'd never do herself in, but you might get her killed."

"White Fox has got nothing to do with me anymore."

"All right then."

Crawford held out the shotgun and the bandolier with the new shells. "Dragon's Breath. Anybody tries for you, that's the taste of hell."

Bishop took the rig and ammunition, tucking the gun under his left arm "'Taste of hell.' They can use that in the *Gazette.*"

"Your idea," Crawford said. "However this ends up, it's going to make history some way."

"Maybe you can sell the marker for a few dollars."

"A *few* dollars never interested me, Doc." Crawford kicked at several bent and twisted Colt pistols stacked behind the grave markers. Scorched pieces of twine were attached to the triggers, dangling loose about a foot. "What's all this?"

"Found them when I was rounding the horses. Colby tied pistols to the trees, cocked them to fire with the force of the grenade blast, give him some cover. He knew what we'd be using."

"But we still got the best of the little bastard. He wasn't no warrior." Crawford spit long. "You leave me all his fancy guns?"

CHAPTER TWENTY
Burning Down

The gold tassels hanging from the Temptation Wagon jiggled back and forth as Hunk braked on the side of a small road that gave them a clear view of the prison in the distance.

It was a squat outline against blue mountains, with the blasted-apart towers and falling-down walls giving the impression of ruins, just as intended. There were no riders approaching it, no stray horses running.

Hunk said, "Like nobody's there."

Bishop was tying his bay to the back of the wagon. "Which means they're all there."

"Yah, probably. And getting ready for a big operation. Lots of money, lots of promises."

Bishop took the shotgun rig and the bandolier with the Dragon's Breath shells from his saddlebag and handed them up to Hunk on the driver's bench.

"You captured me and my arsenal. That should restore your standing with the Riders."

"My what?"

Bishop said, "When they haul me out of the back, just make sure you go along, carrying the rig. We've got to get inside the main building, then follow the tunnels."

"Maybe I find gold, and you find your brother."

"Lock me up."

Bishop moved to the back of the wagon, throwing open the half-doors and climbing inside. He got around Colby's body, which was wrapped and tied, and made it to a corner. The explosives, kerosene, and shrapnel were all in their places around him and properly covered.

Hunk was at the door. "So now you're *my* prisoner."

"Just get us inside. And when the battle starts, don't be near this thing."

"How we get to be comrades?"

Bishop, decapitated by the deep shadows, said, "A common enemy. Something Mr. Chisum believed in."

"So does your brother, believe me."

"What's your name?"

"Bogdan."

"Hope I see you again."

Hunk snorted, shut the doors, and bolted them, leaving Bishop in total darkness.

The string of fresh horses came first, followed by a howitzer, and then two flat wagons of cavalry rifles. Red-hooded riders flanked the stolen weapons, riding in a showy circle around the prison yard as Chaney fixed his camera to a tripod.

He was focusing on ten Fire Riders standing with guns shouldered and sabers drawn, the horses and cannon passing behind them. He was experimenting. Trying to catch motion as an energetic blur, offsetting the posed Riders in the foreground.

Chaney had told the prison telegraph boy, "I'd like to leave one image behind with my name on it. It'll be worth more than the price of a tacky newspaper. Hell's rings, they're going to kill me anyway, so why not try?"

He opened the lens exposure, and extended the bellows to its full length, before changing the position of the flash pans to throw optimum light. Chaney thought for a moment, eyed the Riders, then moved the pans again.

Dev Bishop watched the yard from the small, barred window in the old warden's office, with Tomlinson beside him, his two daughters wrapped tightly around their father's legs. "This will be on every front page."

Tomlinson said, "The howitzer's a good addition and very effective for certain assaults, but you have an entire town to think about. That's your income stream."

Dev glanced back at the open ledger on his desk surrounded by a pile of notes and summaries. "Your world's on the desk. The howitzer, maybe that's my world."

Both girls pulled on Tomlinson's knees for attention, and his hands went gently to them. "Begging your pardon, Mr. Bishop, but you're not seeing what change is coming."

Dev was looking down into the prison yard again, past the horses and men to connect with Smythe. "I do, accountant. You do not. Not the way it matters."

Smythe gave Dev a wave from where he was by the open front gates, leaning on his crutches. He was watching the road that led to the entrance, seeing something fast approaching, and had to grin. "I'll be a cockeyed son of a bitch." Then he yelled, "Pickets! Make a line!"

* * *

Hunk steered the Temptation Wagon into the prison yard. Even seeing all the familiar faces pointing rifles and pistols, he didn't snap the team into a run. He slowed. The bay, still hitched to the back, slowed too, snorting.

His wounded leg was throbbing, and he felt moisture around the stitching where his ear used to be, but Hunk ignored those nerve stabbings, and brought the wagon to a stop beside the target range. He tossed a hand to the red hoods aiming at him.

He listened for a sound from Bishop inside the wagon, but there was nothing, just the gold tassels rapping against the purple sides. Guns followed Hunk climbing off the driver's seat, landing stiff-legged, just as Smythe dragged himself over from behind the Gatling gun, taking a small-caliber Colt from his belt as he moved.

Smythe said, "Well, this is like seeing a Highland ghost."

"Because you send those *câini* to kill me?"

"I know some of your talk, boy-o. Those were your brother Riders, supposed to bring you in, but you didn't give them much chance."

Smythe leaned by the horse team, the pistol casual in his hand. The other guns were moving in closer to Hunk, a foot at a time. One kid pulled off his hood, wiped the sweat from his eyes, but never dropped aim of his rifle and bayonet. Hunk disregarded all and walked to the back of the wagon.

Smythe said, "You're travelling in interesting style, boy-o."

Chaney turned his camera around, focusing on Hunk and all the weapons pointed at the same target as if aimed at a giant rattlers' nest.

Hunk brushed a Rider aside with a massive hand, stood beside the bay, and said to Smythe, "You know this fine horse?"

He threw over the bolt, opening the doors, then took Colby's body by the ankles, pulling it out, and letting it sag to the ground at Smythe's feet. It was a tangled bundle, with Colby's head exposed, face slack, and eyes filmed over.

"The fancy talker. You give him special job to get the man what belongs this horse. And look." Hunk pushed on Colby's sagging body with the toe of his boot. "Look how he failed."

Smythe said, "Killing Mr. Colby, now that's a bold move."

"Yah, and this." Into the back of the wagon, Hunk barked, "Get out of there. Now."

Dev was leaning into his office window, palms flat against the wall, watching the yard as his brother climbed from the wagon.

John Bishop's only hand was in the air, surrendering to his brother's men.

Dev's breath caught somewhere deep inside him.

By the wagon, Hunk said, "See. I'm the one didn't fail."

John Bishop finally lowered his left arm and looked to Hunk when the first rope wrapped around his neck, pulling him off his feet. He clawed, the rope being pulled tighter by one Rider, choking, while another lashed his ankles tight.

Dev shouted the order through his barred window. "The Tomb!"

Some Fire Riders heard him.

Excited and laughing, Chaney captured it all, switching out negative plates as Bishop was dragged across the yard, twisting in the dust, Riders running alongside.

Victory shots popped the air while the old bullet maker tossed empty brass like it was confetti bouncing off Bishop's chest. Smythe said to Hunk, "Very well done, boy-o. I'd give you full marks."

Hunk watched John Bishop for a moment—a roped prisoner struggling before he was hauled into the old cell block—then reached under the driver's seat, taking out the double-barreled rig and the ammunition bandolier. He said to Smythe, "Everything, all from this Shotgun."

"Devlin will be most appreciative. I'll see to it."

With the Colt aimed at Hunk's gut, Smythe pulled the rig away from Hunk. "How many of my men did you get killed in Myrtle? You had a case of grenades, and still lost everyone. Didn't even bring back Chisum's herd."

Hunk felt a bayonet's jab at the base of his spine.

Smythe split the breech of the rig and examined the shells. "How many of my men, boy-o?"

Fire Riders took the horse team bridle, and led the wagon to the other side of the yard.

Hunk watched his prize capture rolling off and said to Smythe, "He wanted the brother more than anything. I figured that would be enough to make me all right. Take me inside so I can show my prisoner."

Smythe shook his head in wonder. "Aye, you've got as much brains as a mountain of slag."

The giant's moves were unexpectedly fast. Hunk

turned, grabbing the rifle and bayonet from the Rider behind him. Wrenching it upward, he nearly bent the barrel. The Rider fired, shooting wild. Hunk pounded him down with the butt of the gun, spun, and buried the blade deep into the chest of another Rider attacking.

Hunk's voice was a roar, jerking the speared Rider off the ground, then pitchforking him across the yard. His dead weight smashed into the red hoods by the rifle targets.

The moment of silent shock offered only breath and heartbeats. as Hunk swiped his stiff leg into Smythe, taking him off his crutches. He freed the bay, swung on, and charged.

The Riders opened fire. Gunshots flew and orders were shouted. Smythe rolled onto his hip, shoving his dead legs aside with both hands, then leveling the Colt, shooting twice. A slug blew Hunk's shoulder, spraying red, knocking him sideways. He stayed on the horse, leaping over the howitzer, and running beyond the prison gates.

Across the yard, Chaney clicked the shutter release on the bellows camera and threw his head back, shouting, "Yes, yes, indeed!" He looked up to the warden's office window, and Dev Bishop was gone.

The broken-stone floor sliced John Bishop as he was pulled through the corridors and down the steps to the main cell block, the rope tightening around his throat. His eyes rolled and pain in his head erupted as they let him lie, a crowd of Fire Riders moving in around him.

He saw the little girl with the breathing device over her mouth, watching.

The device he'd made.

April Showers waved, saying something into her mask as the trap door opened. Bishop was picked up by the shoulders and ankles and hurled to the cells below.

She could hear his falling as she drew again through the tube attached to the oxygen box.

Beside April Showers, Dev also watched his brother. Holding a Navy Six, he said, "That's not the man to favor, little girl. Not to help your papa."

"He helped me." She looked up at Dev and kept inhaling deep.

The Fire Rider with the German accent kept his right arm extended, aiming the rifle as he brought his horse closer to Hunk. The two flanking him rode up, then fell into step beside the German, waiting for orders. They had all sprung from the hidey-holes outside the gates, and had trailed Hunk to this point.

The German was straining, but had his aim. "That was a good shot, a good one the English made, but not for killing."

One of the Riders, the scalps of Union troopers hanging from his belt, nodded toward Hunk, who was now barely on the bay, bloody arms dangling, eyes closed, his chin pressed against his chest.

The German said, "That's not all his blood."

The Rider said, "He's bled out deader than Honest Abe, which is the only honest thing he ever did."

Hunk blew a hole in the Rider's chest before he could turn and share the laugh with his buddies. The other Rider flanking the German was surprised, never even getting his gun above the leather before Hunk shot him perfectly between the eyes.

Both fell from their horses, leaving the German

pointing the rifle at Hunk, who, in turn, had one of White Claw's specialty .45s pointed at the German. The recut grip fit perfectly in Hunk's large hand, and the new trigger guard accommodated his fingers.

The barrel of the pistol seemed inescapable, and Hunk said, "You're not shooting, Karl."

"I can, still."

"You'd have already. You see how they turned on me. They can do the same for you."

The German kept the rifle up. "Ride out, Bogdan."

"Ride with me. Let me show you something. You'll have the rifle." Hunk urged the bay to a run, and the German followed, holding the Winchester out to his side, aimed at Hunk's bleeding shoulders. The two men rode for a time, circling back toward the prison, then taking their horses down a series of grassed hills to a small road that led to the oldest part of the structure.

Like the rest of Rawlins Penitentiary, the stone wall was fire damaged, with large sections taken down by the cellar explosion from years before. Rock and corroded steel were piled up, forming their own new wall.

Hunk got off his horse, taking a few steps to where a trench had been dug along the foundation.

The German asked, "What are you showing me?"

"Money, Karl. All Bishop's money, buried in the tunnels here."

"A fairy tale I've heard before."

"A kid was here. He told me. Explosives also buried here, like we used in the mines."

Hunk knelt, grabbing at large sections of muddy earth inside the trench and digging it out with his fingers, revealing the edge of a dynamite case. "See? He's right about the bombs. He said there could be gold, too. Help me find, and I'll give you share."

Karl had the rifle aimed downward from his saddle. "They promised a reward for you."

"Dev Bishop or the English with no legs, they ever pay extra? For anyone? Or given us fairly for what we stole? No, but they shot me quick enough. There's a crawling tunnel there. That's how they get out. Leave us to hang."

Karl quietly housed a shell, cocking the repeater.

Hunk moved to him, the end of the rifle barrel almost flush with his chest as he looked up at his friend.

The German said, "I only know what they tell me to do."

"If you're not joining, I need another gun." Hunk grabbed the rifle, jamming it inward, then yanking it hard, snapping the German's arm at the elbow.

He screamed as Hunk took the weapon, checked it.

"I didn't shoot, Karl. Gave you a chance. Get more men if you want, but I'd go home to my wife. Now." Hunk swatted the German's horse, watched them dart back up the hill, and away. Then, he pried open a case of dynamite.

The young woman and the boy were smeared with blood.

"—*as beautiful as the day I married you . . .*" John Bishop's voice was a drifting whisper in his mind. His mouth parted, thinking he was speaking, but words were a dried nothing. Pain streaked behind his eyelids as he turned his head, reaching out for the photograph of his wife and son, curled into a loving embrace. It was his favorite.

But wife and son were soaked through red, and their image, their faces, crumbled in Bishop's hand as he tried to hold them, the pieces sticking to his fingers.

"You're nearly dead . . . and closer to them now than you've been in years, brother. You should thank me." Dev Bishop was halfway down the iron steps leading from the main cells to the condemned underground where prisoners sat in darkness, waiting for their turn with the hangman. It was called the Tomb because it got them used to being buried. He had the Navy Six and was gesturing toward an old cell, the door twisted apart. "That's where I was the day you came. That last one, remember?"

"Killed—"

"What?"

John Bishop tried speaking again, but nothing came out. He crooked his neck, taking in the empty cells from where he was lying. Bent metal bars became skeletons and the stone walls, stained by blood and fire and stretching upward into nothing but black, gave the feeling of a deep pit. A stench of rotting, something sweet and dead, stung Bishop as he slowly eased himself up, resting his only forearm on the bundle next to him.

It was Colby, still wrapped and bound, with the ripe setting in. His "John Bishop Target File" was littered across him, those family papers and photographs sticky with his blood.

Dev said, "Surrounded by death, but you're a doc. Used to it. That's one of my men, a real professional gentleman, and you killed him. How many dead is it, brother? One story I read declared over forty. I'd double that. I think it's right—you and one of mine that you shot apart—buried in the same pit."

In the tunnel behind the Tomb, Hunk had stopped crawling, wedging himself against a boarded and bricked access way sealed over with mud. His shoulders touched either side of the tunnel walls, and there was no room for him to raise his head as he slipped a quarter stick of dynamite up through his jacket with the tips of his fingers until he could grab it with his teeth and drop it in front of him.

He heard Dev Bishop on the other side of the wall. "Only one life have I personally ended, and I'm the outlaw. You're the hero. Funny world, ain't it?"

John Bishop, surrounded by the cells, could see his brother standing, holding the gun.

"We're . . . supposed to . . . blood."

"Going to try about being brothers? Hell, the day you was born, I was finished." Dev got louder. "Now that's a fact. You got it all, so I made my own way, run territories, command these men."

"Mae . . . maniacs."

"Yeah, a few locos, but mostly soldiers nobody needed anymore, and raw-backs looking for work, half of those not talking American. Hell, I couldn't read or write till a year ago. Not bad."

Bishop was sitting up. He slapped his right hand in a puddle of rainwater, brought it to his face, drinking what he could. Aware of movement—something in the dark beyond him, he said, "I did . . . nothing to you."

Dev had raised the pistol a bit, but stayed his place. "Nothing *to* me, or *for* me. Dumbest thing, you comin' here to visit. Getting yourself set up. A leader can't have no family ties. That's one way he gets brought down." He took a step down with his right leg, bracing himself on the landing to absorb the kick of the Navy Six. "You had your fine time, and fine life. I had this."

Bishop's words cut against his vocal chords as he moved his left hand beneath Colby's wrapped body. "Kill . . . killed my family."

"You've caused me a hell of a lot of trouble, and all because I couldn't put a bullet in you my own self."

Bishop pulled Colby to him as Dev fired the first shot, punching the corpse in the back and legs, thudding dead tissue and bone.

The gun flames lit the Tomb, the sound bouncing off the stone walls a thousand times, colliding every moment.

In the first jail cell, the access panel from the tunnel split open, pushed out by Hunk's knees and elbows.

Dev fired again, the slug biting Bishop's leg as it tore into the cloth wrapping Colby's body. Bishop reached in to free the gun he'd put in the dead man's hand.

Red hoods charged from the back cells, shooting wild. Bullet strikes ripped the floor and Colby's body. John Bishop still shielded himself, trying for the gun.

Hunk tossed the quarter dynamite, the explosion blowing apart the wall, sending pieces of the cell, section of the door, flying. A hood turned, as a bent iron bar spun into him, piercing his chest and knocking him dead off his feet.

Hunk jammed the Winchester through the access way and opened up, taking down two Riders who were trying to stand after the force of the blast.

Outside rang the clanging of a general alarm.

Dev stumbled on the stairs. Holding Colby's body, Bishop couldn't free the pistol, so he squeezed the trigger with Colby's stiff fingers. The shots blasted through the corpse bag, cutting Dev at the hip.

Hunk tore through the access way into the Tomb, shooting a Rider charging from behind the iron stairs.

Bishop brought Colby's arm up and shot the last Rider in the chest.

It was over in seconds, Hunk's and Bishop's ears were ringing like church bells as they made it to the iron stairs. Spots of Dev's blood led to the trapdoor, which was closed and barred tight.

Bishop crawled back to Colby's body, pushing aside the torn bits and pieces of the target file until he found one of his wedding pictures with only its edges stained. He slipped the picture into his shirt. Hunk gave him White Claw's pistol before clearing the wood and brick from the tunnel access.

Hunk went in first, scraping his way against the earth walls. Bishop took himself along on his one arm, the slug from Dev's gun working deeper into his leg.

The alarm was constant, but dulled by the tunnel.

They hauled forward, rats running across their shoulders, then down their arms. They kept moving. Faster. Bishop's amputated right arm shook the rats off, his left propelling him to the tunnel's end.

The crawl dumped them into an open area, part of the original prison's root cellar. Hunk twisted himself onto the floor. Bishop rolled out, rats scattering after.

The room's damp was years thick, and what light there was snuck in around the old trap for the slide that had been the vegetable scuttle.

Bishop said, "We can't have them using that."

Hunk lit a full stick of dynamite and threw it into the crawl.

CHAPTER TWENTY-ONE
Detonations

Minutes before, Smythe had adjusted his crutches, bringing himself a foot closer to the Temptation Wagon parked on the yard near the bullet maker's.

Chaney was checking the image on his wet-plate camera, directing four Riders behind Smythe to hold their rifles, "in that Geronimo pose." He said to Smythe, "Hoist your victory. Be proud, now."

Flash pans were aimed directly at the subjects, and all had eyes strained open with expressions frozen— serious. Smythe smoothed his suit lapel and held the shotgun rig high.

The pans burst white-yellow, exactly as the first dynamite explosion from the tunnels rumbled the ground.

A kid asked, "Are—are we being attacked, sir?"

Smythe ordered, "Sound the general, and all Riders to defense positions! Battle ready! Now, ladies! NOW!"

The kid rang the alarm bell standing in the corner of the yard.

Riders snatched guns from the racks, ran to stations along the walls, and climbed ladders to sniping perches, hoisting extra ammo cases by rope and tackle. Tarps were lowered, disguising potential targets as the bullet maker slapped pistols into the hands of Riders running for the corral, saddling horses, bringing them out.

The howitzer was rolled into place, aimed through a port in the front gate, facing the oncoming enemy. It was loaded and primed.

Smythe raised himself on his crutches, pleased, before taking himself to the main building, the rig hanging from his shoulder. Riders dashed around him, taking up weapons and throwing salutes that Smythe returned with pride. He got himself to the top of the main cell block, looking down as Dev slammed the trapdoor to the Tomb shut, then bolted it.

Pain threw Dev off balance, blood from his hip painting his right leg. He recovered. "Call off the alarm!"

"You need doctorin'."

Dev went up the main steps, favoring his leg and cocking a glance. "I know you gave the order so take the men off the wall, Smythe. I'm in command."

"I know, but I ain't ignoring that blast or who shot you. The men are at the ready and damned fast."

Dev wiped his blood onto his hand. "They're still not like the Apache. That's what we need for raids. How you need to train them."

Smythe chose his words. "The men are ready for *this fight*, son." He held up the shotgun rig.

Dev dismissed it as if talking about his brother. "He's in the Tomb, dying. Means nothing now." Before Dev reached the metal landing, Hunk's second dynamite charge exploded in the crawl tunnels.

* * *

Bishop and Hunk came up from the cellar by the old service stairs and moved into the main corridor, Hunk with the Winchester, Bishop with the specialty pistol. Both took a few steps then held, listening for movement in the maze of narrow halls and accesses. Bishop wagged his arm, getting used to shooting lefty. Thumbing the hammer, Hunk turning quickly from the waist, firing two slugs into the throat of the Rider at the end of the corridor.

The Rider was collapsing to the floor as Bishop fired down the hallway, laying out two more running up from the opposite side. Clean head shots to both. Coming around, he killed a third, brandishing a saber.

Again, it was over in seconds. Hearts stopping before the last of the gunshot echo faded off.

Bishop left most of the third red hood on the wall, quickstepped around Hunk, and walked deliberately down a far length that turned into the open hallway of the second floor. He stopped, suddenly looking down at the black-haired little girl holding the breathing mask to her face. They were feet from the door to the warden's office, Tomlinson standing behind April Showers, with May Flowers' arms wrapped around his waist.

He carried a small satchel, and they were all in their travelling clothes. April Showers' device-breathing was as loud as the alarm. "Are you coming with us?"

"Later."

Bishop nodded toward the door. "My brother?"

Tomlinson said, "Smythe went in with your gun. That's all that I saw. I'm taking care of my family."

Bishop scooped April Showers under his left arm and carried her to a small alcove away from the office. May Flowers ran after her sister, with Tomlinson beside.

He looked to Bishop, then called out, "Smythe! I need to get in the office!"

Smythe said from behind the door, "I told you to scoot you and your girls out of here!"

Bishop and Hunk took places on either side of the door, weapons raised. Bishop, coiled, eyes washing red, signaled Tomlinson to try again.

"Is anyone there with you? Devlin, is he there?"

Gunshots ripped the door and frame and into the corridor, hitting the walls. Tomlinson pulled his girls to the floor, covered them both as Bishop shot the large hinges apart, the iron sparking.

Hunk sledgehammered the wood, splitting it in half, and they plowed into the office. Bishop fired over Hunk's shoulder, hitting Smythe at the warden's desk.

Smythe got off two more shots, one slug skidding against one of Hunk's ribs, the other missing. With Bishop and Hunk before him, he let the pistol sag in his hand. The office was wrecked, their guns casually aimed.

Everyone was wounded.

"You aimed high, Doctor. Hit my shoulder. That was on purpose, I'm sure." Smythe, his face pulped, looked to the safe in the corner, door wide, and money gone. "Aye, you're too late."

The shotgun rig and bandolier were laid out on the desk as trophies, and Smythe pushed them toward Bishop, his movement opening his jacket, revealing the wound in his stomach, blood spreading wide and dark. He slumped back in the leather chair with the bullet hole. "Your brother didn't shoot high. You really set him off. You're the one man he can't seem to kill. He beat me with your rig, then shot me for good measure. After cleaning us out, of course." Smythe actually laughed at this last.

Bishop said, "You've got a chance to survive your wounds, if we get you out."

"Can't help being a doc?" Smythe pounded on his

unfeeling legs. "I'd not be looking forward to more of this. Struggled along, goin' home a rich man. Maybe buy me-self a new pair of legs, or at least a sweet strumpet for a bride."

Smythe raised the pistol.

Hunk pulled up the Winchester, cocking it.

"You're taking it all down, are you? Everything we built?"

Bishop said, "This place should be ashes."

"And then his little town?"

"If that's where he's hiding."

Smythe said, "When I was chief guard, I called this the Abyss, from *Dante's Inferno*, running the last circle of hell. Then your brother started talkin', and I helped him take over. I was conjuring something great and followin' a man what couldn't read or write. My old dad's laughin' from his grave at a fool son."

Bishop fit the rig over his half-arm and bloody shirt, settling into the amputee cup.

Smith said, "These fellas trained well and are finally gettin' it. It won't be no easy battle, even for you, Doc."

"I never wanted it to be," Bishop said, slipping his left arm through the shotgun brace, bringing the trigger lines tight.

Hunk opened a box of cigars on the desk, and grabbed a fistful, saying, "But we will be inflicting pain."

Smythe had the pistol angled to his temple and said to Hunk, "Of that, I have no doubt. Never seen anyone stronger than you, boy-o, or more tilted than the doctor. Accountant, you're keeping your girls in the hallway, yes?"

Tomlinson gathered the girls to him, but April Showers twisted away, trying to see, as Smythe fired the shot.

"You've protected my girls so far. I just want to get them to safety."

Bishop said, "And the satchel of money."

"There'll be more men coming."

Bishop was tying off the bandolier as they made their way down the corridor, Tomlinson and his girls leading.

Hunk said "The kid, he showed us where there could be treasure. Made a map."

April Showers ran ahead and around the corner to the open landing that brought all the lead ways to the old and new prisons together. She stood in front of one of the fire-scorched portraits in the gallery of previous wardens. "I also told that lady-talkin' man about this place. Go ahead, you're the scary giant."

Hunk took hold of the painting and lifted, removing it and an attached section of the wall, wood painted as stone, that hid the way to the old execution chamber.

Tomlinson said, "Warden's escape."

Bishop's head was down, pain increasing with his heart beat, eyes flooding red. "The stores?"

Hunk kept the cigar in his teeth. "And treasure."

Tomlinson said, "You'll find what you need."

April Showers tightened the ties around Bishop's arm "Sometimes, thinking about you gives me night-mares. Other times, okay."

Tomlinson took the hands of his daughters and quickstepped them away. The sisters turned, wrinkled their noses, then ran with their father.

Out of sight, May Flowers started to sing, the beauti-ful sound drifting back.

Bishop and Hunk went through the false wall and onto a dirt slope that had been graded by the wheels of carts weighted by stolen weapons. They made it halfway.

Standing guard, a Rider with two revolvers stepped out from behind a stone arch. He tried to say some-thing cocky as he shot.

The flash of the Rider's guns and the magnesium-fire explosion of Dragon's Breath from the shotgun collided in midair. The flame swallowed the Rider, then the black powder and buckshot blast tore his chest and threw him backwards off his feet, his body open and red tunic on fire.

He rolled off the slope to the chamber floor.

Bishop pulled the shell and reloaded from the bandolier. "Blood on the claw."

In the prison yard, Riders separated themselves into patrol units, charging the main building, following the gunfire. They broke on either side to close in when ordered.

His daughters on either side of him on the driver's bench, Tomlinson braked his prairie schooner with the wildly colored canopy at the main gate. Two Riders standing with the howitzer blocked the way out.

"We have business to conduct for Mr. Bishop. Open the gates," Tomlinson ordered.

One of the Fire Riders stepped forward. "Yeah, and where the hell in creation is he?"

Sweaty and with his hood pulled back, the other one said, "Somebody's giving us what for!" He pulled the cannon aside.

Tomlinson pushed his glasses up on his nose and gave the reins a quick jostle. The wagon lurched forward. Chaney ran up from behind and crawled in. Rolling back, he tucked his legs under his knees, camera and negatives cradled in his arms like newborns.

Tomlinson had the team out of the prison gates, his snout-nosed daughters singing, *"Yes, we will gather at the river; the beautiful, the beautiful, river—"*

Tomlinson patted the valise next to him. "That's good, dears. Give them one last chance to hear it."

In the old execution chamber, rotting nooses hung above a gallows platform. Empty grenade casings and cannonballs were stacked on its thirteen steps.

Hunk said to Bishop, "Stretch the neck. Your brother, he'd threaten that some days."

They managed around the crates labeled PROPERTY OF U.S. CAVALRY, THE ARMY OF THE CONFEDERACY, THE UNION NAVY, THE NAVY OF THE CONFEDERATE STATES, VIRGINIA VOLUNTEERS, SMITH & WESSON GUN WORKS. Hoods and tunics were in a large pile next to Apache spears, next to machetes, next to clubs, next to battleship shells, and next to mines.

"Your brother thinks he's a conqueror. I just wanted money."

Bishop said, "This . . . place can't be his monument." He tore open a box of .12-gauge shells and filled his pockets. "I'll get the front gates, take the cannon. You set off this lot and bring down the cells."

"Doctor, maybe a better way. Your bay's on the other side. Get it. Find your brother. I'll do this." Hunk's wounds spattered the top of his boots. He wiped them on his trouser legs. "I'm not going nowhere." His words weren't reaching Bishop.

The doctor loaded a regular shell in one barrel of the rig, Dragon's Breath in the other. "I can give us two minutes. Cross the yard then get the wagon."

Hunk watched him reach with his left arm and put two fighting knives into the right side of his belt. "This is what you always wanted, I think. I see what you are now. *Răzbunare este pace.* Revenge is peace."

* * *

Moving as they did when raiding houses with Quantrill, shooting innocents, Fire Riders with rifles ran the hall to the warden's office, then held by the smashed doorway, ready to shoot to pieces the first thing that moved, or made a sound. For that moment, everything was still.

One Rider gave a nod, and they peeled into the office, stepping over the wreckage. They found Smythe, a bullet hole in his temple and all the money gone.

The same Rider said, "In on this attack, took the easy way, knowing we'd hog-hang him and cut his throat."

Hunk crouched by some barrels, leveling the Winchester, covering Bishop from behind. The rifle felt heavier to him, his hands and eyes wet from strain.

Bishop looked over his shoulder and touched the brim of his hat before stepping through the blown-apart section of the old wall. He threw aside the disguising canvas and walked into the day, the rig leveled from his hip, White Claw's pistol held confidently in his left hand.

It took seconds for him to take in the positions of the Riders around the yard, the closeness to the horses, the howitzer, and his final target, the Temptation Wagon. He'd work around the base of the high wall, taking out any men there, reload, keep moving toward the wagon to get underneath.

Bishop hadn't taken his next step when a Rider scaling the back wall shouted, alerting the yard, then opened up with a revolver. Bishop shot once, cutting him through the eye.

Hunk cracked off cover fire.

Red hoods charged from behind the med tent as Bishop moved, firing the first .12-gauge barrel to the chest of one, turning and then shooting the Dragon's Breath.

Fire erupted from the barrel, slamming a second Rider backwards, his hood on fire. The buckshot tore through him, then burning and wounding a third.

Tunics were in flames as Riders dragged away the dying and dead. Screams and confused orders. Hunk didn't let up, pumping shots into two more. Bishop fired precisely with the pistol, dead-hitting four Riders running for horses. They spun to the ground.

Bishop made it to the old barricades. He reloaded the pistol and the rig. Slipping a Dragon shell from the bandolier, the oil from the beaver skin pelt sliding the brass into the double-barrel, then making a single movement snapping it shut.

The blood washed through his eyes, completely staining his vision. Riders' red tunics were gray moving targets. Gray uniforms. He waded in, not waiting for the first shot or giving surrender any chances. Attacking and advancing on the enemy.

Moving from the cover of old stones, Bishop fired a Dragon shell at a stack of ammo cases, blowing them apart and igniting them. Moving again, he leveled another Rider with a .12-gauge blast from the second barrel.

Brass shucked, he reloaded one-handed, but faster than a rifle shot.

Bishop tore into Riders coming from all corners of

the prison, trying to surround him. It was turn and fire—shotgun, pistol, then shotgun again—hoods hitting the ground, dead before weapons could even be aimed.

Quick-moving to the wall, Bishop got closer to the Temptation Wagon. Reloading on the way.

The ammo boxes were burning, brass casings heating.

Gunfire burst from the top of the walls, along the barbed wire. Hunk emptied the Winchester, punching a sniper with shots to the chest. Body jerking forward then back, the sniper fell screaming.

Bishop kept to the ground, sighting his target, then, moved for the wagon.

At the same moment the sniper slammed to the ground, the ammo cases exploded.

From the chamber, Hunk fired off the last cover round from the Winchester, grabbed a box of ammunition from a shelf, then stopped. His eyes fixed on what was behind the boxes, and he gave a shake of disbelief at what he was seeing.

Silver, light beading from it, neatly stacked in rows.

Hunk moved to the shelf, holding his hand against the bullet wound in his belly, ignoring his knee, and picked up one bar. ALFRED NOBEL COMPANY was pressed into the silver foil.

Hunk's smile straightened. Breaking the silver wrapping with his thumb, he revealed the caked white gelignite underneath. He ran a finger along the edge of the explosive, then had to laugh to himself. "The silver he found."

He took the Cheyenne necklace from his pocket, saying quietly, "*Soţia mea.*"

Exploding ammunition from the yard filled the chamber with smoke and the shrill of bullets as they bounced off empty iron shells of rockets and grenades.

Hunk ducked the ricochets, the necklace back in his pocket against his heart. Blood stuck his shirt to his body, and he had to grab hold of an old Confederate standard pole to steady himself.

Hunk stiff-walked to the gallows where the stolen percussion mines were placed side by side on the fifth step.

Ammunition rain covered Bishop as he ran around the side of the wall. A slug pierced his shoulder, tearing him sideways, but not slowing him down. He was behind the hay bale targets, the Temptation Wagon directly across the yard from his position.

His rested his right half-arm on a hay bale, the barrel of the rig searing hot. The hay started to smoke. He angled the rig straight from the shoulder and a little downward at the fuse protruding through the iron plates under the wagon.

Behind Bishop, a Rider ran in fast on a new pony, drawing down with a Colt to shoot him in the skull.

Bishop cocked around, swinging the rig up and sending buckshot through the Rider's gut. His body sloped from the saddle, the horse breaking across the yard as guns along the walls opened up, slicing the air with a barrage of rifle fire.

Blood ran down his arm, soaking the rig, but not affecting Bishop's aim. The double-barrel was directed, the thin chains from the trigger tight across his back, and through the harness to his left hand. A slug ripped next to his face, but he didn't flinch.

He couldn't.

Bishop pulled the line, the Dragon's fire exploding from the rig like a spear. Flames lit the fuse, the buckshot ripping the wagon's purple wood and iron.

He pulled himself around the targets, the rifles pinning him down. He loaded two .12-gauge shells, dove from behind the targets, and shotgunned the top of the wall, pushing the riders back from their positions, away from the wire.

The fuse burned to its end.

Smoke burst from the bottom of the wagon, the burning powder sprouting into black wings before the first explosions hurled the wagon into the air, the sides blasting apart in large, razored pieces.

Red hoods were beaten by the shrapnel, the flying wheels cutting them off their horses, an axle pinning another to the ground. The force blew through the prison wall, collapsing one side, throwing Riders from their sniping perches, burying them beneath rock and metal.

The second blast was the fireball, the kerosene jugs igniting in burst after burst. Flames ate the air, spitting shards in all directions. The fire ignited the bullet maker's tent. More powder blowing it apart. The medical tent burst into flames that snake-jumped to the training area.

Guns, staffs, and bows, all devoured.

Riders were still shooting, trying for Bishop through smoke and panic. They broke from the side buildings, not running fast enough, the charges around the walls exploding inward. The ground erupting.

The howitzer keeled over, the cannonball pulverizing the gates as the horses crashed the corral, leaping through the burning ruins to the open road.

Surrounded by the last of the running horses, Bishop pulled himself onto a stallion and raced out as more fiery debris fell, spiking the ground like volcanic ash.

In the chamber, Hunk stood over a flat percussion mine that he'd placed on top of silver gelignite bars he'd stacked on the gallows. Holding himself by the thirteen steps, damaged and bleeding, with the last bit of strength in his massive body, he thought of family, life in the mines, and treasure.

Riders burst in from the upper halls and came down the dirt ramp. With rifles shouldered, they dropped to their knees as a firing squad. One of them shouted, "Betrayer!"

Hunk regarded them with, "*Răzbunareaestepace,*" before using his last strength to bring down the butt of the Winchester on the mine's trigger.

The trigger clicked. And there was a flash.

CHAPTER TWENTY-TWO
The Trail

A thick fog had rolled in from the mountains in the afternoon, but split away as the sun went down and a steady snow began falling.

Widow Kate bunched her fur collar around her chins, one hand on the pistol in her lap. Mayor O'Brien pushed her wheelchair to the edge of the front porch of the House of Pleasures, giving her a wide view of Paradise's main street.

The freshly painted saloons and hotels threw out some light and a little music, but that's all. There were no fights or raised voices. Just some random sounds. Seemed most were waiting.

O'Brien touched a match to the bowl of the opium pipe Kate was holding.

"The cold comes on, and I feel everything ten times worse." She drew on the smoke. "I've got to be taking care of that. This year. Get some of my health back."

O'Brien said, "We've got a lot to tend to."

Kate nodded, watching John Bishop ride his bay from the opposite end of the street, pausing at the corral by the train depot, then bringing his horse to the hitch post directly in front of her. He didn't climb down.

"God have mercy," Kate said. "Look at you. Face all scarred. That gun and those are your damned eyes? You're the image of death, Doctor. Just the image of it."

"His horse is in the corral."

"The beauty he took from John Chisum? Likes to brag on that. Too much."

O'Brien said, "Your brother's here, and he isn't. It's his town, but the man could be anywhere."

Bishop said, "Mister, you're taking a real chance I won't shoot."

Kate drew the last on her pipe. "We heard about Rawlins. There being nothing left but a hole in the ground. Devlin didn't know if you were killed or not. I bet against it. He was taking care of business until less than an hour ago, then he lit out."

"Kate, you knew me once as a patient man. Don't count on that now."

"You settling family business, that's good for me, but then it's settled. You're not to come back here, stepping into my affairs."

"I'm not a lawman."

O'Brien said, "There's one waiting. If that goes bad, well, Tucker knew the risks."

Bishop said, "Where?"

Kate smiled, drew out the pistol from her lap, and pointed it toward the coffin maker's place.

The double doors to the coffin maker's were open, breathing just a bit on their hinges with the night snow.

Rig poised, Bishop stepped into the dark of the front showroom. The rows of pasteboard caskets seemed like the shadowed shapes of gunmen standing in the corners, against the walls, or playing possum laid out on a table.

The first drops of blood he saw were gathered in a pool, the imprint of a boot drying along the edges. Fine repeated drops went farther into the showroom, making a pattern around the rows of coffins.

Bishop said to the dark, "My brother. That's all I want." He took a step, following the blood, when Scalped Outlaw leaped from a far corner, tackling him from behind, slashing with a long blade.

Bishop was halfway around, smashing Outlaw down with the side of the shotgun, sending him to the floor.

Scalped Outlaw crawled to his feet again, his jaw wobbling free and yowling, "You're the most famous man I ever kilt!" He charged, waving the blade, and then the knife from Bishop's belt was in his chest, buried to the hilt, a move so fast, Outlaw didn't even see it. He touched the knife's handle, trying to believe what happened, then dropped his own weapon before stumbling backwards into a paste coffin, legs dangling over.

Bishop said, "Tucker! Your man's done!"

No response. Only faint music from the street.

Bishop kept the rig up, his eyes back to the floor and the droplets leading into the workshop. He stayed with the blood, rig locked from his hip, and called the sheriff's name again. Even more than in the showroom, there were places to hide—rows of leaning caskets, large sections of lumber piled against the walls, coffin lids propped with them.

The blood continued but was smeared as if the wounded had fallen to one knee, then crawled through it. Bishop followed the direction toward the back where he could see the edges of a handprint against a wall.

Jags of memory cut through him—*gun against his temple, the whip across his face.* "It's not your jail now, Tucker. You got paid for tonight. Don't try anything. Maybe live to spend it."

He took another step and saw the reflected movement in the polished surface of Widow Kate's green-lacquered casket. The lid of a coffin by the doorway moved just enough for a pistol to emerge. Chromed, the barrel caught the light.

Bishop fired, tearing the coffin and Sheriff Tucker in half, scattering them on the floor. He cleared the shells from the rig and reloaded with buckshot and his last Dragon's Breath before going to the back wall.

More than a single handprint showed above the opening that had been broken through and then shored up, leading into a small shaft from the played-out gold mine. Someone had lingered at the break, supporting themselves as they gave orders or prepped a trap for anyone following.

The shaft was dim yellow, lit by small, fluted oil lamps that had been mounted on the rebuilt walls. The blood was harder to see, drying and mixing with the color of the earth.

Stepping in, Bishop drew the rig in close.

Dev using the mine for escape wasn't a surprise. The papers had written about his getting out of prison twice before by digging tunnels. Bishop had been a surgery student when he read about his brother in the same dreadfuls that now wrote about him.

On shoring lumber, he found more blood and another handprint slick and wet with the mountain damp.

Or new, which meant that Dev could by lying in wait around the next turn.

Bishop turned down each lamp that he passed, making his way farther along the shaft, keeping his own pace despite the bullet in his hip towing him back. Crouched, his hat scraped the mine ceiling.

He doused another lamp so not to be a silhouette-target, followed a blast of snowy cold coming from the mine opening just ahead, and stepped into the bases of a series of small, black-rock mountains.

He wrenched the lamp from the wall before ducking beneath the last support beam and walking into the blue winter night. He stood by the mine opening, peering at the crags of the rocks, trying to sense movement.

The clear sky and mountains were still, meeting just right. The cold coming from them hit Bishop clean and felt good. Pure. That he could draw deep into his lungs.

He knew he was bleeding again and figured his chances of getting the job done before bleeding out. In a moment of instant knowing, he dove into a mountain crevice before the first shots tore at him.

He found his place under a ragged cliff, the gunfire coming from an outcropping above. He scrubbed the snow from his eyes and saw the cast of Dev's shadow before him, backed by the light of the winter moon.

Bishop watched the shadow of Dev's movements on the ledge above, his inching along the side, gun aimed downward, trying for a back shot.

Dev said, "You're trapped, John. You ain't gonna hit me with a shotgun blast from there. You can hide and freeze or come out. Hell, you've wrecked everything I built, killed my men."

Bishop was eyeing the shadowed moves, setting the

aim of the rig from his elbow and angling it upward. He saw just a bit of his head, then a bit more.

He called out to his brother. "All I wanted was what I had. You could've left me alone."

"No, I couldn't." Dev laid down three shots in quick succession, rapidly firing down to the rocks, but leaning forward on the ledge. He broke his shots, waiting for Bishop to fall out dead before him. He took two deep breaths and thumbed the hammer again.

Bishop swung out from the crevice, letting fire with one barrel, catching Dev in the arm and gut. Spinning him over and off the ledge.

The winter air held the smoke of the gunfire as a thin fog that Dev fell through, hitting the rocks, ripped by jagged edges, then rolling to the base of the small hill.

Bishop walked down to him, the rig extended, and the lamp in his left hand. Dev still had his Navy as he stood, everything about him sliced to the bone, but still reacting when he saw John Bishop's solid blood-red eyes.

"Jesus—"

Bishop said, "There was a time, I couldn't even recall your face." He cracked open the lamp and hurled the broken well at Dev, soaking him with the oil. "Now, I remember everything."

Dev almost laughed through his bloody teeth, using what he had left to bring up the pistol and shoot as the Dragon's Breath shell erupted from the shotgun rig.

The flames engulfed him, the buckshot blast blowing him back and down the rest of the mountain. A fiery heap, rolling yellow and orange, the oil leaving a burning trail of acrid smoke behind the dragon's tail.

There was a scream, and Bishop glanced to see

Soiled Dove standing at the end of a small trail by the mountain base, holding Hurricane by the bridle.

She screamed something at him again, but he didn't hear as he watched the fire at the bottom of the hill burning smaller and smaller.

The apple tree was bare, but the branches had reached out in all directions since the time Amaryllis had planted it. It was her favorite thing, caring for that tree, and Bishop liked leaning against it, his back to the grave marker of his wife and son.

The bay was drinking from a trough and reacted when White Fox ran her hands across his back as she passed. She was wearing her leathers, her hair straight and tied in long braids to hold it against the wind.

Bishop looked up at her but couldn't stand.

She said, "I didn't know what I would find here."

"That letter you wrote, all in Cheyenne . . . I figured it out."

"You remembered your words."

Bishop said, "Eventually."

She bent down to him. "Everything the woman said to you, she predicted?"

Bishop gave that a moment. Without looking at her, he said, "I don't know."

White Fox put an arm under his shoulder.

Turn the page for an exciting preview.

Before there was SHOTGUN: THE BLEEDING GROUND,
there was the first story of Dr. John Bishop . . .

A DOUBLE-BARRELED AVENGER IS BORN

Dr. John Bishop thought he'd seen his share of
death on the battlefields of America's great Civil War.
Then his quiet life was shattered when a gang of
outlaws invaded his home, killed his family,
and tortured him within an inch of his life.
John Bishop's soul may have died that day, but his
mangled body lived on. A beautiful Cheyenne
named White Fox nursed him back to health—
and a gunsmith outfitted him with a special shotgun
rig where his right arm *used* to be. A strap across
one shoulder fires it, while the chip on the other
fuels his quest for vengeance. Now the man called
Shotgun rides deep into the Colorado winter to find
and kill the men who murdered everything he once
held dear. The hunt will lead him straight to the heart
of a fiendish criminal conspiracy—and force him to
confront the violent legacy of his own outlaw brother.

SHOTGUN
by C. Courtney Joyner

"You damn well know I'll do it."

"Major" Beaudine's spit-shined boot was flush against John Bishop's right arm, pinning it down, while he turned the blade in the moonlight to heighten the threat.

Beaudine said, "So, your choice?"

Bishop managed, "You're thinking I know something I don't. I swear, I've told you everything. You got no reason to touch my family."

Beaudine gripped the handle of the long cleaver, saying, "A liar always boils my blood."

Bishop was on the edge of consciousness, trying to take in the faces of the other men holding him to the frozen ground. They were dirty fragments: mustaches dropping into beards, fresh burns, and one curtained eye. Their names were nothing but jumbled noise, while the screams of Bishop's wife and son cut through everything to reach him. Their voices didn't even sound like them anymore, though they were just a few feet away. Bishop cried out, twisting his head to see,

as Deadeye and another man gripped him by his ears
and jaw.

"Them ears'll come right off!"

Deadeye asked, "Why are you tryin' to look, anyways?"

Beaudine let Bishop know, "They're breathing. I see
her little bosom moving in and out, but it's not honor-
able for you to make your wife and boy pay for your
being contrary. Do you understand the penalties, what
it means to incur my wrath?"

Exactly fifteen minutes before, Amaryllis Bishop had
joined hands with her husband and son for a Methodist
grace. John always gently rubbed her fingers with his
thumb while his wife asked for blessing, and she flashed
her blue eyes in a way that was supposed to be annoyance, but was something else.

Their son giggled as he reached for a piece of
chicken before the plate was offered. Mama issued a
smiling warning. "I know somebody's birthday is in
three days, but it may not come at all, if—"

Amaryllis's voice was cut off when the front door was
kicked off its hinges.

"Major" Beaudine and his men exploded into the
house, tossing the dinner table, splintering a bookshelf,
and slapping the youngest to the floor. Bishop sprang
at the "Major," but heavy fists from behind pounded
him down, and Beaudine's heel cracked his ribs with
little effort.

Beaudine warned one of the others not to do more.
"Show restraint, gentlemen. Our friend is essential to
our mission."

He knelt next to Bishop, measuring his words. "I am
aware of the gold you and your brother liberated, one
half of a million dollars. Don't deny it. The letters he

wrote you from prison, finalizing your confidential plans? I wrote them. You know your brother could neither read nor write, and so he trusted me to set down his thoughts. Devlin and I were cellmates, until the morning he was hung. He took me into his deep confidence, which I honor. You have all that money, John, and you need to share. Your brother is departed, but I am here. Death's arrived, and I want paying."

"I'm swearing, I don't know a damn thing about any gold. There's nothing between me and my brother. Never was."

"No, that's not the answer."

"Where's my wife?"

"You must think clearly now, about the gold. Nothing else matters at this moment, I promise you."

The man with the trimmed mustache and salvaged gray Confederate tunic, who spoke as if he were reading holy scripture, pressed his knee deep into Bishop's back. Bones cracked. Beaudine asked again about the stolen gold.

"If anything happens to my son . . ."

Beaudine pressed his knee again and Bishop couldn't move, his thoughts slipping away with his bleeding.

Beaudine said, "There's a Foster Brothers cleaver with a polished blade on a thirty-one-inch handle resting across my saddle. It's a thing of beauty, but you do not want me to fetch it."

Beaudine put the last of his weight on Bishop's spine, dropping his voice. "You need to concern yourself with gold. Try again."

The outlaws waited for the answer, and Amaryllis swung a pork-fry pan from the Crawford stove, spattering hot grease across the face of one of them, sending him screaming into the cold. Time stopped for a few heartbeats as Amaryllis Bishop scooped up her son, his arms around her neck and their tears mixing on their cheeks, as she whispered a kiss to him.

That's when the first shot was fired.

CHAPTER ONE
Nothing Dies Like a Man

Huckie's Saloon, with its caving roof and sides, was a whipped dog cringing in front of the Colorado Mountains, ready to snap. It was the only place John Bishop saw with any signs of life, and he angled his horse toward it.

He was navigating a tough trail winding out of the steeper foothills that led to what was passing for some kind of a town. Bishop's bay horse was cautious with her footing. The snow on the trail wasn't deep, but a layer of ice beneath the white cracked under each footfall, throwing off her steps. Bishop patted her neck to tell her she was doing well as she managed a narrow cut between some tall pines.

There was another rider following, about half a mile back, but Bishop didn't even turn to see, his mind and eyes locked straight ahead, the reins steady in his left hand to keep the bay sure. She responded.

The frozen white was blowing just enough that he

had to squint to read the battered sign that declared
Huckie's. A pack mule snorted out front, and a mutt
scratched at the front door, until someone let it in.
There was loud, drunken talk followed by laughter.
Bishop figured there had to be at least five in the place,
including a cackling woman.

Bishop clenched the reins. His memories from
months ago, the ones that beat hell out of him every
other minute, had brought him to this place, but now
he had to put feelings away. He was going to do this,
and had to be clear about it. No backing down.

Chester Pardee liked Huckie's. The drinks and the
one woman were so watered and worn that even he
seemed like a big shot in the place. He took another
swallow of no-name whiskey and tried to fan his cards,
but they were too ear-bent to separate. Pardee then
studied each of them, pausing for a sip, making a show
of what a fine hand he was holding.

Chaney, who had killed someone someplace, was
getting tired of the put-on. "You ain't droppin' anything
on the table, Chester."

"I like to think my bets through."

"Nobody's got that much time. Play or fold."

Pardee adjusted his fingerless gloves, and reached
into his pocket for the last bit of paper he had. He'd
gotten the coat from a dead man, and it was stained
with his fortune, but the money was his own, and he
placed an old Union twenty on the torn felt like he was
presenting a king's crown.

Chaney said, "The bill's got blood on it."

"What doesn't? I know'd every one of ya and your
dirty habits. I say can't none of ya match it."

Chaney nodded. "Things are temporarily lean, but I

have twenty-three in silver, and this banker's watch you've always admired. You're being raised, Chester."

Pardee reached into his jacket, and took out a letter that had been roughly folded into five sections, the words smudged by whiskey rings. Too many reads had frayed the paper, but Chester Pardee waved it at Chaney like a red verónica in front of a Brahma bull.

Pardee said, "You know what this is?"

Chaney didn't change his expression. "You jaw about it enough."

"Right, it's a goddamn treasure map. I'll throw ten percent—no, one percent—into the pot. One percent. One."

Chaney said, "You might as well say you wipe yourself with it."

"You won't take that much of a chance, Chaney? You ain't a gambler at all."

Chaney looked up from his cards.

The Colorado snow eased as Bishop rode to the hitch rail. He threw his weight to one side, angling his right arm from its special sling on the saddle, almost turning in the stirrup, before dropping to the ground. Here, the snow was slush under his boots, as he listened again to the voices escaping from Huckie's. Bishop rolled his shoulders and said something like a prayer before walking the last steps to the batwings that were banging against the front door.

The glass in the front door had a little split, and for some reason, Bishop almost knocked. Instead, he opened it with his left hand and let the door swing free inside, the glass breaking in half to announce him.

Pardee turned in his chair to see Bishop standing in

the doorway. One of the others at the table belched, "You're gonna have to pay for that."

Bishop kept his head down with his arms straight at his side, his black duster a size and some too big, hanging scarecrow loose, but it gave him the freedom of movement he needed. The first time he saw himself, he thought he looked like a specter from Poe. Bishop cleared his throat, but didn't speak.

Huckie's was all whispers and mutterings; guesses about Bishop passed from the drinkers who sat at the old silver exchange counter that now served as the bar, to the laughing whore on the straw bed tucked away in a corner, with the pull curtain above it. Bishop had their attention, until he raised his eyes. The whispering stopped, and then started again, punctuated with loud snickering.

Bishop's face was softly round, and not protected at all by his blond beard—the kind of face that made men like these laugh among themselves before trying something.

"Chester Pardee."

Pardee paid no mind. He slipped the letter back into his jacket, and said to Chaney, "You can't kill me for tryin'."

Chaney said, "Find somebody to stake you, or fold."

Bishop hadn't moved; he tried again. "Chester Pardee."

Pardee said, "It's freezin' in here."

"That's all you have to say?"

"We've got a game, jackass."

Bishop took a single step closer to the table. "Then you don't know me?"

Chaney said, "You lost, Chester."

Pardee said, "Hold up! You say you know me? Stake me to this pot. I got the cards, amigo."

"You really don't remember?"

Chaney said to Pardee, "I called, that's it."

Chaney laid out two pairs of faces, while Pardee tossed a weak five-high straight on the table. Chaney gave Pardee a smirk with some pity.

Pardee faced Bishop with, "Whatever the hell you're on about, it didn't mean nothin'! You just cost me!"

"Slaughtering a man's family doesn't mean anything?"

"What man?"

The first blast ripped through Pardee's shoulder and sent him spinning out of his chair, spurs catching the edge of the table, sending the whiskey, cash, and five-high flying. Pardee twisted on the bowed floor, screaming out for Jesus, but Jesus didn't make a move. Nobody did.

The whore burst into tears because she'd never seen a shooting up close before; everyone else rubbernecked for a look, not exactly sure what had just happened.

Bishop stood over Pardee, gun smoke drifting from the end of his sleeve where his right hand should have been, but wasn't. Instead, the two barrels of a Greener shotgun poked from the ragged cuff, which had been singed by the blast. Burning threads danced from the cuff to the floor.

The double barrels were in place of Bishop's right arm, attached somehow at the elbow, and held waist-high steady. He shifted his weight from one leg to the other, keeping the weapon dead-centered on Pardee's chest.

Pardee was still crying out for Jesus as he struggled to stand, red spreading across his jacket. He tried drawing his Colt with fingers that wouldn't work. "You ain't given me a sloppy Chinaman's chance!"

"What kind of chance did you give my wife and son?"

"Jesus Lord."

"I've still got the second barrel."

"Can't you just let me out, Bishop?"

"So you know me now."

"What happened wasn't my doin', I swear. That's not why I was there."

"I can barely see where my wife threw the grease from that hot skillet."

"Please, let me ride out and you'll never hear my name again."

"Beaudine."

Pardee said, "If I live another twenty years, it won't matter. I'm already dead."

Bishop had to shift his weight again, but, with effort, he kept his voice calm and the shotgun aimed at Pardee's chest, "You wanted to know about gold I didn't have. Well, now I want to know something. I'm counting."

"Beaudine's crazy, and I fell in with his gang. That's all it was: us tryin' to eat. Nothin' personal."

"I'm only going to five."

Pardee stammered through tears, giving up a crossroads where Bishop could look for Beaudine, and kill him, if that's what he intended. Pardee even gave his permission.

Bishop said, "You know what retribution is?"

"It means I'm done."

"If you can get off the floor, I'll let you try."

Pardee didn't move. Bishop said, "I'm not a murderer."

"You're a blessed man, Doc. Better than I'll ever be."

Pardee dropped his words as he grabbed Bishop's left hand, and yanked him forward, slashing him with a rifleman's knife he had strapped to his boot. The blade sliced deep, from earlobe to the corner of Bishop's mouth.

Pardee whooped, "How you like that—?!"

Bishop heaved backwards and brought up his right arm in a single motion. Buckshot 'n' fire erupted from the sleeve a second time, rag-dolling Pardee into a stack of empty beer kegs. Wood and bone shattered together, then settled into silence. Pardee's eyes stayed wide and his grip on his pistol never relaxed.

Everybody froze for a moment, and then the talk started, along with nervous laughter. One old boy said something about a "nice killin'" and spit a stream of tobacco juice that spattered a brown halo around Pardee's head.

Bishop waited for someone to try something, but no one bothered. The mutt in the corner wagged his tail and barked his approval. Chaney, the card player, scooped the poker pot into his hat as Bishop took careful steps to the shattered door.

Chaney said, "You blew both barrels."

Bishop jerked his arm, and the shotgun breached inside the duster, the sleeve tenting the open barrel. Bishop reached inside the sleeve, coming out with two spent shells, and dropped them on the floor. He grabbed two fresh from his jacket, and reloaded, before bringing his arm upward in a motion that snapped the barrel shut.

This took moments, with everyone watching, their eyes wide and "goddamns" whispered. Bishop aimed the rig directly at Chaney's gut. Chaney showed his palms. "Hey, nobody gave a shit about Chester, except you."

"You going to bury him?"

Chaney shrugged while winding his watch.

"The railroad's probably put up a price."

Chaney said, "Knowing Chester, they're offering the lowest bounty in history."

Outside, the midnight wind stung Bishop as he checked the cinch on his bay, but his one hand was shaking, and his chest pounded. A lot had led up to this, and in a few moments it was over. Well, Pardee was over, but there were still the others. At least now Bishop knew he could go through with it; he had to keep that in his mind, the knowing, no doubts at all. He had to.

His face was sticky with the wash of blood from his sliced cheek, and as Bishop calmed, he started to feel the pain. The batwings creaked, and a few drinkers poked their heads over the doors. The whore moved to Bishop, holding out a lace handkerchief. "It's clean."

Bishop wrapped the handkerchief around his face to soak the bleeding. He felt the girl behind him tying it off and caught her heavy perfume. Bishop thanked her and she nodded before wiping her wet eyes on her sleeve.

The others hung back on Huckie's porch, watching as Bishop hefted himself onto his saddle, again throwing himself wide and keeping the shotgun clear of any tangle. He played it slow for them, settling against the leather, and sliding his double-barreled right arm into the canvas sling.

The bay was ready to run, but Bishop kept the reins tight around his only knuckles, holding her back.

Old Spitter hollered, "Hey! You busted some good bottles killin' that piece of sheep dip! Plus the door, and a couple of chairs!"

Bishop took fifty from his vest and tossed it. "You're going to tell folks about this, right, friend?"

Spitter gum-grinned. "I'll be talkin' about tonight for the next five years, five months, or five days. Dependin' on how much time I got left."

"God only knows, and I'm obliged to you both."

Bishop brought his horse around slow for that last look, and then heeled her. The bay took off toward the blue-black silhouettes of the rising hills, and the high Colorados beyond.

Spitter whistled with gums and two fingers, but Dr. John Bishop didn't hear it. His horse was running strong into the winter night, knowing where to go, even if his mind was taking him someplace else beyond the hurt—maybe back to his wedding day, or the birth of his son.

Behind him, a rider was charging hard to catch up, a Cheyenne war club in hand.

CHAPTER TWO
The Fox

White Fox kept her body low and tight against the painted stallion. They moved as one, racing down the trail, the snow kicking up around them like bursts of brake steam. She grabbed the horse's mane, fingers tangled in wiry brown, and gently pulled. The stallion slowed as the path through the trees widened into an easier slope that led to the "town" just below. It was a mule squat for drifters who still had hopes for the played-out silver strike at Cherry Creek—stop for a drink or an ash hauling, and ride on.

But this was where Bishop had to go, so White Fox had to follow.

She pulled up to watch Bishop's silhouette pause outside Huckie's, say something with a roll of his shoulders, and then go in. White Fox dropped from the horse, and walked him around the burned skeleton of an old barn to a water trough thick with ice. She broke the icy surface with a kick and tossed away the pieces.

The horse inspected the trough with his nose, then drank.

While he watered, she scraped packed snow from his hooves with a six-inch blade. She had the feeling everything in this place was dying or dead. Two loud voices from Huckie's stopped her.

White Fox stepped into the moonlight, craning her neck toward Huckie's to hear. A voice she didn't know was yelling about Jesus. Two shotgun blasts followed; that low rumble mixed with those louder cracks that ring in the air and ears.

The painted lurched as the blasts smashed against the hills. White Fox said, "*Nâhtötse,*" close to the stallion's ear, calming him, before swinging herself on his back, and circling around the far side of the barn. She saw Bishop on his bay, talking to the Spitter on the porch. White Fox dug in, and the stallion broke into a run, while Bishop rode off without looking back.

The Spitter whistled loud after Bishop, before looking up to see White Fox charging toward him. It was either an image from some kind of holy book or his best damn whiskey dream ever: the beautiful Cheyenne woman, onyx hair spreading behind her, riding out of the night just to take the old man away. White Fox pulled a war club she'd tethered to her belt and held it high.

Spitter closed his eyes and smiled, thinking, *This is a hell of a way to go, and why not?*

White Fox rode close, swinging the club into the skull of the drunk standing next to the Spitter, creasing his head. The drunk fell forward, the revolver in his hand hot-blasting the muddy snow instead of John Bishop's back, where he had been aiming.

Spitter grabbed the pistol for a trophy, and White Fox threw him a stony nod while the horse galloped toward Bishop. Bishop turned at the sound of the shot, just as White Fox rode up next to him, still holding the war club. They rode side by side for a moment, the legs of the painted and the bay falling into sync.

White Fox said, "*Hetómem.*"

Bishop spoke through the bloody handkerchief, "He remembered me."

White Fox pointed to the nearest mountains with the club, and broke ahead. Bishop heeled the bay.

The cave was a huge, yawning smile beneath a jagged slope of blue rock, sheeted by snow and protected by daggers of ice formed by the water flowing from up-mountain. Bishop followed the barely there trail for more than a mile, guided by a small fire White Fox had left burning inside the cave's mouth, its drifting heat melting hanging icicles. Bishop felt comforted by the distant, flickering orange, even as a raw burning raced across his face and down his right half-arm.

The painted was tied to a Rocky Mountain birch, eating fresh snow, when Bishop reached the cave. White Fox stood just inside, waiting to see if he could get down from the bay by himself. He did, a scream jamming the back of his throat. Fresh blood specked Bishop's sleeve and the shotgun barrels. She took a step toward him that he stopped with a raised hand. He nodded that he could beat it, allowing himself a moment to let the throbbing from his arm and face ease with deep, cold breathing. It didn't.

White Fox slipped herself under his shoulder and helped him to the fire. "Bi-shop."

Bishop smiled at the way she said his name, breaking it gently in two, as if each syllable had a spiritual meaning. She eased him onto a blanket on the cave floor, where he stretched out, propping himself on his right elbow, the shotgun rig resting on his knees.

White Fox pulled off the blood-flecked duster and folded it carefully, before putting more wood on the fire, sparking the flames. She then opened one of the redware jars she'd arranged around the cave, along with bedrolls, a cook pan, a coffeepot, a lot of ammunition, and a small leather satchel that had Bishop's initials stamped on it in gold.

Bishop said, "You're nesting—Jesus!"

He cried out raw as she peeled the pink handkerchief from the drying blood caking his cheek. White Fox tossed the rag, and dabbed the wound with a soft cloth she'd wetted with melted snow. It was cool, and felt good against the damage.

Bishop said, "Stitches. You know how."

White Fox ran her fingers along the inside of the jar, gathering yellow salve. She smeared the mixture on the wound, then cut a piece of yucca in half, opened it flat, and pressed it against Bishop's face.

She took Bishop's left hand to hold the plant in place and he said, "This won't be enough. *Ma'heo'o Ôhvó'komaestse.*"

Bishop got the words out, but White Fox didn't hear them. Her jaw was set, which meant that she would take care of him in her own way; she didn't need white medicine.

She unbuttoned his shirt, and he automatically leaned forward so she could pull the right sleeve free, gathering the rest around the shotgun rig, then slipping it off. The shirt caught on the hammers, and White Fox yanked it.

Bishop swore in Cheyenne, and White Fox gave the back of his head a gentle slap before allowing him a swallow of mescal.

Bare-chested, he leaned to one side, his back toward her, so she could unhook the canvas strap that was tight across his shoulders and connected to the two triggers of the Greener .12 gauge. The strap dug into him, leaving marks like the bite of a whip, and was connected to a looped piece of fabric that ran down his right arm and anchored to the triggers, so that the action of bringing the shotgun up to waist level would pull on the strap, firing either or both barrels.

The bleeding started around the leather cup that was fit to Bishop's right arm just below the elbow joint. It was a standard prosthetic that rebel and union boys now wore as a battle prize, but had been modified to allow the short stock of the Greener to fit where a metal hook would replace the patient's hand. The stock was secured in the cup with small metal bands that joined the shotgun and prosthetic together as one.

White Fox loosened the ties that held the cup tight to Bishop's arm, and pulled the entire rig away, revealing a bleeding stump. More mescal from the heel of the bottle, and Bishop's head lolled back, his hand still holding the yucca against his cheek as she checked the arm for fresh wounds.

He said, "Nothing's opened up?"

She examined the corrupted skin and muscle that was a knot around the bone, and saw that none of the crude surgical scars lacing it together had ruptured. The blood was smeared from small wounds around the elbow, where the amputation point met the healthy rest of the arm. White Fox swabbed away the streaks of wet red.

Bishop said, "It's not setting right, rubbing raw. I know you don't understand everything, but you did a fine job. I'm the doc, but you're the surgeon."

White Fox dressed the wound with salve and wrapped it, saying, "I still am, Bi-shop."

"Not always, not always."

White Fox allowed the corners of her mouth to turn up, as she settled Bishop down on the blanket. A last bit of mescal and he closed his eyes at her touch treating his wounds.

"Where's my medical bag?"

"Close."

Bishop barely opened his eyes to see the small, black leather bag, age-cracked, with Lt. Bishop embossed in flaked gold on one side. It was Bishop's field kit, blood-stained and heavy with instruments. White Fox had arranged it among the other supplies, but knowing that piece of himself hadn't been lost eased Bishop, and he closed his eyes again.

Bishop said, "You take care of me."

White Fox rested the shotgun rig between the medical bag and the stacks of ammunition, all the time watching Bishop as he drifted, his words folding into each other.

"When your husband stabbed you, I sewed you up. And when he broke your arm? You were a good patient."

White Fox treated the slice on Bishop's face with the last of the yucca pulp. His eyes were heavy with sleep coming, but his thoughts were fighting the peace.

"Pardee had never seen anything like me. Nobody had."

Bishop lifted what remained of his right arm to reach out to White Fox, but he couldn't. She touched the side of his face, lightly tapping the pulp onto the wound so it would dry in place.

Bishop said, "I've watched a lot of men die, but I never killed one. Not even in the conflict."

White Fox lay next to Bishop, pulling a blanket over them both, keeping one hand on his chest.

Bishop said, "It felt different than I thought it would."

White Fox understood but didn't react; she just lay next to Bishop, feeling the still-excited, rapid beat of his heart and quietly murmuring his name until his body eased, and he fell, peacefully, asleep.